Bad Hair Days

D. C. Paull

LeRue Press
www.leruepress.com

This novel is a work of fiction. Names, characters, places and incidents either are the product of the author's imagination or are used fictitiously. Except for obvious historical figures, any resemblance to actual persons, living or dead, businesses, companies, events, or locales is entirely coincidental.

FIRST EDITION

Printed on Green Seal Certified, Acid-Free Paper

Library of Congress Control Number: 2010938016

ISBN 978-0-9797460-6-2

10 9 8 7 6 5 4 3 2 1

I dedicate this book to my friends and family; what would life be without them? Special thanks to Jan, Ruby, Kathy and Lenore of LeRue Press for believing in me. To Jim, Ethan and Jessica, thank you for keeping our home filled with laughter. To my folks, Dottie and Mel Swingrover, thank you for your continuing support (and first edits)! To my brother Greg Swingrover, and his wife Richel, thanks for trying to keep the family unit alive..

To my extended family, Vicki, Hugh and Michaela Wuelfing and Kathy Paull, a thank you and shout out for Washington (someday!). To my friends, Kathy McGann, Tammey Stewart, Renee Gloyd, and Shawna Lovett, your unconditional friendship is so appreciated. To my most "mature" fans, my uncle, Gayle Swingrover and Ruby Szudajski, and to my youngest fan Peyton Kosman, thank you very much for your kind feedback. Of most importance, thank you to our Father above. Through Him ALL things are possible.

1

Bright lights flashed through the limousine's darkened windows, creating a surrealistic shadowy, strobe light effect. The result was almost eerie, as the people that were visible through the windows seemed to move in a wave of slow motion.

Between the blinding flashes, I could just make out throngs of people in the distance behind a roped off area. They were cheering, waving signs and banners, and in general contributing to the tremendous noise level we heard at a deafening intensity inside the car, despite the protections of its luxuriously padded interior.

It was finally our limo's turn to stop in front of the event's entrance and red carpet. The process was more like the landing of a plane than the curbside parking of a vehicle. Three people directed the car into the exact space it needed to be to ensure we could make a truly grand entrance.

The car finally rolled to a stop. "Ready, Sara?" Alex asked.

I sucked in a deep breath, "It's your night, Alex, and I'm just glad to be a part of it. Thanks for inviting me. It's just so exciting!"

"Let's do it then," he said putting up a closed fist. We did a knuckle busters gesture and both laughed, albeit with a tad of nervousness hidden under the humor.

I nodded just as our chauffeur opened the door, and his hand grasped mine in an elegant gesture that made me giggle. I slowly stepped from the vehicle so that my posture remained lady-like and my dress would neither hike up nor rip in the transition from the car. I carefully ensured that my feet and body were properly positioned so that I looked comfortable walking in high-heeled shoes. I had spent two weeks practicing walking in them to ensure I could pull it off, and was grateful I wasn't wobbly as I walked onto the start of a long length of carpeted sidewalk. This was the proverbial "red carpet", and I prayed that my first and very public visit to it would not be face down.

My appearance from the car elicited no response from the crowd,

1

and more of a feeling of wonderment at who in the world I might be. When Alex followed, though, the level of noise increased ten-fold as soon as his face became visible. Screaming, cat-calling, and even crying could be heard from among the crowd, who were now pushing at the rope that kept them away from those of us on the red carpet. Several security guards buzzed about the lines to keep the mass of people under control.

Alex and I looked at one another and grinned in anticipation. He took a deep breath. "Here we go, Sara." He squeezed my hand, and then took my arm to head down the red carpet, following other well-known people through the path of reporters, cat-callers and star struck fans. I felt completely lost and clueless as to how to act or what to do.

"Smile," Alex said, and demonstrated his own well-practiced technique, a semi-open mouth with all teeth showing. I followed his example, but it took a lot of effort.

"Good. Now relax."

I realized I'd been holding my breath since we left the limousine, so I let my body relax and tried to allow natural functions such as breathing and blinking appear normal, although I still didn't know what to do next. I was still worried that I'd stumble in the heels I was not quite used to wearing.

Thankfully, Alex kept me steady, and indicated by touch when I was to stop, turn, smile, or do anything at all. Each time we stopped, I turned in the direction Alex indicated, and smiled as light bulbs flashed in my face.

It was like a dream. There were VIP's on the red carpet ahead of us, and more to follow based on the endless line of limousines, each awaiting their turn to stop and provide an "entrance" for the cheering crowd.

I recognized some of the people in the red carpeted area, but there were many I didn't know by sight or name. There were a sea of people wearing gowns in various styles; from the most gorgeous I'd ever seen, to those that seemed a little ridiculous. For as many bona fide stars, there were twice as many media type folks milling in and out of the stream of people. They were taking pictures, holding cameras, and some reporting directly into the camera, submitting live TV footage, as the action continued.

I was a guest at a Latin American Awards show. This was like the Emmys, but for Latin Americans whose work had impacted the community the most. The star power slated to attend the event was huge, and the fashion statements made by those around us validated the fact that this affair was no small shindig.

After just a few painfully slow steps down the carpet, Alex had a microphone stuck in front of his face. Before I knew what was happening, Alex began conversing in Spanish with some reporter. I just stood by his side, cameras flashing, and feeling rather awkward, like a freshman that had crashed the senior prom. Alex's gestures and words were perfectly mannered as he answered question after question, and taking time to look directly into the camera and even giving an impish wink, which made the watching crowd ooh and aah with adoration.

He was a star in the making, and was one of several guests of honor to the event for a small part he was now playing on a Spanish soap opera. Alex said they called them "telenovellas" in Spanish, and millions of people watched them in the states and Mexico. His small part on the show had made a big splash in a very short period, and the crowd called out his name in almost a chant.

It was such a shock to be here, insignificant me, as a part of such a major event, when just a few months ago Alex was working as a teller and trying to get modeling jobs and I was out of work. Through a bizarre recent chain of events, Alex and I were featured in a local media interview that received nationwide coverage. It seemed that within hours of the national broadcast, he was signed by an L.A. agent and immediately started working as a Calvin Klein underwear model. He was gorgeous, well built, and had "the look" that made this overnight transition seem natural. Then, during one of his first shoots, he met one of the stars of the soap, was picked up for a small role, and now here he was, on the brink of being a star in his own right.

Since his first appearance on the show, women all over the world, and some men too, had gone gaga for him. Alex could ooze manly sexuality right through the TV screen. I didn't even understand Spanish, but Alex definitely had proven his natural acting ability to me despite the language barrier. Heck, sometimes I even got a little hot and bothered when I saw his scenes.

Unfortunately for those adoring women, Alex preferred to play for the other team. His acting must be really good, as Hollywood had obviously not noticed this fact yet. He was receiving oodles of mail from thousands of the show's fans, mostly from women who swore their undying love for him. Along with the letters, some sent him everything from flowers to underwear, and sometimes even naked pictures of themselves. Even some of the actresses on the show had thrown themselves at him as well, but he'd held them off somehow without offending them. He was naturally good at dealing with the politics that came with the entertainment world.

I would've thought this industry could tell who went which way from miles away, but the gaydar in Hollywood appeared to be broken when it came to Alex. It was probably because he was so good looking; he'd appeal to just about anyone.

Alex nodded in my direction as he was speaking, so I gave my brightest smile and nodded to the camera. I got a brief shot, and then the reporter went back to Alex. In another moment, it was time to move down to the next "station" on the red carpet. We passed an area in which the reporter didn't show any interest in speaking to Alex, and then another came by and practically grabbed him by the arm to ask a few questions.

It was just like I'd seen on similar events for TV and movie stars a hundred times before. I even felt like I looked the part, in a sparkly ruby red dress that showed off everything good about my tall, somewhat slender body, and hid the fact that I had a small chest and that my hips were a bit wider than my shoulders. The dress was nearly backless, ending appropriately above my rear end, and showed off my back. I was pale, but felt I looked best in red, so I didn't care. My dark brown hair and scarlet lips seemed to make pale look elegant.

The front of the dress draped down glamorously in the front, not too far, as there wasn't any cleavage to feature. It was more of a billowy drape, with the side coming up my shoulders and all was held up with a strap that went across the back of my neck. The length of the dress went about halfway past my knees towards my feet, and had enough give to allow me to walk with regular strides without waddling.

I'd borrowed the dress from a good friend, Shelby, who attended glamorous parties all the time. Alex had gotten offers to wear designer clothes, but I was on my own, a nobody, and not about to buy a pricey dress for the event. Shelby's closet was full of fancy clothes, and I was happy to let her pick one for me since I was fashion challenged in addition to being frugal.

Of all the choices I had, this was the one that said "Wow" when I tried it on. It was a little small, as I was several inches taller than Shelby, but I felt like a million dollars in it. I had sparkly red high heels that matched the dress. They made me think of the shoes Dorothy took from the Wicked Witch of the East in the Wizard of Oz, but with killer, spiked heels and fashionable.

My make-up job had been professionally done by Alex's cosmetic artist friend, and included false eyelashes that made my green eyes even more intense. He also gave me a hair style that I couldn't duplicate on my own in a million years. My mid-length hair had been swept back with gel in a sleek style, and held in place at the nape of my neck by a gorgeous rhinestone clip, borrowed from the set of the show. I felt good, looked great, and thought just maybe I could blend into this sophisticated crowd for this one night without giving away how awkward I really felt.

It was just a one time thing for me, until Alex met other industry folks that would be more grateful to attend an event like this. Regardless, I planned on enjoying tonight to the hilt, and could not hide my happiness to witness firsthand the instant success that my good friend had achieved in such a small amount of time.

"Alejandro, bebito," came from somewhere from within the sea of beautiful people. A stunning woman approached Alex, and smothered him with air kisses and an unnecessary amount of attention. "I'm so happy to see you came after all," she hesitated, "with your, ur, little friend."

I recognized her as Cecelia Barbaron, the lead actress on Alex's show. She was decked to the hilt in a silky white dress that hugged all of her ample curves. She was rather short, and had her normally long, dark tresses piled on top of her head. She had a white feather boa around her shoulders, and I could not help but think a bird could confuse the hair and boa for a nest and dive in.

Her make-up was also professionally done, and no one could deny she had lovely features. She also had a sensual appeal that couldn't be dismissed, and I saw many glance her way as she spoke to Alex. Her personality matched her attire, so big that her small body couldn't seem to contain it. Alex returned her affectionate pecks as gentlemanly as he could, and then turned her to greet me.

"CeCe, this is the friend I was talking to you about. Her name is,Sara"

"Jes," she said, her accent suddenly getting heavier, "Mucho gusto, Sara."

She made the same air kisses to each of my checks, embracing me with forced feeling. Then, instead of turning to include us both in the conversation, she placed herself in between Alex and me, with her back now roughly two inches away from me. She tossed her boa around her shoulders and it smacked me in the face. I gently moved it away from me, a little miffed at her rudeness.

Alex had already told me she had been trying to bed him since the day he arrived, and he had used me as the "girl back home" excuse to get her to retract her claws and leave him alone. I had expected her cold shoulder treatment in advance, and was prepared to accept it gracefully. Despite this, I could not help but enjoy a moment of guilty pleasure when I realized her lovely white boa now had a two inch red smear from where it had brushed against my mouth.

Good luck with the dry cleaners on that stain, sweetie, I thought to myself, and then felt rather catty about it. *Get over it, Sara, this is her world, not yours. Just enjoy the moment.*

Luckily, I had little more to endure, as it was over as quickly as it had begun. CeCe was off to spread her love and affection to others in the crowd. We moved down the red carpet again, and more stars were appearing. There were TV and movie actors, singers, writers, politicians and more.

I gazed around when we paused again. We were getting closer to the entrance of the complex, so I could look back at the crowd of the power players, all made up for a night out. We stood still for what seemed like five minutes to me, so I soaked it all in. It was too much; famous faces, beautiful appearances, excited greetings to see one another. I could not help wonder what power struggles, competition for camera time, and other problems lie beneath this surface of pretend perfection.

After several minutes of gawking and supposition, Alex brought me back to reality by tightening his grip on my arm. He had started conversing with a reporter from one of the entertainment shows whose name I actually recognized, and this time in English so I could follow along.

I recognized the woman, having seen the show a million times, but I could not remember her name. Short blond hair, professional clothing and appearance, perfect teeth. She blended into yet stood out from the crowd in her own way. It was exciting to see her in person, and Alex answered her questions in a casual manner that I knew he'd prepared for in advance. He came off like he had done it a hundred times before.

Suddenly, the buzz of the audience became even louder; someone VERY important had apparently just arrived. Could it be J. Lo and Marc Antony, George Lopez?? It was rumored that Madonna might even attend. From our position at the far end of the red carpet, it was hard to tell, but is seemed that catching the first picture of whomever had arrived was a big deal.

Catching the buzz, the reporter left Alex in mid-sentence, running off, and the media portion of the red carpet crowd rushed back down the carpet towards the curb. I could hear from others around us that a very famous singer had just arrived, but not who it was.

A group of people standing just to the side of us pushed in between Alex and me in a rather rough manner. Alex started to laugh and said "What a bunch of cutthroats" when it happened.

It felt like a ten minute process, but it must have occurred in just seconds. After being pushed, I'd stepped back awkwardly on my heel and it snapped right off of my shoe. Being off-balance, I started to fall backwards.

We were so close to the building's entrance that I fell into the wall that had a large banner attached to it, naming the event in huge letters. As I fell backwards, Alex attempted to keep me upright. My back hit the edge of the banner that had a nail or some other metal fastener that held it to the wall. It stuck out from the wall quite a bit. I felt pain in my back as it scraped upwards, digging into my skin. The pain was pretty intense. Alex kept me from fully falling, but then the WORST thing of all happened.   The neck strap of my dress got caught on the sign's fastener. As Alex tried to get me loose, my hair clip came off, and then the strap snapped.

In a slow motion of horror, I watched as the front of my dress fell down to my waist. Despite the majority of the crowd ogling over the big stars, there were enough left to ensure that the entire event was caught on both camera and video. Being small-chested, I hadn't worn a bra, and I was completely exposed.

Light bulbs flashed, and a video or camera or two was turned in my direction before I could cover myself. I heard loud gasps from those nearby who sympathized with the situation, and laughs from those who apparently didn't.

Alex quickly grabbed me, and placed me between himself and the wall so no one else could take pictures. He then started yelling at the camera crews and photographers to back off. One of the cameramen shouted something in Spanish. Alex made sure I was covered and standing upright, then shouted back at the man, gesticulating wildly in apparent outrage.

The pain in my back was unbearable, and I could tell I was bleeding profusely. I closed my eyes and clicked my now uneven heels together three times, thinking "There's no place like home" in a vain wish to get away. I was still there when my eyes opened again. *Toto, we're still in Kansas,* I thought to myself.

Someone apparently on the event team took my arm quietly and indicated that I follow her. She led me away from the scene to a side door of the building. As I walked away with her, I saw Alex hitting the shouting man square in the jaw, resulting in his camera's hitting the ground with a loud crash, barely heard amongst the louder crowd. A full-on fight had now broken out, and I saw police officers coming to break it up as I was whisked inside.

2

The sun was just coming up as I left the hospital. It shone weakly, half hidden behind a haze of smog, but I was grateful to be out of the irritating, artificial lighting of the hospital.

I'd spent the last twelve hours in the emergency room. The first six hours had been wasted waiting time. I thought the wait at ER's in Reno was too long, but this hospital had a new emergency more serious than the last in fifteen minute intervals. Gun shot victims, serious car accident injuries, and worse had come and gone while I waited to be seen. When the horrors of life in Los Angeles ceased for at least one fifteen minute period, it was finally my turn to see the doctor. Actually, I only rated a physician's assistant, but I got a tetanus shot and thirteen stitches in the back as a reward for waiting so patiently.

Another two hours of waiting got me a visit from a bona fide physician, who checked me over, issued me some prescriptions for pain and possible infection, and then released me back into the world. After the tedious process of checking out, I walked through the hospital's huge revolving doors to wait for my ride.

One of the show's producers had let me know that another employee would pick me up and take me to Alex's apartment. I felt odd, standing in front of the hospital, alone and still dressed in the red dress that had assisted in turning an accident into a disaster. I was barefoot and shivering cold in the brisk morning air, now thinking that bare and backless wasn't all it was made out to be.

I felt eyes on me from every direction. Those being delivered to the curb in wheelchairs stared, as did others going in and out of the hospital's entrance. I must've looked a fright, and hadn't bothered looking in the mirror before leaving.

I dug through a plastic bag the hospital had provided for my personal items. Rifling past Shelby's now useless shoes, I found the small handbag I had taken to the event. I found my cell phone and powered it on. Yikes! There were 17 messages for me. I shuddered, wondering how word got out so fast, and dreading the thought of listening to even one of them. There were several messages each from Shelby, my sister, Alan, June, Eckert and my Mom. I put the phone back in my bag. I couldn't deal with this now.

Within ten minutes or so, a car pulled into the hospital's circular driveway and parked. A man walked towards me, apparently able to figure out that I was the one to pick up based on my now inappropriate attire.

"Hello, I'm Carlos from "Dime Que Me Amas". His English was perfect, and contrasted with his perfect Spanish pronunciation of the show's name.

"Dime Que Me Amas" is the name of the show Alex was appearing in. Translated into English it means "Tell Me You Love Me", or so I had been told by Alex. I'd been watching the show since Alex started appearing on it, and knew that Carlos wasn't one of the actors.

I got out a weak greeting as he eyed me up and down, and I caught a look of wonderment, or was it bemusement, behind his glance.

"Are you okay?" he asked, and with a very soft yet concerned tone that touched me.

"Yes, thank you. Only thirteen stitches," I added, pointing to my previously bare back, now bandaged to the hilt.

Carlos helped me into the car and closed the door. After he had fastened his own seatbelt, he said, "I was at the show last night but I didn't see the accident footage until this morning. It looked pretty painful. Did ya want me to take you to Alex's place?"

"Footage?" I questioned, simultaneously nodding my response to Carlos as he carefully navigated the early morning traffic.

Shock and horror overtook my mind as I realized that this incident had been part of a televised event. I'd just assumed that it would be cut out of what was televised, overlooked or tossed aside. Footage? This meant to me more than just being mentioned over the course of the show.

The tears I'd been holding back welled up in my eyes. I had avoided thinking about what this could have done to Alex's options for the future. A rising star, fizzled by his klutzy friend.

Is it possible I could've destroyed his chances for continuing with the show? I thought to myself. *Was he in jail over the fight? Would the show's reputation be damaged? Would Alex be mocked in the industry?*

All these questions came to mind at once, and I suddenly felt nauseous. The tears then poured from me, uncontrollable, with my sobs too loud to comprehend anything Carlos was saying. In between heaves I heard, "Sara, it's going to be okay. Worse things have happened on these shows." He went on to tell me about some other mishaps, but I wasn't really listening to him.

I sat silently in the car once I stopped crying, and soon we arrived at Alex's apartment complex. Carlos took my bag, and led me to the apartment. It was in one of those complexes surrounded by a pool. All the residents could hang out on the walkway leading around the complex and be involved in group activities such as barbeques. It was quite a hip place. I felt fortunate it was still pretty early in the morning, so there weren't too many folks outside to stare at me.

Carlos knocked when we reached Alex's door. Someone I didn't recognize answered and quietly ushered us in. Carlos whispered something to the man and quickly left.

Alex was seated on his couch with Jorge, the man that had done such an artful job on my make-up for the event, his roommate Kevin, and the man who answered the door, who I later learned was Rodrigo Valdez, one of the producers of "Dime Que Te Amas".

When I saw Alex, I fell apart all over again. He practically leapt from the couch to comfort me as I sobbed apologies and condolences. Alex led me away from the group, and sat me on the bed in his room.

"Are you okay?" he asked quietly, then checked me from head to toe, and spent the most time looking at the major bandaging job on my back. "Wow, you really did a number on yourself. No one would tell me what happened after you fell. They said you went to the hospital."

"Did, did, did you get arrested?" I choked out in a stutter, still trying to keep my emotions in check and losing the battle. "I wasn't sure you'd be here when I got in. Thought I might have to bail you out of jail or something."

Alex laughed lightly and shrugged, "I'll tell you everything, but first, are you okay?"

I nodded as Alex checked out the bandaging job.

"Let's clean you up."

He led me to the bathroom and I had a first glimpse of my appearance since Jorge had turned me from a plain Jane into a semi-goddess. What was left of my make-up was smeared, and black streaks ran down my face. I guess Jorge forgot to use waterproof mascara. I suppose most guests don't cry at awards shows or have to spend an hour lying on their face to get stitches in their backs.

My previously sleeked hair was the biggest shock. Jorge had used a wax product in my hair, and it now stuck out at severe angles all over my head. I looked scary, maybe like a character I'd seen before in one of my favorite scary movies after spending an evening at the prom running away from a killer with a chainsaw.

I gasped. "Holy crap! I must look like I escaped from an insane asylum or something."

"Something like that," Alex said in unwanted agreement, stifling a chuckle. He brought out my suitcase and selected some clothes for me to wear.

He looked away as I slipped off the dress, and put on the jeans he'd selected for me. I felt about six years old as he cleaned off my mess of a face for me and then washed my hair in the sink. I couldn't shower for another day due to the stitches and bandaging.

When I was fit to be seen by others, Alex sat me back on the bed. "Better?" he asked softly.

"Much," I replied and started to go on. He put his fingers on my lips to stop me.

"I'll tell you everything. Just sit back and get cozy. When we're done, I need to get back to the living room to wait to hear what is going on from my agent and the show's producers."

I propped up some pillows, but couldn't seem to get comfortable in any position. I decided to act comfortable so Alex could tell me what had happened after I left the scene.

"The guy that I hit..........hmm, how do I say this. You didn't understand what he said because it was in Spanish, but he said some things that infuriated me."

"Like what?"

"Well, uhm," he stammered and I just kept looking at him, eyes widened in anticipation to hear the details of what made my calm, cool and collected friend lose it, in public and on film to boot.

After a moment of Alex's brain thinking in overdrive, I couldn't take it. "Will you please just spill? After what we have been through, it can't be much worse."

"He commented on your, uhm, lack of assets," he finally got out slowly, and his eyes went to my chest, "and that he had seen milk with more color than your body, AND that of all the people this could happen to in front of his camera, he had the misfortune of it being you."

I took it all in. Small breasts, white skin, didn't seem too bad. "So he was laughing that I have no boobs and a pale white body? It's not very nice, but it doesn't seem all that awful."

"It's more of a cultural thing, I guess," Alex said, grabbing my hand, stroking it softly. "You don't comment on another man's woman in front of him like that. You have to react and set it right. He had no business commenting on my lovely date, especially in light of the incident. This man has no respect, and he'll have to answer for his behavior."

I was touched by his response. I could never be Alex's woman in that regard, but that he thought that highly of me and reacted as he did made me proud of him. I just hoped the results would not lead to a quick exit from Hollywood and subsequent return to Reno.

"Is that a touch of machismo I detect, Alex?" I asked laughing, as Alex and machismo were not two concepts I'd normally consider in a connected thought about him.

"I guess that about sums it up," he admitted, also chuckling at the thought. "No one insults my best girl and gets away with it. You know that." He kissed me on the head and released my hand.

'Okay," he continued, "Now for the other part of the story. I was arrested, as I did hit the guy and bust up his camera. At least the crowd was on my side. They were cheering for me, and probably would've attacked the guy too if the police hadn't gotten in between us. We both got cuffed and put into police cars. I heard he was released after fifteen minutes or so, but I was taken downtown. I heard he took enough verbal lashing from the crowd to make him leave the event too."

"So you missed your big night after all. I'm so sorry, Alex," I said, almost crying again over the thought of his missing something that might not be a future option, not to mention the potential legal and reputational repercussions.

"It's okay, Sara; it might actually turn out well for me. I'm expecting news anytime now about how this will effect my job. Publicity for the show, good or bad, can be a good thing. I'm choosing to think positively about it."

"Is that supposed to make me feel better?" I asked, and he nodded. "What if you lose your job on the show? Your friend, the klutz, gets you kicked out of Hollywood. I feel awful, Alex. I'm sorry."

Alex took my face between in his fingers. "You," he emphasized, "have nothing to be sorry about. It was an unfortunate accident. It wasn't your fault, and I won't have you blaming yourself for any of it. It was the media that ran us down to get to someone higher on the ladder in the entertainment world. I only wish I could have gotten in front of you faster, or done a better job of keeping you from the wall. If this costs me my job," he shrugged, "then I get to come back to Reno and be a teller again."

"Could you live with that?" I asked

"Of course," he practically retorted. "We've been friends for a long time. This is fun, but would never be more important than the well being of one of my favorite people in the world."

I sniffed a little, again touched at Alex's views at what was important in life. He was probably the most balanced of all of my friends. "Do you want to go back to the living room now and find out what is going on? At least I look human again."

"Wait," he said, and stopped me from opening the door, "I'm still not done yet." I sat back down on the bed. "First, about the arrest. It is not an official arrest yet. One of the producers got there before they booked me. I'm not to leave town, but the matter is pending additional investigation. Apparently, the people behind the show have some influence in Hollywood, so I have been released on my own recognizance until the investigation is resolved."

My worries for his job now returned to the reality that he could face legal recourse for having a rare show of temper, again on my account.

"Gosh, I hope it will be dropped," I punched a pillow half-heartedly in protest. "The jerk asked for it. What about the others that pushed us? Do you know who they are?"

"The show's staff is looking up the names of the reporters and cameramen that pushed through us. I have a feeling that there'll be a lot more said on this topic."

"Is that a good thing?"

Alex shrugged. "It will play out however fate decides."

"Well, I hope fate decides in your favor, and hopefully leaves me out of it."

"Too late now, Sara, the world has now been "exposed" to you. Or should that be "by" you?" His eyes laughed as I gave him a murderous look. Anger, pain and worry had me wound up as tight as a drum again.

"Relax a little would you, Sara? What happened is already done and over with. It's how we handle the aftermath that could make the difference for us. Did Pee-Wee Herman hide after his embarrassing incident? No, he turned it into a positive and made fun of himself over it."

"What a horrible comparison," I said, having disgusting visuals of the little man in one of THOSE theaters, caught doing something better left to the privacy of one's own home.

As strange as the analogy was, it worked. I got up from the bed with a renewed attitude and a little more courage. "Alex, despite the puns and the bad comparison, I get your point. Let's go face the music together."

"You're on," he said, taking my hand and leading me back to the living room.

When we entered the room, we found a large group of people had settled into various parts of the room. Alex's agent, Ethan Smithson was the first to notice our re-entrance. Alex and I looked around the room. Faces from those associated with Alex's show were glum.

"Alex," Ethan said in greeting, shaking his hand. He nodded at me in acknowledgement. "I have been meeting with the producers of your show while you were assisting your friend. Again, he only nodded in my direction. I felt like an "it", the source of the problem. Things didn't feel good to me at all.

"That's nice, Ethan, don't you care to know if my friend here," he nodded at me, "is okay?"

"Oh of course I do," his face said, splitting into a false smile. "I got a report of the incident and heard she would heal up fine. Right, little lady?"

I tried not to roll my eyes at his false sincerity. "Physically, yes," was all I said, but he choose to ignore my comment. He was anxious to spill something to Alex.

"The studio opened their offices early in anticipation of extra phone calls over last night's incident."

Alex now stood with his arms folded, waiting for the knock out punch that could end his career. I placed my hands on his back in a gesture of support. After a moment's pause that felt like a century, Alex finally interjected, 'And?"

"They did the right thing; the phones have been ringing off the hook!"

I could see Alex was restless over this limited disclosure of information. He gestured his arms in a manner that indicated Ethan was to keep talking. When he didn't, Alex put the questions right to him. "Is this a good thing? Are the calls good or bad? Why do Rodrigo and Wally look so down?"

"This incident has hit the major media, kiddo," Ethan said smirking as if he'd just won the lottery. He looked first at Alex, then me; almost as if he was enjoying watching us squirm.

"You're killing me, Ethan; spill it all! Am I going to be arrested? Am I going to be replaced for my last week on the show?" Alex was exasperated, as was I, wanting to hear all the dirty details at once.

Ethan laughed. Alex and I looked at one another, not sure if we should choke or hug him.

Finally he dropped the bomb, "The charges have been dropped, and the public is out for the head of the guy you popped, AND the group that ran you over to get to J Lo's entourage."

Huge sighs came simultaneously from Alex and me. The legal ramifications were gone; one down, one to go.

"Well, that's good," Alex commented and questioned at the same time, 'Isn't it?"

Another huge smile erupted from Ethan. He was having trouble maintaining his enthusiasm. "Forget good; it's great! The public is loving this whole knight in shining armor thing. Besides an apology from the jerk that you decked, the public is screaming for the heads of the evil paparazzi in creating a situation in which this poor gal," he paused, again nodding at me, "was hurt then victimized in front of the entire world just so yet another picture of someone on Hollywood's "A" list could get sold to some magazine."

I tried not to faint as he included me in the same sentence of "the whole world" in the discussion of "the incident". This was not about me though; this was Alex's future on the line, so I reverted all thoughts back to the task at hand.

"The public is in love with you, Alex!" Ethan said beaming, his hands now moving excitedly. "We have to jump on this train and let it run its course. This could lead to huge things for you. HUGE," he emphasized. Ethan looked very pleased with himself as he said this.

"Why are Rodrigo and Wally so glum then?" Alex asked with good reason, as they remained in another area of the room talking quietly among a group of people from "Dime Que Te Amas".

"Why?" Ethan said beaming, finally ready to share the trump card I'd figured he'd been holding back. "I'll tell you why. Your contract with them is up in a week, and your character was set to get knocked off for messing with the wrong man's wife. After just the preliminary publicity from this incident, they want to write you into the show permanently."

Alex looked stunned. "Well that's great news," he said, his face showing a sincere smile for the first time that morning. "I'm so excited. I love the show, and the cast, but...." He stopped himself, thought, then said, "So why are they down then, don't they know I'd love to stay on? I need the work."

"I'm sure you would love that too Alex, but I've had calls from two soaps and one prime time series. There's going to be a bidding war to get a contract with you. You just might be the hottest ticket in Hollywood television right now!"

3

Jorge dropped me off at the airport a few hours after Alex had gotten his stunningly terrific news. I was so happy for him, but now had to face my own realities. I checked my bag, and went to the waiting area for my flight. I'd turned off my cell phone since the accident, but now grabbed it from my bag to see how many messages would be waiting for me. There were 30. I was pretty sure that meant the message box was full, and I confirmed that fact as I saw about 50 or so calls on my missed call log.

I bit the bullet, and dialed Mom's cell. Better to get the hardest one over with first. I had taken a double dose of my pain medication to deal with the flight. I thought the effects might help me get through this call too.

She answered on the first ring with a pounce, "Sara, we've been so worried. Are you hurt?" Her tone gave me instant relief that her concern for my physical and mental health was greater than her embarrassment.

I started to reply, but only managed to choke up and begin to cry again. I looked around the airport to make sure I wasn't going to make a public nuisance of myself once again. I moved to an unpopulated area, unable to contain any hint of outpouring emotion.

"Oh, honey," Mom said soothingly. "I don't know how I can comfort you from so far away. I wished you'd called earlier, but I can imagine you've had quite a night. We can talk details when you're ready. Can you at least let me know if you are okay?"

"I'm okay Mom," I weakly managed to get out between a few sobs. "I'm sorry I made su-such a mess." I wanted to tell her everything, but knew this wasn't possible right now. "Can you pick me up a-at the airport please?"

"Your father and I are in Sacramento until tomorrow. Some friends invited us over. A last minute thing. I'm sorry we won't be home in time; I sense you could use a little mothering right now. Can one of your friends get you? What about Stephen or Shelby?"

My heart sank. All I wanted to do was to go home, curl up and sleep for a day or two. My condo was still under renovations, and although I loved staying with my employers, Sam and June Westin, it just wouldn't be the same as being with family. It was just now that I realized I had no real place to call home right now.

"Okay," I replied. I had pulled myself together some, and collected my thoughts enough to communicate some of the recent events, "When I fell, I scraped against a sign post and tore up my back pretty good. I have 13 stitches to show for my Hollywood presence. Did you see the awards?"

"Like I'd miss the chance to see my daughter on TV," she said with pride. "We started with the pre-show, hoping to see you and Alex on the red carpet. They didn't show the actual accident, but we did get a chance to see you before. You looked beautiful." I could tell from the sound of her voice she was beaming; she was always begging me to dress up. "I always said red was your best color."

My Mom and her color coordination fetish. I managed a weak "Thanks, Mom."

"During the show, the emcee kept referring to the incident. Alex and you, the mystery woman of the night, made quite a splash. We caught more on it during today's entertainment news." Mom paused, then quickly added, 'Don't worry sweetheart, they fuzzed out the bad part." She hesitated as she said "part".

I hung my head in shame, but then my call waiting beeped into the conversation. Mom ended it quickly for me, "I understand you probably have some other calls to make. Will you call us when you are safely home?"

Her last words came fast, but with heartfelt meaning, "It'll be okay, Sara. You're a tough gal; if you can catch bad guys, you can weather a little embarrassing press. Dad sends his love and well wishes. Bye."

The call ended, so I picked up the incoming call. It was Eckert. Before I could get out a greeting, I got an earful.

"Why haven't you answered my calls?" he demanded. His less than pleasant tone made the water works start all over again. He waited in silence for several seconds, and then changed his tone. "Sorry Sara," he said more gently. "Are you okay?"

I recovered more quickly this time. "My back's a mess, and I'm not yet certain how embarrassed I should be. Are you angry with me? And if you are, why?"

"Yes, I am," he said with a cough, "But only for not knowing if you were okay. You wouldn't answer your phone and I called everyone I could think of to see if they'd heard from you. In the meantime, I have been getting endless questions about it here at the station. I'm about ready to do some hitting of my own," his voice intensified on that last statement. I knew he was getting some flack.

"We can talk more later, please?" I said in a tone to indicate that I'd tell him everything, but now was not the time. "Could you call Shelby and have her tell everyone else I'm okay? I'll be ready to talk more tomorrow."

"Of course. Do you need me to pick you up?"

"Please, I'll fill you in then."

"Gotcha. Take care, Sara; this too shall pass," he quoted dramatically in a well meant cliché that sounded more wise-ass than wise.

"Bye," I said to the sound of a click I hung up determined not to make or take any more calls until after I got home. Stephen Eckert is a Lieutenant with the Reno Police Department. We'd met a few months ago when he was still a detective and I'd gotten a job as a commercial property manager. Since then, we'd been dating on a casual basis, more friends than anything else I could describe, but he'd been there for me when I had gotten myself into a big mess right after we met. My old career instincts and my new job had collided in an odd combination.

To make a long story short, my previous career had involved the requirement to have the means to detect financial activity that might indicate money laundering or terrorist financing. This was during my banking career as Compliance and BSA Officer. In the banking world, "BSA" does not stand for "Boy Scouts of America", but rather for "Bank Secrecy Act", which includes other laws that collectively make sure banks know with whom they are truly doing business and the sources of their income.

In my new career as a commercial property manager, a murder and a new tenant whose financial statements showed what bankers would call "red flags" indicating money laundering or terrorist financing, had led to my investigating on my own to find out if these flags truly indicated anything suspicious.

The results of my snooping had led to the fire-bombing of my condo, nearly cooking me and my golden retriever Rusty into crispy critters. Then, Alex and I barely escaped death in a warehouse as we tried to find out what the bad guys were doing. But, at least, it ultimately resulted in a huge drug ring bust. One for the good guys! Eckert got the credit for the bust before the Feds took over, largely thanks to our connection, and it had gotten him a promotion.

In the fifteen minutes of fame our part in the event had garnered, Alex had received notice from Hollywood and his anemic modeling career to a Calvin Klein campaign. From hot model, he quickly found more work as a smoldering actor and heart throb on the soap opera. He had previously been working as a teller to meet the bills, but now Hollywood seemed to have opened their arms to him.

As for me, the attention was not productive, but I felt good finally being able to use my prior skills to make a real bust. Before it was just paperwork to the authorities, but the final arrest was real, in fact more real than I ever want to experience again.

I was happy to get back to my daily job duties. I'd led a fairly normal, quiet existence until Alex had invited me as his date to this event. I only hoped Alex's star would rise, and whatever embarrassment I'd endure over my accidental flashing the world would be over quickly.

I was still deep in thought as I walked by a snack and souvenir shop at the airport and viewed the newspaper and magazine rack. One paper caught my eye immediately, as the front page showed Alex in full swing at the offending camera man. It was a Spanish language paper. I purchased it and a handful of other newspapers and went back to my seat. My flight would be boarding shortly. I tossed anything that was not about entertainment, as my curiosity was piqued over Alex's front page, larger than life photo.

Just as my flight's boarding announcement came over the speaker, I spotted my own picture on the second page of the Spanish paper. There was an inset of a photo of me and Alex before the accident, and then one of me, looking shocked as my dress had fallen down. Thankfully, the area of "interest" was fuzzed out, but my hair had taken a beating in the fall too. It looked frightful, and stuck out where my head had rubbed down the wall. I silently vowed never to use a wax based hair product again.

As I boarded the plane, someone brushed my back very roughly. I turned white and nearly passed out from the pain, dropping my newspapers to the floor. I stepped aside from the crowd flowing through the tunnel to the plane to make sure I wasn't bleeding.

A flight attendant had seen the incident and my physical reaction. She put her hands up to stop the flow of traffic, completely halting the boarding process, and hurried to my side. "Are you hurt? How can I help you?"

"I just had stitches in my back," I explained as she stooped to pick up the papers for me. "They're still very fresh and quite painful."

She looked at the papers, the top still opened to the 'before and after' pictures of me. She paused; mouth opened, and looked me over in disbelief. She pointed to the picture.

"It's you, isn't it?" She seemed excited at the possibility. I was less than thrilled at the recognition. It had never crossed my mind that anyone might connect my glamorous personage last night to my plain look today. My stomach churned in discomfort.

I finally nodded meekly in acknowledgement of her question. She smiled as she led me into the plane. "We have room in first class. No charge, of course. I think you are going to need some extra room to ensure your injuries are not exacerbated."

I was impressed with her medical language terminology, but shook my head. We were pretty much alone at the end of the boarding ramp, so I didn't feel the need to whisper, "Please, don't make a fuss. The last 15 hours of my existence on this planet have been the worst of my life. I just want some peace and quiet."

"No problem, I won't tell a soul," she then hesitated, "Until after the flight of course. I'll ensure you're comfortable and that no one bothers you during the flight, but I have to tell all of my friends later that I got to see the famous awards show flasher in the flesh!" She giggled at her pun, and her eyes quickly glanced at my chest area.

It took everything in my power not to roll my eyes at her thoughtless comment, but I knew it was the first in many, many more to come. I falsely smiled at her and got seated.

Once she had made me as comfortable as possible, she allowed the rest of the boarding to continue. I got several stares from passers by that had been forced to wait because of me, but no one seemed to pay any special attention to me other than minor annoyance at my causing their delay. I was grateful. I could now understand the anonymity that the famous must crave.

4

An hour and twenty minutes later I arrived at the Reno-Tahoe Airport. I was happy to be away from the metropolis called Los Angeles and back in my biggest little city. Now if I could just get home and into bed without further fuss.

During the flight, the flight attendant had kept her promise. She took great care of me in first class, and even offered me some free drinks. I could not risk the side effects of alcohol with a double dose of pain medication, so I'd declined her generous offer. I was not a fan of flying at all, and normally would have welcomed the liquid escape.

I had put away my papers during the flight, so I wouldn't point out the fact to my fellow passengers that a party to the front page story of every entertainment page was a flight companion.

I could care less who the flight attendant told about having me as a passenger after the flight. More power to her for thinking anyone would care. I was the first off the plane, as she stopped the flow of passengers until I was off and well away from the doorway. I'd declined the wheelchair she'd offered to have sent for me.

Unfortunately, the time in the air had reminded me that I had just a week before I was to accompany June and Sam Westin on a trip to England. When Sam had hired me, he'd mentioned that he'd been planning a trip there for June as soon as she was physically up to the challenge. A stroke she'd suffered had kept her from enough mobility to make the trip enjoyable. Sam wanted to golf, and she, of course, wanted to enjoy the gardens and art. He'd postponed the trip several times, then suddenly sprang it on June as a Christmas present. June wanted to wait until the spring time, but Sam had insisted that they leave in January.

We had a lot to do before we left. We'd made the travel arrangements earlier, but I still had to get some additional items to take on the trip for June and me. I'd declined the awards show invitation from Alex originally citing the demands of the upcoming trip, but June had waived away my protests and as usual, insisted I accept an invitation as unique as this one. She said the week before the trip was plenty of time to finish up the minor details. Of course, I acquiesced, and the rest is now history. I hoped I hadn't thrown a monkey wrench into the Westin's plans with this mess.

I picked up my carry-on bag with a painful grimace, made a quick trip through the tiny airport, and exited to the central island designed just for the pick-up and drop off of passengers. I didn't see Eckert's car, so I sat on one of the concrete benches. It was a chilly December day, and the stone-like bench seemed to absorb the cold and transfer it to my body. In the hunched over position I had to get into to stay warm, my back screamed in pain.

I expected Eckert to be here on time. I grabbed my cell phone from my purse and turned it back on. I was groggy, tired, and wanting to hide somewhere. My cell phone rang as soon as it powered up.

"Sorry, Sara," Eckert's hurried voice came over the line. "I've got an emergency that I'm en route to now. Can't talk, but I contacted June and she's sending someone to get you. Probably Alan."

I detected a tone of distaste in his tone as he said Alan's name. Or was it jealousy? "Sorry again; gotta go." I heard the siren go on as the phone call ended.

It looked like it was going to snow any minute, and I didn't have a jacket. I put my phone back in my purse, deciding to sit and wait instead of calling June to cancel and grab an immediately available cab.

Great, I thought, and tried to hide inside of myself as masses of people passed by the nearby walkway between the parking garage and the terminal. I was forced to pay attention to the endless string of cars driving through the area, as I wasn't certain what car to expect to greet me.

Fortunately, within 10 minutes I recognized my SUV in the line of cars crowding for a turn to pick up or drop off passengers at the curb. The car wasn't really mine, but was the one I drove every day. It really belonged to Sam and June; a rather nice perk of the job had been the unlimited usage of the very nice vehicle.

It pulled in to a space right in front of the bench on which I shivered. Alan popped out, opened my door and tossed my bags in the back in complete silence.

I crept into the passenger seat and shut the door. The pain was sharper than when I was on the plane, and I couldn't even pull the seatbelt across my body. As I struggled, I felt Alan's body reaching across me to take hold of and fasten my seatbelt for me. From the driver's seat he pressed a button to roll the window back to a fully closed position

"Thanks," I weakly managed to utter. I searched his face for any characteristics that might give away his emotional state at being here with me. I wondered if he was annoyed having to fetch me at the last minute.

Alan gave me a soft smile in response to my thanks, and placed his hand on my knee as we drove off. I took it as a measure of support and comfort, and I was relieved.

"Mom said I wasn't to ask you about what's happened," he finally said as we got into a steady stream of traffic on the freeway. "She did want me to tell you that you're to go right to bed when you get home. She's gathered the troops for dinner so you don't have to repeat your experience a hundred times for all of us that care about you and want to know what happened."

He then squeezed the knee his hand was resting on and put it back on the wheel. "I'm keeping my promise, but I have one thing to ask, and that is all."

'Ok," I answered, too tired to disagree and grateful for June's usual foresight in taking care of my needs instead of my taking care of hers.

We had to change lanes to get to the correct exit. There was a comfortable pause until we got off Highway 395 at Damonte Parkway and then made a left onto South Virginia, practically a straight shot back home.

Now that he was comfortable with the traffic, he turned his head to look me in the eyes. "All I want to know is if you're okay." His tone was soft and the concern was real.

Tears welled in my eyes, and I nodded my reply to keep from sobbing. Droplets landed on my shirt, and I wiped them away in silence.

"Okay then. Enough said, but I'm putting you to bed when we get home. If you need or want *anything*," he emphasized the last word for effect, "*Anything* at all, just ask. I'll get it or do it for you without further question. Mom promised she'd leave you alone until dinner time tonight. Unless you're hungry of course, and you know that she has enough food ready to feed an army. A snap of the fingers will get you anything your heart desires."

He stopped talking, looking for any reaction I might have to indicate I was tired, hungry or wanted to talk, but I couldn't muster one.

He squeezed my arm this time. "Sound good?" he asked.

I nodded again, fighting off another torrent of tears, which were brought forth by the range of emotions I currently felt, which now included appreciation for June and Alan's thoughtfulness.

"By the way, your eyes are the greenest I've ever seen them," he said. "Tears become you."

I ignored the comment but it made me smile a little inside. I turned my head to give him a sign of assurance, and I felt a sting on the right side of my scalp. Instinctively, my hand reached up to touch the source of pain, which no longer hurt and all seemed fine. I'd managed to restrain myself from saying something, but turned to the right to see what in the world has caused it.

Expecting to find a seatbelt or metal piece that had smacked me, it was startling to see a small chunk of dark brown hair hanging from the closed window. It took a moment to realize that some of my hair must have gotten caught in the window when Alan closed it. When I turned my head, I'd ripped it right off of my scalp.

Alan, still unaware of what happened, looked over as I loudly sighed, then made a mock-pigtail out of the strands still connected to the window. He put two and two together quickly, and wisely made no comment. Any sudden moves could have made the waterworks come back on in a fierce flow. I made a valiant effort to keep myself together, and lowered the window just enough to get the strands loose. I wondered what effect the loss would have on my overall hairdo, but it really didn't make a difference to me at that moment.

The rest of the journey was silent, and soon I was home, at least the place I currently resided within. June, Sam and Alan had made it a home, and I knew I was wanted there, which helped since I could not escape to either my condo or my Mom and dad's place.

Alan grabbed just my purse for me, then took my hand and led to me to my first floor room; June and Sam were no where in sight. Planned, I'm sure to give me some peace and quiet.

Alan placed my purse in my bathroom, then pulled back my bed covers, and closed the curtains. He opened the French doors to the outside garden and let Rusty into the room as I slid off my shoes and fell onto the bed. As he left the room, he kissed the top of my head and whispered that he'd leave my bag in the outer family room.

Rusty, excited to have me back, wagged her tail in excitement, but seemed to sense I was in pain. She jumped up on the bed with my coaxing, and gently nuzzled my face. She sniffed at the hair in my hand and then the stitched area of my back, and looked quizzically at me. I set it down by the nightstand and reveled in her unconditional love.

June had been thoughtful enough to have a steaming pot of herbal tea and a teacup waiting for me on my nightstand. I drank a cup of soothing chamomile and peppermint brew, then Rusty and I snuggled under the covers just as I'd been dreaming about for the last several hours of my life.

5

It was dark outside when I woke up. I must've slept for five or six hours. My back was on fire. I needed a pain pill badly, and my first instinct was to scratch at the stitches, which alternately itched and hurt.

I hobbled out of bed to let Rusty outside and use the restroom. It took me a minute to find my purse in the bathroom, where Alan had put it for me, then dug through its messy contents to find a pill.

As I came out of the bathroom, a gentle knock sounded at the door. I jumped, momentarily forgetting I was not alone in the house.

"Come in," I called out with as much energy as I could muster.

June entered the room, and the gentle spirit oozing from her soothed my addled brain.

"Hey there," she said gently, extending her hand to squeeze mine.

"Hi," I responded, now giving in to my emotional state. I started crying yet again, and June brought me into her arms, careful not to touch any part of my back.

"It's okay, Sara. Get out a good cry or two," she stroked my hair and sat me on the bed, her arms still comforting me. "All of your friends are here to see you. They're here for your support. You are not to be embarrassed or feel weird about this," she said with a firmness that made me believe it. "It could have happened to anyone. It's what we call an accident with unforeseen consequences due to the stupidity of others."

"Why do accidents always seem to happen to me, June?" I asked between sobs. "I'm like the Murphy's law when it comes to accidents or incidents. If one's going to happen, odds are on Sara."

June laughed slowly, trying to relate to the humor of my outlook without really agreeing it was a fact. She spotted the clump of hair on my nightstand, and to make my point, I told her a short version of the event in the car, and she assured me that the loss was unnoticeable, but it made my point that I attracted all things odd or bizarre.

"I know it seems that way. You're not a magnet for accidents, Sara." She got up and went to the window. As she moved the curtains aside, the winter moon shone brightly in Nevada's unpolluted sky, but a cold haze of clouds lessened the intensity of its glow.

She looked back to me. "It's really due to the type of person you are. You aren't afraid to put yourself out there."

I looked into June's smiling face. She was a lovely woman, and her heart matched the beauty she wore on the outside. She may be tiny in stature, but huge in presence. Her words were meaningful, and I was touched that she cared as much as she did.

"I'm afraid we've eaten already. I couldn't bring myself to bother you until I heard you stir. Are you hungry?"

My stomach churned. "Heavens no. I may be starved after I get this over with, but I kinda feel like throwing up at the moment."

June laughed again, "Fair enough. Ready for the troops then? They're all very worried about you, and," she chuckled, "They're all dying to hear what in the world happened last night."

I nodded, determined to tell my tale, so I followed her into the house's huge sitting room to talk to my friends. I knew they'd be supportive, but it would be hard to talk about it. For the last few months, it seemed like every gathering was to discuss something I'd gotten into or done that required explanation and some type of damage control.

Ten minutes later, I told everyone my story. Everyone had looked at my war wound and comforted me with hugs and well wishes. My emotions were under temporary control.

My spirits were lightened as my friends rallied behind me as I went through the details of the night. First the amazing highs, then the lows of the incident and its aftermath.

Shelby Matthews, McKayla Dwyer and Megan Kevorkian had been my closest acquaintances, along with Alex of course, during my years of banking. Alex was missing, still in Hollywood fighting his own battle over the same matter, but it was usually the five of us against the world. Alan, Sam and June were there with us too. Eckert wasn't there, as I'd expected, but June explained he'd arrived for dinner, and left on yet another urgent call with a promise to return later tonight.

Now that I'd spilled my news, it was question and answer time for them.

"You made E TV tonight," Shelby spoke up, breaking the momentary silence we'd lapsed into. As usual, she shone like a diamond, sparkly and shiny, and spreading her bright spirit to lighten the mood. Too bad the usual didn't fit with that comment.

My mouth gaped in horror as the comment sunk in. *Dear Lord, nationwide embarrassment*, I thought

"I think it was on the Insider too," added Megan.

McKayla spoke up too. 'I saw the whole thing on YouTube. Unedited." She added for emphasis.

My thoughts race again, *Make that global humiliation.*

"I think you should sue the journalist that knocked you down to get to J. Lo," she added, tossing her long ebony braids to emphasize her anger. "Those paparazzi types are a bunch of animals. You should know that the E TV piece said there was an investigation being launched since you were hurt."

"Yes," June chimed in. "Apparently the public is behind you. There are those who will enjoy your exposure, literally, and the aftermath from the incident, but there are many. many more that have rallied to your defense. The famous are prepared for being media prey, but the public is upset that an average person could be treated as tabloid fodder."

"Really?" This was piquing my curiosity; an aftermath occurrence that had never crossed my mind.

"Yes," said Megan, "and there'll be more to come too."

Shelby led us back to an item of equal importance. "Don't forget about Alex; he almost got arrested." She giggled; hand over her mouth and her eyes unable to hide the mirth of her thoughts. "Imagine him playing the macho man to save the honor of his damsel in distress."

The room laughed, and I shared his sudden rise in demand by the Hollywood heavyweights.

"His name has been everywhere today. He's certainly getting a lot of exposure over this too," Megan added.

"But Sara has definitely had the most exposure," McKayla punned, "Hands, or shall we say "dress" down?"

This time the sound of hearty laughter filled the room, and I felt more like myself again. At least like myself with a gouge out of my back. I laughed so hard it hurt, and I feared I'd popped a stitch.

June and Alan came to my aid as my eyes registered the pain. A quick check revealed I hadn't ripped out any stitches,and wasn't bleeding, but I had to bring it down a notch.

"Clever McKayla," I said once my medical examination was completed. "By the way Shelby, I'm sorry about your dress."

She waived her hand, "Oh please, it's nothing. I'm just grateful you're home and okay."

"Shall I get it fixed or toss it?" I asked.

"Neither one," Shelby responded more quickly than usual. She had a guilty look on her face as the comment came out, so all of our attention was now on her.

She looked at each of us, then confessed, "Think of how much that dress would fetch at a charity auction. It's a famous gown now."

"Shelby!" Megan hissed. "You should think of Sara!"

"Yes, I am thinking of Sara, that is of asking her to model it for the show," Shelby said. "Think of how much we could raise for the Juvenile Diabetes Foundation with the incredible story behind that dress.

It'll be the showcase piece!"

It was Shelby's way to think ahead like this,, to make lemonade out of lemons as some say. Unfortunately, I only had horrid thoughts about wearing the dress and being in public again.

"Come on, Sara. This is a great opportunity. What did Peewee Herman do to get past his humiliation? He didn't sit at home and cry about it; he made an appearance and mocked the incident and his, um, involvement."

We each looked at Shelby with varied looks. Mine, one of amazement that she'd chosen the same incident as Alex, and everyone else that she'd chosen such a bad example to use in making a good point.

"Well, you know what I mean." She put her hand up to stop any negative or joking comments about it.

Everyone was looking at me, waiting for my reaction. Too many amusing mental images came to mind. I laughed, and everyone else did too.

"Can you guys believe this? Alex used the same example as Shelby. Peewee Herman I mean."

"No way!" McKayla exclaimed.

"That gives me the total chills," added Megan.

"Alex and I are such kindred spirits. And you know what they say girls," Shel said with false grandeur, "Great minds think alike." She made a bow to pretend applause, so Megan threw a pretzel stick at her.

A half-hour later Nurse June announced I needed some rest. She was right, as always, as I was tired and needed another pain pill.

Eckert arrived just after everyone left. Alan was still in the sitting room, and June was milling about straightening up. I didn't want to speak to him in front of others, so I took him to my room, connected to the main sitting room, to speak privately.

I had my own separate little living space. June had redecorated it to suit my tastes. The shades of muted green, cinnamon and beige made the space warm and inviting. My sitting room had a door to the rose garden. I was too tired to do anything but sit in the most comfy chair and wrap my fleece blanket around my legs.

Stephen gave me a light hug of greeting before I sat. It felt perfunctory, and without the warmth or sincerity I'd expected He let me go, and then sat on the couch across from the wing chair I sat in.

"Well, here we are," he said, slapping his hands on his lap, and looking uncomfortable.

"Yeah, here we are," I replied, not liking where I guessed this might be going.

"How's your back feeling?"

"Oh, it was nothing really, just a gaping wound that needed 13 stitches. I'll be good as new in no time." I said, sarcasm dripping from every word.

"Hmm. How are you taking the publicity? Can't seem to turn on the TV without some reference to your escapade with Alex, and of course your accident and exposure."

His tone indicated that this was a problem for him. Until now, all of my fears of disapproval and shame had been unfounded. My face burned with embarrassment and anger.

"Sounds like it's more of a problem for you than for me," I said quietly, but with an edge sharper than I should have used.

Eckert jumped at my baited words. "Well, it gets a little old hearing about it all damn day long," he snapped. He stood up, pacing the room and looking tired, irritable, as he kept rubbing his hand over his face.

"Then, everyone is showing me the live video online. Unedited video," He enunciated every syllable of "unedited" like it was a term for something dirty or pornographic.

"This went on all day," he grunted is distaste. "Even at crime scenes people were shoving their cell phones in front of me to watch it yet again. Let's just say I had a hard day."

I got up and made an exaggerated effort to plump the couch pillows for him. "We'll I'm so sorry you had such a hard day," I retorted, beckoning him to sit. 'I can't imagine the embarrassment and humiliation you felt," I went on.

"Sara, really.."

"Really, what, Eckert? Could you be any less supportive of a friend, especially a friend who's been through quite a bit more than just a hard day at work?"

"Look at it from my perspective," he started, but I wasn't going there.

"I'll try," I cut him off hard. "But I don't see that well with my head up my ass."

'Ouch," he said, shrinking back from the sting of my words. He sat down on the couch, crossing his legs and fiddling with his shoes. He was still dressed in a suit with jacket, and I could see his gun holster under his jacket from where I sat. He looked good in his work attire, adding a professional edge to his demeanor. It was late, so he must have had a long day too.

I suddenly felt a little selfish and mean, the same way I'd pretty much accused him of being to me.

"I'm sorry," I said more calmly. "That was a little harsh."

'Maybe I deserved it," he said, still looking down, anywhere except at me.

"Remember what you said to me? You said "This too shall pass." Has this suddenly changed? Why are you mad at me?"

"I'm not mad, not really," he said with enough conviction that I knew he would finally reveal his feelings to me. This was not something he was very good at.

"It's just, well," he hesitated, "Every guy in the department was ogling your bare breasts today."

That reality hurt a little. My face flushed in response.

"You know, Sara; I haven't even seen your bare breasts before, before this video thing anyway. I was embarrassed. For you too," he added quickly.

"With this and the fire, and then the drug bust events, I guess what I'm saying is that I can't handle being with someone who is always out there. You know, living on the edge and taking risks a normal person wouldn't."

His words were almost meaningless. He couldn't mean me. He was describing a sky diving, speed racing, out to all hours of the night type of gal. I liked to watch movies and be at home. How was I edgy?

"You get so involved in things; you probably don't even get what I mean here."

With this comment, I did get it. Although it was not purposeful, I kept putting myself in the limelight. Whatever I did seemed to garner news media, whether being the subject of a billboard ad, being snoopy, or innocently attending an event. I was an attention seeking media disaster waiting to happen as far as Eckert was concerned. I was a little disturbed with his thinking only of himself, but that was life.

"I think I do see," I said, stopping his response. "No, I do. You need to devote your leisure time to someone whose biggest excitement of the day is dinner and a movie. Someone who's less, hmm, busy."

Steve looked at me, his brown eyes furrowed together in a type of frown. He nodded his head. "Yeah."

"You know, I've always thought of us as friends before anything else," I added hoping to end this in a dignified manner that let Eckert feel like he'd handled things well, considering I wanted to punch him in the jaw.

"Can we at least be friends?" I asked.

He seemed relieved that I'd been the one to say it. I sensed he was glad it had been easy to break up a relationship, not realizing I felt it had never really taken off in the first place. Maybe he'd been serious about me, and perhaps that's why things had happened so slowly.

"I was hoping you'd say that," he responded, giving a little smile. "It sounds so cliché when the one doing the breaking up says it."

"True," I said. "Besides, with the way my luck's been going lately, I'm going to need some friends on the force."

He laughed, and said, 'You have lots of friends on the force. You could call some of them fans now."

Now he was making light of the situation. I didn't get him at all!

"Simon's party is Friday. Will you still be my date?"

Eckert's partner was retiring from the force. Eckert had asked me to the party right before I went to Alex's.

'Of course," I replied, but wishing I'd say no and make him find another date. "If you still want to take me, you know, considering that your friends will probably tease you about it all night. Pick me up at 6:30 p.m."

He nodded in acknowledgement just as his cell rang. He took the call, replying in one word answers. He ended the call a few seconds later.

"Gotta run," he said looking at his watch. "You gonna be okay?"

'I'll manage," I said, glad he was leaving and resisting the urge to push him out the door.

"I'll see myself out," he said while giving me another insincere hug.

I walked out the door of my room into the sitting room and watched him leave. Alan was sitting in front of the now blazing fireplace. They said nothing to one another, but exchanged the looks of two males fighting over a herd of females. The front door closed and he was gone.

I was filled with emotion all over again, most of it anger at Eckert's insensitivity. I couldn't believe I'd made it through that conversation without killing him. With friends like that, who needs enemies? I was just glad that the formerly "undefined" relationship was finally defined for me as being over.

As I walked back into my room, Alan's voice quietly stopped me.

"You okay?" he asked. As I turned back, he leaned forward from where he sat on the stone hearth. "I mean really okay. I'm sorry; I couldn't help but hear some of your conversation. None of my business, but that was pretty cold."

"I will be," I said with some hesitation. "Okay I mean." I hung my head down, taking in what had just happened. "Thanks, though, for everything. You're a good guy."

He held up his glass of wine as an offer for me to join him.

"Not tonight," I responded to his gesture of company and drinks. "I think I'll mull things through and then get some more rest. Thanks for considering commiserating with me though, and especially thank your Mom for getting everyone together tonight for me, okay? You guys made this much easier for me."

"You got it," he moved to the couch nearest the comfort of the fire, the flames mesmerizing me with their flicker and inviting me to partake in their warmth.

"I'm going to hang out here for a while if you decide you need some company. At least if that's okay with you, you know being so close and all. I don't want to bother you."

D.C. Paull

"Of course it's okay. It's your house; relax and enjoy," I said, and as I closed the door to my room for the night, I added, talking nearly through the door, "You're very thoughtful, Alan. I really appreciate it."

6

Searing pain greeted me as I arose with the morning sun. My back not only burned from the recent stitches, but now itched as well. There was no blood on my bedding, so the stitches had done their job. I hoped they weren't getting infected.

I stretched and headed for the pain medication in the bathroom, when my stomach rumbled and stopped me cold. I hadn't eaten at all the prior day, and I was not sure it was safe to take pain meds on an empty stomach.

As I popped the pill, I spied a bowl of fruit that someone, probably June, had placed in my room sometime after I'd gone to bed last night. I munched on an apple, and sat on the couch of my personal sitting room.

A mixture of emotions surfaced again. I was very disappointed in how Eckert handled things last night. Not so much about ending our relationship, but more about his self-centered attitude regarding my "incident". A little chiding at work couldn't match what I'd been through the last two days. I'd suffered a pretty nice injury for the trouble, not to mention unwanted media attention and pictures of my bare breasts available for anyone with a TV or internet access to see.

"Good riddance," I thought to myself, and then my thoughts responded on their own with a *"Not so easy."* Eckert and I had formed a kind of friendship that was worth salvaging in some form. I guess I was willing to overlook his short-sightedness to keep the friendship despite his failure to support me when the chips were stacked against me.

Looking around the large room, I reflected on the last few months of my life as I finished my apple. My eyes stopped on each piece of furniture in the room. Each one was of a distinctly fine quality, only the best that money could buy. They were all tasteful and each piece added to the overall appeal of the room. Nothing in the room was my own though, and I sensed nothing of myself in the room. I suddenly felt very alone.

Here I am, 31 years old, single and living in my employer's

gorgeous mansion. I am paid to manage Sam's real estate properties and spend time with June. These are some of the most wonderful people I've ever known. What more could someone ask?

Taking in the events of the last two days, I knew the answer to my question. Privacy, and some sort of separation of the facets of my life would be nice, especially when things hadn't gone right, like the last few days for instance.

Just a year ago, I'd been out of work. I'd lost my job as a compliance officer when the local bank I worked for had been bought out by a larger, sexier corporate banking conglomerate. My position's functions had been relegated to a more "efficient" centralized source, a common side effect of such an acquisition. My job prospects had been slim until I'd reconnected with Sam, who had been the president and CEO of the purchased bank. Sam made the wise choice of retirement at the time of the acquisition. I hadn't seen him since the time we said our goodbyes at his retirement party.

He called me one day to propose this working arrangement. He'd gotten a kick out of the "job wanted" billboard stunt Alex had done to get me noticed. He knew me and my good work ethic, and connected his need with mine. The billboards had made the local media buzz for a few days, and had put my search for a job into the right forum to have employers seeking me out. It sure worked better than the unsuccessful groveling and responding to want ads I'd been doing until then.

I soon found that Sam had been kicking around ideas about some assistance he needed, and after seeing my ad and subsequent media discussions, thought I'd be perfect for the unique position he wanted to create.

The position gelled perfectly with my skill set, and Sam and June had become like family in the months I had worked for them, with all of us benefiting from the arrangement. Best of all, I enjoyed the work. My "working" relationship with June had blossomed into a real friendship.

This was not the first time I'd made a mess of my personal life since working for the Westins. My regular residence, a two bedroom condo, had been destroyed by arson. This heinous act was committed by one of Sam's property tenants, and was done to stop my incessant snooping. The fire had almost burned my dog Rusty and me to a crisp. Sam felt partly responsible for the mishap, and both Sam and June had insisted on taking me in during the repair phase on my place.

It'd been a more attractive proposal than moving in with my folks. I also gave my temporary premises, provided by my insurance company, to the neighbor I'd displaced thanks to my unintentionally bringing the arsonist to our condo block. I loved the Westins dearly, but let's face it, once you've been on your own, you can never go back into your Mom's kitchen without dire consequences if the rules are broken. A dish can stay in my sink until I wash it, but at Mom's house, there was a five minute rule; unless it required soaking, it had to be washed, dried and put away immediately.

It'd been very generous of Sam and June to invite me to live in their home. In fact, June had vehemently insisted until I accepted. Since then, I'd created another minor sensation by bringing down a drug ring, also connected to Sam's tenant. Now this little incident had once again thrust me into the public view. I wondered if reporters would be knocking at the door soon, invading Sam and June's lives to catch a few minutes of the girl who'd flashed the world on TV.

I couldn't keep the Westins free from my messes while I was here, and I couldn't sulk and be truly away from work during the time I wasn't officially working. I think I was letting it get to me today.

My condo would be ready in a month or so. Then I could get back to my own little space. This house was gorgeous, huge, and had amenities that most people can only dream about. I loved it here, but felt I could never be one hundred percent relaxed as myself while I lived in such close proximity to Sam and June. For instance, sometimes I liked to sleep in the buff. I wouldn't think of doing that here, and it had made for some uncomfortably warm nights.

Another distraction was Sam and June's son, Alan, an amazing person who I'd been spending considerable time with, primarily because of our shared living space. As a computer networking executive working on a freelance basis, Alan traveled frequently. When he was in Reno he stayed in an apartment over his folk's garage.

We'd taken to playing tennis together until I'd burned my hand in the fire. I still found that he often sought me out for companionship. I enjoyed spending time with him, but felt a little weird since I was attracted to him. It was in a nervous, girlish way that wasn't typical for me. He had a huge heart, an incredible mind, and a to-die-for body. It took everything in my power not to stare when he joined me in the pool or hot tub. I loved his sense of humor, as he saw irony in every situation and had yet to encounter a situation in which he didn't have a snappy comeback to cover.

I also appreciated the way Alan treated his Mom. He was devoted to her, but without being a sissy or a momma's boy. It was with deference and respect he showed her whenever she was around. He was a character I'd just not figured out yet. His flirtations seemed genuine, but I was not sure how sincere he really was. I suspected he might be a player in this field. It was just, well, hard to figure out.

This might not seem like a problem to most people, but until last night, I had been dating someone else. He and Eckert had met one another on several occasions, none of them comfortable, as each seemed to stake a claim on me.

Even though my relationship with Eckert had never been

serious, it had been exclusive. Because I'd been dating Eckert and that I was working for Alan's parents, I felt uncomfortable with his constant flirtations, which he often did right in front of his parents or anyone else that might be around.

It isn't that I didn't like it; in fact the opposite was true. I felt guilty about it. His attention made me feel desirable and alive. He seemed interested in what I liked to do, in anything I had to say, and listened to my opinions without judgment.

Alan was a few years younger than me, which felt wrong. Overall I just felt that he was off limits, especially while we all lived together. Unlike Eckert though, he'd been the one to show care and concern for my well being yesterday, and seemed to have his mother's affinity for thoughtfulness. This was not a bad quality in anyone, let alone a man.

The ringing of the phone interrupted my thought trance. It was my own phone, not the home's main line.

I answered on the second ring. "Hello?" I asked, not recognizing the caller identification number displayed on the phone.

"I got it!" exclaimed the voice on the phone, forcing me to become alert and focused.

"Huh?" was my response, trying to figure out who was calling and what was so great about "it".

Soon enough, I realized it was Alex. His excited voice was so loud I had to keep some distance between the phone and my ear. "I got it; the role on *Night Trials* is mine! I had 3 offers to choose from, and this is the one for me." I could tell he was doing a little victory dance even though I couldn't see him.

"Oh my gosh!" I said, registering the meaning of his news. As far as his participation in the "incident" had gone, it had obviously not hurt him professionally. Instead, it had led to a part on a prime time television show. *Night Trials* was a drama that had a good mixture of crime and romance. It had great ratings, and was known for showcasing the hottest stars.

If this wasn't Alex's ticket already, it was another step up the ladder of success in Hollywood. I had chills running down my spine as it fully hit me, and I got up from the bed and started circling my room, forgetting the pain that radiated across my back.

"Your hot ticket took barely two days to punch. I'm so excited for you. Tell me everything." I grabbed a chair and sat down to get all of the details about Alex's exciting life in L.A.

"First an update on you. Take it you saw the E TV spot?" he asked quietly.

"Just heard about it, and some other one, and the online video outtakes."

'I'm so sorry, Sara. I can't even imagine how you're feeling, and yet you can still share in my joy. You're a true friend. Are you feeling okay/"

"Um, well, the itching is taking hold today," I complained. "I'm not sure if it is a side affect of the local anesthetic or the stitches as they heal. No matter which one is causing it, I hate it."

"Ouch, that sounds like a drag. I wish I could be there for you, Sara," he sounded like he was fighting back emotion.

"I'm going to be fine, Alex. I have some pretty good support here. Plus, you're always with me. I have your Calvin Klein poster on the wall," I said as I walked over to the closet and opened it to peer at the poster taped inside of Alex, of course looking gorgeous in a black and white shot of him in the famous underwear.

"Still, I'm missing you, in general, for the everyday stuff, you know what I mean?" I asked quietly, and then felt bad for raining even a little on his parade.

"I really miss you too. I'll be visiting soon though, promise. My soap gig ends this week; you should see my death scene. Way awesome!" Alex went on, counting down the events after his soap stint. "Then I have a modeling shoot, a few magazine covers and interviews, and then a month of freedom before we start publicity stuff for *Night Trials*."

"That's all?" I said sarcastically, but his cheerful news seemed to lift me out of my funk. "That sounds great. Too exciting for me, though. I'll ask if you can stay here. We can have an old-time slumber party again!"

"I'll be doing an exclusive interview on E TV tonight. I have to be hush-hush on the prime time deal though. No one who's not on the show knows my character is getting offed. The public thinks my role will go on for a while. Promise you'll watch? The E TV thing, I mean?"

"Of course I will. The gals are coming over too; we can watch together."

"Awesome. I won't reveal your name. By the way, in case it comes up, for the record you're an old flame of mine."

"Got it. I hope they focus the story on your little hot self though, instead of Sunday night's "incident". Please keep those animals away from meas much as possible. If I see a camera anywhere near me, I might just kill whoever is holding it."

Alex laughed, "No doubt. There's tons of controversy about what happened. People here think you should sue."

I heard Alex's cell phone ring. I paused while he checked to see who it was.

"Sorry Sara; gotta go. It's my agent."

"I hope there aren't too many more jobs lined up. You won't ever get any sleep. Call me when you're up." I promised him I'd tell Shel, McKayla and Megan the exciting details he'd shared during tonight's follow-up dinner. We made arrangements to speak again after his interview and signed off.

Alex had instilled his usual enthusiasm in the call, but when I put the phone down I felt sad, for myself anyway. I was beyond ecstatic for the fast moving changes in Alex's life, especially since they were all such good ones.

Why was I so sad then? Let's see…..Alex had probably been my closest friend for the last several years, and I flat out missed having him around. He's been the light in my often dull life. My only recent excitement had been at his party debut. It ended up in disaster for me, but it had been a pretty thrilling ride.

Alex had been my soul mate and constant companion for the nine plus months I'd spent unemployed. I missed our movie nights, accompanied by innocent cuddling on the couch. He'd been another that enjoyed my affinity for exotic foods and trying new things. In fact, Alex was fearless.

He had gone to great lengths to get me back to work, even putting up two billboards in our small city to attract the attention of employers in need of quality help. Finally, he'd been the one that had been there for me on the night I'd about gotten myself killed. His call had saved my life, and he put himself in danger to help get me out of the warehouse.

He was someone who I knew loved me for myself, no strings attached. If anyone could help me get over the embarrassment of this situation, it was Alex. I was glad he was doing well though. I guess these are the things that make friends become best friends. Selfish or not, I couldn't help but wish he were here.

I'd have to make do with gawking at him on TV at night with the rest of the nation.

7

I decided before Alex's call that I was too sore to travel today, so Mom came to see me around noon. June had fussed over me all morning, but I still wasn't up to eating much. I 'd been sulking in my room since Alex's call, and was finally starting to get hungry when she arrived.

Mom had brought along one of my favorite homemade comfort foods to share with me for lunch. Her macaroni and cheese had always been my favorite of her many unique recipes. It had about 1,000 calories per bite, but was worth every last one. It contained sour cream, Velveeta, sharp cheddar and ricotta cheeses. It was pure heaven and was definitely the right thing to offer to help bring back my usually hearty appetite.

As I practically licked my plate of a huge helping, Mom hurried me along, wanting to see my wound and discuss details of the event.

"Ouch!" she exclaimed as she changed my bandages for me. "It's looking a little infected. Did you get a tetanus shot? I think it's been a long time since you've had one."

"The hospital gave me one since I didn't remember when my last one had been. It's been itching like crazy. Can you put some something on it so the itching will calm down?"

'Ah, you've been scratching at it. No wonder it's so red around the edges."

She rifled through the bathroom cabinets and came up with something to spray on the wound. It stung, but provided relief from the itching immediately.

"Much better. Thanks."

She re-bandaged me, and I got my shirt back on.

"So, I have to say that you have given your father and me more near heart attacks and sleepless nights in the last few months than during the rest of our lives combined. First billboard advertisements, your condo gets blown up, and then you break into a criminal's lair and get caught, and now this." She shook her head in disbelief as she rattled off the events of the last several months of my life. It did seem a little unreal.

"We can only imagine what is next at this pace. At least all

Brooke does is get pregnant," she looked at me, and we both started laughing. "Why don't you try that route for a while? At least we're more used to it. Your dad is relishing the thought of being a grandpa for the second time. Make it a third; although get married first if possible," she added with a look of warning. "I loved planning Brooke's wedding. What about that police man, Stephen something or other?"

Her bringing up Eckert's name made me feel like I'd disappointed her again, but I didn't respond or react to her thoughts. Then, completely out of my control, the pent-up emotions came out, resurfacing yet again. Before I knew it, I was in Mom's arms, crying like I was 7 years old.

"I'm sorry, Mom." I sobbed as she held me, stroking my hair.

In the same motherly tradition of my past, she made a gentle noise of "shhh" as she held me, reminding me of the comforts of being a child once again.

"Sara," she finally spoke, and very softly, "Don't be silly, there's nothing to be sorry about. You had an accident that happened to have unusual consequences. And, it just happens that it was caught on film and broadcast on national TV."

"Don't forget the internet too," I choked out between sobs, not knowing if she were aware of this fact yet.

"Oh yes," she giggled, probably without meaning too, "We mustn't forget the wonders of modern technology. Still, the ones who should be embarrassed are the people that caused the accident as well as the media with the audacity to publicize it. I'd like to give them a piece of my mind."

I could imagine Mom going off on the paparazzi and media for their lack of judgment. The image made me smile, as they'd be sorry.

"It's bad enough that the rich and famous are subjected to this treatment, but an average citizen?"

She let go of me, and led me over to the couches. It was a more comfortable seating arrangement for us than the bed had been.

"I'll bet if this had happened to J. Lo there'd be hell to pay," her eyes narrowed as she thought this through. "What was the reaction of the others at the event?"

"I got whisked away too fast to tell. Alex says he's being interviewed tonight on E TV. He said it's likely to be a topic of conversation; heck it's been a wonderful career booster for him. It's nice to see something good come out of it. He promised to keep my name out of it, but hopes there is some way to vindicate me."

I blew my nose, and wrapped myself tightly in a blanket, another favorite comfort of mine. I had Rusty in, so she climbed up with me to snuggle.

"It will do you good, too. It's a character building experience.

Hold your head high. You don't have to laugh with those that find it amusing, but don't hide from it."

"Both Alex and Shelby compared it to Peewee Herman's appearing after his incident."

"That's about the worst comparison I can imagine. You weren't committing a crime or some sexual act in public for heaven's sake," she said as she dished herself some of the macaroni.

"I'd compare it to a fire victim that made it out of a fire but lost a garment, or a drowning victim whose bathing suit top fell off during the rescue. The public, or some of the public anyway, is reacting like it's one of those funny videos instead of a tragedy. The laughs won't last long, and soon they'll be on to scrutinize the next incident. You'll be forgotten before you know it."

Her analogies brightened my outlook considerably. I threw my arms around her, at least to the best of my ability before the shooting pain halted it.

"Thanks, Mom. I feel so much better. I've been so worried about letting you, Dad, June, heck everyone down for embarrassing myself publically."

"Like I said, hold your head high, honey," Mom said, kissing my head. "You could never embarrass us in any way that would make us mad at you. Your Dad passes along the same sentiments, BUT asks that you refrain from being blown up or from putting yourself in other dangerous situations long enough for his blood pressure to return to a normal level.

A smile crossed my face, as I could picture Dad relaying those exact words to Mom.

"Fair enough?" she finished, looking me in the eye and holding my chin up for me.

I nodded, feeling even better and ready to face the world again with my head held up. Not held high, but at least up.

"Okay, what's next?" she asked.

"Can I please have some more macaroni and cheese?" I asked, putting out my empty plate.

'Now that's more like my Sara!" Mom exclaimed, happy to fulfill my request.

We spent the next half hour discussing my wardrobe for my upcoming trip to England with the Westins, and she'd even brought me a few items that are prime for travel, being both light and wrinkle proof. Better, she'd agreed to take Rusty so that I didn't have to board her as Sam and June were doing with their dogs.

Mom explained that Kierra, Brooke and Greg were coming over to dinner that Saturday, and was insisting I come along when a soft knock sounded on the door.

"Come in," we announced in unison, then giggled.

"Finally, you got her to eat!" June exclaimed in relief as she saw me shoveling mounds of delicious food into my mouth. "All she needed was some of her own Mom's home cooking."

"Sara's told me how good yours is too. Looks like she's put on a few pounds since she's been with you." She patted me on the rear to convey her point.

"Mom!" I protested in embarrassment, although the statement was completely factual.

"Well, Dottie," June said to my Mom, "I was hoping you would join me for some tea. I have a set up in the kitchen all ready for you. I have freshly made cookies, too, three different kinds."

"Thank you, June, I'd love to. Sara has told me how much she's been learning about tea from you as well. She's so excited about having high tea at the Dorchester during your upcoming trip; although the cream tea at the Ritz is nothing to sneeze at either. What kind of tea are we having?"

"I thought you might like an Oolong after seeing what you brought for lunch. It helps digestion. The one I'm currently favoring is Formosan, and," June paused and peeked back into my room. "Did you want to join us too, Sara? I didn't mean to steal your Mom away; I set three places."

"You go ahead," I said, glad to see the two have some time together alone. "I'll join you in a few minutes."

June nodded and went back to telling my Mom about the Asian grown tea, its origin and qualities.

Enjoy, Mom, I thought happily.

8

After having food brought in for the dinner the previous night, June had insisted on a home cooked meal for my friends and me that night. I was still digesting my Mom's Mac and cheese from that afternoon, but June had made her version of Shepherd's Pie as an homage to our upcoming trip to England. I couldn't resist another meal of pure comfort food, so I gorged again, making up for the day I'd gone without any food at all.

Sam had opted to be out for the evening, and Alan had wisely decided to make himself invisible during the female invasion. I knew both would be watching the E TV show on their own, or would join us later for the event. .

The girls loved June's dinner, and made it known that they were jealous of my having gourmet quality food at home most nights with the family. As Mom had so graciously pointed out, I'd gained 5 pounds since I'd come to live at the Westin's home, so I warned the girls of the dangers of good cooking to the waistline.

After dinner, we took over the sitting room next to my room to wait for Alex's appearance on the entertainment show. June had graciously retired for the night so I could have private time with my friends. Alan had made a fire for us to keep up and left while we were at dinner. McKayla took on the task of keeping it going while Shelby and Megan fussed to get me in a comfortable position.

I felt so lucky to have such caring friends, and as I looked at them, I realized that each was perfect in some way. Megan was the perfectly efficient assistant; the one to help others succeed, and quite content standing far outside of the limelight. Her ability to handle the stress of working for workaholic Shelby and making time for her children always amazed me. She never complained and was always prepared.

McKayla was a perfect physical and mental specimen. She'd never been truly ill a day in her life, and her approach to all things was with a balanced mind that carefully thought things through. My total anti-thesis.

Shelby was the social and fashion wise one of the group. Her attire was never anything but sheer perfection down to every last detail, whether it be shoes, a scarf, jewelry or whatever accessory it took to make clothing an outfit. Comfortable in any social situation, she could make a dull party come to life, or the most boring seminar interesting with just the right touch of conversation to get the speaker to connect better to the audience.

Then of course there was Alex, the missing piece to the puzzle for this group. He'd been the one that had sparked our friendships with one another and had been the glue that held us together since then. He was perfection in spirit, and was never one to let anything get in the way of his enjoyment of a moment.

I looked at my friends, here again to show their friendship and understanding as I dealt with my current mishap. I don't know how I fit into this picture of perfection that surrounded me, but I was glad to be a part of it. Fortunately, they were thrilled that tonight also brought Alex's good news to share.

Finally convincing everyone I was comfortable enough to quiet their fussing, Shelby poured some wine and we all settled in to chat. It was like old times, all of us there catching up on life, love and work. We all admitted that Alex's absence made it less than perfect.

He was one of the girls through and through, and he made our group fun with his semi-male perspective on the girly things we talked about. We made a toast to him and his continued success, and then relaxed into typical conversation

"Where's Alan?" Shel chided as her head searched around the room. "I could just sink my teeth into him." She made a motion with her mouth as if she were snapping up something with a bite. My friend the cougar.

"He is darn good to look at," McKayla agreed, looking round the room at Megan, who nodded her agreement. "Is he still available?"

"Will you all stop it," I insincerely ordered. "I work for AND live with his parents for gosh sakes. There is no hanky-panky or anything like that going on."

"Too bad for you," Megan chimed in, the words oozing from her mouth as if she were talking about some mouth-watering morsel of food. The comment seemed out of character for our most shy and conservative friend. We were unsure whether we should laugh or be shocked.

"Come on, ladies," she said as she glanced over our varied expressions. "I'm the only one in this room with children. I think I know a thing or two about the birds and the bees."

"Girl, you are going to have to fill me in on your love life later tonight. You may be the only one getting any regular action." Shelby said to Megan, her eyebrows rose in wonderment at her typically reserved assistant.

Her tone turned a bit catty as she directed the next words to me, "At least she has some hormones; some of our group has given up on men altogether, or so it seems."

"I've been dating, gals," I retorted with a snap. "At least until last night, anyway. I was still seeing Eckert when he had time to go out. He's been pretty busy since his promotion."

"What do you mean until last night?" Megan asked.

I wasn't sure how to nicely put that I'd been dumped. "He was having some difficulty dealing with seeing someone who always seems to be making a spectacle of herself," I said, hoping that I got the point across.

"You mean he dumped you because one paparazzi jackass knocked you off your feet, and another one filmed the resulting incident?" Shel retorted. "I hope that's not true, or someone's going to get a piece of my mind!"

What could I say? "Well, yes, sort of I guess," I stammered for words, "but I'm not that hurt about it. We were still just friendly dating."

"So did he ditch your friendship too?" McKayla asked, "That would be way cold."

"No, he still wants to be friends. So do I. Maybe he thought we were on track to having a relationship, but it never really took off anyway."

"No bells or whistles for you then?" Megan asked, looking perplexed that I'd be in such a relationship.

"That's right; it never progressed to the next level or anything, but the companionship was nice. We both like exotic food and movies. We can't seem to agree on movies we both like though"

I laughed as I rattled off points on our lack of commonality, and then the whole "break-up" in general. The girls all looked kind of surprised at my revelations, like they'd thought there was more going on in our relationship than I'd shared.

"Sounds way exciting....not! You weren't getting any, then?" Megan asked, once again to my shock and surprise. Everyone laughed, but then looked to see if my eyes would give up any information that I'd not been sharing with them.

My face reddened. I didn't want to talk about the intimate details, or the actual lack thereof, regarding my relationship with Eckert. I offensively turned the topic towards McKayla.

"And when was your last date?" I asked

She gave me the once over with her gorgeous eyes. "What year is it?"

"Well here's a chance to meet someone. You promised to come with me to Simon's retirement party. It's going to be quite a bash."

"Sara, you know parties are not my thing," McKayla protested, her head shaking to emphasize her dislike of social events. "I only have to go to one a year, for work, and after that, forget it. Heck, this year the bank isn't having one to save money. Like I care."

"Come on; I'll be alone most of the time since there'll be so many cops around. Eckert will probably leave me with the other women or old folks anyway, so I'll be bored too. Can't we at least be bored together?"

"Shel will be there."

"Yeah, entertaining the troops," I said with a scoff. "She'll leave me cold in the corner faster than you can say "men"."

Shelby acknowledged this as a fact with a simple nod, and a "You know it sister. I gotta use it or lose it. Maybe I'll even score with some young stud."

Coming from Shelby, this was not shocking. She was older than the rest of us by about 10 years, and prided herself on dating many, and mostly younger, men. She was the role model for the term of "Cougar", which has long replaced Mrs. Robinson as the name to call mature women disregarding age when dating. Our own secret joke was that she was an "Equal Opportunity Dater", a term that played upon one of the compliance regulations I used to hammer into her head whenever I had the chance.

"See, I'm still going to be alone. I promise you won't have to stay long. You can bring your own car and leave if you hate it."

She hemmed and hawed for a moment and then relented, agreeing to go with Eckert and me that Friday night.

As we finalized arrangements for the party, Shelby shouted in excitement, "Everybody shush. It's coming on. Quiet!"

June, Sam and Alan entered the room as the familiar music played. The men apparently wanted to brave the event with the gals, which made sense since this room had the best TV. They found chairs and sat with us, eyes glued to the set. The show's hosts covered the highlights of the night, with Alex being the last one.

"Tune in to hear about an up and coming hot star's disastrous date at the Latin American Awards and what it means for his future," said the perky brunette hostess right before going to commercials.

"Disastrous date?" I moaned, "Oh Lord, what's next?"

'Maybe you'll make the "least" dressed list!" Alan commented, obviously not too shy to participate in conversation with the girls.

I tossed a pillow at Alan to show my lack of appreciation of his gest at my expense. The laughter in the room softened me up though, and I couldn't help but laugh too.

"Cute and a sense of humor," Shelby growled, scooting closer to Alan on the couch they shared. "Are you free later?"

The color drained from Alan's face, and I have to admit it was the first time I'd seen him uncomfortable or unable to reply with an immediate snappy comeback.

After a few seconds of silence, more laughter ensued, and Shelby let Alan know she was just kidding with him.

"See, don't mess with me or I'll sic Shelby on you," I warned Alan, who took his own moment of embarrassment with good humor.

"Point noted," he nodded, with an extra respectful glance towards Shelby.

From the look on Sam's face, I think he enjoyed the moment the most of all of us. He'd known Shelby for years, and no matter how much of a ladies' man Alan thought he was, Sam knew Shelby could eat him whole, and reveled in the opportunity to see it happen.

The music sounded again, and we sat through a few minutes before Alex's interview began. Alex's segment was being broadcast live from the set of his soap.

"Here's Alex Rodriguez, a hot young Hollywood actor on his way to stardom. His story is different from an actor's typical road to making it in Hollywood, with a recent incident at the Latin American Awards show moving his notch on Tinsel Town's ladder even faster and causing a sensational media controversy. Hear about his rise from bank teller, to Calvin Klein model to soap star in a record breaking 3 month period."

The on-the-scene reporter, Courtney something, turned to Alex to start the questions. "Alex, what has this been like for you?"

Alex looked at home in front of the camera. He was impeccably dressed, of course, and he spoke with confidence that wasn't cockiness.

'Thanks for asking. It's been a whirlwind the last few months. I'm so grateful to be working in an industry I love so much, and the fans have been very supportive."

"Tell us about your attendance at the Latin American Awards, Alex. What a rare opportunity for a new-comer to the Spanish soap industry."

"I was delighted just to be invited to the occasion, but unfortunately the ensuing events prevented my attendance. I was taken into police custody at the time of the altercation with the photographer, and my friend was taken to the hospital at the same time."

"So what the public wants to know is what exactly happened on Saturday?"

"My friend and I were getting ready to leave the red carpet area and enter the building when a very popular star made a curb appearance. The reporters and photographers pretty much ran over my friend to get to the celebrity to take photos as she exited her limo. In doing so, my friend was knocked off of her feet. The wall behind her, which prevented her from falling to the ground, had a metal fastener of the event's sign sticking out from it. As she fell, her back was ripped open from the fastener.

"Is that what tore her dress too?"

"The dress connected behind her neck, and it ripped during the fall, causing it to drop down. I couldn't help her fast enough. It was either grab her or the dress. For her sake, I wish now I'd made a different choice. I think the fall would've been preferable to her now national embarrassment."

"No pun intended, but she's gotten a lot of exposure from the event."

"Although I appreciate the pun, Courtney, there is nothing funny about it. This lady is my friend, who wanted nothing more than to support me at this event. She's not a public figure, doesn't want to be one, and now will likely never visit me again, even on the safety of the set. Because of the broadcasting of this accident, not "incident", she's endured pain and humiliation at the hands of the media, and sadly the public too."

Alex turned to the camera, a sincere look on his face as he addressed the nation.

"I appreciate all of the support you've shown me with your calls and letters to the studio. I only hope you'll continue to show your support for me by leaving my friend alone. I don't want to alienate any of you out there who might be watching, but this person has nothing to do with the entertainment industry. Please respect these wishes. There are plenty of other things going on to keep you entertained. She's hurt, upset, and no one has even apologized for running her down and ruining the special night we had planned together. She wants nothing but to be left alone. Please."

"We'll get more into the controversy in a moment, but, Alex, what happened to get you arrested?

"One of the photographers had the audacity to insult my friend when her dress fell down. I'm a calm person, but I'm afraid I lost my temper with him and let my fists do my talking for me. It happened so quickly, and I'm so new to all of this. I'm shocked at my own behavior."

"Were you charged with assault?"

"No, formal charges weren't pressed and I was released from custody at the station, but not in time to get to the event. I'll have to hope for another invitation sometime."

"Well we're glad you don't have to add criminal to the long list of current titles you have. Calvin Klein Model to meteoric Spanish soap star. What's next?"

"You'll have to stay tuned to *Dime Que Te Amas* this week and find out, Courtney."

Courtney turned to face the camera, obviously pausing for a commercial break.

"'We're talking to Alex Rodriguez, a hot young soap star, who made quite a splash at the recent Latin American Awards. Stay tuned for more, including the media controversy coming right up."

June made popcorn during the break, and we giggled and whispered about how great Alex looked on camera until the show started again.

'We're back with Alex Rodriguez, Calvin Klein model, Spanish soap star, and most recently in the news for his appearance before the Latin American Awards Show."

"Alex, there has been a lot of reaction to this, and not just by those watching the show. Other guests were very upset with the accident and the media's reaction. J. Lo herself has apologized to your friend on behalf of the media. She feels awful that it was her curbside appearance that started this chain reaction of events."

"Wow, that's so kind of her. J. Lo, if you're listening, on behalf of my friend and me, thank you. That's so thoughtful."

"She's not the only one seeing red over this incident, and this isn't the first time the paparazzi itself has been at the center of the storm. There's still litigation pending over the Princess Diana car chase and crash case over 10 years ago."

"Well no one died in this case. Let's face it, Courtney, we need the media to make the entertainment industry what it is. I just think that there are limits."

"There's talk in the industry about resetting the standards for physical proximity when paparazzi is not invited to photograph or interview. Photographers have sued over being hit by the personalities they wish to photograph, but the invasion of personal space has got to be frustrating. What do you think is crossing the line?"

"Well besides this, and anything that jeopardizes someone's safety, I personally think that when stars have babies, no one should approach them or take photos without asking first, and in no situation should there be any rushing or crowding around someone. I'm new at this, and it was an overwhelming experience to have so many people so close to me."

"I know many people who agree with you. In a recent incident, a photographer was hit by certain celebrity's car. In that case, the celebrity claims she was blocked from leaving the parking lot. There's definitely a pending civil suit here, and it will be interesting to see the legal interpretation of these events. We're waiting to see if it is considered unlawful detainment, assault and battery or maybe both. What about your friend? We've learned she had a lot of stitches in her back. We have a picture of the wound. It's pretty bad. Will she sue?"

"My friend? Sue? Gosh, I don't know about that. She's a pretty level headed lady. She's got some hefty hospital bills to cover, I'm sure. Like I said, she's not a celebrity, and a night in the emergency room in itself is a burden on an average person's salary. I'd hope that the injuring party offers to cover her out of pocket expenses that have resulted from this incident.

Courtney turned to the camera again, addressing the audience directly.

"Our sources confirm that Alex's friend is Reno, Nevada resident, Sara Blake, who worked for many years with Alex in the banking industry. In addition to a college degree, we've found out she has a paralegal education as well, so watch out media personnel! "We haven't been able to locate her current whereabouts, but I'm sure we'll be hearing more from her soon."

She turned back to Alex, who was as stunned as we were by the public revelation of my name.

"Alex, do you think we could convince her to phone in for tomorrow night's show?"

"I'm assuming "we" means me? You've placed me in an awkward position, Courtney. You didn't mention you knew or would reveal her name. I promised her that I wouldn't mention her name, and you've included her hometown, too. Must she face more publicity over this?"

"We're hoping that Sara will give us her side of the story tomorrow. Plus, we'll reveal a slow-motion showing of the events, and a surprise revelation of who's really responsible. Will you ask your friend to call in to the show tomorrow? We'd arrange to have her flown in, but I think you've indicated that would be unlikely."

Alex stammered, "She'd never agree to be on the show. I'll ask her about the call, but I don't know."

Courtney cut him off before he could say anything more. My heart broke for him as I could feel the pain of his being blind-sided by the media as much as I'd been. I knew he wanted her to agree not to pursue it, but the camera was no longer on him, instead it remained in a close-up of Courtney.

She wound up the story by inviting the public to return for another juicy segment the next night, highlighting Alex's torment over my pain and humiliation, then enticing viewers with hopes of an exclusive talk with me for my side of the story

She concluded the story but the camera remained on Alex, who looked emotional as he silently took in her words. It was purposeful, showing viewers the personal connection he felt to the story. What vultures!

"We think that Sara will want to give her side of the story. Plus, be with us live when we reveal the events as they unrolled that night. Tune in tomorrow for part two of our interview with Alex Rodriguez and for the behind the scenes look at the awards show incident that is taking the media by storm. Until tomorrow then, Lauren, back to you in the studio."

    Welcome to Hollywood, Alex, I thought. He had what it took to get there, and now I prayed he had the stomach to stay.

9

June, being a quick thinker, had given Alan my cell phone and asked him to field calls after the first show had revealed my name. As she foresaw, the phone began ringing immediately, and didn't seem to stop for the rest of the night. Alan handled conversations with my parents, my sister, Eckert and others for me, and took messages on all calls so I could review them

Megan, Shelby and McKayla were upset for me and Alex, but offered their unconditional support in however I chose to handle it until it was over. They left in a flurried exchange of hugs and well-wishes immediately after the show finished airing to let me sort out the aftermath.

I'd personally taken Alex's call when Alan informed me he was on the line. He was in near tears and very angry at the way the interview had been handled. He was ready to leave town and come home. I convinced him to stay, and told him it was his first lesson of how the entertainment biz worked.

During the airing, Alex refused a second interview the producers planned as a follow-up the next night. Somehow, I convinced him to go through with it. The attention would continue with or without our cooperation. As impossible at it seemed, our participation might help control where it went and prevent additional damage to me. He finally agreed, and I said I'd better call in to be his support.

"Guess we're still in this one together Alex," I laughed nervously, "Besides, what more could they do except show up at the front door?"

"Don't think they won't!" he snarled. "If they try that and I'm on camera, I take no responsibility for my subsequent actions."

"I'll have someone watching," I said in soothing words. 'Promise. Just move this out of your head for a few hours and think of the positives. By the way, get some sleep. We don't want our hunkasaurus having bags under his eyes before the show."

He finally chuckled, ending our call on an upbeat note.

Now that I'd calmed down, I returned a single call Alan had fielded for me. Everyone else could wait, but I knew my Mom would be worried about me, and I also wanted her to have a heads up that I would likely be calling into the show tomorrow.

Everyone went to bed while I was still on the phone, so I took it into my room and ended my evening with her positive thoughts and encouragement I needed.

The next morning came quickly, and I reluctantly made arrangements with the studio to be patched through to the show that night. It seemed like the day dragged by, and I spent most of it alone until the time came to make the call.

I was tense as I dialed the phone, barely hitting the numbers in the correct order. For my efforts, I was immediately greeted by name, thanked for my participation in that night's program, and asked to wait in a holding queue until it was time to start my segment of the show. I was given a quick overview of how tonight's events would unfold, and was promised to be on within 5 minutes of the start of the program.

As I waited, I tried hard not to be nervous, and to think of what I wanted to say. As I didn't control the questions that would come, I would have to find a way to make my points fit into their questions. I hoped I could make the strategy work, and I scribbled down some last minute points I wanted to make.

I hadn't wanted the girls over with me tonight, and opted instead for the sole support of June and Alan. I knew my folks were watching, and they'd said a prayer for me that this would help bring an end to this now out of control situation.

Alan provided me a small earpiece so that I could hear the TV from across the sitting room. I sat at my usual office desk, and June and Alan parked in front of the set, keeping the volume low so there would be no feedback interference during the call.

The music started, and a commercial followed the host's overview of that night's show, which included my exclusive interview and a revelation of the cause of the accident.

After several minutes the show had returned and the host turned over the reigns to Courtney, once again live on the set of Alex's soap.

"We're back with Alex Rodriguez. Although new to the entertainment industry, his popularity has exploded through his role as a love interest of the entire cast of *Dime Que Te Amas*, and more recently by a partial appearance at the Latin American Music Award. During his walk down the red carpet, his guest, Sara Blake, was injured during a media mob rush to meet the arrival of a major star. To top off the 13 stitches necessary to fix her back, she had a major wardrobe malfunction that has been shown repeatedly on news and entertainment shows across the nation. Just three days since the incident, online statistics now show that the video of Sara's incident is the number one online search."

Finally coming up for air, Courtney looked at Alex, who meekly smiled as she continued.

"Tonight we'll hear from Sara herself about the impact this incident has had on her, and from industry professionals who have their own opinions on the topic. Finally, some exciting news about what's in store for Alex."

I hadn't watched Alex's show that day. I wondered if they'd killed him off already so this story would be more sensational.

"We have Sara with us tonight, live on the phone from Reno, Nevada."

Courtney pronounced Nevada as "Nu-vah-da" instead of "Nu-va-da", a major ear cringer to anyone who lives in the state. We hadn't even spoken yet and she was already on my nerves. I heard a clicking noise on the phone, and realized this was the cue that I was on live with the show.

"How are you tonight, Sara?"

"I've been better Courtney, but thank you for asking."

"We've been told that you had 13 stitches in your back as a result of this incident. Is this fact correct?"

"Yes, it is. I spent hours at the emergency room waiting to be seen while those with more urgent needs were handled first. It was appropriate, but made for a long and uncomfortable night."

"What other residual effects has your evening at the awards event had?"

"Wow, where to begin on that one. Let's see, besides the injury and its expense, I broke the heel on a new pair of shoes and my good friend's dress has been destroyed. I missed a chance to see my friend, Alex, amongst his new peers, and, of course, pictures of my breasts have been plastered all over the internet. The picture of me outside the hospital the next morning was less than appealing too. Besides that, just a major interruption of life in general."

"So, I gather that this is unwanted attention?"

I almost threw the phone across the room. Could she actually be serious? June and Alan looked over at me, mouths open in disbelief at the question. On the screen, Alex, put his hand over his face, and hung his face down in shame.

"Well, I suppose that there are some out there who would love any kind of media attention, Courtney, but let me tell you I'm not one of them. If I never step foot in Hollywood, or even Los Angeles again, I won't be sorry in the least. I spent several days feeling ashamed of what happened because of the embarrassment to my friends and family. I even worried it might have ruined Alex's chances of staying on his soap or getting other jobs, and he's so talented, the thought crushed me. I've changed my mind since then, Courtney. I didn't do anything wrong, but I let myself feel like I had. With what's happened since, well, honestly, now

I'm just plain mad."

'Explain your feelings, Sara."

"If an actress at the Oscars had her head split open by a falling boom camera, and her top fell down, would that be newsworthy? What if she were in a car accident, and required medical attention and her breasts were showing, would that be? Would it be different if it happened to an on-looker?"

I was on a roll, and she hadn't stopped me, so I continued. "What it boils down to is that an accident happened, as they often do in life. This one just happened to have embarrassing consequences that have been capitalized on and deemed as newsworthy. What's worse, is that no one cares that a fellow human being was hurt, only how funny it is that someone's top fell down on camera. "I'm a nobody to the entertainment industry, just an average Jane who no one cared about yesterday and will likely be forgotten tomorrow. I'd like for tomorrow to be now so I can concentrate on healing and getting back to work. Don't we have better things to talk about than this? "

Courtney seemed to understand that my tirade had ended, and that the questions were back in her court. "You know it's hard to tell what would classify anything as newsworthy today, but it certainly has generated a lot of public interest. That seems to be today's standard."

"Yes, Courtney," I interjected, "But in a "isn't this funny" manner. I was hurt physically and financially. Instead of someone apologizing for causing the accident, it's a source of amusement for everyone. I guess I hadn't realized that as a guest of a public persona I was fair game to a media blitz. I never expected my name and city of residence to be released as public information. This is a small place, and now anyone could find me, although I don't know why this would be of continued interest to anyone other than a passing "I can't believe that really happened." I just want life to continue moving forward. That night, and even this story, should be about Alex, with just a side note about these consequences. If such a big deal hadn't been made about this, once my back healed, I'd be laughing with everyone too."

"Well, there's no doubt that you definitely have an opinion on this matter. E TV certainly hopes that our release of your name has not caused additional stress on you as you heal. On the good news side of things though, we have footage of the event that will reveal to all just what happened and who's responsible. Another part of the story viewers have been buzzing about is Alex's fighting for your honor. More on that, heated responses from those in the entertainment industry, and some major news on Alex Rodriguez when we return after these messages."

I heard the click in my ear as I got put back on hold or shut off so I couldn't continue my tirade. I hung up the phone, as I had nothing more to say.

'Did I sound like a bitter, angry person?" I asked Alan and June, who muted the TV as I joined them on the couch.

"More like the only sane one," June said, spitting mad herself. I'd never seen her like this before. "I hope that Courtney shows up here for an in person interview. Her lovely cheek has a date with the back of my hand."

Alan and I were stunned, and starting laughing as we visualized the tiny woman smacking the tall, lovely reporter.

"Go, Mom!" Alan said, giving her a hand in the air to high five.

She complied, of course only in the most ladylike manner possible.

"Well, let's at least finish it and hear about Alex's news."

We watched the final 20 minutes. Alex's character had been killed off that day on the soap and his role on *Night Trials* was announced. Huge amounts of fan mail for Alex, lauding his chivalry in light of the event were also shared.

Opinions of the head of the awards show, a famous cameraman, and J. Lo herself were aired over the final ten minutes of show time. The head of the awards show announced that my medical bill would be paid for by the show and offered me an apology on behalf of the event staff for not helping in preventing the accident. He hoped that I had been taken care of by his staff behind the scenes in an appropriate manner. I was invited as an honored guest for next year's show, if I changed my mind and would return to Los Angeles in the future.

I appreciated his comments, and made note to thank him if the opportunity ever arose, as his staff was great at extracting me from the scene as fast as possible.

The cameraman explained the side of things from the perspective of those taking pictures of the stars. A shot of the right star at the right time could earn a photographer enough money to live on for years. The public paid billions every year for entertainment magazines and regularly watched shows such as this one. He apologized to me, and called what happened to me "collateral damage" in an industry that minimizes humanity for true stardom. I couldn't disagree, and appreciated his perspective.

J. Lo was a call in. I was floored as she hammered the "stalkarazi". She made a point of saying as a public figure, she always plans extra time before events to pose for the photographers, and that no one needed to be run down to get to her. She gave me both her own and her husband Marc Antony's personal apologies that their appearance triggered this incident. She alluded that she'd found a way to make it up to me that she thought I could really use.

I was practically in tears, and felt like an idiot for lashing out as I did. I called back into the number, and once again · it was answered immediately. I told the guy I wanted to make just a quick comment, and I heard the clicking sound and was live on the air.

"Back with us is Sara Blake, who disconnected after making her initial statements. Sara, what do you have to add?"

"I just want to say thank you to all three of the guests that just appeared. Each of you has put this into perspective in a way I can now accept and move on. Thanks to the studio for covering the bill, and also that the event staff was very fast in removing me from the scene and getting me to the hospital. I don't see how they could have prevented what happened, and dealt with it very professionally as quickly as they could. To the cameraman, thanks for sharing this incident from your perspective. Anyone who has bought a fan magazine, including myself, has to take some responsibility for building this animal. Finally to J. Lo, probably the most photographed and stalked of all stars, thank you for caring enough to make a statement on behalf of someone you've never met. I hope you'll make a point of meeting Alex sometime. In your crazy world, he's the kind of friend you can count on."

"Um Courtney, I'm going to hang up now. I was so angry before, but now I'm ready to move on no matter what happens in your world. I think I'm ready to start the healing process. Thank you."

'Do you want to stay live while we reveal the culprit?"

'I think I'll watch from home, thank you. I've had enough of your time. Congratulations, Alex. You've always been and will always be a star to me."

As I hung up, Alex's face brightened, and I knew everything would be okay.

10

The next day, I decided I was done being a victim and hiding away in my room. Despite last night's media blitz, I entered the kitchen like I would on any other day to enjoy my coffee and interact with June, Sam or Alan. Disappointed to find myself alone, I helped myself to some breakfast and thought about the past two nights.

I'd handled last evening's events before without overreacting. Although I'd been horrified at having my name and hometown revealed on national TV during the first show, I did manage to keep my emotions in check for a change, at least while I was on the air.

. Last night's call in had taken a bad turn when Courtney made it appear I was some attention seeker. I think I set the record straight, and after listening to the cameraman and J. Lo's perspectives, I was ready to move on

Despite the emotional pull of my personal drama, I decided that some work was in order for the day before I went out. Technically I had the day off, and planned on badgering Eckert to take me to lunch to discuss some unfinished thoughts from my side of the relationship. I doubt it would make a difference to him, but it would make me feel better. Then, I had to pick up some final items to complete my packing for the trip. I wanted to be ready far in advance, showing what a novice traveler I was, I'm sure.

I looked around the area I called my "office", which was just a desk off in the back of the sitting room. There wasn't a lot to do really, except to e-mail or call tenants to let them know we'd be out of town and where to call if something came up.

I had gotten Sam's business so organized that it only took a few hours a week to maintain, unless he were buying or selling one of the properties. Most recently, I'd completed the sale of Sam's downtown center, the one with the dry cleaning facility that had been at the root of the recent crisis we'd endured.

One of Sam's tenants had been vandalized and later killed. After my own probing into the matter, I'd learned that the murder had been orchestrated by a potential tenant who desired to obtain the subject's precious dry cleaning facility. These properties were hard to come by since they posed an environmental hazard, and the potential tenant really needed a fully operating plant as a cover to manufacture meth amphetamines. My nosing around led to the fire bombing of my condo as a warning to back off, and had nearly gotten me killed when I refused to stop. With a history like that, let's just say Sam was happy to remove the property from his portfolio.

He was now searching for a suitable property to add to his mix of retail, office and residential real estate holdings. Once he found an acceptable investment, things would get a little more heated for me in taking care of every last detail. I'd have to arrange for property inspections, building or parking lot improvements, and understand the current lease arrangements any existing tenants had in place. I would then need to create a legal entity, probably an LLC, to use to buy the property, draft a sale agreement and get it through escrow. Most importantly, all of these things had to be done in a certain timeframe for Sam to maintain the tax advantage of a 1031 exchange. No problem!

Until he found just the right property though, I found I was spending most of my "work" day with June. She was like a second mother to me, but without the constant poking and prodding around in my life regarding areas I didn't want to deal with.

We shopped, read, cooked, worked in the garden, watched movies, and more together. Best of all, it was a part of my job. Life was good here. It was a nice solace after my most recent injury and media woes.

I still wished for a little more privacy. I wasn't sulking over it like I was yesterday, but my bedroom was 15 feet away from my office. There wasn't a lot of separation here. I was missing my condo and being able to have my own private space. When we got back from England, I should be ready to move back into my condo. I just wondered how June would take the news.

When the "out of town" e-mail was out to all tenants, and calls made to the few without e-mail addresses, I settled on the couch with a map of London to review the events we'd tentatively planned. We'd all promised to let each day run its course naturally, but we'd set out things to see by proximity for efficiency.

Officially off for the day, Sam threw me for a loop as he tromped in the sitting room.

"Sara, I need you to form a new LLC for me right away," he said as he entered the room. He was dressed for golf, which on a cold day like today meant indoor golf at the Grand Sierra Resort. His tone meant business, so I grabbed a pad and pen from the desk.

"All the usual suspects as members, same set up, standard docs," he rattled off, gesturing the entire time to indicate nothing special was necessary. He opened the closet to get his clubs and favorite hat.

"Ok, but what about a name?"

"Westin Investments, LLC," he said as he slicked down his gray hair to put on a ball cap.

"Got it," I said as I made notes, familiar with the process. "All legal activities as its primary purpose?"

"Yes," his voice trailed as he opened the hall closet for his clubs. "I need a bank account too."

"Right away?" I asked since this definitely deviated from our standard procedure.

"Yes, please. Can you have everything ready tonight for signing, then drive to Carson tomorrow and pay for an expedited filing?"

Sam was referring to the legal and formal processes involved in the formation of a legal entity. It wasn't hard once you knew what to do and had the right legal forms and necessary clauses to make the entity work as its originator wanted.

Sam had never had me get a filing in person though. For a nice sized fee, the Secretary of State would process your entity in an hour, which meant I could technically get a bank account opened tomorrow as well.

'Ok, no problem. I should have signature cards for you tomorrow afternoon."

Sam hitched his clubs over his shoulder, and rubbed me on the head on his way out. "I knew it, of course. My Girl Friday makes things happen! Bye," he said as the door slammed shut behind him.

Although this represented Sam's typical way of giving me work outside of the daily routine, this time the work itself was unusual. I was hoping to squeeze lunch in with Eckert before I did more shopping for the trip to England, so I got on task right then and there.

"Eckert," was the curt greeting I received as he answered his direct line on the first ring.

"Hey," was all I could muster to start the conversation.

"Hey, yourself. How are you?" I could hear papers ruffling on his desk. "Are you mad?" he said in his usual short but to the point manner.

"No, it's only been two days, I'm fine and calling now," I rattled off. "You said we could still be friends. I want to talk about it. Are you free for lunch?"

"Hmm," was the first part of the reply, and I knew he was scanning his calendar for the day to ensure his schedule would allow for time out of the office. "I saw Alex's interview last night," he said with a note of sarcasm.

"Noon, at Taste of Thai, then?"

'Affirmative," I sarcastically replied, ending the call and not jumping to his baited comment. His mannerisms had become even more serious and professional since his promotion to Lieutenant in charge of the Robbery and Homicide division of the Reno Police Department. This, I could forgive, especially since he picked a restaurant that served fantastically exotic food. His sarcasm and unsupportive reactions to recent events were not the acts of a true friend, and I planned to tell him so.

As for the promotion, I couldn't be happier for him. His part in helping Alex and me when we were held hostage by the Finnuto gang had been noted by his superiors and he had been well rewarded for his efforts, even getting the credit for the bust when the Feds took it over.

It had been my own meddling that uncovered the plot, and Alex's bravery in saving my life initially, but hey, all's well that ends well. Plus, I got free lunches with Eckert whenever I could get him to go out.

Even though we were now officially just friends, I wanted to see him. I was still mad as a hatter at him for being so insensitive about my current situation. The party was tomorrow night, so I wanted the air cleared first. Well, at least after I gave him a piece of my mind about his reaction to my Hollywood incident. Instead of helping me get over my embarrassment, I felt he was punishing me for embarrassing him in front of his peers. He'd hear more about that at lunch time, but I had to make it so that we could remain friends after. I thought of it as helping him be a better man for his next relationship, because no woman I knew would tolerate a man that didn't back her when the chips were down.

It wasn't as if my heart was hurt or anything that we "broke up" either. I think my ego suffered the biggest blow since no one had ever broken up with me.

Our relationship had been a coupling of convenience for us really, and I'd repeatedly thought about its lack of forward movement. The lackluster conversation and non-lustful thoughts had been endured to have something to do and to keep my parents from inviting endless strings of men over in hopes of marrying me off to one of them. With Eckert, there'd been no hanky-panky past an occasional deep kiss. No harm, no foul as they say.

As we ate, Eckert took the lashing well, and we both had an opportunity to share thoughts and feelings about our "relationship". We both agreed that we had different wants and needs at this point in our lives. He needed a woman behind him, and not one constantly traipsing into trouble. I wanted a man to jump into all that life had to offer with me, and not just bail me out when there was trouble.

He actually took my advice on being more supportive for any future relationships, and admitted that he'd taken out his frustrations on me due to his being the butt of jokes at work. All was forgiven, and he agreed to pick up McKayla and me for the party the next night.

After lunch, I made time to pick up some last items for the trip and get home in time to prepare for my phone interview tonight.

Over the last few weeks, I'd been running all over Reno in preparation for the trip for everyone else. I had dropped off and picked up dry cleaning, made sure everyone's prescriptions were filled and had to pick up some new luggage for June.

June and I had also spent several hours at a local boutique that features clothing made to hold up under the stress of packing and extended travel wear. We each got six or so matching pieces that would resist wrinkles. Best for me, stain resistant too! With these and the ones that Mom brought, I felt I had clothing covered except for shoes.

I needed a pair for walking, and a dressier pair that was still comfortable enough to wear around town. I opted for a classier than normal shoe store, since their specialty was comfort. Despite the hundreds of styles, I made my selections and was out of the store in fifteen minutes flat.

I had to hit the mall for specialty items from the travel store, as I hoped to get an adapter for my hair dryer and curling iron to use with the different English electrical current. I found one, a simple looking thing that held the appliance plug in one side and had the two pronged plug required. The clerk was less than helpful. After I spent the time finding it, he insisted it was fine for what I needed.

My last destination for the fun part of the day was the local bookstore chain to replace a great travel book about England that had some great maps. I'd about destroyed it deciding how to map out the days with June, so ordered two more copies to take with us on the trip. I was set now, and still had three full days before the trip to consider anything else we might possibly need.

My next errand was to the County Recorder's office in Carson City to set up the limited liability company. The Westin's home was closer to Carson City than to Reno, so I saved this effort for the end of my day. I'd give the clerk the paperwork, the extra fee for the rush filing, and go get coffee during the hour that it would take to retrieve them.

I called the bank on the way to Carson to start on the bank account so I could pick up the signature card for Sam in the morning, or drag him to the bank to get it signed and have it done with. I needed the paperwork that I was getting done today to get the actual account opened, but Sam's relationship with the bank warranted faster service. All in day's work, or in my case, part of a day's work anyway.

11

It was a beautiful morning; sunny but chilly, just the way I liked it. I did a quick appraisal of the events of the night before as I got out of my warm bed to let Rusty take care of her business outside.

Sam left the house at the crack of dawn to take care of few final details he'd needed to do before the trip. He'd been acting funny about the new LLC, and didn't want to talk about it. He'd signed and left the paperwork I needed to get his bank account opened without a word to me before he went out.

Ready for the trip long before the rest of us, June spent the previous evening engrossed in a marathon of old black and white mystery movie classics. She'd been up until the wee hours of the morning. Worked for me, as I craved some alone time and gladly left her in peace.

Knowing I had the run of the entire downstairs area to myself that morning, I put on a "barely there", silky nightgown over my bare body and headed out to the kitchen for some coffee. Night clothing had been difficult due to the stitches in my back, as whatever I wore always seemed to catch on the fabric as I turned and moved during the night. I opted for sleeping in the buff to accommodate this inconvenience, although I'd previously sworn I'd never do it while under the Westin's roof.

I yawned and stretched my way through the family room, and arrived at the kitchen to the smell of the coffee that Sam had graciously set to brew within the last hour or so.

I poured a cup, opened the refrigerator for a bit of my favorite coffee creamer, and turned to go back to my room. Out of the corner of my eye, I saw a newspaper rustle at the far right side of the kitchen, the breakfast nook area.

I knew Alan was away for the day, so when I saw the head full of brown hair, I just about dropped my cup of coffee.

"Hello?" I mustered out, not sure what I should do.

The newspaper dropped, and a handsome man peered from

behind the paper. He had a roguish smile on his face, like he'd been caught hiding but just didn't care.

"I tried not to scare you once I realized you thought you were alone. Guess I failed," he said in a quiet but authoritative voice. He tossed the paper aside and put his full attention on me.

I recognized the man as Adam, Sam and June's older son. I'd seen many pictures of him around the Westin's house, and the pictures did no justice to him.

"You must be Sara," he said, looking me up and down. 'It's nice to finally meet you, in person," he said, slowly emphasizing the last part as he gave me another head to toe review, and not acting shy or shocked about doing it either.

I remembered the sheer nightgown I'd put on and was horrified that I was as good as naked.

How could I not be flustered when I was exposed in front of a complete stranger? I set my coffee mug down on the counter with a clang. Coffee splashed out of the cup, but I didn't care.

"I'll be right back," I stammered as I ran off to my room. I found a very solid terry cloth robe that zipped up the front and put it on over my practically see through nightie. I felt the need to go back and complete our introduction, but I was mortified that once again I'd let myself get too comfortable in someone else's house.

I re-entered the kitchen a minute later. I quickly cleaned up the spilled coffee, retrieved and filled my coffee cup and sat at the table next to Adam.

"Sorry about that. I thought I was alone," I said meekly and put my hand out. He extended his own hand and gave me a slow handshake. His eyes seemed to pierce through me, and I felt like he could still see exposed body parts.

I thought it best to just continue as if nothing unusual had occurred. "I am indeed Sara, and it's a pleasure to meet you in person as well, Adam." As he released my hand, his eyes twinkled with an underlying laughter of catching me off guard and maybe getting an eyeful.

"Your dad didn't mention that you would be visiting."

"It was a last minute surprise. I got in right as Dad was leaving. He told me you would be out and about soon, and to stay out of the way." He smiled broadly. "What a nice morning surprise for me. I caught your interview last night too. It seems you've had lots of exposure lately."

I turned red again, and gave him a look of disgust. He had his brother's sense of sarcastic wit, but the timing and lack of sensitivity of Eckert.

He looked a lot like Alan too, or vice versa since Adam was older than he by several years. He had a sleek haircut and no facial hair. His jaw line was angled just like Alan's, and his eyes were a warm honey brown color, the same as his hair. He was dressed in full business attire, and had an elegant appearance that fit his position as an attorney. He was a business Ken doll, while Alan was the sporty version. They were both just too good looking for words.

This was not how I envisioned our in person introduction at all. What's done is done though, and I just hoped I hadn't embarrassed Sam or June due to my casual behaviors around their home. After the last few days though, I didn't think a revelation of this would be too much for them to handle.

If I had been in my condo, I would have come out naked, so I could at least be glad I had enough common sense to put something on.

I knew that Adam was living in Northern California, and had recently divorced his wife. He was licensed to practice in both California and Nevada, and I'd spoken to him on the phone several times regarding various legal matters relating to Sam's business dealings. I'd received a legal education and earned a designation as a paralegal some years ago. Adam and I had worked well together over the phone and e-mail so far when I needed legal advice. I hoped this would continue, but it would be hard to maintain a professional relationship when someone has pretty much seen you in your birthday suit.

"What brings you to Reno?" I asked, sipping my coffee slowly and attempting to pretend that all was well.

"I'll be back and forth a bit for the next few weeks. My daughter Peyton is taking ski lessons this season, so I brought her up to get some new equipment at the local ski shop."

"Is she here now?" I asked, my heart dropping again that I could have made the same entrance in front of June's granddaughter. I knew Peyton was about eight years old, and his other daughter, Ella, was six. June talked about them often. In fact, so often I almost felt like I knew them.

"No, her mother is bringing her and her sister Ella down tonight. I just came up from a business trip in LA." He got up from the table to pour himself some more coffee. I couldn't help but notice that his clothing was well made, and fit him perfectly. The rear view of his body was again similar to Alan's, but Adam was slighter, and probably less athletic than his brother.

I tried not to stare, but I couldn't help making continual comparisons between the two brothers. I looked away when he turned back around, hoping he hadn't noticed the place my eyes had been looking.

"I thought I'd take Mom to lunch, and also go through the new entity papers you drew up and leave the 1031 paperwork with you while I'm here," he said.

"You too, by the way," he started, and when I looked at him with an odd expression, he finished, "For lunch I mean."

Sam was diversifying his real estate holdings to offset the recent devaluation of local property. The whole nation was feeling it, but Reno's real estate market had accelerated at an insane pace a few years ago, and was now hurting from the corrective decline that had been bound to follow.

The downtown retail center had been sold, and Sam needed a 1031 exchange to be set up to maintain the proceeds of the sale until Sam found another property to buy. It was a very common tax vehicle for real estate investors such as Sam, but I was a little new at facilitating them and was grateful for Adam's assistance.

As for the new entity, I was fine with setting up the paperwork, but it was wise to have Adam review them for accuracy.

"Sounds great. Your Mom won't likely be down for a few hours."

"Was it an all-nighter of reading or movies?" he asked, apparently used to June's marathons of either activity.

"Movies. I think it was a Thin Man marathon. All six of them on TCM in one night, and she had to see them all. I'm not sure if she made it, but I know it was very late, or rather very early, when she turned in."

Adam laughed, "Yeah, she sure is a night owl." As if sensing I was ready to finish getting ready for the day, he added. "Go on, do whatever you need to do. If Mom isn't ready, how about we go at 11:30?"

"You mean without your Mom?"

"Mom's not up, so I didn't get the normal breakfast feast she prepares. I'm famished so I'm going with or without her. Since I'll be here overnight, she'll have time with me later anyway. Probably some tea thing." He finished with one eyebrow raised which told me that this was not a favorite activity of his but one to be endured for his Mom's sake.

I returned to my room to get showered and ready for the rest of the day. I hoped it was full of less surprises than the morning had held. Just as I was starting to get over the fallout regarding my public embarrassment, something like this happens. I was a magnet for awkward situations. I was really wishing my condo was ready so I could enjoy the secure serenity that only came with being the only one at home.

Since I had a while before I was expected to be Alan's "date" for lunch, I thought I'd treat myself to a hair oil treatment. Between the wax product my hair had recently been plied with to losing a nice chunk of my brown locks in the window of Alan's car, deep conditioning seemed a necessary luxury.

I pulled out bottles of hair and body oil that had been given to me as a gift. *Might as well soften up the skin some too* I thought, and immediately decided to run a bath instead of the shower. When the temperature was right, I added some oil and sunk into the water. I used a bath pillow to keep my stitched places away from the hard surface, and promised myself I would not stay in too long or risk ruining the healing process.

I used a hand held shower to rinse my hair, washed it, then put in a generous amount of oil. I sulked over my unintended introduction to Adam, and came to the conclusion I didn't like him one bit. How could he be a product of Sam and June? Maybe Alan got all of the good things, and Adam the worst.

I decided I was being too judgmental of someone I'd only spoken to on the phone and met for a few minutes in person. I made a vow to give him a chance at lunch, but hoped June would be joining us.

I did two full rinses of my hair, then got out to dry off and pick something loose and comfortable to wear. By the time I got dressed, the clock indicated I had about 45 minutes before Adam would want to leave for lunch.

I applied a minimal amount of make-up and dried my hair. Normally, my hair took about 8 minutes to dry to a level that was workable with a casual style. It didn't seem to be working, and finally I turned off the dryer and ran my fingers through my hair.

It was dry, but felt greasy and hung limply on my head. My eyes rounded in surprise, and I snatched the bottles I had taken to the tub. It was hard to be sure, but it looked like I used the hair oil in the bathwater and the bath oil on my hair. Crikey!

Jumping back into the shower, I shampooed two more times before trying to dry it again. The end result was the same. I now had just minutes before I was expected to go to lunch with Adam, and my hair looked like it hadn't been washed in a year. The amount of oil left in the hair made it impossible to be truly dry, and it hung in limp strings. How was I going to fix this?

12

What's the matter, Sara? You aren't yourself today," June said, startling me, as she entered the living room later that afternoon. She cozied up on the couch, and watched me filing the paperwork on the new LLC and the bank account I'd opened for it after having a too long lunch date with Adam.

I was surrounded in quite a mess of paper at the moment with new file folders all made up to go into the proper areas of the drawer so that Sam could have anything he needed at his fingertips.

"How was lunch with Adam?" she asked when my initial response had been little more than a shoulder shrug.

"Fine, June," I said less than truthfully, as the lunch had been all about Adam. Topics ranged from how great he was in law and life, how his ex-wife just didn't understand him, and covering in detail every interest he had. We never did manage to discuss anything work related, and his hard sell approach of himself went over poorly with me.

When we returned home, Adam had been surprised when I declined his request for another "date". I knew I'd be seeing him around the house later, and that was enough for me. I was surprised that he'd expected I eat up his self absorption, and then I felt bad like maybe he was trying too hard since starting over was no easy feat.

On the plus side, he'd been a good sport about my hair. I'd put on a ball cap and tried to decline the date, but Adam insisted, and I had to run other errands for Sam anyway, so I went with it. I'd have to find a way out of the party that night though

I was also thrilled to see June so upbeat about getting an opportunity to spend time with Peyton and Ella before we went abroad. I planned on pretty much steering clear of the family for the rest of the day until that night's party. I hoped she wouldn't ask me specifics, as I think telling a Mom that one of her sons is a selfish jerk may not go over well.

"Everything's just fine. Lunch was fine. I'm just thinking about what I still need to get done before the trip," I answered safely, closing the drawer once all the new files and paperwork had been filed away neatly.

"Can I get something for you?" I asked in hopes of changing the subject.

"No, thank you," she replied in her most polite tone. She changed chairs, and made herself comfortable on one of the recliners. "No, thank you though," she replied in her most polite tone. She changed chairs, and made herself comfortable on one of the recliners. June took a hard look at me, realizing that my hair was not wet but greasy. "What happened?" she sputtered, fingering the strands to see if her eyesight had played a cruel trick.

"Accidental application of body oil instead of hair oil," I stated nonchalantly, "Told you I was a magnet for accidents." Adding a sigh, I finished, "At least this one's just hair related. I'm supposed to go to that party tonight with Eckert and McKayla. I hate to cancel, but I don't think the ball cap will suffice to cover this mess up."

Giggles erupted through the room. June actually shook in her mirth. "You do find your way into and out of the oddest things, Little Miss."

I couldn't help but let a small smile peek through my blue mood.

"Sometimes you remind me of Anne Shirley," she stated as she directed me into the kitchen. She shuffled through cupboards until she found what she was after.

"Do you remember the scene in which she accidentally dyes her hair green, or when she fell off the roof and walked out of her way so she could avoid getting assistance from Gilbert?"

I nodded, as the movie was one we'd watched several times together. "She ended up hurting her other ankle falling into a hole."

"She sure did. Your accidents are not Murphy's law, they're more like Sara's law. Someone is going to have to save you from yourself. Fortunately, I've had a few hair accidents in my lifetime too, and this one," she stopped and tugged on my greasy locks. "Just so happens to be one I know how to fix."

"I just thought it would take a few days and a few hundred more washes before it came out."

June held up a bottle of apple cider vinegar and closed my bedroom door. "We'll get you good as new for the party tonight," she said pointing to my shower. "In," she commanded. "If this doesn't get it out, we'll try lemon juice, but this should do it."

A short time later, the application of vinegar was followed by washing, towel drying and then a short blow dry. My hair was nearly back to normal!

"Wow, you're a lifesaver June. Don't think I'll be trying hair oil in the near future, but I'll have to remember that just in case."

June was sitting patiently in one of the chairs, watching me and still smiling. I'm glad I could be a source of amusement to her. I personally thought I'd be sick of myself with the amount of attention I'd required recently.

Sniffing the air, I gagged, "Gross, the vinegar smell didn't come out with the shampoo."

"It will take a day or do for that, but at least you don't look like you showered in grease."

I couldn't disagree with her logic.

"Come, sit with me and let's talk," she beckoned, motioning for me to sit at one of the other seats. "Now that this emergency's been dealt with, let's discuss other matters at hand. Shall I make some tea? How about some Geinmaicha?" she asked, referring to a Japanese green tea with roasted barley in it that had always succeeded in lifting my spirits.

"No, I'm not in the mood for tea," I said, finishing a comb through my hair to ensure that I was oil free while I sat on the chair she kept patting.

"Okay, we'll pass on the tea then," she said gently, and then added more firmly, "I can tell something's bothering you though, and I want to talk about it. You seemed to be doing so much better yesterday regarding the "incident", so it must be something new. Is there something you need here at the house? Or maybe," she queried rather slowly, "Are you missing your own place?"

I looked up, caught off guard that she had nailed it, and without much digging either. Why did my face have to give away anything and everything I thought? She knew immediately that she'd struck the heart of the issue.

"Ah, that's it. This is a great house, but it's not the same as staying at your own place is it?"

"June, I hate to seem ungrateful," I replied in automatic apology mode. My mind quickly thought through the most appropriate response to the question. I could really stick my foot in my mouth on this topic if I weren't careful.

"You've treated me with nothing but respect since I have been here. You've gone above and beyond what any employer and even most friends would do for each other.
You've helped me through this crisis, had my friends over, and taken care of me when I should have been doing the same for you. I love your house, and you have made me feel at home. It's just…"

"It's just not the same as having your own place," she stated factually, adjusting her already impeccable hair. "You know, I actually feel that I've been kind of selfish with you."

"What?" I replied, mystified by her response.

She laughed, and elaborated for me, wringing her hands together a little nervously as she revealed her own motives.

"I never had a daughter, and I think I have been mothering you too much. I just love having you around. Sam is so pleased at how well we get along. I've been taking up a lot of your days though, so you don't get to work on Sam's things until late."

"I haven't been getting much done at all for the last week, June. In fact, the past week, I've been taking up much of your days. In regards to the job, though, I don't mind the hours. I have never had such..." I motioned around the room, "Such freedom and such a lovely place to work, or such great people to work for."

I wasn't fooling her for a minute. "But?" she asked, wanting to pull out the rest of what I had on my mind.

"But, I start to feel too at home sometimes, and get a rude awakening that this is not my own place."

"What do you mean? What kind of rude awakening?"

Should I tell her, or should I gloss it over? I decided to be honest, and told her about what had happened with Adam. I turned red as a beet, mortified that the details might somehow shock her. Instead of a display of distaste, she responded by laughing so hard, I thought I was going to have to hit her on the back.

This went on for a good minute, and she finally slowed down, going from a position of rocking back and forth to once again settling on the sofa.

"Sorry, Sara," she said as she finally regained her composure, "but that is good. More than good, it is destined to become a family classic. Adam will tell that story every chance he gets." She added, 'To change the subject for just a sec, can I tell this story to Sam before Adam gets to? He will love it."

I was stunned, and said nothing, so June went on. "Oh honey, Adam will tell him anyway. That boy is not shy, and he probably relished every moment. You played it off pretty cool too. I wouldn't have come back and pretended all was well."

She started giggling again. "I don't think this house has ever had as much excitement since you joined the clan. It's been interesting and fun. There's never a dull moment around this place anymore."

I said nothing, and June got serious, speaking in soft tones of comfort and understanding.

"I do understand though, I mean about getting too comfortable. Your home and work are one and the same. There's no separation. You just want to let loose without the mother hen looking after you. Dance naked. Eat ice cream for breakfast, or follow any wild hare you might have."

Once again, she zoned in for the kill. June didn't beat around the bush. I should take lessons from her in getting to points of conversation quickly and tactfully, as she was now the master in my eyes.

"A little," I admitted, "I was lonely on my own, but I got used to it. Now I have company 24/7. I love it, but I don't feel I can really and completely steal away or miss a meal."

I pinched my middle to show her the roll of fat that was trying to form there. "Those five pounds will turn into more from eating so much of your fantastic cooking."

"You were too skinny anyways, but again, I get where you're coming from. I was once a lovely, single lady like you. Once you're grown and gone, you love to visit home, but not to stay forever. It's supposed to be that way. Isn't the condo just about ready?"

"I think they're just finishing with the painting before the new carpet goes down, and then it's good to go. June, it is not going to be that easy to move back either."

For the third time during this conversation, she knew what I was going I say before I did. "Rusty's had the best months of her life here, hasn't she?"

"Yes. I'm afraid to uproot her and bring her back and forth again. She's never been so happy or healthy ever in her life. What dog wouldn't want a 40 acre playground and friends to play with?"

"It's more than that too," I said softly. June looked inquisitively into my eyes.

"Yes?"

"This may make no sense. I want my independence, but I want the proximity too. I like being close, not having to take a 30 minute drive twice a day, and you guys are loads of fun to be around. Your cooking is amazing too; I don't think I've eaten so well in years."

"That makes perfect sense to me."

"That I want to have my cake and eat it too?" I laughed over my use of the tired cliché.

"Doesn't everyone?" June laughed. "Well, I have one possible solution. No matter what you decide, Rusty is welcome to stay here with Ruger, Sheba and Cleo."

I knew she was thinking in a forward fashion, but this was not my idea of a solution. I didn't want to be without by best friend, or alone at night. On the other hand Rusty would have her friends to play with until they all crashed for the night too. Selfishness was going to have to take the lead on this one though.

"June," I started, wondering how to say "no" nicely. I didn't have to say anything else, and June snapped her fingers, and jumped up out of the chair. She had an idea that was about ready to explode out of her head. I hoped it was better than her first one.

"I've got it!" she got up from the chair and headed into the kitchen. She was talking to herself the entire time, and I had to get up and follow her to make out what she was saying.

"A good cleaning, new décor, it's perfect!" she twirled around, expecting to find me behind her.

She grabbed some keys from the rack by the back door and dragged me outside. "What is it, June?" I asked, my wonderment growing with each passing second.

"You can have the best of both worlds, have it your way, have and eat the cake, the whole thing," she rambled.

We walked by the pool area, through the garden, and headed out for the back of the property.

"Are you going to tell me your idea, or do I have to guess?" I asked impatiently. "You're killing me here, June."

June laughed, and slowed up. She linked her arm through mine and pointed to the back of the property. The gardener's cottage, a small empty place, was nestled at the far end of the property.

The cottage had its own front porch area and a white picket fence completely surrounded the place, giving it a quaint, country feel. The back pond was close by, too. There had been a flower garden out in front, but this hadn't been kept up since no one had regularly stayed in the place over the past decade.

It took us a several minutes to cross the grass, and fortunately there were no patches of ice left from the last snow fall. She unlocked the door and made me pause before entering. The porch was about six feet across, and some patio furniture was off to the right next to the railing, covered for the season.

I could tell June was tired from the walk, and I don't know why I hadn't insisted on driving her out here.

"Are you alright?" I asked. She'd shown such tremendous improvements in health that I often forgot she had to be careful. She'd suffered a stroke a little more than a year ago, and still had some residual effects when she over exerted herself physically. At least for our London trip, she'd conceded to my insistence that we use a wheelchair during museum visits and long outings.

"I'm fine, Sara, just had to catch my breath for a minute. What do you think of the place? I haven't updated it for a while now, but it's in just fine shape."

She started opening cupboard doors and checking about to assess the affect the years had taken on the place.

"Adam and his wife would use it while they visited, at least for the few times they could arrange time to come up. I offered it to Alan last year, but he insisted he was perfectly happy in the apartment over the garage. He's pretty low maintenance you know."

I nodded in agreement at that. Alan's place was practically bare. The quintessential bachelor's pad without proofs or frills. At least it had been tidy on every occasion I'd been there.

"This is far enough away from the house to give you the feel of it being yours, and close enough to the house so I always know you're here."

Inside was a nice sized living area, small kitchen and dining area. The place was dusty, and June profusely apologized that the cleaning staff hadn't been sent out to the cottage for the last year.

The carpet and walls were in blue tones, and a nautical theme was evident in the décor. A navy blue couch and matching chair faced to the left of the room. This was both to show a nice view of the pond, as well as to face the fireplace which was off to the far end of the room.

There were two bedrooms, also fully decked in shades of blue. Each had a small closet. There was a hallway in between them, with a small coat closet or linen cabinet right outside the bathroom, which was the very farthest door on the right. The bathroom had a full tub and shower.

One bedroom was larger than the other. Overall, the place was about the same size as my condo, but with a fireplace and killer view to add into the mix.

June fussed about, talking about how this or that could be changed, the color scheme. Finally she realized that she had been talking to herself.

"Well, what do you think?" she asked.

"The cottage is nice," I said giving it a second appraisal.

"Would you consider staying here for a while if I get it fixed up?"

"June, it's fine the way it is."

"No way. If you decide to move back here, it will be completely redecorated for you. The furniture hasn't been replaced for a while, the carpet, oh and the color scheme has got to go. Don't know why I went on a nautical kick that year. So 1980's."

She kept going, ignoring me again. "There's an outside phone line, and we can get updated wiring for cable, internet and that kind of stuff. The fireplace needs to have its chimney swept. Oh, and we'll need to put the golf cart back into use, or maybe get another."

She looked out the front door. "You see how this lines up with the garage and the house? We used to have a road of sorts so that guests could drive up to the house in a golf cart. Maybe I'll get it paved this time."

There was no stopping her thought process, so I didn't try.

"Well?" she asked.

"June, it's an awful lot of trouble to go to. What if I changed my mind and moved back home after the winter is over? I can see the benefit of staying during the snowy months. The drive through Pleasant Valley is quite a bear when it's icy."

"There would be absolutely no strings attached whatsoever. You can stay two days and go back to the house or to your condo. This place needs decorating anyway; this decor is so outdated. I think a modern

Bad Hair Days

touch is in order even if no one ever stays in it."

Her eyes twinkled and I could almost see her brain whirring as she thought. She was an unmovable force when she got any sort of bee in her bonnet.

"I enjoyed doing your room in the house so much; a whole cottage would be that much more fun. Unless you want something different, we'll do the light greens, cinnamon and beige tones again. Leaf and pine cone accents, similar to your room in the house?"

"Well you could just take most of the stuff from my room at the house."

"No, honey, we'll leave that as it is. It turned out so lovely."

"I think other guests would like it too. You did a great job."

"We have plenty of other rooms for guests," June said emphatically. "Although we don't have many guests, other than family of course. That room is still yours for as long as you choose to work for us. Now you'll have two places of your own!"

We were still standing in the living area, and I was gazing out at the pond, remembering how lovely it looked in the autumn.

"Alex can stay here with you when he visits too. Your friends are welcome anytime, you know. Other guests too, err, you know overnight guests, boyfriends," she added trying to be tactful yet shake off the stigma of discussing such private details.

"I can understand this is a lot of to think about. If you don't want to answer right away, will you at least think about it?" She squeezed my hand and caught my eye to show her sincerity.

"Of, course, June. This would be a lovely place to stay. Alex and I could get into lots of trouble out here on our own; you might regret it. One thing though, don't you think Sam would be upset at your spending so much money on my accommodations again?"

June's face looked puzzled, and then she laughed, sounding like a tinkling bell.

"You don't know?"

"Know what?" I asked, feeling like I was overlooking something in front of me.

"Oh, honey, you don't worry about Sam's money. He makes his for fun. I inherited mine. You've lived in Reno your whole life, right?"

I nodded.

"Does the name "Culver" mean anything to you?"

"You mean like Culver Ranch?" I replied, my answer referring to a huge section of land that included the piece this house was on.

'You got it. My maiden name is Culver, and my dad owned this entire valley, and areas of Spanish Springs and Cold Springs. The water rights too. I made a mint when development took off. I still own the largest amount of water rights held by a single person in the entire county, and I still have plenty of land holdings too. I'm holding onto them for a rainy day."

She laughed, "Heck, that's how I met Sam. He was the banker who helped me decide what to do with the land. Some was sold, and some was held back. The boom that happened before the current downturn was the best of all. Sam decided long ago that his best bet on reaching retirement before death was marrying me!"

I helped her close up the cottage as she talked, then we headed back towards the house.

"All the money I spend is mine. I'm not one for diamonds or gems, fussy parties and the like. My art pieces are the only thing I'm really extravagant on in my spending. Sam can stick it if he thinks I'm being silly in re-doing the cottage. He likes to see me busy though, and when my garden is out of commission for the winter, I need something like this. When I get bored, I start asking questions about his businesses, and he hates that. I wouldn't be surprised if he thinks it's a grand idea," she laughed. "Anyway, I'd be amazed if he didn't forget about it the minute after I tell him. He could care less, and besides, he knows I'd do it with or without his stamp of approval."

As we got closer to the house, I agreed to think about June's proposal and let her know in a day or two. The dogs ran across the great field to greet us. With all four dogs running full speed right at us, it was hard not to think we'd be knocked down by their unabashed affection.

I made sure they didn't jump on June, and stayed outside to play with them after June made it quite clear her bones had felt enough of the cold weather for the day. She insisted that she could manage the rest of the walk without assistance, and headed off to put together some items for that night's time with her granddaughters.

She was excited to spend the evening with Peyton and Ella, and had made all kinds of fun plans. There were enough homemade sweets around to feed an army.

Getting some exercise with the dogs gave me time to think about my living arrangement options and what they could mean for the future.

It was a little cold to be out without a jacket, so I said my goodbyes to the pack of loving beasts after a few minutes and went to clean off the dog scent that was now more pungent than the vinegar smell, and prepare for that night's party for Simon's retirement.

I couldn't be less thrilled about my first public outing since my return from L.A. I didn't want to go, but I'd promised Eckert and begged McKayla to come too. The last place I wanted to spend my evening was at a social event, and as the date of my ex-whatever to boot. At least I couldn't do anything to make things worse, could I?

13

There were trays of langoustine, exotic cheeses, vegetables cut into exquisite shapes, and a variety of wines being brought through the small but growing crowd of people by elegantly dressed servers. This was no ordinary retirement party; Simons was going out wanting to make a big impression on his friends and guests. If the intended impression was that he had money to burn, he was succeeding.

I made my best attempt to be invisible, as I wanted no recognition by the guests. I wanted to blend in and stay out of the way. I don't even know why I'd agreed to come considering the TV interview that had identified me by name. On top of that, there were still photos of me in the gossip sections of the paper. Even the latest edition of a major magazine released today showed photos of me continually in "before", "during" and "after" phases that showed me in the glamorous, klutzy and disgraceful moments from the pre-show to coming out of the hospital.

I got a few "that's her" looks from some of the guys on the force and the wait staff, but no one seemed anxious to rain on my party parade, at least not right away.

I was happy to be ignored. The less fuss and spectacle, the better. Eckert had insisted that I come, and promised that he wouldn't be upset if I got noticed, called out, or otherwise made to publicly face the "incident". He hadn't added that he'd come to my defense if it happened though.

Apparently Eckert could handle the humiliation of a friend, just not of a girlfriend. I was still disappointed in his less than chivalrous actions when I came home from LA. Not being particularly hurt by the break-up though, I'd decided that being his guest at the party as just a "friend" would be okay, and in turn I'd invited my own friends to come too.

I was conservatively dressed to hide my back wound, which was now healing quite nicely, but was too unattractive to wear anything showy. It was still painful, too; I made a point of shaking hands instead of hugging when possible in hopes of avoiding any reference to the injury or the event that caused it. Hugging would also repel the giver, since I still smelled of apple cide vinegar, a fact Eckert had let me know when he'd picked me up. Fortunately, there were not many people I had to meet or make nice too, so I could avoid most contact all together.

Shelby made a grand entrance to the party, her personality entering the room before her. She acknowledged me with a showy peck and a hug. Perfectly at home in a crowd of people, Shelby recognized several of the guests, and immediately excused herself to mingle.

She could not turn off her business development persona for even one minute, but I loved her for always being on point, forever looking her best, and seizing any opportunity that presented itself. She became the center of attention within minutes of her arrival, and I watched in awe as she worked the guests, making each one feel especially connected to her in some way.

Simons' house was fairly large for a single man. It was spacious, with most of the living area open and airy. The living, family and dining rooms were decorated to appear as one large space. Furniture was modern, and sparse; only placed where necessary. The setting of the extra tables and chairs had been easy in the large space, and hadn't required anything to be moved aside that I could tell, although Eckert had alluded to a pool table being taken to the garage for the night. The walls and carpets were all done in shades of blue. A total man pad.

A sommelier sat in the back of the large room, inviting party guests to participate in a wine tasting. Several guests were swirling glasses and sniffing bouquets of the wines. I walked back to join the group. Learning more about wine would be beneficial, and I could still stay out of the way. Eckert lingered back, looking around for Simons or some friends on the force he could engage in conversation.

With Eckert looking so uncomfortable, and the wine tasting area pretty full, I rejoined him to keep him company. Eckert wanted to pay his respects to Simons so he could say he'd been there and then we could leave. I was completely up for leaving, so I agreed to help look.

I found him in the middle of a buzzing cloud of well-wishers. He was rather enjoying his role of host, and was all smiles and laughs. Despite what was in front of me now, I had a hard time envisioning him as anyone but the strict and serious police officer who had recently run me through the ringer when Sam's tenant was murdered.

Eckert spotted him at the same time I did, and butted right into the crowd. He grabbed Simon's hand in both greeting and congratulations and thrust a bottle of wine at him. Well, that was done and over with. I only got in a wave of initial greeting myself before the mob once again reformed itself around Simons to listen to some fascinating story he was telling.

McKayla had quietly set herself on the couch. In her usual keen but quiet manner, she preferred to observe others instead of participating

Bad Hair Days

in the eclectic mix of things. Despite this wish, she stood out in her electric yellow dress, and she was a vision of beauty unlike I'd seen in a long time. This was not the fake beauty like those I saw on the red carpet at Hollywood; this was the real thing, radiating from the inside out.

Her hair was free of its normal braids, with long curls hanging down her back. A matching yellow hair clip kept the hair from her face, and her angular features were on display. High cheekbones, dark eyes, reddened lips, and flawless skin made her natural beauty stand out. She was a summer daffodil in a winter storm.

Once he had greeted his partner, Eckert spotted Simon's collection of cds, opting to peruse the titles instead of our making a quick appearance and early exit. He found one he liked and put it on the nice home system tastefully held behind a lovely wood cabinet. Sounds of gentle jazz music filled the room, creating even more of a party atmosphere.

Eckert seemed oblivious to everyone else in the room, comforted somehow by the familiar music and the quality of its sound on Simon's excellent stereo system. Without paying attention, he sat on the couch roughly, forcing McKayla to scoot over, and began reading the cd liner notes.

McKayla looked a little put off by his lack of manners. As the music began, she noted the liner notes he was reading. "You're a fan of Miles Davis?" McKayla asked.

Eckert jumped a little, oblivious that she was sitting next to him on the couch. Treating the question as a personal challenge, he rebutted, "*Blue Train* is only the greatest jazz album ever made."

"Okay, glad you have an opinion. I prefer the old classics from the early days of jazz though. Do you like Jelly Roll Morton?" McKayla cocked her head, wanting to see his expression as much as hear his answer.

Eckert jumped to the bait, pleased to debate on this, or any topic for that matter. "I love the way he used swing and especially ragtime influences in his work," was his reply. "Are you a fellow jazz fan?"

"Yes, sir. I have to admit I'm a bit surprised you are. I think I kinda guessed you as a classical music man."

"And what is wrong with that?" he raised his voice defensively, but it was a put on. "I happen to be a huge fan of classical music, and most any type of music for that matter." He lightened his tone, "Music soothes the savage beast, you know."

McKayla laughed, obviously now feeling relaxed with Eckert, and relieved at finding a topic of mutual interest to discuss with someone. She turned her body towards him, which I knew was an indication that she was inviting more conversation.

"I love the ragtime influence in jazz too. James P. Johnson is a favorite of mine."

"Me too," added Eckert emphatically, "It was my love of big band swing that introduced me to jazz, and I went from there."

"Okay then, I have a test for you. This will tell me what kind of jazz fan you really are. Once we get this straight, we'll bring in the more modern era for comparison. Do you prefer the sounds of Lee Konitz or Charlie Parker?"

"No question, Parker for me. I enjoy bebop over experimental sounds anytime."

"You passed the test. In my eyes, you're a true aficionado of jazz," McKayla put her hands together in a semi-clap as if Eckert had won an award.

I tuned out of the conversation for a moment, lost after the first artist was mentioned. Despite my own boredom, I had to admit I was pleased she had found something of interest to discuss tonight. With a person as quiet and intellectual as McKayla, it was a big feat to engage her interest. I watched with curiosity as they spoke, and they seemed completely oblivious to my proximity. I was definitely not invited into this conversation.

"I love most types of music, but jazz is my favorite," McKayla offered, "especially live. It's like an entirely different experience than listening to a recording."

"Me too, and I agree with the difference," Eckert added, repositioning himself on the couch in indication that he was quite comfortable. "I even go to Sacramento to some of the clubs and events. Do you attend the local jazz festival?"

"Every year, and Tahoe's too when I can get away. I go to the local jazz bar on occasion. I'm not much on going out, but I'll make an exception if it's a favorite performer," she said softly. She was smiling brightly, and her eyes were alive. This conversation was definitely going somewhere.

I decided I was intruding now, pretty much eavesdropping, so I looked around for somewhere to go and let them carry on their music discussion without me. I know very little, if anything, about jazz music, so I had nothing to add to the conversation anyway.

I enjoyed seeing McKayla open up. She rarely shared personal information with those she didn't know well. Seeing her converse with Eckert was a sight I'd never imagined, but it was always good when mutual friends became friends too. They'd only met on two occasions before, which is probably the only reason McKayla spoke to him at all.

14

I made my way back through the room to the wine tasting area, glad to leave a place I wasn't wanted. It was still rather crowded, but there was a place at the table for me. As I took the seat, the sommelier placed three glasses in front on the counter, and nodded for me to take a specific one.

"How about a buttery Zinfandel for the lady?" he asked and poured as I nodded. He rolled the bottle slightly as he poured. He filled a few other glasses for the guests and then invited us all to sniff the wine.

It smelled rather acidic, and I didn't think I'd like it. He instructed us to swish the glass and then taste the wine. I made the same circular motion he did, then took a small taste anticipating an acrid flavor, but the wine was smooth, and had a buttery after taste, just as promised.

"This is a 2001 Zinfandel from New Zealand." He indicated and then provided some facts about the wine and New Zealand's entry into the world of serious wine making. The crowd listened intently to the information, but was ready for another taste as soon as he finished.

For several minutes, I swished, sniffed and tasted several other wines, and listened to the comments of my fellow tasters about each one. Some of my thoughts were in line with theirs, and others weren't even close. Since I drink wine from a box in reality, I didn't trust my own opinion about any of the wines except if I liked it or not. As the sommelier discussed the average bottle price of each as we tasted it, I knew I wouldn't be partaking in any of these wines again in the near future anyway.

I ended up trying four wines, all red, before I decided I better hit the food tray or risk being carried home. A sensation of relaxation came nearly instantly with the wine, quite a different experience than with the same amount of the low quality stuff I drank. I didn't think it would make me as light headed and giddy as it did.

I made a plate of food, making sure to try at least one of each item, and located a seat at the dining room table. I found I was alone, and

I didn't mind. The food was quite good. As I enjoyed it, Simons, finally free of a crowd, came to greet me.

"Thanks for coming. I'm glad to see you again. Eckert talks a lot about you," he said, his eyes monetarily wandering to my chest, and I made my best effort not to roll my eyes. I was sure Eckert had taken lots of jabs about my little incident at work. Until now, I'd been fortunate enough to endure no recognition from the party guests, even in glances or whispers, yet that evening.

"Thanks for inviting me and my friends." I replied as nicely as I could, and re-directed his eyes to McKayla, still engaged in conversation with Eckert, and then to Shelby, who was still center stage at the party. She was surrounded by a crowd of people, mostly men, and they were laughing at every word she said.

"No problem," he said adjusting his very stylish and probably very expensive jacket. As he pulled up his sleeves some, I noted the cuff links. They were nice, in the shape of a police badge and looked like solid gold. Swanky.

"It looks like everyone is having a good time," he added, "Are you?"

"I think I've had a little too much of those fantastic wines. I had to catch up with some food or I might need to take a nap here."

Simon laughed, and he pulled out a chair to sit next to me. I'd never heard him laugh, but had never spoken to him on much of a personal level before. He was definitely more relaxed than any time I'd seen him previously, but he was off the clock for good now. He'd been stiff and suspicious when questioning me about the murder at the dry cleaners months ago. Who wouldn't be relaxed once retired from the chains of daily employment duties?

I asked the question that was on everyone's mind that night. "So tell me, since Eckert could not explain it well, how is it that a 40 year old can retire from a job with the local police? Did you hit the Mega Bucks at one of the local casinos?"

Simons laughed again, "No, something even better." He looked uncomfortable for a moment. "Geez, maybe I shouldn't say that, oh dear. You see, it's that a relative of mine passed away and has left me a good sized chunk of money."

"Oh, I'm so sorry. About your relative I mean"

"That's what is weird. I didn't even know this relative. I knew I had relations in Europe, but apparently I had a distant uncle in England I'd neither met nor knew about."

"Well, congrats on the good fortune then. Are you investing it well? You know my friend Shelby is here with me. She's a local banker and can help make sure your money is put to work for you," I said in a spiel like tone, trying to sell for her while she wasn't even around. I spied around the room, visually locating her if the conversation went in that direction.

"Eckert told me you used to be in banking. It kinda makes sense with the recent situation we helped you with," he said and I knew he was referring to pulling my butt out of the warehouse. "One of the reasons I wanted to talk to you was to ask for advice on what to do when the remaining funds get here." He paused and took a drink from his own wine glass.

"No problem," I said with confidence, "I have lots of friends in the industry, and as I said, my friend Shelby is here tonight. She's one of the best business development officers in the industry. You have lots of options right now," I replied, wondering how much his inheritance would amount to as I tried to match up options for him.

I tried to beckon Shel over to enter the conversation, but she didn't seem to notice my waving madly at her. I stopped as soon as Simons spoke again.

"I don't have the funds just yet. A wire's been sent, but it is going through a process at the Federal Reserve Bank of New York. I got a check from the solicitors to cover some of the expenses of getting the money moved. I already wired funds for the security clearance of the funds, and spent the rest on the party."

My mind cringed; my hackles arose. I wanted, no needed, to know more about Simons' transaction. I hated to seem nosy, but I had a bad feeling that he might be the victim of a scam I'd seen happen to many good people during my years as a banking compliance officer.

I kept my voice together, not giving away my suspicions yet. "So, why is the money held up in New York. Wires are practically instantaneous once sent."

"I had to contact a representative of the bank today," Simons continued nonchalantly, pausing to greet a well-wisher before he continued.

"In international transactions, apparently the funds have to be proven to be from legitimate sources and not as a result of terrorism financing and the like before they're released. One of the things I had to pay for was the expense of an anti-terrorism certification."

I was certain this was a scam now. "So you cashed the check at your bank, wired funds as directed, and took the rest in cash?"

He nodded, still casual and relaxed. "Yeah, pretty much like that. This party is a result of those funds. I spent $20,000.00 on it. It's pretty cool too, huh? I always dreamt of giving a killer bash like this. The cost is a drop in the bucket compared to the 15 million I'll be getting from the estate."

I was rendered speechless; I couldn't get any words to come out, as he kept on going. "I'm still trying to figure out the tax consequences.

Apparently, the UK requires that estate taxes be paid prior to the release of funds. I may have to cash in all of my retirement funds to pay the taxes. I don't know why they won't just offset the funds for them, but I don't know much about these things."

Unfortunately I do, I thought, *now how am I going to tell him before he sends more money to these crooks?*

"Can I call you later and get some advice on where to place my money. You know, reputable inventors, best banks, and stuff like that?"

I managed a nod of affirmation.

"Thanks, you're a sport," he patted me on the back, obviously forgetting or oblivious to the fact I was injured. I jumped in pain, but he didn't seem to notice. His game, or rather party face, was back on. "Gotta get back. See ya."

I let Simons slip away from me as he continued to meet and greet the party guests, being the quintessentially cordial host. I had to think about this. How could I tell him tactfully, and without putting a damper on his night, that he was being victimized? Even harder, how was I going to tell him without hurting his male pride?

This scam is a variation of a common scam known as a Nigerian 419 scam. These scams originated in Nigeria and are named after a section of law that prohibits them. They began with the enticement of riches to those who would help some official government figure in Nigeria "move" funds to an American bank. The reasons are usually stated as some political coup, but had the scam kept changing to catch a wider net of victims. I'd seen more variations on this scheme than I could even count, and all had ended up in the financial destruction of the victim and often caused the victim's bank to take a loss as well.

The most common form this scam takes on these days is through official communication to a person, usually in a letter or overnight type package after the victim responds to an e-mail sent to a wide net of people. I've never found out how names and addresses are obtained by the crooks, but they send official looking documentation to people indicating that they have won a lottery, and inheritance or some other prize, of which the value is great enough to get many to nibble on it. It seems to be provided willingly by the victim after e-mail correspondence promising a nice chunk of a big financial pie. It's a cruel play on the American dream, but as my mother always said, "If it sounds too good to be true, it probably is."

Once a victim has nibbled, additional communication comes in with more documentation. The victim thinks he or she is very close to getting the funds; however, right before the funds are to arrive there is some obstacle. It could be for payment of taxes, fees, or some other "reason" that requires the victim to cough up their own money to take care of it. Most, thinking that the fee is a temporary inconvenience which will soon be offset by the funds due, scramble in an effort to get the funds out in anticipation of the larger sum, which of course is never received.

Some victims are given multiple obstacles to jump over. If the victim pays for one lie, why not another, and another, and as many as it takes until the victim gets wise to the fact that the funds are never coming. Simons had fallen for the first one, and I knew that the next one would be coming at any time, and I had to stop him from losing more than he already had.

Another huge tip off to the fact that this is a scam is that the Federal Reserve Bank, whether in New York or any other city, is a bank for banks. No one at the Federal Reserve would contact a customer directly regarding a transaction. The Fed is only a middleman, facilitating requests sent in by other banks

Simon's case has a component of this scam I hadn't seen before. A check, undoubtedly a fake or forged check, was sent along to entice Simons to send off funds. The check will come back as bogus, and Simons will be liable for the entire sum.

A lot of people assume that banks know if a check is good or not upon its receipt from the customer. With advancements in computer technology and criminal techniques, it is sometimes impossible to tell an item is false until the bank it was drawn on sends it back as such.

I didn't ask Simons how much his check was for, but he said he'd paid over 20 grand for this party, so I'm pretty sure the check was for at least $50,000.00. Wires, unlike checks, are only sent when backed by guaranteed bank funds. Once a wire is sent, there's no getting the money back. Simons had unwittingly participating in sending $30,000.00 of guaranteed funds to a crook because the $50,000 check was bogus. He was funding this party out of his pocket. This news was going to hurt.

I decided I needed to talk to Eckert before breaking the news to Simons. I prayed that my scam sensors were off, but they'd yet to steer me wrong in those I'd sniffed out in the past. At least we could prevent future financial harm to him, if I could convince Eckert I knew what I was talking about.

15

I found Eckert where I'd left him. He and McKayla were now discussing mountain biking, and I overheard a bit about the desire to enter an ironman competition someday. I knew it had been a wish of McKayla's, but Eckert's too? This multiple connection thing was almost eerie.

Each was so into the conversation, I'd almost say they were entwined. I felt bad, at least a little bit bad on McKayla's behalf, to have to break it up.

"Sorry Kayla," I said with a sweet smile, then turned to Eckert and rapidly ordered, "Eckert, I need to see you right away. It's important."

He looked a little put out at the unwelcomed interruption, and let me know with every gesture he made as he followed me from the room. I went into what must have been a spare bedroom, and then shut the door behind us.

'What?' Eckert barked. "Am I being insensitive for connecting with your friend?" He sat on the edge of the bed, the sole piece of furniture in the room.

"Uh, well yeah, but I could care less about that," I choked out with a near laugh. "That goes without saying these days, although what nerve to bring it up like that. This isn't about you," I emphasized on his continual egocentric sentiments, "Or me either. This is about Simons."

Glad that a fight was not going to commence, but apparently still irritated over my interrupting his blossoming friendship with McKayla, he threw his body fully on the bed.

"What about him?"

"Have you ever heard of a Nigerian Scam? Maybe they've been taught to you as "advance fee" scams?" I did my best to quickly get to the point in terminology he could relate to.

"Yeah, so what."

"I think that this inheritance is one of them. I believe Simons has

86

already lost $30,000.00 plus whatever he spent on this party, and when that check he deposited gets returned to the bank, he's going to be completely astonished, and possibly even send more money out to try to fix it."

Eckert was sitting at attention now. His face was contorted, like he was thinking deeply, or about to let me have it.

"What in the heck are you talking about?   Nigerian scammers take people's money; they don't give money to their victims."

"Earth to Eckert. Just because his bank gave him immediate credit on an item, in this case a check, doesn't mean the check is backed by good funds. It can come back unpaid, forged or fraudulent item, stolen even. When he wired funds from his account to pay for bogus security clearance fees though, that was good money," I got red as I explained. Eckert's face indicated he didn't get it at all.

"It's a lot easier to get someone to wire out money to a scammer when the victim thinks he or she has money to start with. I could write a check off of your checkbook for a million dollars, and my bank might take it, and it's even possible that they'd let me have access to it right away due to the way I've handled my account and the length of time I've been a customer with them. Prudent banks would put a hold on the funds, which basically allows the item a little time to clear before the funds are released for me to use. In this case, the bank didn't restrict the funds."

This time, I knew he was following the story, so I continued, "So my bank lets me withdraw funds against that million dollar check I just put into my account. Great, I get to spend it. Yipee for me. What is your bank going to do when it's presented to them for payment?"

"I don't have a million dollars in my account."

"Of course you don't, so your bank will refuse to pay the bank presenting the item for payment because your account has insufficient funds. Then what happens?"

"Your bank will get notified?"

"Right, the item will be returned by your bank to my bank and charged back to my account. But I already spent the money, so I can't cover the check. I have a gigantic negative amount in my account, and now I'm in trouble with my bank."

The lights went on for Eckert, and his face fell. "Oh crap. Are you sure this is the deal on Simons' money?"

"99% certain. Eckert, I've seen this happen many times before. The worst part is that Simons will be sending more money to cover the taxes supposedly due. There'll be continuous attempts to get money from him until he figures out that there's no inheritance."

"But the check will come back?"

"It could take a week or more, much longer if it was drawn on a bank outside of the US. Even then, there'll be explanations, excuses, promises, or whatever it takes to keep bleeding him."

Now pacing around the room, I could tell his mind was whirring away.

"I don't want to embarrass him in front of his guests or ruin the party Sara, but I don't want to wait. He needs to know right now, or show us that we're wrong." His eyes were sincere, and his affection for his partner was evident in his expression, which was torn by having to rain on his big night.

"Bring him in here, and I'll explain. I just wanted you to understand first so that we can explain together, make sure he doesn't send any more funds, and maybe even work it out with the bank before the check comes back."

I waited while Eckert sought out Simons. Ten long minutes later, Simons joined us in the room, not happy at being pulled away from his big night.

"What's this about," he joked, beaming exuberance and rainbow party cheer in all directions. "Lover's quarrel again?"

Stepping on this kinda of sunshine was going to be tough.

I explained in the same manner as I had to Eckert, and although he got the overall understanding of what I was explaining, he laughed it off.

"Wait here, I'll be right back."

He re-entered the room with several neatly organized files of information. Each contained communications detailing the inheritance, the transaction, and the sudden hold ups that required immediate rectification. In a new one to me, this time the solicitor indicated he was sending his own money to cover the first expenses since the principal amount of the inheritance couldn't be touched until its final release by the Federal Reserve Bank of New York.

A very formal letter from the Federal Bank of New York indicated it was indeed holding a wire from London on his behalf, and that final international processing steps were being made to ensure that the funds were not the result of terrorist financing or other illicit proceeds, as well as that all applicable taxes had been paid.

Simons had a smirk of complete satisfaction on his face. It was so believable, that Eckert suddenly seemed to doubt my prior convictions, which were now only solidified by this written evidence.

I looked between the two of them. I was now sitting on the bed, and I indicated for each to sit next to me.

His nose wrinkled, "Sara, what perfume are you wearing? I don't usually comment on this sort of thing, but I don't recommend it for you."

Eckert and I laughed, and Eckert took this one. "It's not perfume, and you don't want to know."

His face was blank, so I took the opportunity to get to it.

"Simons, you're a detective. You investigate, evaluate and usually resolve a case upon reaching the probable conclusion. Right?"

He nodded, and I put a hand up to indicate neither was to speak. "I was a kind of detective too, only specifically for banking transactions. Not the same job, but the same methods. Let me give you a few clues that might help you see the conclusion I'm coming up with."

"First, the largest legal firm in London contacts you by e-mail. Although this is not impossible, it is improbable that your personal e-mail address is easily attainable through standard channels."

I held up an e-mail, "Second, would a solicitor from this well known firm use a g-mail address in official correspondence with you?"

I handed the document to Eckert. He noted the sender's e-mail address and gave it to Simons.

"No, official correspondence would be made from an e-mail account somehow associated with the law firm. It would never be done using a throw away account such as those offered by g-mail, Hotmail and Yahoo."

I kept going since there was no interruption or laughter now. "Third, would an educated solicitor, from England, have as much difficulty with the English language as this guy?"

Clearing my voice, I read a line from the e-mail aloud. *Dear Sir, It was with our most respectable pleasure to inform you of a situation that is one of mutual beneficiality, although through unfortunate circumstances has this contact been made.*"

When I finished reading through that grammatical mess, I read from another section of the e-mail, *"It is our sincere conviction that you will handle this transaction with absolute confidentiality, maturity and utmost sense of purpose."*

I couldn't go on. "Guys, these scams are perpetrated with promises of contracts, promises of fees for assistance in getting money out of the country, lottery schemes, and about a hundred or more other variations. The commonalities are most often the disposable e-mail address and the poor use of grammar. Even with these similarities, you have the clincher here."

Simons grabbed the document I held up. It was a letter from the Federal Reserve Bank of New York.

"The other stuff you said is remotely believable, but this is an official document. I've even verified that the person that signed the letter works there. And that the English lawyer is for real too. His name and picture are on the firm's website."

"Yeah, and that's pretty easy for anyone to do to add validity to a fraud. The problem is that wires are not sent and then held as indicated in this letter. And more importantly, this bank does not do business with individuals."

"But I called and spoke to this person," Simons protested.

"There are several Federal Reserve Banks in the United States, each serving a specific geographic region of the country. They've been consolidating recently, which makes this easier. You won't find any branches on street corners like you do for all the big box banks though. These banks are set up by the government to act as banks for other banks. The Fed is the clearinghouse for all items that are processed."

"But I called," Simons again protested, but with less resolve.

"Let's try a phone number from the internet's listing of the bank and not the one on the letter.

Eckert was back on track with my thinking. "She's right Simons. If by chance she's wrong, what harm's been done? If she's right, you won't lose more money, and we can do some upfront damage control with your bank."

'I received a check though," he said sitting down to think it through. "You said that the scammers require victims to send money, not to send money they gave you"

"True, but you used the check to wire money to the scammers. Who do you think will be responsible for the funds once the check is returned as a counterfeit item?"

"You mean that the bank can't tell that there are no funds behind a check, or if it's forged or fake when it's deposited?"

"No, and your bank should have placed a hold on those funds before giving you access to them. There's a banking regulation that addresses the problem this situation has now caused. This is out of the ordinary for you, right? I mean receiving a check of this size?"

Simons nodded, as most folks don't deposit checks for $50,000.00 often, if ever, in their lifetimes.

"When you wire money, those funds are good when they leave the bank. The bank is liable for the funds behind a wire. Wires can't be stopped either, and it can't bounce like a check. The check you deposited to back those funds is not a good item, and when it is returned, a large negative balance will hit your account and you'll be responsible for it."

He finally grasped the full gravity of the situation, and I could see that it ate him up. His face was white and his fists were clutched into tight balls.

I have seen many people, usually seniors, get caught up in these scams and lose hundreds of thousands of dollars paying for costs and fees in order to get a huge inheritance or lottery win that is nonexistent. It is a cruel play on the American dream, but it keeps working for the bad guys so it continues in an endless cycle.

"I'll help you as much as I can, I promise," I softly said with the intent of being supportive now that he understood.

"Hey, where are you going?" Eckert shouted as Simons peeled

from the room, like a fire had been suddenly lit in his pants.

"The wine," was the desperate response that drifted back, the sound getting smaller as he got farther away from the room. 'I can still return whatever's unopened. At $50.00 a bottle, I'm starting damage control right now.

16

I'd received two calls from the local news stations requesting an interview already that morning, and then a call from the city paper. It wasn't even 10:00 a.m. yet, and last night's party had ended up being anything but festive. Thank the Lord for coffee.

Situations like this had been discussed with the girls and the Westins after my interview on Wednesday night, and we'd decided that saying a little something about it was better than providing a flat "no comment" and allowing their elaboration in any direction they chose to take it .

I'd decided to provide some minor details to them about the incident, giving them just enough information to make it seem boring. This was in hopes of their quickly dropping it for follow up questions due to lack of interest. I declined offers from both of the TV stations to appear in their studios live that night.

The day the first reporter and her camera person showed up had caught me off guard. I was still in pajamas when she showed up, if I recalled the events correctly. Getting caught off guard when someone has a camera is not something I'd relished at the time. In retrospect, I'd rather be caught off guard at home and just looking less than my best than be caught looking my best with my dress falling down. It gave me some perspective now.

The doorbell rang, and I thought maybe one of them was going to be persistent and insist on camera time at the studio or try to get me to answer questions in person for that night's show. I was preparing to give Rusty a bath, and looked as grubby as possible, but I answered the door anyway.

"Delivery for Sara Blake," announced the driver, his van taking up most of the driveway, touting the famous overnight delivery service it was best known for. He brought a huge box into the house for me as I signed for the item on his electronic pad. As usual, it felt like I was signing a document with a crayon. I thanked him, and he was off to the next delivery for the day.

June came in from the kitchen, her gray hair coiffed neatly and outfitted to perfection as usual. The only time I'd seen her remotely grubby was in her gardening clothes, and they still matched.

"Oh, what could it be?" she asked. "The return address is from Los Angeles. Maybe it's from Alex, or his studio."

"One thing's for sure, it's much too big to be my dignity," I laughed, "that's the only thing I left there."

Alan came in through the front door, surprised to find both of us in the foyer. June put him right to work.

'Sweetie, can you put this on the table. It's too heavy for us to lift," her voice followed her as she left and quickly returned with some sharp scissors.

Alan hefted the box onto the table, and I slit it open with the scissors June had handed me. On top of some lovely tissue wrapping, was an envelope. Under the wrapping, were several baskets and boxes of luxury items, each wrapped exquisitely in various see through cellophane patterns, and some topped off with bows of fine material. There was a basket of fancy cheeses and food items, one full of fine bath soaps, oils, perfumes and lotions, one of skin care items, several boxes of expensive chocolates and cookies, a basket of various designer make-up products, a gorgeous, luxurious red terrycloth robe, nightgown with matching slippers and satin sleeping mask, dozens of fragranced candles, and the last item, a huge porcelain tray that included a tea pot, accoutrements and a dozen tins of teas that I could tell were only the finest based on June's reaction.

We rifled through the goodies, oohing and aahing over the fantastic score. It was like getting the entire Summit Mall, one of the few places in Reno where most of this finery could even be purchased, in one box.

"Open the card."

Another envelope fell out of the one I opened. Alan retrieved it from the floor, while I read the aloud from the card.

"Marc and I hope that these small tokens of luxury will help erase some of the embarrassment you've recently suffered. We hope to meet you someday so we can personally apologize for last week's unfortunate incident during our event arrival. Alex indicated that these were your favorite kinds of things. PS – he is kind of hoping for an invite in regards to the second envelope. God Bless, J. Lo," I finished reading with a widening expression of joy.

June's mouth fell open, as did Alan's when I'd read the name on the card.

"I wonder what's in the envelope," Alan said, handing it over. "Maybe it's a note from Marc Antony."

I pulled out the contents, and had to sit down. "Oh my gosh!"

"What is it?" came simultaneously from the two, each trying not to grab them from my hands.

"It's a 10 day trip to Oahu, including first class airfare and accommodations at the Kahala Mandarin Oriental! Look a brochure of the hotel too. A private beach, wow!"

We all sat in amazement over the tremendous gift that had been so generously provided. Tears glistened in my eyes, as happy emotions started to come forth.

June gave me a warm hug, "It's nice to know that there are still some good people out there.

"She said she'd make it up to you somehow. This is a new definition of "somehow" in my eyes. Way to go Sara!" Alan was excited for me. "Tell Alex I'll be his date next time he gets an invite to some swanky event. Heck, I'll even streak around the red carpet for this kind of prize."

June gave Alan a mild motherly spanking in response to his bad behavior, but the visualization of his promise made me laugh. Besides, if Alan promised Alex a date, Alex might get his heart broken, as he'd made it no secret that he thought Alan was a hunk and a half.

"Call your Mom and Alex too," June fussed with the baskets and boxes, still reading out some of the names of the brands and products they contained. "I'm sure you want to. I'll get these things to your room."

I picked up the basket of fine teas. 'At the risk of being viewed as having poor manners in re-gifting, I think that this should be yours."

Alan rescued the huge tray as it almost slipped from my hands. There must have been a dozen fine teas, each in four ounce tins, and an exquisite teapot that looked like it was of Oriental origin.

"I couldn't," she protested.

"No, I couldn't," I said, giving her a huge hug, "I couldn't have made it through this week without you. You took charge, coordinated everyone, and in general made it easier for me to handle. Remind me to hire you as an agent if I ever get famous. Your damage control efforts are rather effective."

June laughed, "Oh Sara, thank you, this is so lovely. Do you have any idea how rare and expensive some of these teas are?"

"Not even a clue, June. That's why the only way I'd really enjoy them is by sharing them with you. I'll get to appreciate them when you serve afternoon teas. Plus, I'll enjoy the experience so much more from an expert's viewpoint."

"Oh stop," she blushed, and headed off to the kitchen, her last words floating in the room after her, "Thank you Sara, I can't wait to open and smell them all!"

Alan had returned to the foyer to taking the next item to my room. "That was very nice of you Sara," he half whispered, and I followed him back to my room holding another basket.

"Mom loves that stuff. I'd buy it for her, but I can't tell grocery store quality from any other. This tea stuff is like art to her. I know she's secretly thrilled to get it, re-gifted or not."

"Your Mom means the world to me. She can have anything from this lot."

"I know she feels the same about you, too."

"You know, speaking of sharing and good will, I'm not so sure I should tell my Mom about this until I get back from London, or maybe not even until I get back from Hawaii."

Alan looked at me; an amused expression told me that he considered this unusual. "And what would the reason be for the omission of such exciting information from your own mother?"

I smiled with a guilty expression. 'I've always wanted to go to Hawaii. Mom will probably hint on how much she and Dad would love to visit there again." I held the tickets in my hand, and waived them like a fan.

"But I'm not about to give these babies up. Which basket should I give her instead?"

17

Since Rusty was going to be spending two weeks with my folks while I frolicked in England, I wanted her to be especially fresh and clean. Mom and Dad didn't have any pets because my mom hates the smells that come with them. I'd promised that Rusty would be well behaved during her visit, and that she'd smell like roses so Mom's house didn't smell like dog.

I couldn't come through with the promise of the rose scent, although I had found a wonderful lavender fragranced dog shampoo at the local pet store chain. I figured she wouldn't take me that literally on the point, and that the smell of any scent indicating clean would be sufficient.

I thought about using one of the several fantastic scents J. Lo had sent. There were perfumes and bubble baths in each of her signature scents as well as many other well known designer brands. When I realized that a bottle of this kind of bubble bath probably cost $50.00, I selfishly thought the lavender shampoo was a better option for the task at hand.

I got Rusty into the tub in my bathroom, and realized as I scrubbed her down that it had been longer than I thought since her last bath. The water was a gross murky brown color; evidence of the amount of fun she'd been having running around the huge property with Ruger, Sheba and Cleopatra. The winter had not been very snowy yet, but there'd been plenty of rainy days that had produced fabulous mud puddles for the dogs to frolic through.

Dismissing feelings of guilt over my lack of hygiene for Rusty, I instead appreciated that she'd been living in dog paradise for the last several months. In my condo, she had been cooped up all day, and having to bring me her leash to remind me to take her out on more than one occasion.

Rusty had been my constant companion for the months I'd been out of work, and remained the one friend that I knew would never judge or be angry with me no matter how many stupid things I did.

Rusty reveled in the vigorous massaging of my fingers as they scrubbed through her fur. She did manage to give me a shower once or twice when she halted the process to shake water from her fur. I'd be cleaning the bathroom once we were done, as the walls had evidence of the incidents from the floor to the ceiling. I hoped June wouldn't mind I'd washed Rusty inside, as I didn't want to take her to a groomer.

After two thorough shampoos, I towel dried her, then spent quite a while brushing her golden hair. She patiently sat, tongue out in indication that she was enjoying every minute of her pampering.

'I think you'd enjoy trips to the beauty parlor more than me," I teased her. "Maybe if you did it for me, I'd like it better than having a stranger do it."

I kissed her head, and led her to the luxurious dog bed I had for her next to my bed. I made a mental note to take it with me to my folks' place later. The spoiled pooch usually snuck in bed during the night anyway. I only hoped I could keep her clean until tomorrow night, or I'd be doing this exercise again.

Eckert called mid-morning to thank me for meeting Simons at the bank and for offering to help him out. I was surprised to get this call out of the blue, and I wondered why he'd really called.

"I just wanted to make sure you and Simons have the time down, to meet you know," he defensively replied when I'd asked him what he really wanted.

"Okay, I did have an ulterior motive for calling. You already let me have it for being insensitive to you when we had lunch Wednesday, but you said that you weren't really hurt or disappointed. I think we agreed that our bond had always been more friendly than anything else."

"Wow," I exclaimed in surprise. "That is the most accurate assessment of what's happened than I've ever heard pass your lips. What's led to this laying it out on the line today?" I asked, and suspected the answer before he confirmed it.

"McKayla and I had a great time last night. We'd met before through you," he stumbled a bit, "but we'd never really spoken before."

He coughed, and I could tell he was a little nervous. "We really hit it off, and I think it could be more than friendly with us. We have common interests and outlooks on life. She's always been so quiet; I never knew her brains matched her looks."

"I could tell you two enjoyed your jazz music discussion," I added, wanting to string this out enough to make him a little uncomfortable.

"There's that. We both cycle and we both want to finish an ironman competition someday," he said, his voice indicating he wanted to get to the point sooner rather than discussing why he liked her further. I asked her out after the party.

"And," I added for my own benefit, "She's not always stirring the pot like others you've dated. That's a plus too."

"Ha-ha Sara," he retorted, throwing off the sarcasm. "Bottom line is I asked her for a date. She said she'd love to, but wanted to make sure it was kosher with you. I knew it would be, but she gave me another earful over my lack of judgment when I came to see you on Monday," his tone was sincere. 'I was a jerk and I'm sorry."

My ears were pleased as punch. "Yeah, you were a jerk. To be fair, I can appreciate your outlook. If you are ever insensitive to McKayla though, I'll hunt you down and do the most embarrassing, horrendous things I can think of to you in front of as many of your colleagues as possible. Understood?"

"Wow," was his surprised reply, and I knew that he was fully aware that I could, and would, make good on the threat if necessary. "I think that is fair enough. I've learned from the experience. I think having less of a media hog as a date will make the lesson easier not to repeat,"

I laughed at this fantastic reply. "Nice dig, Eckert. One point for you. I have one final condition that both you and McKayla have to agree on to earn my full blessing though."

"Come on, already! You're not her mother for gosh sakes, but to play along, what condition would that be?"

"That you remain my friend, and that we can go to lunch occasionally, and that McKayla won't think that it is weird, or that I have to ask permission to do it."

'I don't think that will be a problem. She'd just about die for you, you know that?"

"I surely do and feel the same. I'd kill for her too, including police officers. Don't you forget that!"

"Cross my heart, Sara" he laughed, but I knew that he understood I was serious. "If I don't talk to you before, have a great time in London."

"Thanks," and before I ended the call, I added, "Do you realize that this is the longest phone conversation we've ever had?"

'Enough already," he said sarcastically. "Don't be late to meet Simons. He's a nervous wreck. Take good care of him for me."

"Will do; I'll call when I get back from London."

An hour later, I was in front of Simon's bank. Of course he would have to bank with one of the national chain banks. I didn't have any close buddies working at the main office of the bank, so this would be a little more difficult to explain without coming across like a loon. At least I knew a few of the officers there, and I could get them involved if this couldn't get moved along right away.

Simons opened one of the large glass doors leading into a cold foyer, and soon we were telling the story to the branch manager, Madison Atchison.

"Wow, that's a large return," she said in reference to the check that Simons had deposited and would be hitting the bank's cash letter as a forged or fraudulent item any time now.

"We're giving you a heads up on this, and want to deal with it before it becomes a problem for the bank or Simons," I said, but knew Madison thought I was nuts or trying to pull a fast one on her.

I went on anyway, "I was thinking Simons, I mean Edward, could qualify for a loan to cover the item. The bank would then have options in place in anticipation of the dreaded event. I'm sure your credit administration would be on board with this."

Still no reaction. She didn't smile, frown, twirl her hair or do anything to indicate she'd even heard anything I'd said.

She might be wondering if Simons were mentally vulnerable since I was doing the talking for him. I probably would be thinking the same thing if I were in her shoes. When someone talks about getting a loan for someone else, it's weird. Plus, no one fesses up to screwing up like this before they're called to the carpet. Still, I had to finish the sordid tale, and Simons was not about to open his mouth. He was a sorry sight, just sitting there listening to the ramifications of his error and wanting this conversation to be over. I felt badly for him, but had to push ahead.

"I know it is out of the box, but being proactive in situations like fraud calls for this kind of forward thinking."

I could tell that this was still not quite sinking in with her. I was shooting fast and straight, and had explained my banking past. It might seem suspicious to her somehow. Unfortunately, the laws had us so worried about being able to identify what did and didn't constitute suspicious activity; many like Madison treated anything out of the ordinary as just that.

Simons still sat there like a lump of nothing. I don't think my inability to get a reaction from Madison added any to my credibility in his eyes. I had to go higher up the food chain, and I only knew one person at the bank. I hoped he was in today.

"Madison, can you please call Earl Sampson for me? He knows me from a previous bank where we worked together. I understand he's the Credit Administrator here. Maybe he could offer a solution that works for everyone?"

I hoped she took it as an offer to fix the problem at hand, and not one of running over her own authority.

She chewed her lip, and after a moment of thought, agreed to make the call. Just a few minutes later, Simons and I were in Earl's office. There were frogs everywhere, just as I remembered. He mentioned that he liked frogs maybe once in his whole career and every gift he'd received since had something with a frog on it. I recall someone even gave him a cd of Christmas carols sung in frog sounds.

"Good to see you Earl," I said as I gave him a large hug.

"What's it been, like 8 years now? What trouble have you been getting into lately?"

"Now that's a story for another day," I remarked with a high note and a cough. I knew he'd had to have seen the papers, although not much had been done locally on my "incident". Maybe he didn't know about it. One can hope.

Once again, I explained the check Simons had deposited, that he'd been given immediate credit on it, and immediately wired out most of the proceeds. I then told him that it was likely part of a scam, that I'd reviewed the underlying documentation Simons had, and that a line of credit could be placed to cover the item when it was returned.

"Simons," I stopped, "I mean Edward, has good credit, a decent sized savings account with you and a home practically owned outright. I know this is out of the ordinary, Earl. I'm leaving the country in a few days, and I thought I might help move this process along faster in order to mitigate the risk to the bank. Underwriting expectations must of course meet the normal standards of banking safety and soundness."

I had let Earl know that this favor didn't include anything that could place the bank in jeopardy. Simons was probably one of the most creditworthy loan applicants a bank could see. I was only asking for a shortcut on the amount of time to review the application in order to meet or beat the check's return.

Simons had been looking at his feet during my conversation with Earl, and I could tell that he was embarrassed by my retelling of the story, which Earl recognized immediately as a scam too. I hoped he appreciated that this was the best way to go at this stage of the game. With a line of credit in place, when the check came back, there was no need for calls and scrambling. It would simply go against the line, and be done as far as the bank was concerned. If the check never came back, the loan would never be advanced. Once again, no harm, no foul.

Simons would have to make monthly payments if the check were returned, but at least they would be nothing more than he could handle since he'd already resumed his job duties with the police department that morning. A one day retirement. It's more than many of us will ever get.

Last night, I'd promised Simons I'd do my best to track down the recipient of the wire while I was in England, and make every effort to help get his money back. The truth is though, the fruition of whatever efforts I made were not likely to result in recapturing the lost money. I now had a copy of the actual wire documentation, and the name and address of its recipient. If it were real information, which was unlikely, I'd have a chance to catch one guy in the chain of this long and winding web of a scam. The chance was slim at best, but was at least there as a glimmer of hope that I could offer to Simons.

Earl quickly reviewed the application we'd completed for Simons.

"If his credit is as good as you've indicated, and he can supply proof of his reinstatement with the police department, I don't see why this should be an issue. We'll do it as a Home Equity Line of Credit loan. Even with the debt, your loan to value ratio would only be about 40%, even in this market. I'll take it to one of the processors."

"Thank you, Earl," I sighed in appreciation. 'Edward would have taken care of this, but I thought an explanation from a former colleague might help since this is extraordinary."

I looked at Simons. "And if there is any reason that I'm wrong about this, it hasn't cost you anything but spending an afternoon with me and filling out an application."

"Drop off the application, copies of pay stubs and a phone number to verify his employment status with Renee downstairs. She's in charge of our consumer lending. We should have an answer by tomorrow, and loan docs the day after that if it's approved as is."

Simons shook Earl's hand in appreciation, and waited a minute while I took a few minutes to catch up with Earl. We dropped off the information with Renee, who also asked for his homeowner's insurance provider and gave him a package that included some required disclosures. I was proud of her for remembering.

I was about to head home, and I told Simons I'd see him when I got back from London. It was unlikely that I'd be seeing him before then, and I had no plans to see Eckert again either.

"Sara, I'm sorry I've been so sulky," he said in a voice softer than I'd ever heard him speak before. He looked defeated.

"This is really a lot to handle, and I haven't wanted to believe it. I thought I knew better, especially as a policeman. I'm supposed to be able to smell this stuff out, not fall for it. I guess I'm embarrassed, and I feel so stupid. I've taken it out on you when all you've tried to do is help me. Can you forgive me?"

"Of course I can," I replied as I put my arm around his shoulder in a gesture of sisterly affection.

"I'm kind of an expert at doing stupid things myself. Damage control is practically my middle name."

He gave a semi-smile as a response.

"Other than my own public humiliations though, I hope you can appreciate that in my work experiences, I've been through this before many times. Every instance has been awful, each with its own complications and unknown variables, but each incident has left its victims feeling just like you do now. I've had people argue with me, and in this same situation, even insist that they knew what relative had left them this money.'

I looked him in the eyes, "And unfortunately, on every one of those occasions, I was right. Everyone wants to win the lottery, per se, and when it seems like it's your turn, you want to believe it."

He nodded, and gave me a hug.

"Thanks for helping me out. I don't deserve it," he said, and ended the sentence with a giggly sounding laugh.

'What's the laugh for? This is anything but funny."

'Yeah, I know, but I was thinking about what Eckert said yesterday, and it is pretty funny. He said you were just enough of a pain in the butt to actually track down this guy while you were in London."

I frowned and gave a sound of disgust; figures Eckert would say something so tactless.

"He also said if there was one person in the world who could get my money back, or bring at least one person to justice, that you were it."

Okay, so he could say some nice things too. He was insensitive, but nice. "Well, I've been able to verify that the address on the wire is legitimately traceable to a residential area outside of London. There's a chance, a very small one, that this could be the actual bad guy's name and address."

"Or it could be a false name and address," Simons stated glumly.

"Could be, but one can hope. Most never bother to track them down, so it could be we fall into an unlucky mistake of a crook and I find him while I'm there. I'm making arrangements to stay a few extra days so I don't interfere with the Westin's plans while I check this out."

"Thanks Sara, I appreciate it. I'll make it up to you somehow."

I waived him off. "It'll be exciting doing something other than writing up reports on these for a change."

"Heaven help Alfred wherever he may be," Simons said as he read the wire recipient's name from the form he'd filled out to send the wire. "If he is a real person, he doesn't know what's about to hit him," Simons said with almost a sense of sorrow for Alfred.

We both laughed, said our final goodbyes, and got back to our busy days.

18

I had promised Mom I'd join the family for dinner later that night. This marked the first time we had all been together since Greg and Brooke had gotten married; I cannot say the wedding planning had been much fun. I was excited about getting to see Kierra, and I felt like I'd been neglecting her some since the wedding, but I wanted her to enjoy her new family without any undue interference.

I had brought Rusty with me, and planned to keep her with my folks tonight since we would be leaving in just two days. I was so grateful that Rusty would have familiar folks taking care of her while I was gone, and I knew she'd be missing the huge near 40 acre backyard that had become her personal playground. Both Mom and Dad had promised to walk her every day so she wouldn't feel too cooped up in their small third acre yard. How spoiled she'd become since we'd been staying at the house. I didn't know how she would be if we moved back to the confines of my condo again.

Everyone was already at my folk's by the time I arrived. I was grateful knowing that there would not be any "company" for me to deal with on this outing. I had quit coming around despite my mom's great cooking because she was always inviting a single young man that she hoped would sweep me off of my feet.

I was grateful that Brooke's pregnancy and marriage to Greg had taken these awkward events out of the limelight, plus Mom and Dad thought Eckert was just wonderful for me. During our recent lunch event, I hadn't shared with her that the "relationship" was over now, and I was going to avoid the topic for as long as possible.

Kierra ran to greet me right as I walked through the door. She threw her arms around me, almost swallowing me whole with her affection.

"Auntie Sara," she said as she finally let go of me. "I've missed you. Did you know I'm going to have a baby brother named Ethan?"

Brooke had joined Kierra in the living room to greet me. She glowed with pregnancy, with her belly swelling away from her normally trim figure. I hugged her in greeting and gave an obligatory pat to her belly.

'Ethan?" I asked. "That's a nice name. Congrats." She smiled, but Kierra was already pulling me to the dining room. Everyone else was already seated, and Mom came out with a steaming plate full of cuts of prime rib.

Greg and Dad were deep in conversation, but gave me a glance as a greeting. It was just as well, as Kierra was telling me about the new house they would be moving into.

"I'm gonna have my own bedroom, and there'll be a living room upstairs and downstairs too. I get to have my walls painted blue too!" It was a pleasure to see her so excited, and I could tell that theirs was a happy family, and I was very happy for Brooke in finding a good man.

Mom cut right into our discussion. "You're late," she chastised me in greeting. She directed me to sit at the table, and I knew that small talk was out of the picture until food was plated.

I looked at the still steaming food. In addition to the prime rib, there were mashed potatoes, green beans, and Mom's homemade rolls. Yum.

"I think my timing's perfect," I said sneaking a green bean from the plate. "I'm starved."

"Figures," she said, giving my hand a slap when I tried for a second steal from the bowl of green beans.

Mom looked fantastic, as usual. Whether or not she ever left the house, had company or was completely alone, you would never catch her without her hair and make-up done to perfection AND with a completely color-coordinated outfit. She and June were one and the same when it came to this standard.

Dinner was a noisy event. Plates were passed, glasses clinked and silverware moved at a fast pace. I waited until everyone was well into the meal before sharing an overviewof the "incident" and all that had happened since. Thankfully, it did not remain a topic of conversation for long, and normal family activities once were the focal point during the meal.

I had brought some of the fine chocolates, and selected a nice perfume for each my Mom, Brooke and Kierra. The story behind that was a lot more exciting to tell than the reason I'd gotten the gifts in the first place.

The girls were thrilled to have a bottle of real perfume from such a famous person. Kierra insisted on squirting hers as we sat at the dinner table, and the smell of dinner was quickly overwhelmed by a fragrance that we quickly decided was far too grown-up for her. Once the main dish was served, the strong scent had dissipated and the banter flowed on to other matters of life.

Dad started off. 'Are you all packed and ready to go?"

"Yes, I'm so excited about the trip. June and I are going to visit all the museums and the countryside. We even get to stay at a real castle for a weekend. I can hardly wait to feel the history all around me. English landscapes and portraiture have also always been a fascination for me. I can't wait to see a large representation of work. I've only seen a few examples up close and personal, and not enough to compare styles. I can only dream about seeing a whole room of works by Gainsborough, Reynolds and Lawrence at one time!"

Brooke rolled her eyes, "Enough with the culture and history stuff. Yawn already. What about the shopping? European shops are supposed to be the best ever. Plus, London fashion is all the rage."

I shrugged my shoulders as an answer since I had nothing whatsoever to say about fashions or trends. Things of the present didn't intrigue me like things from the past, and fashion and I were not on good terms whatsoever. Her question made me bristle nonetheless.

She's the pretty one, Sara, I told myself, *but you're the smart one that is not making childbirth into an annual event. Let it go.* I love my sister, but she can be so shallow. I don't know why I let it grate me so. I guess she'd be a little sister forever

A piece of meat fell off of her fork as she was eating and landed on her baby bump. It left a nice grease stain on her lovely and probably expensive maternity top. "Now that's fashionable!" Dad commented.

I almost snorted at the timing of his comment, and Brooke glowered at me as I laughed. I mentally stuck out my tongue at her. It was like the old days once more!

Mom rescued us from further fashion speak. "I thought Sam was going too?" she questioned as she dished up more mashed potatoes on Kierra's plate.

"He is, but he wants to take care of some business most of the time. It was going to be a golf trip for him, but when the trip got delayed, the change of season changed his plans. That's why he's so glad that I'm going so I can take June shopping and to all the cultural stuff. I think Sam only cares about the courses, and he'll probably visit some even though it could be snowing for all we know. I think he wants to soak in the atmosphere through the pubs the guys will visit after finishing each course. He says he is meeting some businessmen while he's there. Museums bore him, but he's always taken June since she loves them so much. Now he has me to handle that for him."

"Paid to go shopping and visit museums? Sounds pretty good," Greg chimed in. "I could go for a job like that."

I held the back of my hand to my head in mock protest. 'Yes, someone has to do it. It's just part of the job. I don't know how I'll manage to survive staying in a first class hotel and getting paid to visit some of the best places on earth." I added a sigh. "I'll manage somehow."

Everyone laughed, as it was no secret that my job had definitely come with some amazing perks and privileges. Another one had been that I had been able to get Sam and June to switch from their regular gardener to Greg's company. He was a landscaper, but was able to make a full day once a week just in taking care of the Westin's gorgeous grounds. He did a good job too, and better keep doing so as it would reflect poorly on me if he didn't. I wasn't worried though, as Greg had a great work ethic and was a fine catch for Brooke.

'Kierra, what do you want me to bring you from England?" I asked.

She smiled with excitement, not anticipating a second present, and better yet one from another country. I had no idea what to get for a five year old, so I was grateful for any help. Shopping in another country was not as easy as taking her to the toy store and letting her choose what she wanted.

"A present for me? First perfume, now this, Wow! Well, Grandma made me tea today, like she had with you at the other lady's house. She had such a pretty cup for me to use. I want my own so I can play tea party at home. Can I have one with flowers on it?" she asked with wide eyes at the possibility.

I breathed a sigh of relief, as this was an easily handled request in England "What color flowers? England is famous for its bone china teacups, Kierra. I can probably get one with anything on it."

'Anything? Even fairies?"

"Maybe, would you like me to try to get fairies, and if I can't find one, then flowers?"

"Oh yes. I like blue bestest. Thank you, Sara!" her face expressed her pleasure in being able to get such a grownup present for herself. She threw her arms around me in a tight squeeze, practically spilling her plate. "You're the best auntie ever!"

Kierra was such a joy, and she constantly reminded me of the beauty of youth's innocence and appreciation. Her happiness made me smile inside and out, as I readjusted her place at the table as not to create an event involving spilled food and broken plates.

As she settled back in, I switched up the conversation, and looking from Brooke to Greg, I asked. 'Tell me about the house? When's the move?"

Greg and Brooke exchanged looks that indicated all was not as well as it should have been.

"Escrow has been delayed on the house," Greg said. "The closing hinges on the seller's contingent sale on the house he's moving into, and so on and so on. It could take another three to four months before it is finalized."

"With the current state of the housing market, it could be even longer," Brooke added glumly. "The lease on our place is up, and we have to be out in a month because it has already been re-leased to another family. Greg and I are scrambling for a solution."

She looked down at her belly, and Greg massaged it gently. "I don't want Ethan to be born before we move in to our first family home," he said gently speaking to her belly. Brooke wants to have the nursery all set up first, but it isn't likely going to happen. She's spending her days looking for places. We can't control what's gonna happen though, unless we cancel escrow and buy somewhere else."

Brooke flashed him an alarmed look, and Greg sighed deeply in recognition of what certainly must be an on-going conversation at their home.

"She's got her heart set on that house though," he continued softly, "So until then, we'll have to find a solution and wait it out."

"Why don't you move in here?" Dad asked, after he'd shoved a roll in his mouth. 'We can take you in for a few months until the house is ready."

Mom's fork hit her plate with a clash. She threw Dad a murderous look that told me he'd sprung that one without discussing it with her first.

An idea hit me in a flash. This situation, along with Mom's reaction, made my decision suddenly easy. Never had my indecisiveness ended so abruptly, and I literally felt like lightning had hit me in the head.

"This is perfect!" I announced. All eyes in the room were on me. The looks indicated that I'd just said about the worst possible thing in this situation.

"No, not about Greg and Brooke's problem, but a solution for them and for my own dilemma," I said with my voice rising in excitement that no one bought into yet. "My condo will be released for occupancy before I get back from London."

"And?" Mom asked impatiently as I scooted my chair back from the table so I could use my hands as I spoke.

"And, one of the reasons I agreed to come over tonight was to ask advice on whether or not I should move back in right away. June wants me to stay at their house, and even offered to renovate the back cottage for me, you know for more privacy. I've been feeling like I want my place back, but feeling terribly guilty since June likes to have me at the house so much."

"And?" Mom said again, impatiently wanting the rest of the story.

"Mom, relax, I'm getting there!" I said flashing my eyes since Mom's impatience was raining on my parade of good news.

"Don't you see that this problem makes my decision for me? Greg, Brooke and Kierra need a place to stay, and I have one available. It has two bedrooms too, so it should be plenty big enough for them to use while they're waiting for the close of escrow. Now, I won't have to make a decision as to what I'm going to do yet. I'll have more time to think about it, and can make a decision that's best for me."

Everyone finally caught on, and a buzz of enlightenment rounded the room

"That's wonderful for Greg and Brooke," Dad said, and they both nodded in agreement, obviously thrilled to have their own problem thwarted somewhat, "But what are you going to do when they move out? If you don't live in it, you should rent it. The sales market is too volatile right now, and you almost own it outright."

"Well, that's just it. I don't know what I want to do yet. I may not have this job forever, so I want to keep it. It's my home. For now, even if I'm living there again, I still would be spending a lot of time at Sam and June's. It makes more sense to stay there, plus Rusty loves having acres to run around in all day and having a pack of dogs for friends. I just feel like I need a little distance now and then, you know separation from home and job."

"Hon, just talk to June about how you feel about the space thing. Maybe the cottage thing's a good idea after all. Kind of a happy medium for now," she placed her hand on mine. "I'm thrilled Brooke will have less stress until the baby's born and can get the condo ready for Kierra and Ethan. Sounds like a win-win situation."

Mom got up to clear dishes and get dessert, as everyone assented and started talking about the move into the condo. Kierra lit up in anticipation of the chocolate cake she'd been eyeing in the kitchen.

Brooke and I gathered some more of the dishes from the table. Mom called back to us from the kitchen. "By the way, don't bother Sam with it; men can't deal with getting in touch with women's feelings." She shot a glance at my dad, who intelligently chose not to respond.

"I don't want to hurt her feelings," I said, putting dishes in the sink and taking the first plates of cake back with me. "She's been so good to me, and I want to be there for her anytime she needs me."

"I've gotten to know June a little the few times we have had dinner together, and I know she thinks the world of you. I know she would want you to be happy. You two will come up with a good solution together," Mom added, bringing out more plates of cake.

She set Kierra's down first, much to her delight as she dug in before the rest of us were served. Mom swatted her hand gently and said, "Until then, I thank you for fixing my own dilemma too."

"What dilemma?" I asked and everyone looked at Mom with the same question, wondering what other news revelation would be coming.

Bad Hair Days

"How to deal with your father if Brooke and Greg had decided to move in for a few months. I didn't know if I'd have killed him or just kicked him out."

The room erupted in laughter, although I knew that her comment would make my Dad sweat things out for a while. Mom would be giving him a verbal lashing later for offering before asking her about it. Better him than me any day.

19

I hate flying. Traveling is inconvenient, but being in a metal bus 30,000 feet above the ground and going a zillion miles an hour just didn't thrill me. Multiply that by enduring 14 plus hours of time in the air, and you have yourself one nervous wreck of a flyer.

I hadn't done a lot traveling in my life so far, with most trips being business related for seminars or classes. On those days, I drove whenever I could.

I made my first international trip to France some years ago. As I recall, the flight was a nerve killer. To my later understanding, the flight itself was not particularly bumpy or otherwise more difficult than any other international flight, but I was miserable during the entire trip. Every bump or change in the sound of the engines made me cringe. I found myself unable to sleep during the 14 hour flight, and found myself having reverse jetlag for my first day in the country.

It didn't help that the return flight put us in a huge lightning storm as we got to the airport, and we had to circle around it until it was safe to land. Needless to say, I'd made no additional international trips since then.

The flight from Reno to New York was pretty tame. We left very early in the a.m., and I was sleepy enough to get a few more hours of shut-eye. We changed planes at the JFK Airport in a mad dash. The international plane was much bigger than the one we had just departed. It had three rows of seats instead of two, with a total of about twelve seats across instead of five.

I settled June and Sam into the first class area as we boarded, and then I said a goodbye and Alan and I headed for business class. June had wanted me to fly first class, but I could not allow them to pay the additional three thousand dollars for such a luxury. It was fine for them, but I had insisted and June relented. Alan agreed to join me in business class, and had bought his own ticket for the seat next to mine.

We were in one of the rows with eight seats across. I sat on the edge of the aisle, and Alan just next to me. The flight was not very full, so after take off, our entire row was still empty. Alan scooted over a seat and we made ourselves more comfortable.

Alan bought headsets for both of us when the flight attendant asked if we wanted to see the in-flight show. The plane was showing a Disney animal movie, and I knew I'd be too nervous to read, so I jumped at Alan's suggestion. We immediately inserted the headphones into the plug so we could listen to the radio until the movie started later during the flight.

For a while, I went through the travel magazines the airlines provided. In a sudden movement, the plane dropped about ten feet. My stomach dropped about a 100 feet, and I found myself clutching Alan in a death grip.

"Whoa, girl," Alan said. I don't think he had realized I was a nervous flyer until that moment. He moved back into the seat right next to me while the plane continued to bump and move.

The overhead speakers came on, and the pilot announced we would have a bumpy ride for the next few minutes. The seatbelt signs went on and the stewardesses went to buckle themselves into their own seats.

"The flight attendants are sitting too. Should we be worried?" I asked Alan like a little girl asking her mother if a roller coaster ride was safe.

"No, it's standard procedure, and especially common on these long flights across the Atlantic. No need to worry."

I still had my hand on top of Alan's, and I think he liked it. He patted my hand with his other one, and casually stretched out and put his arm around me. I let him, and appreciated the human contact during the moments of extreme turbulence.

It ended ten or so minutes later. "Excuse me," he spoke as a flight attendant, now back on her feet, was checking through the aisles to ensure all of the passengers were comfortable again.

"Yes?" she asked, turning to him with her full attention. A pretend smile was plastered across her face.

"Could we please have some drinks here as soon as you are able?" Alan asked nicely.

"I'll just be starting my first round, and soon we'll be serving lunch," she replied in a saccharine sweet voice. She smiled again and walked away, not giving Alan a definite answer to his question.

"This is why first class is worth the price. I'll be right back," he said and sauntered up to the first class area. Within five minutes, he was back with two gin and tonics.

"This will settle your nerves some. I asked Dad to order some more and bring them back."

I gratefully took the drink and pretty much slammed it down.

Alan raised his eyebrows and handed over the other one to me. I did the same thing with that one.

"Geez, if I had known you wanted shots, I would've gotten those instead."

Sam brought two more drinks back to us. "Alan says you're a little edgy." He spied the two empty glasses in front of me. I gave a weak smile and a nod, and jumped in my seat as the plane unexpectedly lurched again.

Sam steadied himself and chuckled, as once again I had a death grip on Alan. Fortunately, the drinks in Sam's hands hadn't spilled, but the two empty drink cups, now filled with just ice and limes, were now in my lap.

"Crap!" I said, shaking off the wet mess. I managed to get everything that remained back into the cups, and Alan pulled out a handkerchief and wiped off my lap. His touch was gentle, and I looked into his eyes as he patted me on my wet spots. His eyes were searching mine, flirting and suggestive. I blushed and looked away. All I needed was to get hot and bothered on this plane, especially after inhaling some pretty strong drinks.

'Well kids, I'm going back to my paper. Come back to first class if you need a refill," he said as he sauntered back to towards the front of the plane.

I downed another drink, which I shouldn't have done so quickly after the first two, and without food to offset the affects. Three drinks on an empty stomach were not a good idea even for the most anxious of travelers. I felt my mind fog over, and my body begin to relax.

I patted Alan's hand. "Bathroom," I whispered and headed down the aisle.

I finished and washed up, now feely a little woozy. I'd have to slow down on the drinks or I'd be trashed in no time. Drunkenness felt better than terror, but I felt rather nauseous due to one or the other now.

Once I felt a little better, I opened the door but it was quickly pushed back in. Alan slammed the door behind us and put a finger to my lips before I could utter any protest.

He put his hand behind my head and put his face to mine. He gave me a kiss, and not just a kiss, but one that was so soft and passionate it about melted my pants off. The kiss was warm, gentle and slow.

I took in his fragrance and reciprocated on the kiss. Excessive alcohol had always affected me in several ways, one of which included fast arousal, an abandonment of good judgment and its subsequent side effect of low morals.

Alan nibbled my ear and put his hand up my shirt. I pushed his hand back down, protesting only now that things had heated up. My back was starting to burn, its odd position arching over the sink towards the bathroom mirror pulling on my not quite healed stitches. The pain killed the mood for me, but I could sense, and feel too, that Alan's mood was still quite alive.

"Let's become members of the mile high club," he whispered into my ear, and continued to nuzzle my neck even though my hand was still covering the one inside my shirt.

'Alan, no," I pulled from the embrace, returning somewhat to my senses. I was really hot and bothered now, and I felt bad for getting Alan there too.

I hadn't yet decided if it were right for me to date Alan. He was Sam and June's son, and I didn't want to risk my relationship with them over one with Alan. I didn't know him well enough for this big of a step anyway, regardless of my temporary state of drunken euphoria.

I indicated to him that my back was hurting, and he immediately let me go with a response of concern.

I quickly opened the door and exited the tiny bathroom, wearing a guilty grin and looking around the cabin to see if anyone had noticed that there were two of us in there. I was met with more than a few sniggers, and I was so embarrassed, I turned red before making it to my seat.

Alan had enough sense, and probably needed to wait a minute or two anyway, before returning to his seat. Upon his appearance from the tiny room, I heard a few cheers and jokes from the passengers sitting around that area. Someone even gave Alan a high five.

Yikes, no matter where I go, I get into the middle of something' I thought. I slammed the fourth drink down and happily passed out for the rest of the flight.

20

My first day in London began with my head pounding from the after effects of the gin and tonics I'd recklessly drunk on the plane. I'd gone right to bed after getting to the Dorchester the night before and barely looked at the place before crashing out for the night.

A knock on the door of my room awoke me, my head throbbing in rhythm with the tapping.

"What?" I called in a voice rather gruffer than my normal morning greeting.

Alan came into the room, looking like he was ready to conquer the world.

"Wake up, sunshine," he practically sang out.

"Please go away, or at least make my head stop beating in time with my heart," I said from beneath the dark safety of a pillow.

"Dr. Alan's got just the thing for you. The blinds are shut, and I'll close the door to keep the light out."

Flopping the pillow off of my head, I decided to obey Dr. Alan or suffer the likely consequences. Alan stuck a gin and tonic in my hand. The smell hit my nose, and my gag reflex took over. I searched for a trash can to vomit in. I couldn't find one, and luckily the heaving sequence stopped.

"Could you be any meaner Alan?" I sniped.

"I'm not the one who drank these like water on the plane little missy," he teased, "but I do happen to know that drinking another one will make the headache go away."

"You can't be serious Alan. I never want to see one of those drinks again."

"Sara, you must trust Dr. Alan It's called "hair of the dog". You feel lousy because of the sugar and alcohol coming out of your system. Put a little of the same back in, and you'll level out."

He shook the glass in front of my face again, and the queasy feeling returned. It sounded scientifically reasonable enough that he could be telling me the truth. He had no reason to want to make me feel any

114

worse.

"Mom's got a big day planned. You'll make it through a lot easier if you drink this. Your hair looks more interesting today than most mornings, by the way."

My head hurt too much to listen anymore, and his snide comment about my fair was meant to gauge a reaction. I grabbed the drink and downed it. I don't know how the liquid made it down my esophagus in between uncontrollable heaves. I managed to keep it down, and felt around on the top of my head to see how bad it was. It felt like a bird had nested in it.

"Yeah, it is bad," he laughed watching my face scrunch up as used my fingers to unknot some of the mess. "Go shower. In 15 minutes, you'll feel alive again. This is a seasoned drinker's staple for survival. Being a sober minded guy, I've been the one to administer it to many friends in my life. I promise." he made the sign of crossing his heart as he said it.

I have to admit that I hadn't known about this trick before, but it actually worked and I felt more like myself fairly quickly.

While cleaning up, I took an opportunity to check out the suite. It was a luxurious dream of a place, and would be our home base during our entire visit.

The main room was about 800 square feet, with a large seating area surrounding a real fireplace. There were four bedrooms, each with a door connecting the main suite. Each bedroom had a private bath, and the décor was as expected. Fine art, detailed wood work, and wine red velvet draperies oozed antique elegance.

A dining area was just off the main sitting room, and could seat eight comfortably. An archway led to the sitting room so it was separate yet a part of it. The table was set, as if dinner were to be served at any time.

I took in the extravagance of the room, momentarily forgetting I was trying to get over the pounding in my head and feeling of nausea that accompanied it. I headed back to my own room to get ready for what was sure to be a fast paced day.

Within the hour, June and I were ready to head out to take our first journey out into the wonderful world called London. Sam was already out and about, and Alan decided to join us for the first day.

The Victoria and Albert Museum was very close to the hotel, and would be our very first museum visit for the trip.

It was cold outside, and I was grateful I had worn the thickest coat I'd brought.

"I'll call a cab," I offered as we headed out the hotel door, nodding morning greetings to the doorman.

June's voice called me back before I'd taken three steps, "Sara darling, we've already arranged transportation."

"Oh, I see. I didn't hear Alan call from the room." I rejoined them with a shrug.

Alan pushed June's chair towards a long white limousine. The driver jumped out and assisted in getting her inside the vehicle and put her wheelchair in the rear.

Holding the door for me, Alan beckoned my entry with a formal "Madame", and we were off for our first day of adventure. He noticed my astonishment at the formal vehicle. The inside was decorated in white leather, and had enough room for all of us to lie down if we wanted. There was a phone, television, and a full bar. This was my second time in a limousine, the first just a week ago, but it was still an unbelievable way to travel. I'd assumed we'd be taking cabs during the trip.

"When you stay at a room like this, it's part of the package Sara," he whispered in my ear.

I nodded, and replied, "I think I could get used to this first class travel thing."

He laughed as I got in, "It's an easy thing to do."

The next few days were a blur. June and I visited as many museums each day as we could in the time allowed. After spending the first day at the Victoria and Albert Museum, we managed to squeeze in long visits to the British Museum, the National Gallery, the Tate Gallery and the National Portrait Gallery. I gained a new appreciation for British portraiture, and wanted to learn more about Gainsborough and Reynolds when we returned home.

In between museum visits, we shopped and had tea or lunch at places like the Ritz. The famous gardens were not in season to visit, but despite the cold and damp, we managed to get into to the Orangerie and Kensington and the Hampton Court Palace.

June and Sam had hired the limo for our entire visit, so we could go where we wanted, when we wanted, and we did just that.

After six days of museums and garden tours, June wanted a day to devote just to shopping. Although I'm not like a typical gal in many ways, I did enjoy browsing through the unique shops both in and outside of the city, and the break from routine sounded fun.

Actually, the shopping was amazing. We must have hit every high end store in town. We went to Harrod's, Burberry's and Barkers of Kensington, which were all on June's must-do list, with Fortnum and Mason our destination for tea shopping and lunch. I loved eyeing all of the fine things, even knowing they would never be mine. I could appreciate their beauty and significance with just a longing glance, which was even more educated after the marathon museum tours.

I must have bought tins of tea for everyone I knew, but now that my circle of friends had come to enjoy tea at the Westin's, it was a must have gift for everyone.

I found fabulous things for everyone back home, and most importantly, a blue fairy tea set for Kierra. I got her two other floral teacups. The set came in a wicker basket with a pot, saucers and cups. Kierra could play with it for hours at teatime.

I'd seen sets with teddies and flowers on them. When I came across one with fairies and color choices of either blue or purple, I knew it was providence!

I had a hard time not spending any money on myself. There were enamel boxes that were replicas of snuff and patch boxes I just adored. Many were similar to ones I'd seen at a few of the museums we'd visited. They had been used to carry snuff or serve as sewing kits for women. They were ornately decorated with scenes of outdoors, portraits, and had embellishments in gold or raised design that made them art works all on their own.

Each box was a piece of art. Even though they were reproductions, they cost nearly $500.00 for the smallest box. Some were very ornate, adorned with portraits of royalty, landscapes or courting scenes. The most lovely was asking a hefty price of nearly $2,500.00.

When we were at a smaller shop, one in particular caught my eye. It was about a one and a half inch square that had been hand-painted on every surface. There was a store display on the artist, an English woman who was trying to revive the craft in its original form. Most of the replicas had transfers or other means of design placement put on the box, but hers were completely painted in freehand.

I couldn't bring myself to pay the $1,500.00 price tag for the box, and opted instead for a porcelain brooch from her collection. It was also lovely, and would serve as my personal memento of this fantastic trip. It was a landscape of the countryside, and reminded me of what the Hampton Court Palace must be like in the summer months.

I also got a teapot and several cups for myself. June had begun a tradition in taking time just to enjoy tea and reflect on life or enjoy company. I wanted to continue the tradition forever and pass on it to those I loved most. I got Mom a set too, and was thrilled to have her upcoming birthday present taken care of, and timely for a change.

June went crazy at a few of the antique shops. While I browsed, she arranged to have a few large items shipped to the house. At one shop, I think she made the shop owner's year with the amount of money she dropped.

"I'm going to re-do one of the upstairs rooms in authentic English antiques. I'll do rich red brocade paper and huge pieces of carved furniture. "Maybe even some of the ornate tapestry chairs," she said to herself as she asked questions about pieces and tapped the ones she decided upon.

As we bought items, we arranged for direct shipment home so we wouldn't have to carry them with us or worry about shipping them in packages from the hotel. The furniture shipments came to a sum that was nearly my entire annual salary. June was not an extremely extravagant woman, but if she was going to do something, it was going to be done correctly.

At the end of the day, our wallets were much lighter as we returned to the hotel. We spent the evening enjoying room service and old black and white British mystery movies in the grand space that had served as our home away from home for the past week.

21

It was a dull, damp, typically English morning. The grey sky exuded gloom, all wet and slushy, and reminded me of being at home in Nevada during this part of the year. We were so far away from home, yet so near to it in weather conditions; it was an odd feeling of familiarity.

June and I were alone, enjoying the large sitting room and an exquisite breakfast, reflecting on the previous day spent shopping and the week immersed in the glorious art and culture of this fabulous country. We sat in silence, as I gorged myself on sausage, eggs and toast that room service had delivered earlier.

June sipped at her coffee and stared off into space. She was far away in thought, and by the look on her face, the thoughts weren't necessarily pleasant ones. I'd never seen her in what must be her version of a sour mood.

"A penny for your thoughts?" I cheerily asked, hoping it would somehow snap her back to the present.

She seemed startled by my question, "Sorry Sara, I honestly think I forgot I wasn't alone."

'Are you okay?" I put down my fork, and wiped my mouth, giving her my full attention.

June looked at me with overwhelming sadness in her eyes. I think I heard my heart breaking.

Tears came out of the tiny woman, and I didn't know what to do. I led her to the couch and held her as she cried, just as she would have done for me. I was worried, since I'd never seen June give into any undesirable emotion before. Had she fought with Sam?

"What's the matter?" I asked in a soothing voice, hoping that for a change I could be the one providing comfort.

She motioned for tissue, so I let her go to retrieve the box.

"Believe it or not," she said with a smile, "that was all I needed. My tear ducts must have been clogged."

I laughed at her joke, just as I knew she wanted me to do; I was not letting her off that easy, though. I decided to take her usual path of

119

polite directness.

"Did you fight with Sam or something?"

"Oh, not really a fight," she said waving off the thought, "but I'm a little upset with him, that's all."

"Enough to make you cry? June, I've never even seen a frown on your face."

"You don't see me 24 hours a day, little miss," she chastised. "I'm not always happy, but I'm glad to say I am most of the time."

Her long robe, a lovely royal blue silk damask, fluttered as she arose from the couch and went back to the table to finish her coffee. She beckoned me to join her there.

"Come and sit down, and I'll tell all now that I've let loose a little."

I went back to my plate and poured some more coffee for myself.

"I've been begging Sam to take me to England for years," she started, looking up as if recalling a memory. "We were finally set to go in the spring, but the doctors wouldn't release me yet. Then we were going to go in the late summer, but business got in the way, you came along and so on."

I shrunk a little, hoping my arrival hadn't been a main interruption in her plans.

Reading me as usual, she reversed herself. "Oh honey, it had nothing to do with you. Sam just got involved in some things that made us change the date again. Now, here we are in the winter, visiting a cold and wet place."

She took her mug and strolled to the window, opening it to reveal another gray morning.

"What's my favorite thing?"

"You mean like to wear, to eat, to watch, to do?"

"I meant in general, but it's a thing to do as well."

"Garden of course," I replied without effort, and then it struck me. She'd made an offhand comment about it before, but who would want to visit the famous gardens of England in the winter?

June recognized that I got her point. "I do love the art and architecture Sara, but it's been a dream to see these elegant places in full bloom."

She gently sat again, "I just should have insisted that we wait until the spring to come. Sam wanted to come right away because of the business he wanted to wrap up. He said he wanted to meet these folks in person before he got more involved in the venture."

I gave her a supportive look.

"I'm just feeling a little sorry for myself, especially since Sam didn't want to do anything with me today. I want him to have tea with me at one of these fabulous places we've been visiting. I just wish he'd experience some of the things I love *with me*. You know what I mean?"

"He couldn't go?" I asked as I nodded my head in complete understanding of her wanting to share her hobbies with Sam. When I saw him, I'd have a hard time now, and at the moment I wanted nothing more than to chew him out for upsetting June.

"No, business meeting again. He's been so secretive about this new enterprise of his. But," she added encouragingly, "he promised a great surprise for me tomorrow. He said it would take my breath away, and that I'd have three days of his complete attention. That's more than I've ever had!"

Her eyes had regained their gleam of sunshine, and I happily joined in her merriment over the fact that Sam was never really fully present, even when he was with you. His mind was always working away, somewhere distant even while he talked with you.

"Well that's settled then," I said, exuding happy thoughts to keep the mood up. I'm glad you're out of the doldrums. I only hope that you never have to go there again. What's on the schedule for today?"

"For you, a day of freedom or a day of spa luxuries with me," she said. "I'm having a mud bath, facial, massage, hair set, manicure and pedicure."

My face fell. I found it hard to hide my disappointment, and I was immediately angered at myself for showing my heart on my sleeve to her when she needed me most.

"I know, it's not your thing, but I wanted to offer just in case. The mud bath and massage might be up your alley. What about a style? An upswept look would be great!"

"I think I'd rather have a root canal," I admitted, although that too would require my sitting still for a long time. "Sorry, June."

Just then Alan sauntered in, having taken his morning walk in Hyde Park.

"Hey," he said to us, rubbing his arms to warm up after removing his coat. He put his freezing hands on June's cheeks to emphasis how cold it was outside that morning.

"I was just telling Sara she was going to have to live without me for a day. I'm cutting the chain so she can be rid of me." She looked at me, and motioned dramatically that I was released from my daily bondage of spending time with her, "Go. Be free."

Alan looked at me. "Do you want to do something together? I remember you said you want to see the Tower of London. Mom wasn't into that. Sounds pretty good to me. Its bloody history is interesting."

Thoughts of the Tower's historical significance flooded my mind. I really did want to visit a few of the more significant places of the Tower. The dungeons would be fun and scary. I think the tours played up the best of the worst events that had happened there.

"Would you really want to go there?" I asked in wonderment. It wasn't on everyone's top ten list, and Alan didn't seem like the history buff sort.

"I want to go anywhere that would please you, my lady," he bowed, kissing the back of my hand.

"Alright, enough already. You're on though. I want to see the Tower Green and the Bloody Tower, and there is an exhibit of armor from the time of Henry VIII. You'll be stuck going through those with me. Plus, I want a chance to see one of the famous ravens, said to protect the tower and the safety of the city itself."

"You got it," he said, and eyed me still dressed in my morning gear. "Get dressed already, would ya? We're burning daylight here!"

"From Prince Charming to General Patton in ten seconds flat. This will be an interesting day," I said, leaving the room to prepare for a day at the infamous tower.

22

I was elated to be nearing the place in which I'd seen Anne Boleyn lose her head to a sharp sword. The scene I saw was from a movie of course, but being here would make one of Henry VIII's legendary tales come to life. I understood that Catherine Howard, Henry's fifth wife, was also beheaded here. Both his second and fifth wives had ended their lives to the sword on this very green, both accused of adultery.

Alan and I viewed the collections of armor and the exquisite crown jewels of England, at least what remained of them. He hadn't said much during the viewing of these collections. When we went through some of the tower sections, he just watched me, as if fascinated more by my reactions than his own impressions of the more ancient parts of the stone palace.

The Bloody Tower was an area evoking emotional and physical sadness, and we visited cells and other parts open to public viewing where prisoners had been held, knowing that the reasons for their imprisonment hadn't always been justified with crimes other than claims to the country's throne.

A famous prisoner of particular interest to me was Lady Jane Grey, an unfortunate teenager whose parents had ambitions of her being named as queen once Mary I died without issue. Jane's claim to the throne lasted about 9 days before she was executed. Merry Ole England had a bloody past that one couldn't help but be fascinated with.

She was killed, also beheaded, as was the man she was forced to marry in her contemplation of coming monarch of the country.

The Bloody Tower was aptly named, and its history was dark, known primarily for the past imprisonment and torture of its prisoners during the long years it stood.

One of my favorite mysteries of the place has remained unsolved by history. Richard, then a Duke, had locked away Edward IV's young sons in the tower while he acted as Protector for England in 1483. He claimed them illegitimate and seized the throne he was supposed to be protecting for them. The two princes, Edward V and Richard, Duke of York, were never to be seen again, and he was crowned Richard III. Rumors circulated that Richard III murdered the boys, but some blamed Henry VII, and still others believe at least one of them lived.

At one point of the visit, and patiently listening to my version of Henry VIII's marital history and other facts of its past, Alan asked, "Just how many wives did he have, and did he kill them all?"

"He was married six times, and history states he only truly loved one of them, the third, who died in childbirth. His sixth wife survived him and remarried. He annulled the first and the fourth, and killed the second and fifth for purported adultery."

"How do you remember all this?"

"A favorite way is a rhyme, just remember "Two annulled, one died, two beheaded, one survived". That's always made it easy for me to remember. Plus I've read fictional and historical accounts of his life, and seen lots of movies about it too." I recounted the numerous books I'd read by Margaret George and Allison Weir, which had brought these tales to vivid life for me.

"Okay," Alan said with a note of sarcasm dripping from it, "I'll just file that fact away somewhere in case I ever need it again."

"You do just that. I'll quiz you tonight," I joked just as we reached the Tower Green.

As with the Bloody Tower, the Tower Green was associated with some of the darker parts of English history. It was an outside area in between the towers, and was a place noted for the execution of nobles and others that were not for public viewing.

The ax was the standard, with some like Anne Boleyn, fortunate enough to have a sword, as the axe did not always get the job done the first time. Margaret Pole, the Countess of Salisbury is the most famous of these incidents. The inexperienced axe man didn't remove her head with the first blow, and it took 10 additional strikes to remove her head. Her cries are legendary. Another grisly fact is that nobles were expected to pay for the services of their hooded henchman, with hopes that a nice payment would mean a quick death.

A plaque commemorated the place where the scaffold had stood, and a chapel, St. Peter Ad Vincula, held the remains of Lady Jane Grey and other notables.

I awoke from thoughts of historical imagery that passed through my mind. Alan was patiently sitting on another bench close to me. Being a rather cold day, the other visitors had been chased back inside. He smiled wanly as I looked at his near shivering frame.

"I'm so sorry Alan. I got carried off by history. I love art as much as your mother, but parts of history, too. The history of the English crown is filled with lurid details that make soap operas seem tame.

Here though, in the Tower, is a place that connects events from many periods of this country's history. There is romance, turmoil, betrayal and tragedy. I can feel it all, you know, just by being here. It's a lot to take in."

"No problem. I'm enjoying watching you; it's just a bit cold that's all."

I realized I'd been looking around as I spoke, so now I gave him a look of uncertainty. "And what does that mean? It sounds a little creepy."

He sat on the bench next to me and put his arm around my shoulders. I didn't protest because I was rather cold.

"I like watching you look at things. I love your wonderment, and the emotional responses that you can't control in your eyes. I've known a lot of people, Sara, from all stations of life. I've never met anyone that appreciates all facets of life the way you do."

"There's so much to learn and do," I answered. "It's just too much for one lifetime."

"You find beauty in art, history, food. It never ceases to amaze me what little tidbits of knowledge you have, but what I like most of all is that you are unpretentious."

I took in his comments, trying to understand what he truly meant. "That's an odd word. What do you mean by that?"

Alan lowered his head, and took my hand in his, rubbing our fingers together to warm them. "You refuse the privilege of first class accommodations, you oh and ah over the room, you're surprised by the arrangements for a limousine in expectation of taking a bus or a cab."

I didn't know what to say. Was he implying I was simple?

"What I'm trying to say, Sara, is that of all the girls I've personally known or dated, you're the only one that does not have expectations of things that come with the privilege of wealth. You take the time to appreciate the things that money can buy, and the things that money can't, like natural beauty. I can see your mind at work when we're looking at art. Even when we're eating at some fancy place, I can feel that you're savoring every flavor. You make what is a meal for someone else an *experience* for you. A real experience to put away in your memory, to remember in the future."

I blushed, and removed my hand from his. I don't know why, but I was equally touched and embarrassed by his comments.

"I don't know what to say. I think you're saying I'm fun to hang out with."

He slapped his hands to his thighs and stood up, taking my hand and pulling me up to him.

"That's exactly what I'm saying. You're one of a kind."

A cawing sound came from above us, abruptly taking precedence to my "moment" with Alan.

"Oh, it's one of the ravens!" I exclaimed, thrilled that my experience at the Tower would end with viewing one of its famous inhabitants. Since the time of Charles II, ravens were protected, with at least six in residence at the tower at any given time. When Charles II was going to banish them at the request of one of his court members, he was told that the White Tower and England itself would fall if the ravens ever left.

I explained their significance to Alan while my eyes followed the bird's flight. It soared above me, probably leaving the green area to land on one of the walls.

It flew directly over me and disappeared just as a wet substance splatted on my head. I felt it hit my head and my clothing. I'd been pooped on by the raven!

Alan's eyes were wide as saucers, probably in uncertainty as to how I'd react. Alan reached out to somehow help, anticipating a show of disgust or my outraged reaction to the incident.

I think I surprised him, as I loudly laughed, and headed towards the door to find a restroom. I wondered how much was there, as it felt a bit heavy. I hoped it wouldn't slide down onto more of my clothing.

He looked at me in complete puzzlement, speechless.

"Alan, how can I feel anything but honored to receive such an offering from one of the famous ravens?" I said, pointing to the entrance to indicate I needed to make a restroom visit. "All I need is to wash it out; there's no need for me to "lose" my head over a little bird doodie!"

Alan groaned at my horrible pun, and then joined me in laughter as we headed inside.

I was ready to leave within ten minutes after the raven delivered its present.

"Are you really ready to go on today?" Alan asked, surprised at my lack of concern over the poop in my hair.

"I got it washed out with soap in the bathroom," I said. "The restrooms were quite capable of accommodating me. I'm ready to roll, unless you are too embarrassed to be seen with a gal with wet hair?" I intimated.

"No, not at all. I'm glad you were able to clean it out so well. I can handle being seen with a girl with an unstyled set of locks. It's being out with a girl who doesn't demand first class treatment that I am unaccustomed to," he laughed, checking over the washed area to make sure I'd gotten it all out. He nodded to indicate no traces remained. "If you're good to go, then I am too."

My stomach gurgled with hunger.

"Do you think we can do something a little different for lunch today?"

"Of course, anything. What are you in the mood for?"

"I have been dying to have a traditional lunch of fish and chips from a street vendor. Not that I've been disappointed in the lovely meals we've been having, but it's a must do on my list. I'll wait until I'm on my own if you're not up for it."

"Who wouldn't be allured by the fancy newspaper wrappings they're served in? Count me in!"

"Let's go!"

We spent the rest of the afternoon enjoying lunch and getting scared in the dungeons in various parts of the London Bridge. A total tourist trap, the set-up made them more like a haunted house of horrors than just a visit to the cells.

At some point, Alan let me know that my wet hair had dried itself in a less than fashionable style. He put his hand to my head and showed me that it poofed out where I had washed out remnant's of the famous raven's present.

He qualified his actions, "I don't care in the least, but I'm not used to hanging out with someone who doesn't go into cardiac arrest if her hair isn't perfect. I just don't want to get back to the hotel and be in trouble for not telling you."

Laughter flowed from deep within. Some former girlfriend must have made his life miserable. "If you haven't noticed yet Alan, my life is a series of bad hair days. You gotta go with the flow, and deal with what comes at you."

For once, Alan was speechless, so I added, "Don't worry, I'll style it before we go anywhere tonight though; gotta care a little about my personal appearance, especially on grand occasions like a night on the town!" We headed back to our rooms to get ready for an evening out with Sam and June.

23

I was very excited about an opportunity to enjoy London's night life, and especially the chance to see a show with such historic importance as *The Mousetrap*, the longest running play in history.

June gave us notice upon our return and I knew Sam had made a huge comeback by coming up with tickets, as June's glowing grin ensured me her melancholic episode was done and over.

You did good boss, I thought, glad that June's morning blues were long forgotten.

The show was playing at St. Martine's theater, a lovely old place located in a part of town known as the West End, London's answer to Broadway. Besides, it was an Agatha Christie mystery, a favorite author of any mystery lover. Sam held back the name of the show as a surprise, and June was thrilled. Of all the glitzy shows that were playing at the West End, we were going to the one that she and I actually wanted to see.

June and I had already bought evening dresses to wear for the occasion, knowing that one would be coming during the trip. Hers was an exquisite peach chiffon gown that made her skin look even more flawless than it was. She wore her good pearls, which offset her lovely gray hair, and her make-up was done to perfection.

I went a little on the daring side, and chose a black velvet dress that skimmed my body to just past my knees. It had been on display in the boutique downstairs. When I saw it in the store's window, I knew it had to be mine for an evening like this.

I'd never spent so much on a single article of clothing before, but I knew as long as I worked for Sam and June, I'd get more opportunities to wear it. I hadn't dressed up since the awards show, and I felt great in the dress. Best of all, it had a full back and no possible way to fall down regardless of what klutzy events I might encounter that night.

June was fussing over Sam's outfit in their room, and I was finishing up in my bathroom. I knew that whatever disappointment June had felt in Sam's behavior had disappeared with his production of these tickets, but she still wanted him to be dressed to the nines.

After I applied some make-up in my room, I left my curling iron and hair dryer in the bathroom for a chance to use them when it was available again. I washed my hair to get rid of any remnants of raven poop. I thought I'd style it in curls for this special occasion.

I got a better view of my make-up in the bathroom light. I hadn't done too badly, although I was rather made-up for my own taste. If I was going to carry off this dress, I wanted to make a real statement, which included lots of eyeliner, high heels and a head full of curly hair.

My hair had already partially dried, but I wanted to run the drier through it so it would take more curl. I grabbed the hair dryer and inserted the travel adapter to the plug end so I could use it in the little round outlets.

I first tried the dryer on high, but I nearly dropped the dryer as sparks shot out of the end. Thank goodness I hadn't pointed it at my head yet. The heating element still glowed. I turned it off, but my heart was beating a million miles an hour.

I tried the lower setting, holding it away from myself. It was very hot, but nothing seemed out of the ordinary, so I gave my hair a quick once over with it. It smelled a bit smoky when I turned it off, but the job was done.

I'd plugged in my curling iron on high as well, and thought I had better put it on a lower setting as well. I left it to cool some, and went to put my dress on in my private room area.

A few minutes later I returned and yanked through my hair with a fine toothed comb before starting to curl it. As usual, I started with the top right section of hair. I slid the iron in and waited a few seconds. Before I could slide the iron out of my hair, I smelled burning and felt the iron come away from my head on its own.

My hair suddenly felt very hot. When I looked at the iron, the entire section of hair I'd clamped into the iron was still in the iron's grasp, but the iron wasn't in my hair.

I looked into the mirror and gave a startled yelp. "Oh no!"

I guess my warble was enough of a distress signal to make everyone come into the bathroom. I was still holding the iron in one hand, and pointing at both the iron and my head alternately as I babbled nonsense.

As soon as Alan assessed the situation, he started laughing. Sam tried to stifle his chuckle, but did manage to comment on the horrible smell of the burnt hair.

"Gentlemen, how could you laugh at a time like this!" June said, blasting them with incredible force in her voice, recognizing the fashion emergency at once. She quickly determined what had occurred and took charge, first physically removing Alan from the bathroom, and giving Sam a look that indicated he'd better do the same, which he, of course, did.

She closed the door and turned to give me her full attention. She took the iron from my hand and put it on the counter, removing the plug from the wall with a swift jerk on the cord.

I was still stunned as she put the toilet seat down and then guided me to sit on it. She looked over my head, I think to make sure there was no burn on the scalp.

"Is it bad?" I was finally able to muster as I touched the area with one hand.

She waited a few more seconds before responding. "Well, there is no burn on the scalp, so that is definitely a plus. The hair is completely burned off, and there is evidence of singeing on some of the surrounding hair. Your hair is dark; your scalp is white. There's sort of, um, uh, a bald spot."

I tried to hold in my distress, not encouraged by the word "bald" whatsoever. Finally I mustered up enough nerve to look at the damage for myself. My head wasn't burned, so how bad could it be? The sight in the mirror was a little sad looking. With my dark hair, the patch of hair that had burned off more obvious than if I had lighter colored hair. The skin of my scalp definitely showed through; the contrast of the dark hair and the pale scalp was quite noticeable, and made for a disturbing look.

"I guess I'll need a wig for tonight," I sighed, quickly accepting my fate. "Or a hat."

Bird poop to burned hair in one day. Forget a bad hair day, I had a bad hair life!

June was cleaning up, and held the curling iron in one hand, the wrapped hair still inside its grasp. "Do you want me to clean this out? We can save it, but it may be damaged from the stronger current."

"Toss it. Right now I feel like I'll never curl my hair again." I looked at the end of the plug I had used as an attachment. "I should have gone for the travel hair items instead of cheaping out and hoping this adapter would work. Not that the store clerk had been any help."

"Never mind that now," June said as she once again led me to sit on top of the toilet. "Let's see if there is anything I can do to fix it. You look fantastic tonight, and I think I can do something with your hair."

June fiddled for a few minutes, her face gestures letting me know what she liked and what did not work for her. "It's difficult since it is the very front pieces of your hair. It's not like we can comb over it, unless…"

I could tell by the look on her face that she'd thought of something new. She was combing my hair straight back, making a new part. Her face showed success, and in a minute she told me to look in the mirror again.

"That'll do just fine," she said as I had my first look at the style.

She had made a new part to bring more hair to the right side of my head. It worked, as the big naked spot was covered and the hair seemed to be thick enough to cover it.

"Thanks June," I said as I gave her a giant hug. "I'm not into being a beauty queen or anything, but I don't relish standing out in the crowd in a freaky way either."

June laughed, and then her face fell as my hair did its own thing, and put itself back as it was.

"Didn't the store display show this dress with a hat?" June asked. I nodded, remembering the entire ensemble.

"A hat and a purse."

June worked with the hair again, trying to get it to stay in the new position, then gave up in frustration. My hair had always been difficult.

"I'll send Alan downstairs to get the hat," she said in defeat.

 **24**

We traveled by limousine for about an hour and a half outside of London. Soon, we were in West Sussex, and the car slowed down to pass through the village of Amberley.

It was idyllic, just as I'd imagined an English countryside village would look, with thatched roof cottages, and old Norman church and plenty of pubs. There was a thin layer of snow on the ground, so we could not see any traces of green in the meadows that were outside of the village.

We stopped in front of a huge stone wall, and finally found our way through its entrance. Ahead was a real, historical castle. June gasped and hugged Sam with so much enthusiasm, I felt like an intruder.

"Oh Sam, this surprise tops it all. I've always wanted to stay at a castle. And this looks like a real one too!"

"Down Mom," said Alan, attempting to curb her enthusiasm in vain. "Dad, time to tell us where we are."

"It is a real one alright. It's called Amberley Castle," Sam said with a smile and handed over a brochure. "It was built over 900 years ago and even Queen Elizabeth owned it at one time."

Our limo doors were opened for us, and we were greeted by the castle's owners and staff, who were dressed in medieval attire. We took in the immense castle and grounds in awe. I couldn't decide if I wanted to see the entire castle or read all about its history instead.

"Welcome to Amberley," said a man who was not costumed. I later learned he was the owner who, along with his family, resided in the castle. We entered over a traditional wooded drawbridge through a grand front door.

Within the hour, we'd been settled in grand suites, which were in part of the dry moat surrounding the castle. The rooms were furnished with authentic antiques, four poster beds and luxurious grandeur. Despite its feeling of authenticity, each suite was modernized, and even had a Jacuzzi. I was mesmerized with the room, but I could not resist a tour of the castle and its magnificent grounds.

The part of the castle we were staying was called the "Bishopric". Each of the five suites it contained was named after a bishop from the twelfth century. The castle had been visited by many nobles and royalty over the years, and the grounds showed evidence of a grand garden that would have been lovely in the springtime.

There were lakes within the walls of the property, a croquet lawn and a tennis court. The interior of the castle boasted large lounging areas, ornately carved mantles, wood inlayed walls and windows shaped in unique patterns

Two restaurants were part of the castle, the Queen's Room and the Great Room. The Great Room had an amazing wood floor, and was decorated with suits of armor and tapestries. The Queen's Room had a ceiling made from barrels. Each offered award winning cuisine, and were open to serve those who were not overnight guests at the castle.

Being the off season, there were few people staying at the castle, and the next few days were a dream. I spent hours going through every area of the castle that we were allowed, and inspecting the layout of the gardens and fountains that would come back to life in a few months. We visited the village, had local fare in the pubs and shopped in .quaint stores.

The stone wall surrounding the castle was 60 feet high. The gate, called a portcullis, was pulled down each night as it would have been for the proper defense of a castle during medieval times.

On our first day there, we took a helicopter tour over a large area called the Sussex South Down. Despite the winter cold, it was lovely and the countryside was extensive and very inviting. Elizabethan minstrels and a short jousting tournament were hosted at the castle the next day, and much of the village came to participate in a lively festival.

There was a wildlife reserve nearby, with beautiful water gardens that again hide their full beauty behind the bleak weather. The famous Bewick Swans were in residence though, and flew from Siberia each winter to reside in Amberley.

June tried to hide her disappointment in the absence of the full glory of the grounds. Instead, she immersed herself in the history of the castle and the casualness of life in the village.

We had tea in town several times, and again on a grand scale at the castle. The local pubs served huge portions of shepherd's pie, and we had bangers and mashers on a second trip in. The dining at the castle was everything we'd heard, and I felt like a queen just being served at the grand table.

It was over in a whirlwind, and on our last day there, June spent time in the castle's library while Alan and I rented horses to ride around the local countryside. To all of our amazement, Sam was as taken with the place as June and I were. Sam marveled in June's enjoyment, and asked if she'd return with him to the castle in the spring.

"Oh, Sam!" she replied in tears at his unexpected offer.

"June, I didn't do this right. I should've waited for the gardens to be in bloom. This is so lovely, but it's not complete in this weather. Watching your face over the last few days has brought me joy."

We hated to pack, but headed back to London for a last night at the Dorchester for an early flight the next day.

I'd broken the news to Sam, June and Alan that I'd be staying an extra two days to see if I could find the place that Simons' had sent his money to. It'd been a real address, so the worst I could do was spend two days looking for a person who'd given a false name and address to get the wire, but I had to try.

June had insisted that Alan stay with me, and had called the front desk to ask if two additional nights in the suite were possible.

I had planned to move to a more affordable room in the hotel, but June and Sam waived it off as "nonsense". And it was done, of course.

Alan had accepted his delayed departure with delight. "Sara and I alone in the great city of London? And alone each night in our suite? Yes!"

June slapped his leg. "You behave now. Sara, you'd better lock your door at night, or you might find out he's crawled in next to you."

25

The taxi led us through some winding roads on the outskirts of the city. I wondered if we would eventually be let off in front of a country farmhouse or a quaint cottage, as we passed by several on the way.

We said our goodbyes to Sam and June a few hours earlier. I was anxious to get going to find Albert, if he was even real, right away.

The taxi ride took so long, I thought we might be in Ireland, but eventually we passed beyond the scenic area. As we went down an incline, the surroundings changed to more of a cityscape. The houses were getting closer together, some with little or no front or back yards visible.

After a few more streets, the cabbie stopped and indicated that we had arrived at our destination.

"Treat yourself to some lunch," Alan said to the cab driver, and handed him far more pounds than the ride and tip could have cost. "We may be an hour or more. Can we just call your cell number when we're done?"

"Suit yourself," the cabbie replied with his thick Cockney accent, greedily eyeing the handful of bills. 'It's your money to burn; take yer time if ya wish."

Finally estimating the total Alan had given him, he cackled enthusiastically, "For this kind of scratch, I won't be takin' off w'out ya."

"Thank you." Alan turned towards the house we were now in front of. My eyes were taking in the place, an old, shabby cottage that looked like it had seen better years. The paint was peeling and the yard was overgrown with weeds and other decaying plant matter that gave off a moldy, wet smell.

"Shall we?" I asked Alan. I was getting a little nervous about going through with this, and I felt so much better that he had come with me. For all I knew, I could be walking into a den full of killers and thieves. This house could be their headquarters, the main hub for international financial crimes. It was probably the house of some innocent senior citizens who'd look at me like I were nuts when I explained to them who I was looking for.

I decided to stop speculating. I was not about to turn back, so I walked through the little gate that Alan had propped open for me. It rebounded back to place with a crash, and I feared that we'd broken it.

"Oops," mouthed Alan.

The porch was rickety, and the front windows were covered with lacy curtains. I rang the bell and heard it echo inside the house. My nervousness grew as we were met with silence,. Alan seemed to sense my uneasiness, and he gave my hand a squeeze.

I was aware of the sound of my own breathing after I rang the bell a second time. No sounds came from inside the house. Alan was trying to peek through the curtains, but the glare of the sun made it impossible to see anything other than his own reflection in the glass.

"I don't hear anything at all. No one must be home."

Alan nodded in agreement, and made his way down the steps to the side of the house. I obediently followed, and we walked the perimeter of the house. I was worried that the neighbors would call the police since we were now rather obviously trying to get a peek inside from the other windows.

At the back of the house, we could view a kitchen. I expected to see a very plain, unkempt area. Instead, it was frilly and homey looking. This is not what I imagined the kitchen of a thieves' hideout would look like at all.

The back of the house was as overgrown and unkempt as the front. I saw a clothesline a few yards back, complete with drying items.

There were men's shirts and underwear on the line, but it was the brightly colored muumuu and the massive bra that caught my attention. The cups were so big, surely watermelons would fit into them.

Alan shuddered when he saw the items. I knew he must be imagining who could wear a bra of that size.

"Are we at the right house?" I asked out loud, worried that we were nosing around the wrong yard. I suddenly became aware of the proximity of the neighboring yards, and felt like an intruder, which technically, I was.

'No, I checked the address many times, and I even kept it in my cell phone for GPS tracking. The street sign said "Covington Circle", and the house number is 1375. This is definitely it."

'Let's go back to the front. I don't want to attract any more attention to our presence here."

Alan nodded in agreement and we'd soon made it back to the sidewalk on the outside of the gate.

"Whatcha wanna do?" he asked, and I knew he wished that I'd suddenly want to go back into London for more appropriate vacation activity.

'I'm waiting. I didn't come this far and get up the nerve to do this, get here and then just walk away because no one's home."

I spied a shelter for a bus stop across the street. "Look, we can wait over there." I walked toward the empty area and sat on the bench.

"There's a perfect view from here, and we won't attract any unwanted attention."

Alan frowned. "What if a bus comes by? Eventually people will think it's weird that we keep missing the buses."

"I'm prepared to deal with that later." I looked into his eyes; he was trying to be supportive and patient. I hadn't asked him to tag along; he'd insisted. I knew my stubbornness was not easy to deal with regardless. "You don't have to be here," I said softly. "I didn't ask you to stay behind with me. I want to do this. No, I have to do this"

I sat on the bench, and Alan continued to stand, hands on his hips like he wanted to challenge my comments.

Alan's tone changed from one of questioning to one of confrontation. "You can't stop every kind of financial crime that occurs in the world Sara. You can't right every wrong. You have to be realistic about the magnitude of bad guys that do this kind of thing everyday. Cleaning up the world is not your personal pet project."

I jumped at the baited words, and my eyes flashed in anger at him. "I never said I could stop any kind of crime, but I can't sit by and watch a friend get into trouble when there is even a little something I can do to help." What nerve he had. Who asked him along anyway? "You may be okay with just letting these things happen, but I'm not."

I crossed my arms and legs on the bench, wanting him to leave. I managed to sit still for about half a minute, but could not yet let it go. I stood back up, my fists balled at my sides, and re-started my rant.

"If I can even do one small thing to help, it is something. The police are no help on these cases, and the FBI and government agencies are after bigger targets. People are constantly being preyed upon and there's no one looking out for them. If I can help just one person, or stop just one victim from losing their life savings, then I feel it is all worth it."

He remained in the same position, but shook his head as if he were disappointed in what I had said.

My anger was not about to subside, but I was done explaining myself to him. I waved my arm in dismissal. "Go into the little town we just passed. It's a couple blocks down. If you won't go back to London, I'll meet you there when I'm done."

"Done with what?" Alan asked smugly, making my blood pressure rise that much more.

I made my best effort not to shout, but my answer sounded so lame when I said it in my head, it came out quietly. "I don't know, but when I do and I'm done with it, I'll meet you there."

Alan was about to retort to my comments, when we both became aware of someone walking toward the house we were supposed to have been watching.

A small figure was just reaching the gate. She was a small woman wheeling a basket full of groceries that she was struggling to get through the gate.

Alan ran across the small roadway to assist her. She looked up, startled by his sudden appearance. For a moment, I hoped she would hit him with her umbrella. Instead, she showed genuine appreciation for his kind gesture.

"Thank you young man," she said as he opened the gate and took her cart up to the door. She smiled up at him and opened the door to give him access to the house.

I had followed, Alan across the street, albeit more slowly, and watched in amazement as she let him in. If this were a city in the US, Alan probably would've gotten her handbag to his head and screams for help would have rung out.

Alan put the cart inside the door, and went back down to the bottom of the steps to give the little lady room to get by.

She thought nothing of it, and gave him a big smile and another thank you. She then saw I was also standing by the gate, and waved me in.

"Good afternoon darling," she said, taking us both in, still not threatened in any way by the sudden presence of two strangers. Then again, maybe she had a .45 in her ample cleavage or would hand us over as offerings to the man of the house. For all we knew, he could be a serial killer in addition to a money laundering crook.

I wasn't too worried though. She was tiny, barely five feet tall, but plump, and wearing another of the brightly colored muumuus like that on the back clothesline. She definitely seemed to be the owner of the bra on the line, and her large bosom seemed to take over her whole body.

She was probably about 75 or 80 years old; she had a short hair style of curly hair that was almost blue in color. She also wore horn rimmed glasses. I could not help but think she looked like Dame Edna or the Queen Mother's sister.

"Mrs. Fleming?" I asked, guessing that she might be the mother of the person I was seeking.

Using her name apparently startled her. "Oh dear, was I expecting you?" Her accent was lovely, English countrified and unrefined, but oozing with sincerity and charm. She peered at both of us, her eyes appearing rather large through her glasses.

"I do so often forget things these days. Please come in," she continued and waved us entrance into her home.

I was exhilarated that I got her name right, and I felt that much closer to finding out something, anything that might get me a little bit further into getting some of Simons' money back and maybe stopping at least one person on the ladder of this scam.

She went into her kitchen, and I followed, recognizing the frilly room I had seen through the back entrance. Alan seated himself on the couch.

"I'll make some tea," she announced as if we expected her to do so. She put on a kettle and set up. I noticed that she was wearing blue Ked sneakers and long white socks in accompaniment to her bright yellow muumuu.

"I'm Sara Blake, and my friend is Alan Westin." I said in a way of introduction.

'From the states are ya? I can always tell. I'm so pleased to meet you. I'm Winifred. Are you here for me or Alfred?"

So Alfred was my mysterious "A. Fleming." Bingo!

"We were hoping to talk to Alfred, but no one seemed to be at home."

"He'll be back darling, and probably rather soon. He hates to miss a good tea time. I just got 'is favorite scones too, maple walnut. I'm sure he won't mind if I share with guests. He's so busy with his business dealings these days. I rarely see him. Such a good boy he is, takin' care of his Mum."

I said nothing in response, and waited while she worked away.

Within a few minutes, I carried out the tray of cups and scones while Winifred managed the tea pot, sugar and creamer. She set up everything on the coffee table in the living room, fussing to get it just right.

The living room was as frilly as the kitchen, but the pervading color of the room was rose. There was muted pink shag carpet and dusty pink painted walls The couches were done in a cream tapestry material with huge floribunda roses woven into the material. Doilies covered the top of every piece of furniture in the room, and several curio cabinets cluttered the room with collections of thimbles, boxes and small figurines.

For all the clutter, there was not a speck of dust to be seen. I did spy a basket of tabloid papers that hinted at Mrs. Fleming's literary tastes. The headline "Queen Mother, Saint or Slut?" was showing from the top of the pile, so I imagined the paper was England's answer to the similar US fodder that told of cows with two heads or hermaphrodites that fathered and birthed a child alone.

My attention came back to Winifred as she held up the teapot, ready to pour. "Do you prefer your milk in first?" she asked.

"No, thank you, no milk or sugar for me."

"None for me either," Alan added as the question formed on her lips for him.

"Just fine, dear," She said and after pouring our tea, poured some milk into her own cup, poured the tea and then added lump after lump of sugar. I was sure she had made syrup out of her tea, but her face showed that the taste was perfection to her as she took her first sip.

"Darling," Winifred said looking right at me. 'Whatever happened to your hair love?"

Alan chuckled as soon as the question was posed, and I gave him a sharp look. I then explained the story, and she laughed so heartily I could not help but join in.

"This'll make for a grand story at my next ladies' tea," she said, chest still heaving from the exercise, and then paused to look at her watch. "Alfred should be home by now."

The front door opened before she had finished her sentence. On cue, Alan took the tea items into the kitchen, not wanting to scare Alfred off with a strong male presence.

 26

"Alfred love," Winifred called out. 'Come in here, you have visitors."

Alfred peered into the room. He was not much taller than his mother, almost gaunt, and was pretty much bald except for a few long pieces of hair which he had forced across his forehead in attempts to cover the shininess. They looked like pasted stripes of brown against his pale face and head.

For all the bad hair days I'd been having recently, I felt I should no longer complain. Alfred looked like he had been having a bad hair day his entire life. Didn't he know it looked better to be bald than to paste errant hairs across your head?

He must have been nearly fifty years old and was rather disheveled, wearing a wrinkled blue shirt and brown pants. He definitely had the look of a little sneaky man that lived in his mother's basement, played video games and watched a lot of television.

He put down a backpack, kissed his mother, and looked warily at me.

"Who ur you?" he asked, looking me over, his eyes pausing at my own bald spot.

I stood up and offered my hand. "I'm Sara Blake. I'm visiting from the U.S. I came to inquire about the United Nations Legal Holdings company."

He had ignored my hand, and as soon as I finished the purpose of my visit, his eyes moved around quickly in his head as he was obviously thinking about what he should do. He said nothing, and instead made a run for the back of the house.

'Alfred!" his mother demanded, "That's no way ta treat company. You get back here at once!"

He ignored her, and in another second I heard a commotion in what must have been a hallway. Moments later Alan appeared, holding Alfred by the scruff of the neck, with Alfred struggling to get loose.

"Lemme go!" he demanded, but only managed to force Alan to

change his grip and pin his arms behind his back.

'Oh dear, what is the meaning of this?" Winifred asked, cowering away from me as if I was going to hurt her. "I don't have much money, but it's yours if ya want it. Please don't hurt us. You seemed like such nice folks too."

"I'm so sorry, Mrs. Fleming. We're not here to hurt you or your son. But we do want him to correct his less than honest business dealing that's hurt one of our friends. We have evidence that he is involved in financial scams in the US."

"Is this true, Al?" She threw the question at Alfred as if she knew this were a fact before we had even told her.

Alfred looked at his feet, and Alan brought him over to the sofa and plopped him down. His guilty look told the whole story in her eyes. "Oh dear. How could you? What have you done?"

I overviewed the basics of the plot, and when I was done Winifred got up and slapped Alfred upside the head. He sat back in the couch like he was trying to disappear into the cushions, apparently more willing to take on Alan than his mother.

"I'm sorry, Mum. I'm just a middle man, I swear. I just accept money and send it on. I only get a little piece of it."

She growled at him. I pulled her aside and asked her if we could talk to him alone. "You won't hurt him, will you love?" she asked.

"Of course not. I just hope he cooperates so I can help a friend out in the US who's lost $50,000.00 to this scheme."

She glowered at Alfred. "You tell them what they want to know. If you do not cooperate, there'll be hell to pay. I shoulda known you couldna changed yer spots so fast. Down 'n out one day, on toppa the world the next. Businessman, my fat arse!"

It was amusing watching the little English woman bully her son. It was also effective as he nodded in agreement. She grabbed a tabloid and sat on the couch.

"You take them to your room," she ordered. He did as he was told, leading us to a back bedroom.

As he unlocked the door, the smell of body odor and unwashed clothes struck me. "P-uh" I spat out. 'What died in here?"

Alan shot me a look that said to shut it, so I did. The room was small and rather untidy considering that it was practically empty. There was a bed and nightstand, but no chest of drawers. A huge computer table sat under the window. The equipment looked sophisticated and expensive, and quite out of place in the room.

Alfred made a protective start towards the computer as when Alan went towards it. For h is efforts, he got pushed to the bed before making any progress and then sat on it in apparent defeat,

I suddenly felt rather fortunate to have a computer expert with me. Alan whipped out a pocket sized zip drive and inserted it into the computer. We hadn't discussed what we would do if we found our guy, but Alan seemed to be way ahead of me.

Alfred started to protest as Alan booted up the system. My question stopped him in his tracks. "How long have you been doing this?" I asked as I rifled through paperwork that was stacked up on his rickety nightstand

"'Bout a year," he said stuttering and nervously glancing around like maybe he could escape. I shut the door with my foot to make sure any attempt he made to get out would be thwarted at least a little.

"This letter is over a year old," I said as I read the postmark on the envelope.

"You asked about United Nations Legal Holdings," he stated matter of factly. "It's been used for just about a year, but it's just one of many. Are you gonna ring the coppers?"

I looked up from the letter, which confirmed communication from some scam artist in another country. "It depends on how much you help us. Who's in charge of all this stuff?"

Alfred licked his lips, thinking before he answered. He was now sweating profusely. He made a useless attempt to plaster down one of the hair stripes by rubbing his hand across it. "If I cooperate then, you might not turn me in then?"

"Return my friend's money first." I demanded, and I gave him the date of the wire he had received from Simons.

"I don't got it," he said with poor grammar and accent clashing enough to make my ears hurt. "I took my piece and sent it on its way."

"Where's your cut?"

"Gave it to Mum for the rent. I'm her only source of money."

'Stolen money. Bet she'll make you get a job now."

"So you gonna turn me in?" he asked. I looked him over, a small man with a small and foolish mind.

I looked at Alan, since I wasn't prepared to take anything to the local authorities. They may not appreciate the tactics we had used to get this far. He gave me the nod I had expected.

"Yes, if you cooperate then I won't contact the authorities. I'm after the guys working my area of the world. There must be local participants to gather information on the potential victims."

He nodded. "I have lots of contacts. The ring's so big you could never catch all of us. What part of the US are ya from?"

"State of Nevada, next to California." I had no idea of the average English person's knowledge of the states, but thought I'd shoot for the one they might know.

"Aye. I think the one you are after covers Sacramento to Las Vegas. He makes great fake I.D. cards." He opened a drawer and showed me three or four different types of identification. I was not familiar with the format of official UK identification documentation, but these looked pretty real.

"If you have these, why did you use your own name and address on the wire? It made it rather easy to find you," I said pocketing the fake cards.

Albert was mortified that I was taking his id cards. My real one's in there too."

I took them back out of my pocket, and found one that showed his real name and this address. I held it up and he nodded, so I gave it back to him.

"Well?" I asked again, wanting a response.

"I accidentally gave 'em my correct last name for the wire," he admitted, his face red in embarrassment at his own stupidity. "There's so much correspondence bouncing around, ya can forget pretty easy. Had to use my real I.D.toget the dough."

"Well your mistake nailed you. It laid down the cookie crumbs leading right up to your door. If you're going to play international financial criminal, you have a long way to go to becoming a good one. If I can catch you, another one of your victims is going to come looking for the name and address on the money order or wire they sent to you. They're not likely to be very nice about it either. Do you want to put your mother in that kind of danger?"

He shook his head, and suddenly started to cry, probably thinking about his Mum. Alan paused, and looked up from the computer. He looked at Alfred, then at me and rolled his eyes. I replied with a quick hand gesture and a look that said. "Just get all the information."

I didn't try to comfort Alfred. Instead, I gathered up communications that I thought were relevant to these kinds of scams.

"Do you contact the victims? Do you tell them you are a lawyer disbursing an inheritance or that they've won the UK lottery?"

He shook his head and tried to regain his composure. "No, not my part. I just send wiring instructions to the patsy, take me cut, then pass it on as told."

"And the banks never ask about what you're doing?" I asked, wondering if the UK had any anti-money laundering precautions similar to those in the US.

He shook his head. "I use different ones, but there's a few bankers in on it too. There's hundreds of folks involved all over the world." He rattled off a list of occupations involved in the racket, and added the bankers into the mix with a little bit of a smirk on his face that I wanted to slap right off. His sadness was apparently shaken off by his attempt to shock me.

"How do you know who the others are?"

'I dunno all of 'em."

How do you communicate?"

"E-mails, letters and a website."

I sighed, as I could see I was going to have to pull this information out of him. "What website? The exact address please."

Alan cut in before Alfred could answer. "No worries Sara, I have everything on his hard drive including websites visited." He turned towards Al with a disdainful look, "except the porn."

Alfred, red-faced, looked away from me, but I pretended not to hear. Alan hopped up from the computer.

"Done?" I asked.

"Yep, ready to roll?"

I nodded and then looked at Alfred. I wanted to move on to the next piece of the puzzle and get back into familiar territory. I also didn't want to leave him with all the materials he needed to continue ripping people off.

I hesitated, but Alan grabbed me by the elbow. "Come on," and as if he knew what I was thinking, "I took care of it."

I left Albert on the bed and glared at him as I left the room. Winifred was still reading the paper as we came into the room.

"He's fine, Mrs. Fleming," I told her in an assuring manner since she had jumped when she saw us again.

"I thank you for your time and the lovely tea."

"You're welcome, love. Is Alfred in trouble?" she asked, looking a little frightened.

"No ma'am, not right now. I think I can keep the authorities away from him if he changes his ways."

'I can promise ya that. It's back to the restaurant for him or I'll put 'im out on his backside."

She bustled back to see Alfred, leaving us to see ourselves out. "Nice meeting you," I called back into the house. No reply followed.

We clanged the gate shut and left without looking back. Alan patted his pocket, indicating that the zip drive was safely in his pocket.

"What did you take care of?" I asked as we walked towards the downtown area of the small place.

"I knew you would be worried that he would keep on going after we left."

'Yeah, so what did you do about it?" My hopes rose as I asked.

"Nothing permanent, but he's going to be screwed up for a long while. He laughed. "I erased his hard drive and reconfigured his computer and all the connected gadgets into oblivion."

I smiled in great relief. We hit the town in a minute, ready to call the cabbie and head back to the hotel. I was pleased with the day.

27

It was late when we returned to the hotel. Alan phoned in a room service order while I took a soak in the tub. Of course, he suggested instead that he join me to help me relax, but I was hungry and tired and he got the hint quickly.

It seemed like just a few minutes later when I heard a light knock on the door. I resented being pulled out my peaceful state of mind, as I felt the day's efforts deserved a reward that could be spent enjoying the amenities of the hotel.

"Are you coming out anytime soon?" I heard Alan's voice when I turned off the jets in the Jacuzzi tub.

"If dinner's here," I replied.

"Yep," was the short reply, although I heard no sound of rolling carts or waiter's voice to support the theory. As I dried off, I viewed the clock and surmised I'd been in the tub for nearly an hour.

Candle light filled the living and dining areas as I emerged from the bathroom. Quiet jazz music was playing in the background, and about six dozen roses had been placed artfully around the dining room area. Covered silver dishes were on the table. In the shadows, I saw Alan seated at the table.

He rose as I fully appeared in the room, suspiciously wondering what Alan's idea of this evening might be.

He pulled out a chair and beckoned me to sit. He removed the cover from a tray of a tureen of soup, and served me up a bowl of clam chowder.

"No worries, Sara, this is my apology for getting angry with you today. I'm sorry I tried to sway you from your mission. I hope you enjoy this evening with me, and know I won't keep pressing myself on you. No strings attached. Promise.' He crossed his heart.

I motioned for him to sit down and join me. The soup was delightfully ordinary. Not too fancy; just a familiar taste and texture I loved. As much as I'd been enjoying the five star dining experience with the Westins, two weeks of fancy food made me crave the comfort of familiarity.

Sourdough rolls and butter were under another platter. To my delight, fish and chips from a street vendor were under the last, and fanciest of the trays.

Alan laughed at my startled expression as I eyed the newspaper wrapped food. "I paid one of the staff to get it for us. I thought you'd like to have this at least once more before we left."

My smile was all Alan needed to know that I was pleased. I splashed malt vinegar over the fish and enjoyed every last morsel of the meal.

He expertly uncorked some champagne as we finished the food. "You prefer Brut, right?" he asked, already filling a glass.

"Yes, I prefer the dry over the sweet, but haven't tried this kind before."

"It's French. Very good stuff."

I nodded in agreement as I enjoyed my first swallow of the heavenly bubbles. "Oh, very good. I'd better not get used to this. André will never be the same again! You bring me the non-fancy food I was craving, and then end it with some extravagant champagne."

"You forgot about dessert!" he announced as he brought another platter over. I was about to object when he revealed angel food cake, strawberries and vanilla ice cream.

"You are a good man Alan," I exclaimed, digging into my favorite dessert items. "Thank you so much for your thoughtfulness."

"You're most welcome. It's getting late, and I asked the waiter to leave everything until tomorrow. Are you in the mood for a movie, TV, reading, or are you ready to go to bed?"

"Boy, you are in a mellow mood," I joked, as Alan had never played the gentleman for this long of a period without some sort of comic intervention, sarcasm, or come on. I went with it, feeling rather at ease myself, "How about we find something on TV?"

We fell asleep on the couch watching a Benny Hill marathon on TV. We woke up the next day huddled together, almost cuddling.

I was embarrassed, immediately putting my hand in my hair and seeing what a wreck it was, and ran to the bathroom to brush my teeth before I splayed Alan with my morning dragon breath or he commented on my hair. This time it would be a bird's nest with a bald spot.

A sound at our door brought our morning lull to full attention, and Alan ushered in the waiter, who brought coffee, some breakfast breads and fruit for us. The slim and elegantly dressed man busily removed last night's items from the dining area, and made extra efforts not to look at either of us directly. Must be a hotel rule or something.

"Mornin' Sleepy Head!" Alan said in a cheery morning voice. Knowing I wasn't a morning person, he'd already prepared my coffee and handed it to me as I sat back down on the couch.

"Sorry for spooning you like that. You're so cuddly when you sleep," he teased as he tipped the waiter, now wheeling our dishes towards the door.

I grunted a response into my coffee, no longer embarrassed and instead just my normal grumpy self.

"You have some great morning hair, Sunshine," he commented as he made himself a plate after the waiter had left. "It's amazing how your bald spot looks twice as big when the rest of your hair is splayed around like that."

I threw a pillow at him. Even an attempt at fixing it couldn't stop the comments.

After two cups of coffee and some food, Alan forced me to consider the day's events. It was our last day in England, and I was going to miss it here. It had been the trip of a lifetime. How many people have stayed in a castle that Elizabeth I had once owned, or seen or done all of the great things we'd done in one visit? Even better, my decision to stay had yielded results. As sad I as I was to leave, I was anxious to dig in to the contents of Albert's computer.

I was closer to being my post-early morning nice self again when Alan asked, "What do you want to do today? It's our last chance to get in another activity or two. What's on your list that we haven't done yet?"

"Hmm," I thought for a moment. I had been spoiled since June and my "lists' had most things in common, and Alan had taken me to the tower for my own personal wished for activity.

"You know Alan; this trip has been all about what your Mom and Dad wanted, and even what I wanted. We've done museums, castles, tea, shopping, the Tower; things that people dream about when planning a trip to England. Seems to me the only one who hasn't had a say in our daily activities is you."

"I'm happy doing whatever. I told you already how much I enjoy watching you take in things. Mom too. It's my fun; it's enough for me, really."

"But if you could choose; what would you do?" I asked. I was serious and Alan knew it. He stepped away from my directness, playing it off by grabbing my arm and kissing it.

"Come on! Be serious," I said yanking my arm back. "Please, there must be something we haven't done that's been on your list."

"Well that's on my list, you know," he smirked, raising his eyebrows up and down in a suggestive gesture. "You asked." In a more realistic, lower tone, he added, "I really like you, Sara. It's more like, I'm crazy about you."

I was going to have to respond to him to get past the topic. "Okay, how about we talk about that later, after we've spent a few hours doing something you want to do?" I huffed. "You say you're crazy about me, but I only know the silly Alan, the sarcastic Alan, or the Alan that cares about everyone else and stands in the background. I want to know more about the real you."

Alan wrung his hands together, something I'd never seen him do. He had a boyish gleam in his eye, and I could see his mind thinking. "Well, there is one, no, actually two, things I'd like to do."

I raised my eyebrows in anticipation.

With soft speech revealing a shy side I'd been unaware of, he said, "I've watched the changing of the guard at Buckingham Palace on TV many times over the years. I'd kinda like to see it in person."

"Perfect, I'm in," I quickly replied, relieved he'd spoken up and thrilled that he'd given in to his wish list fulfillment, "Now what about the second."

"Only if you promise not to laugh."

"Of course I won't. You're making me think of something seedy. I'm really dying to know now."

Alan rolled his eyes at my comment, indicating I'd jumped to the wrong conclusion. He kept to his good mood though, and practically spilled out his second desire.

"Well, I've never even told my Mom this, but of all the mystery movies we've watched over the years, I've always had a soft spot in my heart for Sherlock Holmes."

I picked up on his meaning right away, as the Sherlock Holmes Museum was around to appease the masses who wanted the fictional Holmes and his faithful friend Dr. Watson to be real historical figures in England, and their famous address to be a real place.

Attempting a British accent I said, "Then Watson, it's off to 221B Baker Street. Shall we have a Hansom Cab take us?"

Alan was delighted that I'd gotten into the spirit. "Of course, old chap," he added in his best accent, but adding a Scottish lilt to it. "We're off."

A visit with the hotel's attractions coordinator revealed that the changing of the guard ceremony was only done every other day in the winter time. Unfortunately, today wasn't the day for the ceremony. Alan was only mildly disappointed, leading me to believe at least we'd be doing his number one priority all along. We headed to a destination where we could begin our Hansom ride, and then trotting in the creaky horse carriage to the Sherlock Holmes Museum in the late morning, prepared to leisurely pass our time to take in everything it had to offer.

The main room of the museum was more darkly colored than I'd imagined. Deep red brocade wall paper and dark furniture dominated the room, which was rather busy. As my favorite Holmes' movies had been in black and white, I hadn't recollected this feel, but there was no doubt that its layout had been well thought out to please the world's Sherlockians.

We saw Holmes' violin, his chemistry area, the fireplace. Watson's room was overlooking the back area of the rooming house, and was filled with samples of his writings of their many adventures. Only a few rooms made up the museum, but we spent considerable time enjoying each object that had been artfully placed there for fans to connect to their favorite adventure. We even went to the third floor attic to view the lodger's trunks, which was how rooming houses in these times would have stored them for their guests.

We could have opted to get photos taken sitting in Sherlock's famous armchair, located in the main living room's alcove, and Alan asked if we could come back and get some taken, but I didn't understand why we'd have to return to do it.

Alan was dying to get into the museum's shop, which he apparently was familiar with from their website. He went right for the clothing, and I thought for sure he'd put on a deerstalker cap a la Sherlock. To my utter shock, he picked out a black bowler hat, and plopped it on.

"Why not Sherlock attire? I never took you as being a Watson," I stated as he admired the look in the near-by mirror.

Alan tipped the hat at me. "In case you haven't noticed, I'm more of a side kick guy than a lead. Watson was the strength behind Holmes' brilliant brain, and Sherlock couldn't have been as successful without him."

I didn't believe him. "No way. I don't see that at all. Everyone wants to be Sherlock."

"Who played Sherlock yesterday? Who played Watson? I'd rather observe and help out as needed. Sherlock's the one always in mortal danger. Watson is helping save him. He was the only one smart enough to carry the gun after all."

Chewing on his thought process, I guess I had to agree with him after all. He put the moss green and brown deerstalker hat on me, and then selected a quintessential Sherlockian coat to match it.

At his urging, I lifted my arms and put it on. He then selected a close-fitting long black coat for himself to match his bowler. Finally, he searched out a pipe and magnifying glass from the several types available. He chose the ones he liked, not from the cheap ones in the store's aisles, but from the selection of good ones kept behind glass. The shopkeeper presented them to him one after another for his inspection.

He selected his favorites, which I also nodded at as being the ones I liked too. He gently shoved the pipe in my mouth and the glass in my hand, and then found a fake moustache and put it on himself. He tugged me towards the mirror and smiled widely at our new personas.

"Now this is something I've always wanted to do!" he exclaimed. I

Bad Hair Days

finally understood how he enjoyed watching me take things in, as I was thoroughly enjoying his excitement. I'd seen him playful, but he was acting like a kid who'd just gotten the toy he'd always wanted. It was nice, and so different from his usual laid back approach to things.

I smiled with him as he turned to and fro, and insisted I model mine for him. We then practiced looking serious in the shop's mirror, and made adjustments until we were satisfied. The cap covered my bald spot, and was a plus for me before we took pictures.

"Of course, I want to get our pictures taken in the official attire. That's why I said I wanted to wait to get them done. Besides, we can use these for our Halloween costumes this year, and every year after," he announced to me, and the whole store really, and then in a softer voice, "and we can wear them at home too, you know, for fun. Are you game?"

'Sure," I giggled. "June would love to host a costume party this year. Looks like you'll have to be my date to carry this off."

"Why Holmes, you've discovered my ulterior motive, and so quickly too!"

I started to remove the items to put them on the counter to be wrapped up.

"I'm not done yet Sara, plus, would you wear this for the rest of the day with me? Even after the photos, I mean. We can look like uber-Sherlock nut jobs while we ride in the Hansom cab and get some lunch. We'll take the tourist thing to the total edge."

"For real?" I asked, not sure if he were playing or really wanted to spend our last day in London in costumes. I guess it was no different than wearing hats at Disneyland while you're there, except that London was a real city, not a magic kingdom.

He looked me in the eye, and I knew he was hoping I'd be okay with it. "For real Sara, at least, well, if it isn't too dorky for you."

I guffawed at his near pleading on top of his comment about my caring about appearance. "Alan, I never mind looking like a dork. I do it often, even in the media these days, remember? It's just not usually on purpose," I said putting the pipe back in my mouth. "Regardless, for you, anything!"

"Thanks Sara," He responded with a smile, and a gleam in his eye showing he was pleased.

"Anytime," I said, and Alan squeezed my hand in thanks.

Alan bought all kinds of Sherlock stuff, including a replica Persian slipper (for Holmes' tobacco), a bust, an umbrella to go with his Watson outfit, and tins of tea for June. He bought so much stuff, I didn't see it all as it got rung up and wrapped. Of all the places June and I had been shopping while he tagged along, this was the first place that he spent a good chunk of change. I had separated my Sherlock gear to purchase on my own, but Alan insisted on paying. The coat alone was nearly $200 US

151

dollars! It was well made though, and would be a costume to last a lifetime.

He arranged for most of it to be shipped, and adjusted his outfit to make the Watson look work. The shop keeper looked very happy to bring in such a bundle on a slow winter's day, and treated Alan like a king. He had continued to point out things that Alan may have missed, hoping to get another sale from it. He made good selections, and seemed to have worked a spell on Alan while he was in his buying frenzy. I'd never seen Alan be truly frivolous before, so I just watched as I continued to select some Sherlock branded tea tines to add to the dozens I'd already bought. Everyone would want one of these too!

When he finally finished up, and I had made arrangements for my own teas to be shipped, we were ready to go back into the museum for a final look through. He opted to wear the mustache for the photos, but not for the whole day, He insisted that we lunch at the museum's adjoined Sherlock Holmes pub after we'd had about a dozen photos of us taken in and around the famous armchair and in other areas of the rooms.

"Ever heard of a Watson burger?" he asked, and I shook my head. "I've read online that it's the thing to have here. At eighteen bucks a pop, I hope they're worth it, but we're here for the atmosphere.

I opted for another item on the menu.,The Hounds of the Baskerville, my favorite Basil Rathbone as Sherlock movie. It was a dish of toad sausages in the hold (actually Yorkshire pudding), served with mashed potatoes and mushy peas. Alan chose the Thor Bridge Burger, not finding the Watson burger he'd heard about.

A Mrs. Hudson look alike served us lunch and tea, and the restaurant had its own plethora of Sherlock items. Mrs. Hudson was the boarding room owner of the fictional 221B Baker Street, and was often a part of his stories; her food was always plentiful but rarely touched by the genius.

When we were done it was still early in the afternoon, so we headed to all the local shops still in our detective attire. We got a few distasteful smirks and some smiles from those who appreciated the spirit of our attire.

We road the Hansom cab back through London until its route was complete, and took a cab back the rest of the way to the hotel, still laughing and discussing things like we were analyzing them for clues.

"Well, it's our last night here. I really appreciate your getting me to admit what I wanted to do. I was hoping you or my Mom would bring it up; since you're both mystery lovers and all."

"I'm so glad you did," I heartily admitted. "I don't think I'd have thought about it. I concentrated so much on the art and tea aspects, I'd forgotten about this being a thing to do while we were here. I had a great time."

28

Alan and I decided to eat dinner in the room once again that evening. Later, we took a walk in the nearby park.

I slipped on an icy puddle, but Alan caught me in his strong arms and lifted me up. He led me to a nearby bench.

"You okay?"

"Fine, thanks to you. I didn't hit the ground at least."

It was very chilly, but not yet late. We sat in silence for a while, taking it all in, and then laughing about the day. We were dressed in our normal attire, and had fun going over the day's post- museum shopping in our Sherlock and Watson get-ups.

I hadn't brought a heavy coat and I shivered as a gust of wind blew some of the snow around us in a swirl.

"May I?" Alan asked, motioning for me to allow him to put his arm around me. I nodded, not minding at all and grateful for some body heat.

Alan took out his cell and called the hotel, requesting that some evening tea and dessert items be sent to the room to await our return.

When he finished, I realized I was staring at him.

"What?" he asked. "Did I forget something?"

I shook my head. "No, it's just, well, you're so thoughtful. You're so good about assessing a situation and acting ahead to make things nice for others."

His look was still quizzical.

"The tea," I admonished at his ignorance of his own chivalry. "I'm cold, so you order tea for the room."

"I'm cold too," he retorted, then relaxed with his arm holding me close to his body. I felt odd, as butterflies floated through my stomach and I realized that I'd fallen for him.

He squeezed my shoulder. "I'm kidding. I am rather good at that, aren't I?"

I nodded, and he reached down and touched my lips. "I like to take charge when it comes to the people that I care for. I've told you that

I'm crazy about you, Sara. I know I joke about stuff a lot, but I want to be with you." He kissed my head.

"If it means no physical relationship, I'll take it, Sara," his fingers now rounded the outline of my face. "I'll be happy with whatever I can get, but I want you to be mine."

My resolve melted as his mouth covered mine, and I experienced a first kiss like I'd never known. I wasn't nervous or self conscious at all. I just enjoyed as our lips met and tasted only a hint of what I knew Alan had to offer.

I deepened the kiss, which seemed to surprise Alan, but not enough to stop his response. He brought his other arm around me as my own moved to his shoulder, feeling his muscular arms, and then moving my hands around to feel his tight chest. His breathing quickened as I touched him.

My heart suddenly fluttered with excitement, and other parts of me burned with desire. We paused, only to catch our breath and quickly find our way back to the hotel. My body moldered, and I prayed the waiter had brought the tea and left before we arrived back to our room.

My wish was granted, but when we returned to the room, we ignored the silver covered trays awaiting us.

Alan's beautiful blue eyes burned through mine, and again we embraced and our kiss immediately intensified. His hands cautiously moved over my body, continuing once he realized I wasn't setting any boundaries. I decided that tonight I was going to feel and not think. I cared for Alan as much as he did for me, but I'd let my relationship with his parents stop me from considering my feelings for too long. Alan was just too good of a person, and too much of a man, the kind of man I wanted and needed, to let that concern me now. I was in too deep to care.

He nibbled my ears, and placed kisses down my neck as I explored more of his body with my hands, taking in the feel of parts of his body I'd only imagined touching before.

It was me that made the first move, getting up and leading our interlocked arms and faces towards the bedroom. As we got closer, I pulled at his shirt, and it came off quickly.

"Sara," Alan whispered. "Are you sure?"

I nodded into his chest. "I've got a secret, Alan."

He held my hand as I traced his chest, and looked into his eyes deeply.

"And what is your secret, Miss Sara?"

As I placed my mouth back on him I whispered, "I'm crazy about you too. Have been for quite a while."

Alan groaned with pleasure at my answer, and our lips locked. We went slowly, and he allowed my fingers to touch every part of his bare chest, arms, neck and torso. We both kicked off our shoes, and I stepped back to allow Alan to remove my clothes. His touch was so gentle; I shuddered in anticipation as each piece came off.

We came back together with yet more passion, and I could no longer wait. I tugged at his belt, and he allowed me to unfasten it and remove the remaining articles of his clothing.

His body was beautiful. He was unashamed in his nakedness, as he led me to the bed, and he positioned himself so that we were facing each other on our sides so we could still explore.

His strong hands were surprisingly gentle, and he found my most sensitive place easily. We eyed each other's reaction to each place that we touched, each determined to find and focus on the other's favorites.

Although natural, it seemed like it took forever before we gently joined together, and I cried out almost immediately, my body no longer able to hold back.

I felt like a china doll in his hands, he was so gentle and not forceful at all. We kept eye contact, and again I called out my physical reaction to him, and immediately afterward, he did too.

We lay together quietly, watching one another, and tears came to my eyes.

"What is it, Sara?" he asked with concern, brushing my tears away with his fingers, "Did I hurt you? Are you okay?"

I was so filled with emotion; it was hard to articulate what I felt. "It's just that, that it's never been like this for me," I said shyly, looking down once I'd said it.

He kissed my eyes, then my hands and fingers. "Me either, Sara," he said softly. "I've never been in love before. Before now I mean."

I hated to spoil my mood and think of Justin, but I realized that I hadn't either. I'd only gone through the motions of our relationship. I'd known passion, but not this. Not the full giving of yourself to another, caring more about his needs than mine. This realization filled me with even more emotion, and also scared me a little.

Alan brought me a robe and led me to the couch. He poured tea for us, and we spent the rest of the evening enjoying one another's company with thoughts of no one else on our minds.

Alan filled the Jacuzzi tub for us as we finished tea, and we bathed together in innocent enjoyment. When we finally retired for the night, we held each other comfortably in my bed.

"I love you," he whispered, muzzling his face into my hair.

"I love you too Alan," I replied, knowing I meant it, but now having to decide how to deal with it in relation to my job and his parents. My parents would be thrilled. Would his?

As I drifted off, my spirits were high. I knew one thing for certain. A new chapter of my life had begun

29

I was very grateful to be home again. Just being on the ground in Reno felt enough like home that I could breathe more easily. It was about 1:30 a.m. upon our arrival, and the city was asleep, at least as much as a 24 hour city could be.

The streets were dry since no snow had fallen on the valley floor, apparent as we'd circled the airport to land. The sky was bright white, with the objects on the ground visually set off in black outlined relief. It was typical of a Reno evening before an eminent snow storm looming over the mountainous valley.

The flight back was something I'd dreaded since the day we first arrived. June had left me some valium for the return flight, and I had taken a full one, which gave me several hours of sleep and others a relaxed flight time.

Alan had insisted on first class for the trip home, and I let him upgrade our seats since he'd kept stifling my protests with gentle kisses and whispers in my ear. I thought the ticket agent was going to throw up, so I gave in.

I enjoyed our conversations during the times I was awake, and he had his arm either around me or put my head in his lap for comfort during the time I was asleep. It was nice to feel that anxious tug all over your body when you're in love. Wow, I was in love with Alan!

I felt like I really knew him now, and not just because of the intimacy we'd shared the previous night. I appreciated his honesty regarding his past and the present relationships and how he'd felt about each. Like me, he'd never found just the right person to make a serious enough commitment.

He'd even shared that he'd had a serious girlfriend in Colorado for about a year, and thought she might be the one. He'd been doing work for her father's company, and had frequently gone back and forth to set up the technological needs of the business and spend time with her.

Alan confided that he'd broken it off with her several months ago after I'd come to work for his parents. He said once he met me, he knew that staying with her was settling for something less than what he wanted.

I felt bad for the girl but it made me feel good,. It also explained the frequency in which he'd sought me out for companionship in activities or for just talking since I'd arrived at the Westin household, and his continual flirtations. He said he did that as a nervous reaction to me, but I'm not sure I believed it.

I couldn't deny that he was a catch, or that I loved spending time with him. He made me feel good about myself in so many ways. He actually listened to what I had to say. Now that a more serious relationship had begun though, I was very uncomfortable about how to handle the home front situation.

Maybe I wasn't good enough for Alan in Sam or June's eyes. Knowing them, I just didn't believe they would ever take that attitude. Based on some of the fine girls that Alan had dated in the past though, how could I be considered suitable? Even though Alan and I were alike in many ways, the fact was that we came from different worlds. From the societal position that came with wealth, some would feel I was beneath the family standards.

Even if they approved, would it be a betrayal of friendship, or even a view that I had used my position to get in with their son? My anxiety started to return as I fretted over the situation.

I finally confided my fears to Alan during a layover in New York. His response had been solely one of amusement. He assured me that all of my thoughts and worries were completely unfounded.

Since the effects of the valium had since worn off, Alan had gotten me a few drinks to relax me for the rest of the trip. He made sure to order just enough not to put me in the state I'd been in on the flight over, but enough to obtain my agreement to be inducted into the mile high club. Valium, alcohol and a touch of Alan in between. What a way to fly.

Alan lugged my suitcases into the sitting room for me. I was too tired to see if June and Sam were up, and kind of hoped they weren't. I'd see them tomorrow.

"Please don't stay long," I said as he sat down on my bed. "Your parents."

"Won't care," he interrupted me. "Like I said ten times already, geez! Heck, Mom would have us married off in a heartbeat if she even had a hint that we liked one another. We could live here and everything, in sin, and she'd still approve," he added with a laugh, and then said more seriously; "I know you're tired and feeling weird about this, so I'll respect your wishes."

"Thank you Alan, I, um," I started, but stumbled over what to say.

"Hey, I want you to know that I meant everything I said. You're one of a kind, and I really care for you. I love you." He looked me in the eyes, his bright baby blues boring into mine, and I melted all over again. I'd never get tired of hearing those words.

His attention drifted off, as if he were looking inward to his own thoughts. "You were amazing too; knocked my socks off actually. Better than I ever could've imagined."

I blushed, but pushed the compliment. "So, did you? Ever imagine I mean?" I asked, teasingly as he approached for a kiss. He nodded as we embraced, and as the intensity increased, he eased off.

"Often," he said in reply to my question, and then whispered as he mouthed my ear, "Amazing."

My heart fluttered again, and I knew my body wanted him to stay even if my mind said no.

"I'll come back after saying hi to Mom and Dad if you want me to. I know I sure want to."

"Oh, I most definitely want the same thing, but I'm not ready to put it in your parents' faces yet. Their room is practically right above this one too. I'm feeling weird, almost like I've done something wrong. Taboo even."

He sighed. "You haven't, but I get it and it's okay with me as long as you don't keep me away too long. Or, we could go to my place," he offered as a solution to the proximity issue, his eyebrows rose in a nearly irresistible, devilish manner.

I gave him what had become a standard reply to his sarcastic wit. I threw a pillow at him, but this time winged it at him hard.

'Ouch. Okay already. Get some rest. I'll see you tomorrow." He shut the door behind him and I heard him go upstairs to see if his folks were up.

I opened the sitting room doors that led to the garden and called out for Rusty. I tried to keep my voice quiet, but there were 40 acres of land out there, and she could be anywhere. I hoped she'd hear me without having to call too loudly

Mom and Dad had brought Rusty back earlier that day so I could see her right away when I got home. I was lucky that she scrambled through the door within ten seconds of my call. She was wiggling her tail, excited to see me. After I'd petted and loved her for a while, she was happy to climb into bed with me for some well deserved rest.

30

It's a good thing Alan didn't sneak into my room that night.   It was barely light outside when June knocked then came bounding into my room before the "Come in" had even passed my lips.

"How was the flight home?" she asked, with unexpected enthusiasm. She was fully dressed and coiffed. A peek at my clock said it was just about 7:00 a.m. I'd only gone to bed a few hours before, plus I was recovering from the use of valium mixed with alcohol. Not a good combination.

I gave her a grouchy look, and she handed over the coffee mug I'd assumed was hers. "For you, my dear."

I sat up in bed, and took the coffee. I giggled, with June joining in. I was not a morning person, and there was no way to mask it.

"Obviously there is something you need from me this morning," I grumbled.

"Only your undivided time and attention for the next hour," she said, then clapped her hands together to speed up my alertness and make me jump enough to slosh coffee on my bed.

If it'd been anyone but June, there'd be a heavy price to pay for waking me up so early after a long international flight. I'd gotten about 5 hours sleep.

I knew she was serious in getting me awake and alert when she brought my slippers and robe to me.

"Come on sleepy head. Daylight is burning and I just can't wait anymore. I've been up for two hours waiting for you to stir."

"No mystery movie marathon last night then?" I asked groggily.

June shook her head. "Too busy. Come on now."

I insisted on a trip to the bathroom before I let her drag me off. Then, with coffee in hand, I followed her. We went out the front door. Sam was in the driveway, at the wheel of a new red golf cart.

"Hop in; let's roll!" he beckoned patting the seat of the cart to show the enthusiasm his voice did not quite convey.

June got in next to Sam, which left me to get on the back. I gave

Sam a look that said "this had better be good". He laughed and returned a look that said, "It'll be worth your time, trust me."

Sam whizzed down the driveway towards the back of the house. We passed the garden and the pool. I noticed that the driveway, which had once ended onto a dirt path, had now been converted into a road of crushed gravel. We'd only been gone for two weeks! Either side of the gravel road was lined with brick, and went straight through the meadow as he drove to the back line of the property. He halted in front of the cottage.

"Ta da!" June announced, taking me by one hand and stretching out the other to introduce me to the cottage. I could immediately tell the porch had been painted and the old solid door had been replaced by one with a section of fuzzed out glass.

Sam opened the door, and she led me into the beautifully re-done cottage.

The previous nautical themed room had been transformed into a chic, modern cottage with somewhat of a lodge theme. Colors of the moss green and cinnamon furniture jumped at me, but in a tranquil, tasteful manner.

The carpet was a sandy tan, and the couch a tapestry of leaves in the combined color scheme. The fireplace had been re-done to include a light oak colored mantle. Above it hung a lovely Bierstadt I recognized from the house. It was a stunning oil painting, depicting the sun setting behind the mountains, and a small group of people surrounding a campfire. It was serene, and added just the right touch of class.

"June, I can't believe you're entrusting me to an original like this. You do remember my last placed got barbecued?"

Sam and June both laughed. "It's insured my dear. It fit so well into the theme I asked that it be hung here. I know it's one of your favorites too."

I went through each of the rooms. The living room was large, and the kitchen was just off to the right. The cupboards and countertops had been redone, with the light oak blending in magnificently with the marble countertop in a maze of browns and greens.

A few of the upper cabinets had glass doors, and I could see that the dishes had all been replaced as well. The natural theme carried throughout the kitchen, and the stoneware dishes had a lovely pattern of leaves on them.

June didn't wait for me to ponder. Instead, she lead me to the bathroom, which had a pine cone theme. The old tub and shower had been ripped out and replaced with a nice garden tub and separate shower stall.

The largest bedroom had more of the pinecone theme, and the comforter was again a tapestry blend, but with pine needles and pinecones against a beige background. The sheets were a pale green, and the furniture was again the light oak color. There were both blinds and drapes throughout the cottage.

The smaller bedroom was decorated in a rich brown color with light blue accents. It was different than the rest of the house, yet perfect in its own way.

I couldn't stop gawking, but June insisted I open the living room closet. I couldn't imagine what to expect. I jumped 10 feet back when Alex said "Boo" when I opened the door.

Thank the Lord I'd had the sense to put my coffee down during the inspection, because I'd have made the first mess in the cottage.

"Surprise?" Alex asked warily, gauging my reaction to such an early morning scare.

After a few seconds, I began to laugh, and everyone else did too.

"Sorry, Sara, I couldn't help myself. Alex came in last night and stayed here. You did a great job of making the bed, Alex; I couldn't tell it'd been slept in at all! Before I let you two catch up, do you like the place, Sara?"

"I love it June; I can't believe you accomplished this while we were away."

"It's amazing what money can buy when you pay a premium for quality labor to be done so quickly," Sam grunted, then said "Ow!" when June smacked him gently on the rear.

"Well, I wanted to make sure you'd be happy in here. We're just thrilled you agreed to stay and let your sister's family have your place. I was not ready to have my right hand gal so far away."

June's face shined as she looked at me.

"This is amazing June, Sam," I said. "This is better than a condo any day."

"Oh," June added. The cart is for your use too, so you don't have to walk back and forth. And, later I'll show you the plans for the small garden in back."

She registered my shock at having a garden to care for. "No worries there, Sara, I'll plan it, and the gardener will take care of it. At least if it is okay with you."

"Of course."

Alex had sat down on the couch, and Sam nudged June to head back out.

'We have two carts. The blue one is on the side of the cottage, and I'll take June back in the red one," Sam said, holding out some keys for me.

"I'll leave some breakfast out for you two when you're ready to come back over," June said, hugging me. "Alex can help bring your stuff over."

"Thanks so much, both of you."

"See you soon kids!" Sam said and whizzed off in the cart, with June chastising him for going too fast.

Still in my robe, I grabbed Alex and hugged him in a vice-like grip.

"What are you doing here?"

"I have a few days off before my next shoot, and then I'm getting ready for the new show."

"Tell me everything!"

For the next hour, we filled each other in on the last two weeks. The media had died down in regards to me, thank the Lord, but had continued in a torrent for Alex. He'd been in every issue of the weekly spreads since the event, and was booked solid for TV show appearances for the next two weeks. After that, he would be starting with media shots and all kinds of work before he started taping the new show.

"I've been reportedly linked with every hot female star in Hollywood, and a few of the articles stated how "distraught" my old Reno, Nevada flame Sara Blake had taken it. You even left the country to get over the heartbreak!"

We laughed about the whacked up media in Hollywood and all of the crazy things that had happened after the awards show incident.

"It helped launch you on your way to being a superstar Alex. I'd do it again in a heartbeat!"

'You've paid a high price for this, Sara, and I will never forget it. I'll stay out of the way should you decide to, err, have other company visit, but I want to help you, too."

"What do you mean?"

"Let's hunt down this I.D. guy, check him out and see where it takes us. It'll be just like old times, except this time I won't hit my head on anything and pass out, or let you get kidnapped. Other than that though, all the good stuff."

'I don't want to get you into any more trouble, Alex. A jail sentence might be a bad thing for you, and I may have to break a few rules again."

"But it's for the greater good, just like before. I'm in!"

We spent another half hour figuring out how to find this guy and creating an alter ego for me to use to attempt to buy some fake I.D.s from him. Who knew where it would lead, but it was definitely the next piece of the puzzle to bring any sort of justice to Simons.

31

A FedEx delivery arrived for Sam the next morning. Sam looked pleased as punch as he opened it, and I heard the van's driver mutter in contempt at having to get back out of the long driveway, which was covered with mounds of wet slush from the previous night's dumping of sleet filled snow.   He fishtailed down the driveway, off to the next delivery.

I was answering some tenant e-mails and taking care of some minor business needs that had gone unattended while we'd been away. When I was done, I'd planned on digging into the information Alan had collected from Albert's computer.

"Sara," Sam triumphantly bellowed, capturing my attention from my previous staring out the window. He handed me the contents of the FedEx. "Our first business transaction for Westin Investments is here. Time to rock and roll!"

I did a quick scan of the contents. There was a check for $275,000.00 from a New York company, with a letter containing instructions to cash the check and wire the proceeds to an individual in China, minus a ten percent commission for Sam to keep. My stomach sank; I'd seen this game played before too often.

"Are you ready to explain in detail the purpose of the new business Sam?" I asked, not revealing my immediate concerns. A look at the remittance address on the FedEx envelope made my hopes of this being a legitimate business transaction fall further. It had been sent from Canada.

"Westin Investments, LLC, is now assisting in international property management," Sam announced loudly, as we both knew June was listening in. "We will collect rents from various clients around the world, and send them on to the property owners in different parts of the world." He seemed giddy, and casually sat on the couch. June came from the kitchen, done with her morning duties, to hear more details. Sam had kept her in the dark to these arrangements as well.

"I didn't invoice this client to send its rent here," I asked, "Did you?"

"No, the group from England handles that, and has asked the properties assigned to me to send their rents here." he elaborated, his face now wore an expression of incredulity. "Why do you ask, Sara? This is why I met the group in England. I had them checked out and everything. This is the easiest $27,500.00 I've ever made."

Yeah, too easy, I thought and nearly said it out loud. Should I make some calls first to validate my suspicions, or should I tell him now? What a situation to happen right here on the home front. Sam may have inadvertently involved himself in money laundering or theft. He knew all about what was happening with Eckert's friend Simons, but hadn't recognized that this could be a scam too. He'd heard me report on this topic many times at the bank, but it must not have registered with him.

"Let me just ask you a question, Sam," I said gently as I sat across from him and June. The morning light had permeated the room, but didn't brighten my mood.

"Shoot," he said with a sniff, obviously still feeling like the king of industry.

"Why would a company in England that manages international properties, subcontract out to a company in America for the collection of rent? Why wouldn't they just hire employees to do it?"

June looked from me, then back to Sam, who looked less than pleased for being put on the spot.

'Uh," he started, but I interrupted.

"Also, why would a New York company write a check to you, then overnight it from Canada, and ask you to wire the funds to China? And finally, why would they pay you $27,500.00 to cash a check and wire funds? Even if these events made sense, if the English firm billed them, why use you? They could just as easily have gotten the check and wired the funds."

Sam's face was red. I hadn't seen him get truly angry since I'd been here, although I'd experienced it a few times at the bank. It was not a pretty sight.

"Why don't you just get to the point, Sara? Apparently this is "suspicious" to you," he spat out, emphasizing the word suspicious. "What could possibly be wrong with this? Maybe it's a tax issue with the property management company, or maybe there aren't qualified employees that handle this. Maybe the company hires an accounting firm in Canada to do its payables. That's a lot of if's to ponder."

"A monkey could do this," I said waving the letter. "I don't want to insult you, but I smell trouble."

"Just cash the check and send the wire, Sara!" Sam said strongly. "Like you said, a monkey could do it. Is it too much to ask?"

"Of course not, Sam," I said gently and with a tone of respect that I held for him. "Can I please do a little checking first though? You're paying me to protect your interests, too."

June gave him a look that said he'd better let me do just that, so he nodded. I got on the internet and looked up the phone number for the company, a real one as I soon found, that had written the check. I looked back to Sam and June as I wrote it down.

"Please? Just give me a few minutes."

June glared at him until he nodded his approval.

"If I'm wrong, I'll carry your golf clubs this summer," I added, hoping to improve his mood. It did, even causing him to grin.

"You are so on for that. No tipping caddies this summer. I'll save a bundle."

"If I'm right, I think I deserve another week of paid vacation," I added, knowing I was pushing it. I smiled, then dialed the number and asked for the accounting department. I got transferred twice until I was speaking to the head of the department.

"Hi there. I'm calling from Reno, Nevada. We assist an international firm in the collection of rents from various properties around the world, and I wanted to verify a check we received. It came from Canada instead of New York as we expected. It struck me as odd, and as this is a newer assignment for us, I thought I'd check and make sure the check was valid."

For the next two minutes, I answered a battery of questions, and asked a few of my own. "Troy, you've been most helpful, of course I'll do as you ask. I'm very sorry this has happened and I wish you the best of luck in solving the problem."

I left him my contact information, and added, "Troy, I have experience in this sort of thing from my previous banking career. If I were you, I'd look from within your department first." Listening for another minute, I ended the call with, "Of course we'll cooperate fully. I'll be ready to answer any questions and share any information I obtain during my own search for answers. Have a great day."

Sam and June were still in the room, both sitting stiffly on the edge of the couch. I could tell they'd tried to hear the other end of the conversation, but had only heard enough of what I'd said to scare them with my word usage of "cooperation" and the like.

"What the heck was that about?" Sam demanded.

"Sam, watch your tone," June ordered, "She'll tell us, so calm down.

I cleared my throat, and re-joined them in the sitting area. "Sam, this is a stolen check. It was written to their phone service provider in New York in the amount of $700.00. It's been stolen, washed and re-issued."

"What?" Sam retorted. "There's just some mix up. I'll call Greg or Charles in London."

"Not until you listen to me, Sam. I want to know details about your dealings with these guys, but first, I want to explain what you were almost made a party to."

June poked Sam in the ribs just as he started to reply, then sat back into the couch sulking.

"I'm making some pretty bold guesses, but I've seen this a few times on the bank's end of it when the check gets returned as forged and the customer, or the bank, takes a loss. Just like the scam I'm helping Simons with; these guys operate all over the world. They steal checks from the mail, checks already written by a company, or blank checks they somehow get their hands on. They are then washed, at least in the case of checks that are already written to someone else, or filled out to the party of their choice and sent to that party. In this case, it's Westin Investments."

I had to pause for some water, so I kept talking loudly as I filled myself a glass in the kitchen and re-entered the sitting room.

"The check is sent to the party, cashed and immediately wired elsewhere. As you know very well, Sam, wires are good money and can't be retrieved. Checks can come back for up to three years for forged endorsement."

Sam nodded, aware of these facts.

"If you'd put this in your account and sent the funds to China, the check would have come back against your account. Most banks won't send a wire unless the funds are already good, which is why the crooks prey on professionals like you that already have some money. You have enough clout to get money sent against a check before it clears, but when the check comes back as fraudulent, it comes out of *your* pocket. You could do a lot of these transactions before you get bitten in the butt by it."

Sam put his head in his hands, still red. Then a stream of swear words came out of his mouth in a torrent.

"Sam," June said in a voice that halted the swearing. "No harm done. Sara's caught it before we put ourselves in harm's way." She took his hands and looked him in the eye, "No big deal."

"No big deal?" Sam said vehemently, "These jokers had me pay an upfront franchise fee of $25,000.00! I thought I'd make it back in the first two transactions."

He stood up and walked to the window, speaking more softly now, he said "June, it's more than that though. I miss being a power player of sorts in the world, a mover and a shaker, and I thought I could do something big on my own. Thought I could, well, show you that I can still make money without using yours to do it. Plus, I was the head of a bank, for crying out loud. Like Sara said, I've heard variations of this before many times, yet I don't recognize it when it walks in my own door?

You'd think I'd know better. How could I be so blindly stupid?"

June strode over to him,.I was making an exit to my room in the house so they could be alone until June stopped me with a gesture.

"Sam, you have nothing to prove to me. There are a lot of bad people out there, who prey on the rest of us. You've always been an inspiration to me, not because you rose to the CEO of the bank or handled my money so well, but because you always considered the needs of others while doing it. You earned the respect of your employees, and me too, of course. Not every successful businessman can say that, but anyone could fall for this."

They hugged quietly, and June kissed him with a peck on the lips. It seemed to calm his nerves a bit. I still wanted to leave, so I hovered in the back of the room near my bedroom door to make an escape when possible.

"For the record though, next time you want to start a venture that is out of the norm, please consult with Sara to see if there are warning signs first. If you'd have asked her about this venture, she could have gone along to your meetings and asked the right questions. It sounds like we'll have some explaining to do as far as that company is concerned. I sure hope they haven't lost a lot of money."

They both turned to look at me. I smiled weakly. "Sam, you always said I was the bearer of bad news. Sorry to have to deliver it yet again. On the positive side though," I started.

"There's a positive to this mess?" Sam asked in disgust tone.

"Yeah, Actually two positives," I said as they stared at me, awaiting the verdict.

"First, we didn't facilitate this transaction by sending out a wire, or later we would have the Feds all over your other businesses. Second, one variation of this scam includes visiting the crooks in their country."

"Yeah, well I met with those guys while we were in England. So?"

"And at the time you probably didn't find it odd that you meet somewhere other than at their offices."

"Yeah, guess not. They looked okay though, regular business sorts."

"Well, they would have to look the part to reel you in. You must have been a harder sell than some, and not everyone bothers to meet them in person. Ten percent commission is pretty tempting to most, especially as it's made very easily. Unfortunately, another twist to the scam is that sometimes the bad guys kidnap their party and ransom them back to their family. Sometimes, they even get returned alive. Like I said, there are a lot of variations. Until then, how about we stick to business as usual?"

Sam and June shuddered at the thought. I told them I'd help get these guys caught if I could, but it would be hard, if not impossible. I left them alone to talk things over, ready to find Alan and dig into Albert's computer files.

Although one scam had been stopped in its tracks, I still had the first one to get back to and connect enough pieces to find a related party that was local enough for me to get. On to the next step in getting Simons' his money back. Hopefully, I'll find someone in this endless chain of crooks to answer for these crimes.

32

The next morning, I sat peacefully in the living room area while Alan slept. He needed the rest after last night's marathon love session. Besides just being very physical, it'd been another magical evening, this time more intense and passionate than our first time together. I decided not to count our encounter in the airplane's lavatory as a "time", but rather as a few minutes of silliness that we could laugh about and chalk up on our "I've done that" lists of life.

Reflecting on the physical side of this relationship, I realized what I had been missing in my relationship with Justin. In the combined years we were together, I'd never experienced the pleasure and completeness that I'd had in just the few times I'd been with Alan. With Justin, it had been animalistic, not rough, but more of a biological function of life. With Alan, it was the sharing a mutual enjoyment of one another to ultimately benefit the other person. Heck, Alan seemed to care more about pleasing me than anything else.

I heard Alan stirring in the next room, and it gave me comfort that he was in the cottage with me. It felt good to have a partner share my space, although I felt bad that Alex had picked up on things quickly and had opted to spend last night at Shelby's after helping me get through Albert's information. Alex promised he'd come back this afternoon and help me plan out my next steps.

I started thinking amorous thoughts of Alan as I heard a loud yawn from my room, and was planning a morning attack when the sound of the intercom broke into the silence. It buzzed loudly three times before I could get across the room to answer it.

"Morning, June!" I exclaimed in my most chipper voice.

"Good morning, darlin'," was June's sweet reply. "How are you today?"

"I'm great. Did you want me to come over now?" I asked in my usual nonchalant manner, but behind it was my deepest wish that would allow me to stay here for another half hour or so.

"Whenever you're ready. Breakfast is still set out. Are we still going out today?"

"Of course, June, we'll do lunch, shopping, and anything else you'd like to do."

"Sounds great. Have you by chance seen Alan yet this morning? I can't get him to pick up his intercom."

I heard her say something muffled in the background. It must have been to Sam, and all I heard was "Try" and "cell".

"Uh, no," I stammered, not expecting this question at all, "Maybe he went out for a jog or swim?" I knew how horrible I'd imagined ever having to lie to June would be and it was exactly as awful as I'd imagined. I couldn't do this, but now, at least this moment, was not the time to fix it.

A phone rang in the cottage as I finished my sentence. It was a distinctive ring. It was a ring on Alan's phone set just for calls from his Dad's cell. Crap!

"Well, I'll see you when you're ready honey," June said awkwardly, but at least ending the horrible extended silence after the ring had been stifled.

"If you do see Alan, will you let him know that the early morning FedEx truck dropped off some packages? I need help getting them into the house."

"Ok, will do," I replied, too quickly as my mind tried to anticipate any comments or questions that she might pose. Thank goodness none came. 'See you soon."

After she signed off the intercom, I turned and found Alan sitting on the couch, finishing off my coffee. I leaned over and gave him a kiss. "Mornin'."

"Back at ya," he said, and then noticed my face was too serious. "You okay?"

"Look, Alan, I've made a decision."

"About us?"

"Yes"

He looked playful. "Does it involve you, me, and maybe getting back into bed?" He raised his eyebrows playfully, but then put a hand up to stop the protest that I'd already begun forming on my lips. "Ok, I'll be serious. I'm ready to listen."

I sat next to him on the couch and placed his arm around my neck. "I'm crazy about you."

"Is that versus simply crazy?" he said, laughing. I punched him in the arm. He kissed me on the head in response.

"You said you'd be serious. I'm being serious and this is hard. You said you wanted to be with me, no matter what, including whatever weird conditions I put on it. I'm not ashamed to be with you because you're younger, and I hope I never made you feel that way. I feel ashamed to be in a relationship with you because of my friendship with your Mom.

It's like I'm betraying her, violating her trust. It goes beyond employer and employee. She's treated me like a part of the family, and I repay her by sleeping with her son? Some friend I am."

"I'm glad you're not ashamed of me, just who I'm related to. Hmm, let me think about this." He thought for just a second. "Well it works for me any way you slice it, Mrs. Robinson. What do you want, an employment bonus for services rendered to the son of your employers?" His eyes laughed, but with understanding, and he put his fingers to my lips. "Are you afraid my Mom thinks you de-flowered me or something?"

I could not stifle my own laugh. "Hardly, but I think that Moms don't think of their children as sexual beings at all, and the last thing someone should do to a parent is flaunt that they are." I thought of my folks. "Believe me, I know."

"Are what?" he asked, back tracking to my comment.

"Sexual beings!" I said with frustration brimming over in my voice. "Will you let me finish now?"

"Just wait a minute. There are two sides to every story, Miss Sara. My Mom thinks of you as a daughter, and she'd like nothing more than for you to become one, for real I mean. She'd be overjoyed to know we're a couple. And Dad, well you know, men are happy when other men are getting some, even Dads.

I gave up on even pretending my indignance over his levity on something when I was trying so hard to be serious.

"So, we're, a couple then?" I asked in a soft voice, trying to get past the thought of Sam and Alan doing a knuckle buster to commemorate our lovemaking.

"Hell, yes. No other man better even look in your direction. You're mine now." He grabbed both of my hands in one of his and kissed them, then placed them on his bare chest, near his heart. "I'm crazy about you too, you know that. I love you, and I want to spend every minute of my days, and nights, with you."

"Me too, Alan. There's no tip-toeing around what just happened though. I can't act like nothing's happened and make it through the day with your Mom today."

I continued, "Maybe I'm over thinking and assuming that your parents will be mad; I just hope they're not hurt over it. I have to be truthful with them. However, there's only one way that I can tell them and still live with myself in this situation, you know, and be happy about it."

"What's that? I want you to be happy more than anything else on earth."

"I don't want to hurt your Mom, but I don't know what else to do. I've decided to give notice. I must quit my job here, a job I really love too. It's hardly even work anymore, but if I'm not an employee, I could still be a family friend."

"That's sleeping with their son," Alan finished for me.

"Will you stop emphasizing that part?"

"I put it the way it is. Mom will be crushed that you won't be here from morning to night everyday, but if you're at the house a lot, she'll be okay with it. I don't know what Dad will do. I think he kinda likes playing real estate mogul, and having you around makes him feel like he's financially and legally protected. But, if this gets me out of having to sneak around the grounds to get in your bed, all the better."

He pulled me closer, holding my arms tightly, and rubbing his arms up and down mine. My resolve melted, as our bodies melded together. My point was made and accepted. I felt better, but there were still lots of other considerations, including my finding new employment. I was not going to resort to billboard advertising again.

Alan had the last word, as he ended our conversation with, "Don't you think my parents care about my happiness? You made me the happiest man on the planet 52 hours and 47 minutes ago when you told me you wanted me too. Guys get all goofy inside too, and that made my heart do a flip-flop or two. And frankly, as long as I get to be with you, I don't give a damn." His mouth made sure mine couldn't answer.

 **33**

Sunlight blazed into my eyes as I entered the back of the house. The huge windows all around the front of the house seemed to direct the bright light right into my eyes. I couldn't see as I got through the door, so I bumped into the table on my way to the kitchen.

The kitchen was empty, but the breakfast was still laid out neatly upon platters so I could help myself. I went right for the eggs and juice, and sat down in the nook, eating in silence and dreading the thought of telling June and Sam that I'd have to end our professional relationship.

The job had seemed too good to be true after the first two weeks, and the fairy tale had continued even after that. Once I'd put Sam's information in order, managing it took little time. Taking June shopping, to the theater, or even watching movies with her at home was a part of my "job", and the main part of my job once Sam's business was in order. I got paid for that time. Not exactly like any kind of work I'd ever done before.

I was more of a personal companion than anything else. It had begun with handling the elements of Sam's business, but I had it under such good organization, it took less than an hour a day to maintain most of the time.

June and I spent lots of time together. We'd both shared with one another how comfortable the relationship had become, and how quickly it evolved. June was like a second Mom, and I was like the daughter she'd never had.

As I ate, I hoped that the right words would come. It would kill me if I hurt her feelings in any way, shape or form. I planned on letting her know that I'd still take her out on weekends whenever I could, whenever I was free from whatever position I moved into after this one. I'd do this because I wanted to, not because I got paid to do it.

The eggs suddenly sank like rock in my stomach. As I thought about what kind of job I'd be taking, I'd forgotten the job market in our area. I think the current unemployment rate was 12%. Holy cow! I'd had a hard enough time getting this job, and the economy was far more dismal now that it had been. So much for thinking things through. I still had my condo, though. Even though it was occupied by my sister's family for now, and I brightened when I thought that Alan would be there to help me make it. I don't really know how he made his money, I realized, since he hardly left the house anymore. I hoped he wasn't a trust fund baby or that he relied on his folks for everything. He was a good son to them, but that was hardly a wise choice as a mate for an about to be unemployed person.

"A penny for your thoughts," said June, her voice reaching the kitchen before she did. I rose to give her a good morning hug, and Sam followed after. I scanned June's face for any signs of hearing Alan's phone over the intercom. To my relief, there was none. As I turned to hug Sam, there was no hiding of the fact he knew from the expression on his face. He wore it like the smile of a man who had just high fived the other man.

Confirming this, Alan followed into the room a moment later, with a sly look that gave everything away. Uh oh, now what?

Refilling coffee for herself and Sam, June sat down at the table with me. The silence was a bit awkward. I decided to break the ice and get it over with.

"Do you remember when you said I could tell you anything about how I was feeling?" I directed the question at June, and motioned with my head for Alan to leave. He gave me a look of personal amusement, and got up. Unfortunately, he went to get a cup of coffee and came back to the table as June responded.

"Of course. This is your home too now. Is something bothering you? Is the cottage working out?"

The cottage. I of course had forgotten to take into consideration how much effort, not to mention expense, June had put forth into transforming the cottage into a residence for me. What else had I allowed to cloud my judgment over love?

"The cottage is amazing, June. I really love it there." I hesitated as I looked from face to face, chewing on my lip, and getting no support from Alan who pretended like he knew nothing at all about what I was going to say.

Alan chimed in, "Yes, her first night in it was very memorable, so she said to me." Sam and Alan grinned slyly and I wanted to kill them both on the spot, but I had to keep on track for June's sake.

"I really love being here with you all so much. I love my job."

Sam interjected in a more serious tone," And you're so good at it that you get to spend lots of time with June. It's really been a win-win situation Sara, and we appreciate you too." He put his coffee mug forward in a mock toast of sorts.

"As much appreciation as I have, that is not the purpose of this conversation, just an easy way to start." As I worked on re-gathering my nerve, June gave Sam a look that told him not to interrupt again.

"Something has happened, and I feel it is affecting my job performance, or will, anyway."

I paused again, looking at the faces in front of me, all eager for me to continue. I wrung my hands together and laid it on the line. "I need to give notice. I can't work for you anymore."

Sam dropped his coffee mug, breaking as it crashed to the floor. He wasn't laughing and joking now.

June gasped loudly, 'No! Whatever it is, we'll work through it Sara, I swear. Please don't go unless you truly want to do something else."

Scrambling for some towels, I found comfort in cleaning up the wreckage of Sam's coffee mug and the large amount of coffee that had been in it.

"It's not that I want to," I stated as factually as I could, "It's just that something is in the way now."

"What could be in the way?" Sam was hot. 'Did someone make you a better offer? I knew Evan Cranston wanted you for an assistant. If he offered you a job, I'll bet anything he said he'd pay and double your vacation. That asshole. I'll get him for this."

"Calm down, Sam. Sara will tell us what's in the way, and then we'll try to convince her that it is not an obstacle." June resituated herself at the table as I finished the clean up. 'Really, Sam, relax until you know the facts."

He sat quietly, hands on his face, looking grumpy, and then staring at me to continue. June joined him, her expression grim, waiting for me to go on.

Alan was looking pleased at punch. He sat there with a stupid grin on his face as he watched all of us.

"I feel that I have over-stepped the boundaries of my job, June, Sam," I said, looking intently at each one. "You've given me everything, my job, a place to live, and most importantly, your love."

Holding back my sobs was no longer possible. "And I've re-paid you by," I stammered, "by fa-falling for your s-son." I wailed as I threw my arms around June's neck. "I'm sorry."

June held me for a moment, stroking my hair. Alan let me know he was there for me, finally, by placing his hand on my back.

When I felt able to look her in the face, I hoped she'd say something to make me feel better. Only hope told me she wouldn't be angry or disappointed either in me as an employee and friend, or with her son for his judgment, or lack thereof, in choosing to be with me.

"I'm assuming it's Alan then?" she said, her tone not giving even a clue as to whether this was good, bad or devastating to her.

Nodding my concurrence in between sobs, Alan decided to join the conversation, adding a "Yep." He nodded his head as if his statement of confirmation needed emphasis, and then put his hand in his pants waistband in an unsophisticated Ed Bundy-like style. It was a rather unappealing gesture, as I knew he intended it to be.

To my utter amazement, June starting laughing. Her soft voice giggled, then took on stronger tones as the laugh seemed to emanate from her very core. She had to let go of me as she put her hands to her mouth. Sam then joined in, and Alan could no longer keep his own face straight, and soon I had a chorus of people laughing at me.

Angry, I backed away from the table. Had Alan played me for a fool? Why was this so funny? I felt my face flush in embarrassment, and tears felt hot on my face as they began to flow uncontrollably. I was about to leave the room when Alan got up and physically stopped me, putting his arms around me despite my actions of protest.

In a whirlwind of a moment, he was kissing me, dipping me back in what must be reminiscent of an old movie he'd watched with me or June. Still uncertain of what was happening, I shrugged him off and wriggled out of his arms.

"What's going on?" I demanded, looking just at Alan. I didn't feel right demanding an explanation from June or Sam.

Alan kissed my hand and sat back at the table. Sam pointed at June, apparently giving her the floor to speak.

June cleared her throat, and looked down as she spoke, looking embarrassed herself.

"Bad reaction. I didn't mean to laugh, Sara," she caught my eye so that I'd know she was being sincere. I didn't doubt it, so I relaxed a little and rejoined the group at the table, anxious to hear more that would clear this up.

"How do I start?" she said, clearing her throat and fussing with her hands.

"Like I did, just spill it. I won't interrupt." I shot a look at Sam and Alan that told them not to interrupt either.

"Okay then," June took a deep breath, "I'll spill, as you say."

"It was apparent within a few weeks after you took the job that you were the perfect fit for Sam, and even better, for me too. You had Sam organized so quickly that you were giving me a lot of time and attention I hadn't expected."

She took my hands in hers. "We bonded in a way I hadn't anticipated either." Her eyes misted up, and I could see Sam and Alan squirming over the emotional turn this had taken.

"You've been so good to me and such fun to have around. I'm afraid it went to my head a little, and I got selfish. This is all my fault."

My heartfelt admission and resignation and led to laughter and my supposed humiliation. Now June was admitting to selfish behavior? I was confused, and couldn't imagine how these dots were going to connect.

"I'm getting there," she glowered at Sam, who'd been making hand gestures to her. "Sam is telling me to speed it up, to cut to the chase you might say. I'd been hinting to Adam and Alan what a fine daughter-in-law you'd make. I'm the one that bowed out of the lunch with Adam, made Alan come to England, and stay behind with you, not that either required much effort. I also wanted you to stay here instead of moving back to your condo in hopes of your connecting with one of the boys." She looked so relieved to have it out.

"So you see, I was pushing you together all along. I wanted you to end up with one of my sons. Alan told me a while back that he was intrigued with you, but that you felt you would be betraying your loyalty to Sam and me if you dated. You were involved with the policeman, so I thought it was just something Alan came up with. I never thought you'd truly feel this way about it. Can you see though, why we laughed? Sam and I have been arguing about this for months now. He told me that nature would take its course. Looks like he was right."

I was stunned. Sam and Alan gave the "can we go now?" look to both of us. We had more to discuss, so we both nodded.

"Glad that's over. Come on, Alan. We'll go do something fun while they talk and cry and stuff." Sam patted my shoulder and kissed June.

'Well said, Dad," Alan said, then sarcastically said to me, 'Told ya." He kissed his Mom on the check and me on the lips as he followed his Dad to do whatever while we finished the girl talk.

. June said "Rogue child" to him as he left the room, "Always such a headstrong one." She looked from him to me, "Remember I've got two boys. Adam's a bit conceited for some, but are you sure you want that one?"

34

Alan took his Mom to lunch, as he knew I was itching to find this local guy. Good fortune had continued to follow me as I called the number I'd found for him in Albert's information, and someone answered on the other end.

I told him I'd just gotten into town after vacationing in England for a while, and had made some new friends that told me Reno was the place to be for the furtherance of my "business ventures".

I dropped a few names from Albert's records that lived in England and were somehow connected to Tony. He must have recognized at least one of them, because he told me how to find him and that he could meet my needs. In fact, he emphasized 'any needs' at all that I might have.

Alex helped me cook up the alter ego I was going to use to pull this off. I didn't think that my own vanilla self could pass with a con man's persona. I dropped Alex off half a block away so he could watch me from inside the bar where Tony told me he was out. I was to go into the parking lot and meet him in a van.

I drove my old Saturn, but pulled off the license plate and left it with Alex. I didn't want this guy to have an easy trace to y identity or use the Westin's cars and expose them either.

Just as he said, Tony's van was parked at the far end of the lot, in the dirt area. The windows were tinted in a shade I knew was illegal in the city of Reno, but other than that, it looked like any other van in the area. My heels clicked on the pavement as I crossed the lot. I wobbled a bit as the pavement ended and the heels met sand and rock.

No indications of life came from the van. I had anticipated music, or at least seeing the driver. Nervously, I approached the vehicle which was parked in a head on position.

Just before I could actually touch the car, the side door opened with a force that scared me half to death. No one greeted me, so I walked to the side and peered into the van.

A sophisticated set up was the last thing I expected. There was a full business office in view. A desk, computer, and filing cabinets squeezed into the back. Before I could look too closely, a man's head popped into my view.

"Stephanie?" he questioned. A long stream of cigarette smoke expelled from his mouth as he said my name. He looked me over with a glance that said he liked what he saw. The guy, who I assumed to be Tony, jumped out of the van and extended a hand, his eyes revisiting what must have been his favorite places on my body. .

My nerves set aside, I decided to keep on track and play my part to the best of my ability.

"Yeah," I said, adding my attempt at a New York type accent to complete the pretty-but-streetwise. "And you're Tony?"

He was tall, fairly well built, and was dressed in a casual manner. Jeans, sweatshirt, hiking boots, and he had earplugs that I had a hard time trying not to stare through. I gathered he was about 25. He had a baby face hidden beneath scraggly facial hair. Only after he nodded in acknowledgement did I extend my hand to meet his. In a cheesy gesture, he took my hand in his and kissed it. Although my mind was screaming *"Puh-leaz!"*, I somehow managed to say, "Pleasure" before removing my hand from his.

"What can I do you for?" he asked in an attempt of clever humor while he sat in the doorway of the van. He ran his hand through his mid-length brown hair, then traced his goatee with his fingers. I knew he was still assessing if he could trust me, as much as one crook can trust another crook, I suppose.

"I need some Nevada driver's licenses or state I.D. cards, birth certificates and social security numbers showing I was born in Nevada." I kept it clean and simple, just telling him what I needed. "Enough to establish six verifiable identities. I'll pay extra if you can get me any credit card information to match any of the names."

I shifted in my stance, readjusting my purse to the other shoulder, and toying with my sunglasses. I tried to act comfortable while waiting to see if Tony believed me as a credible identify thief.

Tony laughed. "Wow, whatcha got going princess? Loans, credit cards, romance scams? I'd bet you do well." He apparently didn't expect an answer. He turned his back to me, getting to his feet and moved behind the desk in the van.

"Come into my lair," he invited with a grand gesture once he settled in. He was madly typing away on a laptop that was connected into a port on the desk, ignoring me almost completely.

Relieved that he bought my initial story, I did my best to get into the van. The tight skirt made the step up impossible, so I finally sat down and repeated the same method of getting up Tony had done. Graceless, but avoiding a big step up in my tiny, tight skirt, or fumbling around and risk showing anything more than was already hanging out. I found a fold up chair next to the desk, unfolded it and sat directly in front of him.

"Close the door," Tony gruffly instructed in a tone that meant I should have known to do it already. I banged my head on the ceiling as I quickly stood up to obey. Tony didn't seem to notice, but my ears rung as I swung the heavy door shut. The part of my hair that wouldn't curl decided to settle in the direction of my face, and I fussed with it trying to get it into place with the rest of my hair.

Keys tapping, Tony said nothing for several minutes. Suddenly, he seemed satisfied with whatever information he had in front of him. He looked approvingly at me, then stared into my blouse, his eyes following my fake cleavage as far as possible. This verified that the recording device was definitely not detected, and I hoped it was still on.

Calls had been continually coming into Tony's phone over the last few minutes, but he ignored them. A different ring tone sounded out, and he reached for the phone with immediacy. "Scuse me," he said. He was kind of polite for this kind of business.

I heard a loud voice coming from the other end. Tony listened, the said with a laugh, "He sent more money? Nothing tastes as good as a second lick from the same sucker!" I heard laughter from the other end of the phone too.

'Yeah, I'll get it. What's the cut? K. Same bank and account number? Great, yeah that id's still good."

I perked up to both listen and look around while his eyes were off me. I noticed stacks of unopened mail and guessed right away they were stolen from mailboxes or mail trucks with the hope of stealing important information about people. It was to be expected, but it disgusted me.

One cabinet drawer was partially opened. I could see files neatly arranged inside. I could barely make out some of the nicely labeled headers. All I could make out was "Local Male, 40-50" on one tab, and "Foreign European Female 25-30" before I could tell Tony was adjusting his position.

Repositioning myself to sit straight forward again, Tony completed his slow turn around to face me. He held up one finger as an indication that he'd be done in a minute or so.

"Yeah, I'll go to Sacto tomorrow and pick it up in cash once you confirm it's there. Sweet, thanks, Carlos. Yah, I'll bring it to your house. The King's Beach address? K. See ya. "

He hung up with a snap of the phone. It was hard to fill in what was being said on the other end of the call, but to me it sounded like a Nigerian scam payment pick-up, especially since he called the victim a sucker and used the term "second lick" that told me the victim had fallen for the second of the endless obstacles that made this type of scam so successful. I couldn't help but wonder if it got routed through another of Alfred's contacts in England.

"Sorry 'bout that," he said as he got back to the laptop. "Okay Stephanie, I have information on about 50 locals close to your age. I can give you multiple items you requested on about half of these people. We can talk about which items go with which identity after we discuss price." Tony emphasized the word "after" in a manner to elevate its importance, but it came across like a game show host building up a prize. I made sure my eyes didn't give away the giggle that I was stifling in my throat. I had to stay tough. For all I knew, this guy could be connected to some major crime players and I'd end up in a bag at the bottom of Lake Tahoe.

"Can you guarantee that none of the social security numbers are issued to those now deceased?" I again delivered the line with sincerity and brevity to make him believe I was an experienced professional at these matters.

Tony frowned at the question, and went back to the keyboard with a "hmpf". He tapped away, not anticipating this need, one which I thought a good identity thief re-seller would anticipate. Guess if I take over Tony's business, I'll remember for him.

"K'. Still have 13 individuals, but only 5 with items such as credit cards, utility bills, employment information and other items that can be used to establish identity. You must be doing loan fraud, 'cause no one else checks to see if the social matches a dead person."

'Well, looks like we're still in business then," I said as calmly as I could, "although I'm not sharing what I'm up to. I'll pay $500.00 per identity to include all the bells and whistles."

"A thousand per is standard. Geez, girl, this ain't New York! We don't have as many people in this county to choose from." Tony said to start his end of the bargaining. He raised his eyebrows for emphasis.

"I'll take three for $2,500.00 then. That's all I have today, but I'll be back in a week to buy three more for the same price. The other three can be from California or Vegas, and future ones can be from other nearby states. I gotta have at least three right away."

"Geez, you must have something good going to need that many identities. Yah I know, I 'm not asking," he said as I started to shake my head, "but I am giving you a big break here. I don't usually deal with folks who don't know someone I already know. If Andy hadn't thought you were so cute, you'd never have gotten this far."

I batted my eyelashes in response, and then gave him my best smile. Tony looked me up and down again, and he licked his lips and said slowly. "You're kinda old for me but you have a cute ass. How' bout I give you a fourth one for free? Maybe you give me some love and attention when we're done here?"

I cringed as ripples of both indignation and horror went through me. *What have I gotten myself into this time!* I thought mentally hitting myself on the head, and was pissed as I also thought through his comment that I was old.

His eyes met mine, but I didn't panic once I saw into them. To my relief, I didn't see the cold steel heart or cruelty as I had when Stan, the man that nearly raped and killed me a few month's ago, had done the same thing.

Tony was an identity stealer, a crook of sorts, but not a rapist. There was no indication of callousness or coldness in him. Yet anyway. He was still young. As for his offer, I was sure was one he'd offered and been taken up on many times before. Although my fears were waylaid, I wanted to play this one right, and not offend him since he hadn't given up the goods yet. I wanted to keep this relationship if I needed to come back as Stephanie again.

"Tony, you're so sweet to offer." I said in a false sweet voice, putting my hands on my waist to emphasize the tight fits of both my shirt and skirt. I playfully tapped him with one of my high heeled shoes while giving him the same kind of head to toe appraisal he had given me, taking extra pause on the groin, then the ear lobes. I shrugged my shoulders and shook my head slowly. "Fraid I just can't stand men though. Just can't see my way to play for your team. Not even for money. Sorry, honey."

I hoped he'd catch on to what I was trying to say. Thought I'd play it up a little more to be sure he got the message. I added some breathy sexiness into my accent as I said the next sentence, lingering over each word and running my finger down my pretend cleavage. His eyes followed. "Maybe next time, I'll bring a friend. I'll letcha watch."

Tony's cell phone, ringing again, hit the ground with a thud. A look of awe crossed his face, then a big, knowing smile took over. He looked as happy as if I'd agreed to do him right then and there. "You're so on for that, Stephanie."

He reached over me, and I worried for just a moment that I had played my hand poorly. I closed my eyes tight, not moving until I was certain of what he going to do. I heard a whizzing sound, and his arm came down against my shoulder.

"Sorry 'bout that," he said, stepping back. A blue background was now behind my head, and he had a camera in hand to take my picture. As he lined me up for a shot, he paused. Stephanie, what happened to your hair? You might want to fix that."

I was grateful he didn't expect an answer, and I did my best to cover over the bald spot with other hair without the benefit of a mirror or brush. *I'll never get away from hair problems,* I thought to myself, *not even in the midst of criminals!*

Ten minutes later, I had three driver's licenses and social security numbers, two with credit cards, and one with a paystub and a utility bill. I was grateful to be on my way home and have enough evidence to give to Eckert to maybe earn some information that would get me further along in my investigation.

35

"I can't just verify every piece of information, person or situation you ask me to look into! I'm a public servant, not your personal source of criminal information, and you are not allowed to commit a crime to prevent further crimes." Eckert was spitting mad, and could barely contain himself as I sat across from him at his desk, a large, false wooden corporate representation of a desk anyway. He pounded it for emphasis, as if the volume of his voice hadn't been loud enough to get his point across.

I had just explained what I'd gathered on my English excursion, and how it led to that afternoon's activities. I showed him my newly purchased identification materials to prove I was on track to get someone connected to Simons' money loss. I knew he was mad that I'd put myself in a dangerous situation, again, to get what I wanted. Alex had opted to wait in the car, and I was glad he did, because his involvement would piss off Eckert even more.

"If you want to play private detective, you have to be licensed just like everybody else. Even then, you have a code of ethics to follow. You can't just waltz in and do whatever you feel like to ensure the outcome. You know the law isn't lax on criminal procedure."

I was done with his attitude. "Intent is considered in crimes, Eckert. But I'm not asking for the admissibility of this as evidence in a court case, I'm trying to help your friend get his money back, AND show the world that at least one of these scumbags can be stopped."

My own fury rose in my throat. "For every person out there that has been victimized, and especially for seniors and veterans that are targeted for this type of crime, there has to be some kind of justice. This is a faceless criminal, and a crime that no one seems to care about because the victim handed over the money. I thought you'd see things differently, especially since your own partner was victimized and lost his retirement nest egg. It could have just as easily been you"

Eckert snickered, and I knew it was because he'd never admit he could be suckered like Simons was. "You're not a cop. If you have

184

information, share it, but don't put yourself in danger to try to get more. You could end up putting other lives in jeopardy AGAIN."

I knew Eckert was referring to both the fire and the drug lab incident. I was an overly curious type, but I felt I understood this kind of crime and criminal better than the average law enforcement officer. Nothing ever seemed to happen when financial scam crimes were reported anyway. At least in the situation he was referring to, someone paid the price and millions of dollars in drugs were now off the streets.

In all my years as a banking BSA Officer, I'd never seen a victim of this kind ever recover any money. I'd yet to see the actual face of one of them, not even on an FBI or "Most Wanted" poster. I wanted nothing more than to change that so the good guys could score at least one in the endless game.

He knew he landed a low blow. He ignored his ringing phone. It was probably one of his buddies wanting to dish on our little spat. "You know this is FBI territory again, don't you? Why do you keep bringing federal stuff to me? It was tough getting those guys to help out last time," his eyes indicating he was remembering some past conversation. Then he looked at me with hardness still in his face. "Although they had no problem taking the lion's share of credit for the bust."

"If I can get this local guy, your financial crimes unit can take it and then connect it to the overseas activity. It does have value for you, AGAIN," I landed my own low blow back to him since he'd reaped plenty of rewards for my assistance last time.

"Please be a friend instead of a cop right now, okay? All I want to know is if the police know anything about this Tony guy. I have his license plate number. He's probably been picked up for something before. And also, what about this Carlos guy? He sounded liked he had something to do with a scam too. I have a goldmine of information after just a few hours of trying. Cost me $2,500.00 bucks too. Can't you help me get to the next level?"

His demeanor changed after hearing my pleas. He softened his shoulders, relaxed his mouth and his eyes showed the concern that I knew was there behind his cop bravado.

"I can't do anything officially. You know that." As he spoke, I gave him my best wide eyed look, and he softened even more. "I'm meeting McKayla at the Apollo Grill at 6:30."

I was glad to see that his relationship with McKayla was blossoming, but didn't feel like sharing that I'd been officially seeing Alan now. Eckert was a fun date, but I knew that he and I never would've experienced love on the level Alan and I had already. Not in a million years of trying. I sure hoped he and McKayla could though, more for her sake than for his. She was too good of a person to deserve anything less.

He looked at the I.D.s some of the analysis and information I'd gathered from a review of the contents of Albert's computer, and a paper detailing as much information on Tony and Carlos that I knew so far.

"Show up during dinner and I'll give you what I can."

I kissed his cheek and gave him a big bear hug. "Thanks Stephen. Save me some Falafel if I'm late."

I wasn't late, and the effort was worth the results. Jackpot! I had two full files of documentation Eckert had copied for me. I had Tony's arrest record, driving record, and other information that would make his head spin if he knew anyone had on him. Tony's last name was Balogne, pronounced "ba-loan", but spelled in a manner that made me sing "Tony Baloney" over and over again as I dug deeper into the information.

Tony had been around the block a time or two before. He'd been busted for mail theft, breaking and entering, credit card fraud, embezzlement and evading arrest. All of this by his tender age of twenty-three, which had been easy to find in the arrest records and police reports included in the file. Even with these arrests, he was out on the street able to keep doing it. Justice in action. The criminals have all the rights, and the victims have none.

He had experience of his own when it came to assumed names. I found 4 aliases that he used on a regular basis, Anthony Cardon, William Everson, Chet Ford, and Antonio Carducci. I made a note to call Shelby in the morning to see if her bank had any of these names as customers. McKayla too, as she had access to the entire customer database of her bank since she was in loan servicing. Tony must have accounts at every bank in town to send wires, but most would be under disposable identities, so he might not use any of his "regular" aliases.

I chewed my lip as I thought of approaching Shelby on this. She'd been kept out of hot water the last time I got information from her. I'd had a hard time revealing how I'd found out as much as Sebastian and his gang that I did, but I'd never told anyone that Shelby had given me access to his information at the bank. Even though it was for a good purpose, it could have gotten her fired.

I had to hope she wouldn't think of me as just using her to get data and details again, but it was for a good purpose. I suddenly got an idea. Our mutual friend Heather was Shelby's assistant. She'd gotten very excited about Alex and my participating in the whole drug ring thing. I bet she'd be willing to help, and then I wouldn't have to put Shel on the spot.

Several police reports contained information in the "known associates" field. After reviewing a few of these I came across a name that piqued my interest. Carlos Montana. Could it be the Carlos that had called while I was in Tony's van?

I made another note to check the Secretary of State website to see if any of these names were connected to entities. This would be more sophisticated than I expected for Tony, but you never know the smarts someone might have when it came to ripping off another. Carlos was an unknown factor when it came to this equation, and he could be a mastermind for all I knew right now.

Heaven forbid criminals would use any smarts God gave them to benefit mankind somehow. I've never heard of a convict inventor. I had a flashback to my banking days because the crooks were always two steps ahead of the bankers. No matter what money laundering or terrorist financing detection methods that a market of expert professionals could devise, the crooks could bypass it. With those kinds of smarts, was it too much to ask for a cure to cancer?

I decided to get additional details from the first folder after I'd seen what the other one had. It contained information about Carlos Montana. My mouth fell open in surprise that a connection had been made between Carlos and Tony by Eckert, and that he'd taken the extra time to get me information on him as well. *Kudos Eckert*, I thought.

I started into the pile with gusto, when a noise coming from the bedroom brought my attention back to reality.

Night had fallen quickly, and the room was more dimly lit than I'd realized. Alex was out partying with some friends, and would be getting back later tonight. He'd said he could care less if Alan and I did it till the roof fell down as long as we kept to the bedroom. Alan was working on a friend's computer tonight, and wouldn't be in for a while.

I hit the light switch to brighten the room, and heard the sound again. It was a scratching or scraping noise of some sort. I wasn't frightened because coyotes were constantly running around behind the cottage. I could hit the back lights and they'd run off.

Before I reached the switch to light up the back of the cottage, I heard the back window sliding open, freezing me in my tracks. *Oh crap, coyotes couldn't do that.* Today's events replayed in my mind, and I wondered if I'd made some mistake that had tipped Tony off that I was not who I'd pretended to be.

Was I caught? Did Tony find out who I was? Had he followed me? Oh no, were June and Sam okay? How else could Tony know I was back here?

I grabbed a frying pan off of the stove and waited outside the bedroom door to catch the intruder with a smash to the head. I heard steps in the room, and then nothing. After a full minute, nothing happened and no more sounds emerged. I strained to listen for breathing, creaking, or anything that indicated life was in there.

The frying pan was held up high, and my arms got tired. I waited another minute, but still heard nothing. Maybe it was another fire bomb, or something like poisonous gas let into the house. Rusty wasn't inside to clue me in this time, and I wasn't waiting to find out.

I took a deep breath, and made a dash for the front door. I kept the keys to the golf cart in the ignition, and I prayed that they were there, because I could not run very fast in the frozen grass to get to the house. As I reached the door, a voice stopped me, my hand ready to yank it open.

"Sara, Where ya going?" came from the bedroom. I opened the door as memory started working. I knew that voice.

"Sara, it's Alan. Come here. I need you"

Closing the door, I stomped back to the bedroom and found Alan lying in my bed, naked; the sheets barely covered him and his tanned body delightfully contrasting with the lightly colored sheets.

"Surprise?" He weakly exclaimed, eyeing the frying pan in my hands as if he thought I'd still use it. "I'm sorry, I didn't mean to frighten you. I wanted to see you, so I told Mike I'd finish up tomorrow. Besides I thought you'd enjoy a warm body to sleep next to."

"Damn it Alan! You scared me." I started to feel angry that he could do something like this after today's events, but then I realized he knew nothing about them. In fact, he'd probably be mad at me when I told him what I'd been up to. I was so relieved it wasn't Tony or any of his associates that I let it go.

"I thought coyotes were out back at first. When that window opened, though, I just about wet my pants."

Alan laughed, probably relating to that moment of real fear and my weak yet personal description of it. He could tell I had relaxed, so he pulled down the sheets to invite me in. One look at that body made me forget both my fears and the exciting files of information on Carlos and Tony.

He forcefully patted the area in front of him on the bed, indicating that I should sit. "Come on now. No worries. This is Mom and Dad approved now. You could even say encouraged." He raised his eyebrows up and down in a cheesy come-on that made me laugh.

I reclined onto the bed and into his arms, kissing his lips with passion and feeling reckless abandon in my actions. He was warm, exquisite, and I wanted him to stay. I think he got the hint.

Always one to have the last word, he whispered into my ear, he said "You think too much." He reached above me, and I wondered what he was doing until his hand rested on my still extended arm.

"Can you put down the frying pan, please?" he managed to say as he nuzzled my neck. We both laughed as I realized I was still holding it. I threw it down and my normal caution to the wind as I got under the covers to enjoy a night that required no thinking at all.

 36

"Since I'm driving, where am I going?" I asked June, frustrated, as I started out of the driveway. I still didn't know which way to turn. She had kept me in the dark as to the day's events, but had made me reserve four hours for her. "North or South?"

"South," she answered in a flat tone, looking at her nails and still not giving out any information.

"Are you going to tell me what we're up to today? You're not usually so coy with me. Is it a secret rendezvous with a lover and I have to sit watch so Sam won't come and murder him?"

June laughed in a sing song manner, her sweet voice sounding like a bell. "Sara, you're not that mistrusting," She squeezed my shoulder. "We're doing something for YOU today. If I'd told you about it beforehand, you'd have found a reason not to go. You're going whether you like it or not!"

"So it could be medieval water torture, maybe a root canal? What's your pleasure?" I knew it would be no such thing, but what in the world did she have in mind? It had to be something I hated or she would have told me.

'We're getting that mess," she said, emphatically pointing to my now not-quite- so bald spot, "fixed."

"Oh," I groaned, understanding her reluctance to tell me or I would have coughed up a reason not to go. I hated sitting still just to get a hair cut. It was an hour of being subjected to the insipid conversations of those I knew or cared nothing about. It was a waste of time, energy, and you had to pay for it too. A tip too, or you might get a hack job on your next visit. Hair salons, and beauty shops in general, were a necessary evil in my mind. "Why south then?"

"Because to get quality hair repair you need the best, so you're getting it. We're going to Nyona's Studio 395 in Minden. She's ready and waiting with the troops and all the bells and whistles. She'll fix you good as new."

Within the hour, I was sitting in Nyona's chair, explaining again to everyone what I had done to my hair in England. After the giggles and gests were over, Nyona was all business and ready to go to work.

"We're going to do a weft for this, June," Nyona announced. "She's lucky there's just enough growth that I can weave this in. Otherwise, we'd be in a position to glue, and more often than not, gluing destroys the original hair."

Both ladies fussed over me, tugging and pulling my hair, and talking amongst themselves. My chair was starting to turn a little faster and I was getting dizzy.

"I know I'm just a bystander," I spoke up, putting my feet on the floor to make the chair stop moving and then squirming around to get someone to look at me. "But I do like my original hair. I'd rather be stuck using mascara or even shoe polish to cover the skin tone than losing the hair that grows in." I looked back and forth between them, a serious look in my eyes. "I hope my opinion counts here too."

Nyona gently slapped me on the knee, and June let go of my hair. "Oh, silly girl, of course it does. June just has more experience with, well, hair accidents," she stammered, "so I'm running it by her for a second opinion."

I raised an eyebrow at June, who shrugged, and gave a secretive grin that indicated she'd tell me later. What a relief to know I was not the only one who had perpetually bad hair days, but June? Guess I'd have to wait to find out what stories she'd been hiding.

'Since we're only anticipating needing this for a short period of time, I went with a machine sewn weft. They're not as fine in quality, but they're ten times less spendy."

I nodded my appreciation, having no idea how much money I was spending here already.

Nyona held up the weft to my head. "Looks like I did well in choosing the color too. It was hard based on the photo you sent. Whatcha think?"

June took the weft, a little wedge looking thing of hair, and held it all around my head. "Good," she confirmed. "No need to dye the hair, unless you want highlights Sara?"

"I shook my head. "No thanks. It's hard enough to get me to sit still long enough for a cut. I told you upkeep's a deal killer, June."

"Oh, fine then," she put her hands up in mock defeat. "That's why I love you, Sara. You're so low maintenance, yet you still look just lovely. You make the rest of us look like pampered babies though. Heaven forbid, I want a manicure and a pedicure."

I didn't bother to respond. Let her have her fun picking on my beauty shop aversions. I didn't mind taking her at all, but I hated to have to sit that long and get pawed over. I'd rather go to the dentist.

Nyona brought it back to business. "I'll get this in, and then we'll layer," she stated, monotone, like it was no big deal, then looked at me, big blond hair, great smile and earrings a bobbin'. "Sound good, sugar?"

I gulped. I hadn't had a lot of layers for years. They were such a pain to grow out. Still, I was the idiot that had burned off my hair and I was tired of being a public spectacle of sorts. The missing hair had at least given people a reason to stop looking at my boobs to compare with the on-going public favorite video hit on YouTube, but hair stares were old news too. Glances of pity or amusement had followed my arrival anywhere I went even after my two weeks abroad.

I reluctantly nodded my approval for the layers. June bent down and gave me a kiss on the check. "Good sport. You'll look great darling." Since I was settled, she sauntered off, walking like she hadn't ever used a cane. In a tone of false smugness, she said, "Now that you're off my hands, a massage, manicure and pedicure for me. Oh for the luxuries we pampered types love so much."

"Trade ya?" I whined pathetically, but June knew how much I hated even getting a haircut, and this was like major hair surgery.

"Too late now. Suck it up, Sara. Do it for Alan. You'll come through just fine, and he'll appreciate it," June said, her voice trailing behind her as she was off for the bliss of a massage.

Nyona spun the chair back to face me to the mirror. "You're all mine now," she said then gave her best high pitched, false cackle. June had definitely clued her in on how much I hated this. I'm surprised she did. Hairstylists might not try to hard if they weren't going to get repeat business out of it.

Two hours later, I had to admit I looked pretty darn good. According to the rundown Nyona had given me during the process, I'd had a single track weft sewn onto a single braid made from the hair left on and around the burned spot. She then trimmed my hair so the hair would blend in well with mine.

I have to admit she'd done such a good job, I couldn't even tell I had fake hair mixed in with my own. Any the style was, well, stylish. I knew Shelby would approve. I felt pretty again, and I could give up trying to cover it everyday.

Nyona had provided strict instructions on how to brush, wash and moisturize the hair. I was to come back in six weeks to have it removed and see if I had enough hair to make the style work without the weft.

June was gathering her things, all done with her "luxuries". I whipped out my checkbook, ready to hear the horrific details. Nyona quietly pushed her hand onto mine so that my checkbook went back into my purse. "This is taken care of sweetie," she said quietly. As I turned to protest to June, Nyona continued, "June told me to tell you it's covered by your employment contract's standard hazard pay coverage, whatever that

is. I'm glad I don't have your job if you need that!"
	She laughed and swept up the mounds of hair on the floor.

37

I dialed Tony's number, hoping he didn't have some sort of GPS system that would tell him I was calling from across the street of his own house. .

"Wish me luck!" I commented to Alex, holding up crossed fingers. Tonight's excursion had been his idea, and with Alan out to finish his friend's computer, I was free to act as stupidly as I would have before I'd have him to prevent me from attempting stunts like this one.

"Wishes of luck," replied Alex.

The phone rang. Tony answered on the third ring.

"Yo, Tony here."

"Hey Tony," I breathed heavily into the phone, trying to sound sexy while maintaining my New York styled accent. ""It's Steph."

Alex stuck his finger down his throat, a reaction to the first he'd heard of my voice as my alter-ego Stephanie. I nearly laughed, but forced myself to concentrate on keeping the nasal sound in my voice.

"Hey Stephanie!" Tony answered, his voice making an upbeat intonation. "Are you making good on your promise? Let's hook up tonight."

"Why that's just why I'm calling. Kristina's coming into town to see me in a bit,' I said, having to make a meeting as appealing as possible.

"And me too I hope," he said brightly, and then was gruffer. "You're not jerkin' me around now, are ya Steph?"

"Course not. I got a room at the Nugget for us. Room 1327," I said, reading off the key number. "There's a key waiting under your name. Kristen should be here any minute, so we'll be seeing you in an hour or so I haven't seen her for a while, so tonight should be something extra special for us both."

I paused for effect, and Tony remained silent on the other end.

"Make sure to get cozy in the hot tub before we get there. We like lots of bubbles," I said with a girlish giggle. 'Order some champagne on the room charge too. I think you'll like to watch how we drink it."

"Rock on," Tony exclaimed enthusiastically, his defenses back down and his manly instincts turned up to full blast. 'See you soon then. Out."

Alex squealed when I got off the phone. "Oh, you were so good. Convinced me. I thought I was the actor of the bunch. I should get you a part on the show."

After my own distaste at the visions I had just created for another, memories of the red carpet flashed through my mind and displaced them.

"No thanks, I've had my fill of tinsel town. It's all you, Alex."

Within ten minutes of our call, Tony opened the garage door. He opened the van's side door and went in. He must have retrieved something, because he shut the door a few seconds later.

To our delight, the garage door started to close, and Tony came out, ducking underneath it. He looked like he'd cleaned up, changed clothes, and maybe even showered for the occasion.

We stifled giggles, ducking down so he wouldn't see us. I felt like a high school kid, about to prank a friend.

We heard the squelch of a car alarm being turned off. Tony got into a nice silver Ford-350 and took off down the road.

"Can you believe it worked?" I asked in amazement. And what luck that he left the van at home. I told you, you're my good luck charm!"

"Yes I am," Alex said, bobbing in his head with confidence. "Here's to a major score tonight." He held up a fist, and I bumped mine to his.

We tried the sliding back door first. It was locked, as were the windows surrounding it.

"Look," I called to Alex. It 'd been so dark, we hadn't seen a small door built right into the back of the garage. It was locked too, but there was a huge opening that must have been a dog door.

Simultaneously we scanned the yard for a dog. I imagined that Tony would have some ferocious pit bull trained to attack intruders, and the thought had both terrified and electrified me.

Seeing none, and being neither pounced on nor attacked, we looked more closely for signs that a dog might live at the house.

"No poop," I whispered, after I'd visually scanned the yard.

'What?" Alex retorted, obviously clueless as to the relevance of my statement.

"No dog poop," I said, "So no dog. Even the cleanest house in the world would have some signs of a dog and this isn't the swankiest place in town. Let's go. You first."

Alex easily ducked through the opening. I followed as soon as he indicated all was well inside.

We didn't want to risk turning on an overhead light, so we brought out our flashlights. A regular, everyday average Joe garage met our lights at every angle. There were tools, some boxes holding odds and ends, and a refrigerator. Then, of course, the van itself, probably the mother load of information we needed to officially place Tony in a position to pay for his part in these scams.

Tony had alarmed the car on the street. Had he done the same to the van? Alex and I nodded, knowing we'd be ready to run if an alarm sounded. I tried the back door of the van, and it opened. No alarm followed.

"Yes! Can you hold the light for me?"

I entered the back of the van and was right behind Tony's desk. I sat in his chair, taking note not to roll backwards or meet with pavement. The desk was strangely in immaculate order. Pens and typical desk supplies were in the pull out drawer in the middle of the desk. The drawer to the top right of the desk contained boxes of checks, and I mean boxes as in, *thirty* boxes.

I booted up the computer so it'd be ready when I was. I hoped it wouldn't be a noisy process, as you never knew with computer these days.

Working quickly, I opened my backpack and sat it on the floor. I then opened each box and took the bottom checkbook. I put them back in the same exact order, even though it added a few minutes to the time I intended to stay in the van.

The next drawer contained files of bank statements. There were rows of hanging file folders neatly arranged in the drawer. Each folder had a numbered tab, and each contained bank statements neatly arranged. It was odd.

"Alex," I loudly whispered.

"Yeah," he said. "Everything okay?"

"It's going great. I'm finding some good stuff in here. Remind me of something later though."

"And what reminder would that be?" he asked, trying to hold the light steady to follow my fingers on the files.

"Remind me to hire this guy as an office assistant when he gets out of jail. He is the neatest record keeper I've ever seen."

"You got it," Alex replied sarcastically. "I'll put a reminder on my cell phone for ten years from now."

I giggled, furiously pulling the back page from each statement copy, which were each so neatly stapled together. The back page seemed to contain enough information to identify each account by number, accountholder, the bank and bank's address, and a short summary of activity.

I finished, making sure to place each statement back in the drawer with no edges peeking up or looking askew or out of place in anyway.

In the left drawer of the desk, I found wire records, by date. I knew we shouldn't stay long. Should I try to copy some on the copier, or just take some and hope Tony didn't notice, at least for a while?

I checked the records for the two week period I thought would contain anything to do with Simons. To my great pleasure, I found that the files were small for this period. I found three separate documents referencing Simon's name on them, so I took them all. I grabbed a few other assorted papers from this drawer before concentrating on the computer.

Thanks to Alan's resourcefulness in London, I'd learned about the power of technology and remembered to bring a flash drive with me. Alan had said that a 12 gigabyte one should cover as much data any normal computer could hold.

"Over here, Alex," I directed, placing my hand where I wanted the light to be. I found the port thing where the flash drive went and clicked it into place.

I did an "explore" function to get right to the meat of what was on the computer. I copied the entire G, H and J drives, those that appeared to contain data files, and moved each over to the F drive that recognized my flash drive as being there. Each driver's folder file took several minutes to transfer.

'Hurry up, Sara. We'd better get out of here," Alex whispered to me. 'We've been here about thirty minutes."

We'd agreed ahead of time that thirty minutes was the maximum we should spend no matter what we found. I was in the middle of the last drive, when I got a message that my flash drive could hold no more data."

"Twelve gigabytes is more than you'd ever need Sara," I said in a mocking voice to imitate Alan's comments. I extracted the drive and powered down the computer, careful to remember to turn off the monitor.

"What?" asked Alex.

"Never mind. One more minute please." I directed him to place the light onto the large filing cabinet Tony had retrieved my identification elements from. I made a random grab for a few items, and then grabbed some mail from the middle of the mail stack he had in the van.

As I started to exit the van, I spotted a small cash box under the desk.

'Wait just a sec. Found something."

The box was locked, but had the key still in the lock. When I opened it, neatly stacked packets of cash greeted me. I did a mental count of the stacks. There was nearly a hundred thousand dollars here. I could easily take enough to cover Simons' loss and get my money back for buying the identification. Temptation ate me alive.

"Come on Sara, we really need to leave. Soon, please,"

I closed the lid, cutting off the visual piece of the temptation.

This wasn't the right way to do this. It might be my only chance to get his money back if the other information I'd gathered produced no alternative way. Hesitating, I pushed the box back into place. I couldn't do it. I felt like it was stealing. If I held back now, I could get the Feds on him and maybe who ever really owned that particular money could get theirs back too.

If I took the money, he might be tipped off that something was amiss. Getting Simons' money back any other way was more of a risk to me, but the real goal was to stop these guys from doing this. If Tony took off, there would be no one to catch and the risks would have been for nothing.

"Ok, let's scoot," I said, putting my hand out to Alex.

Alex helped me down from the van, and I moved Tony's chair back to its original position. We closed the van door as quietly as possible, ducked out the dog door, and made our way back to our car.

As we got in the car, we noticed a light on in the living room of the house.

"Was that there before?" I asked.

"No," confirmed Alex, starting up the car. As we pulled away from the curb, we saw the front door open, and a couple come out. They paused in the door frame, too deep in a kiss to notice anything around them. When they separated, it was obvious that they'd been there the entire time, but must have been otherwise engaged and were none the wiser to our presence.

As we made it to the next block, we burst out laughing at how close we'd come to getting caught. I stopped for a minute to catch my breath and allow my heart to resume beating at a normal pace.

"Just one last thing," I said, and dialed my cell.

"Steph, babe where are you?" Tony answered the phone obviously recognizing my number. I could hear the hot tub whirring in the background.

"I got bubbles going in here for you. 'I'm getting impatient."

"Kristina's had an accident on the 80. I'm on my way to get her.," I lied while maintained my accent.

"Damn it, I knew it. Don't screw with me Stephanie. You don't want to mess with me and my friends," he practically shouted through the phone.

"Calm down, Tony. Gees, you didn't even ask if she was okay. We've got the room for the night. Can't you wait for us?"

He seemed placated. "Alright, I'll wait two more hours, tops. I'm going to the movie theater across the street. If you're not here when I get back, I'm outta here and you owe me big."

"I'll do my best to get us there in time Tony. Kristina's looking forward to meeting you. She wasn't hurt, so we should be there unless there's some hold-up with the cops. If we miss you tonight, I'll bring her by tomorrow afternoon. Where you gonna be?"

"Dunno yet, but get here tonight, got it?"

"Got it," I said as he ended the call. I'd have to hunt him down tomorrow or call with a good enough story to get him to come to me. I'd have to set the trap carefully. I'd have to be very thorough to pull this off without putting myself in harm's way.

38

My printer whirred from continual printing of the information Alex and I had scored from Tony's computer. I was surprised that for such a computer whiz, Tony hadn't password protected or encrypted anything. I had anticipated needing Alan to help break into to any useful files, but I'd been able to manage on my own.

Alan came in and saw Alex and I knee deep in paperwork and didn't ask. He said he'd been playing basketball with guys before he'd finished Mike's computer and was wiped out. He kissed me goodnight and said he'd be asleep until his services were needed. He could tell by my look that I was not going to be easily distracted for a while.

I was too excited to think of much else, even Alan's luscious body. I'd been able to create a clear trail of information from Tony's records. His computer storage was as neat as his paper system. This had made for an easier task than I'd anticipated. It was too good to be true, and I hoped that there was not something here that could backfire.

Alex had helped by sorting stacks for different accounts and banks for me, and had finally fallen asleep on the couch for some well deserved rest. We had more than enough information to put Tony away for a long time, and maybe enough to get Carlos as well. There were documents evidencing transfers from certain accounts to others that could be linked to Carlos. As intricate as this web was, its spiral still reached down to name the responsible parties.

We'd identified several other colleagues in this financial web, including Alfred, our English friend who'd escaped legal repercussions from his actions while we'd ransacked his place.

I'd identified more than one hundred fifty different bank accounts held under various names from Reno to Sacramento. After hours of tracing activity, I could determine that some accounts were used for the receipt of money that was sent by victims. I called these "first tier" accounts. These were "throw away" accounts, or ones that would not be used more than a few times before the bank would get wise, and then other new accounts would be opened to replace them.

When funds were received, they were immediately moved out of these accounts, some to a second tier of accounts, and some to accounts I could not identify as being connected to or owned by Tony. Some funds were wired to other banks, even those in other countries, so were probably shared proceeds for others involved in this huge network web, like Alfred in England

The second tier of accounts held a cut of funds. Some money from the first tier accounts came to these, and other deposits were wired in from outside sources. These outside funds were probably Tony's profits from elsewhere in the network. These accounts were also kept at near zero balances. All funds were taken out in cash or through the purchase of smaller monetary instruments to avoid potential detection and reporting as illicit activity.

A third tier of accounts received the bulk of its funds in cash. One account had a lot of funds in it, and a historical review showed a monthly wire to the Cayman Islands, a banking safe haven country. It was a modern day Swiss bank account, money one could hold and be completely unaccountable for.

Each monthly wire exceeded $100,000.00 and was sent to an account for International Funding Inc. Normally, the ownership of this business would be virtually untraceable. It was a foreign entity also set up in safe haven countries to protect the owners of these accounts from being exposed as owning funds and having to account for the sources of the money they held.

Since Tony meticulously kept every document, the actual bank wire form he sent to the bank to request these transactions showed the name "Carlos Montana" on a memo line. Who would have thought that attention to detail could lead to one's downfall, and provide the very information needed for the Feds to finally haul in Mr. Montana.

Several of the second tier accounts matched names Alan and I had gotten from Alfred's contact list when we'd taken his hard drive data. In a matter of minutes, I was able to identify which of Tony's accounts had been credited with a wire that I could trace as being his cut of Simons' money. The date and amount matched what Alfred had told us, and what we'd found in his records, which by the way were no match to the neat records Tony kept. The entry was for $42,000.00, which meant Alfred had gotten a cut of nearly $8,000.00. I'll bet Mum didn't know just how much her precious boy actually had in his bank accounts, and that he could have kept in her queenly accommodations compared to her little, run down place. He certainly could have afforded to live on his own.

The account that Simon's money had gone into had a pretty sizable balance in it. Although I could not stoop to taking cash from Tony's van, I had no qualms about dipping into the account to get Simon's money back. Mine too, for that matter, as I'd dropped $2, 500.00

on the fraudulent identification items I'd bought from him.

I went through the stack of checkbooks I had taken from Tony's drawer during the van raid. Once again, Lady Luck was smiling on me, as there just happened to be a checkbook for that account.

I had originally thought about initiating a wire from Tony's bank to mine, but that would leave a trail I didn't want found. I didn't want to explain how Simons' got his money back. Instead, I'd simply walk into a local branch of the bank, fortunately a nationwide institution, and present a check made out to one of the names Tony had sold me. I had primary and secondary identification he'd provided, so I could satisfactorily prove to the bank that I was the payee on the check under the false name. Of course I'd later turn in all the identification items I'd bought from Tony so that the people whose identities he'd stolen would not be harmed.

The satisfaction of reclaiming the money using the identification he'd provided for me was just too good for words. I'd need to get some help in forging the signature he used in signing the account, which was entitled "Anthony Carbato".

I'd bring Eckert in as soon as possible, and tell him as little as I could get away with so he wouldn't be obligated to pass on information on my own illicit activities. I had to become a crook to catch a crook. It gave me perspective in how hard it was to fight this kind of crime when the rules stacked the odds against the good guys.

I put the mounds of paperwork in order and decided to call it a night. Tomorrow I'd cash the check, give Eckert the analysis of the data from Tony's computer and ask him to find a reason to pull over the van and bust Tony. I hoped that the plan would work. Best case scenario, Simons gets his money back tomorrow and Tony gets taken down. Worst case scenario, I get busted at the bank for I.D. fraud and Tony hunts me down and kills me. How's that for options?

39

If a teller were a police officer, I would've been busted. I'd managed to keep my face even, as if cashing a check for $54,269.00 was no big deal. I had dressed up as Stephanie again so my picture would match my id. I had to remember that I was Karen Bosley while I was in the bank, as I'd brought these identification items with me today to pull this off.

Alan hadn't even asked where I was going when he saw me tease my hair into a pile, get upset when the new hair weft wouldn't cooperate, or put on the most tacky and tight clothing I could find. I think he knew I'd been up to something with Alex, and that he knew further not to ask about it until I was ready to tell him. I was pleased that he was so right, and that he could not be named as an accomplice if I got caught.

The teller, who looked all of 16 years old, couldn't cash a check that large without the approval of a manager, and went trotting to an office somewhere behind the bank's long teller line. I stifled a giggle that she knew from her bank training that this was not an ordinary transaction, and she did just what she should have. *Good girl*, I thought, proud of her for doing the right thing. *As long as I don't give myself away and they contact the police!* my negative voice thought into my head.

The branch manager came out of her office to ask if the bank could send a wire some where for me. She was petite, in a professional looking suit and super spiky heels and had a tousle of black curly hair. She introduced herself as Michele, and showed the kind of concern that she should have as a pretense in finding out why in the world I'd be asking for that kind of cash.

I had several options in how to handle it. I could be obstinate, which would likely raise their suspicions of the origin of the transaction. Heck, they might even call Tony to verify the check if I did that. I could have told a number of stories, but I wanted it to be a believable one that made sense why I needed cash. Fortunately, I'd had Alex include a memo on the check when he'd "re-created" the signature, and it indicated it was for the purchase of a 2009 Hummer.

"Tried to sign this over to the casino, but they wanted cash. They wouldn't even take a cashier's check, even though my boyfriend's been such a good customer there.   His marker got called at the Peppermill," I said as realistically as possible. "His Superbowl bets went awry for him, and they aren't letting him wait any longer to pay it off. He sent me over to cash the check since they wouldn't take it.   They sent a casino employee, a goon really, to be my security for carrying so much cash.   I wonder if they'd break his fingers if he didn't pay, just like the movies."

The teller's face fell in horror, "Oh, I'm just kidding darlin'," I said in my bad New York accent. "He just went over his limit and I think the casino took a bath on the Saint's win. They were the long shot, you know."

I scanned their faces, trying to read them. It was a very believable reason, as we lived in Reno where gambling was legal and the Superbowl betting had been all over the board. I'd only learned about markers while I worked at the bank, so I'm sure Michele knew what it was. Casinos sometimes extend a little credit to their better customers, but they can be called when you're in the red.

"I'm so mad at my boyfriend. He's a professional gambler on a bad streak. I had to sell Anthony my brand new Hummer just to get the money. Gary, my boyfriend, just bought it for me a few months ago too," I said not acting mad at all, but more like a spoiled child who'd had to give back a coveted toy.

They seemed comfortable with the story and by my comfort level with me and the situation, so I kept going.

"Anthony'd been eyeing the car since I got it, so I'll just have to wait until Gary's back in the green again to get another one.   Anthony's been doing very well lately; so good he could probably afford a new one. Too stingy to pay the price for new though. Heck, he's too cheap to even pay the full $55,000.00 we'd agreed on.   He was whining about the taxes he'd have to pay at the DMV on a private sale.   Oh well, he's my cousin so it's all in the family anyway. My loss is his gain, and Gary will be out of hot water.   It's a small price to pay for my man," I shrugged as if it were nothing.

Michele watched as the teller counted out the money to me. She'd had to go to the vault to get the amount.   It took five minutes to count it all for me, then the teller placed it all in a nice packet so that it was secure and not obviously a big mound of money.

I placed the envelope with the money into my purse. 'I really appreciate your concern for my safety Michele. I said shaking her hand, and trying to keep up my Stephanie look and mannerisms through my longer than anticipated explanation.

"I'd be jumpy carrying this kind of cash if I didn't have that goon out there." I walked to the bank's glass doors and pointed to my car. I waved at Alex, and he waved back, visible through the window. Michele seemed satisfied and thanked me for coming in, holding the door open for me.

I couldn't resist one more comment. 'Be sure to ask Anthony about his new ride when he comes in next. It's a real sweet piece."

40

I didn't want to take the chance of calling Tony again in case he'd somehow found out I'd broken into his van. He was such a neat freak; I had to have made at least one mistake that he'd pick up on when he went through his van. .

I had Simons' money and I wanted to get rid of it first. We stopped off at the station and tracked him down. He'd aged in the days since I'd last seen him. His normally punchy, egotistical self was deflated by his being duped and his return to the workforce after it happened. I'd have to venture that he'd been smart enough not to tell anyone off before he'd "retired" or he might not be back to work at all.

He looked up when I stopped at his desk, and did not look hopeful as he stood up to greet me. Actually he was as colorless when I gave him the money as he'd been when I told him he'd been taken.

"What the?" was all he could manage, then he sat back down behind his desk and counted the bills in the envelope I'd given him. He got sidetracked for a moment, and stared at me up and down slowly, and I remembered I was in my cheap Stephanie attire.

"Don't ask," I stated as he kept counting.

'How'd you?" he started, but I cut him off.

"I had some luck in finding the guy you sent funds to in England, and he gave me information that led me to someone back here."

Alex had gotten uncomfortable with the conversation, and headed back out to the lobby.

"You don't need to know any details, but just know that I was able to track and trace this money directly from you through the food chain of these scammers. This is your money. Go pay off your loan and be happy that some form of justice was served."

"I don't know what to say. The cop in me wants to know more, and revenge too, but the part of me that was dumb enough to fall for this is just so grateful I've been made whole again. I don't know if I should grill you or just say I owe you one."

"I'll opt for the favor, as I may need it if Eckert doesn't help me out with this next phase of my plan."

Simons chortled, "He'll be so shocked I got my money back. I'll bet he won't let this rest, Sara. I know he'll be grilling you about it for sure. You are aware of how strongly he feels about citizens taking the law into their own hands, even if it is to serve a higher purpose. He was super pissed when you broke into that building, even after he got promoted for assisting with the bust."

"Well, he can have a turn with me later if he really wants details, but for now I just hope I don't need rescuing again. I want to take the next steps without putting myself in harm's way if I can. That will lessen the chances of invoking his anger, at least a little bit anyway."

Fortunately Simons didn't ask more questions, and I knew he didn't offer to help or dissuade me because of his own potential connection to the events. The less he knew, the safer he was. I confirmed Eckert was on duty before I got Alex and left. He wasn't at headquarters, so I would have to call him to find out what he was doing for the day.

I had a feeling I'd be needing Eckert later if we found Tony's van and had to confront him, or that maybe we could get Eckert to pull him over for some infraction and just happen to find the stacks of stolen mail and call the Feds on him.

Alex and I got frustrated after two solid hours of looking for Tony's location that day. I was starting to wonder if he were in Sacramento or some other location. That would ruin my plans, and I was ready to be done with this. I'd made good on my promise to get Simons' money back, but I just couldn't let Tony continue his business. If we could get Carlos Montana implicated as well, a whole scam ring might collapse. Even considering the best case scenario, it saddened me to know there were many others ready to take over whatever territory got rescued.

Alex was asking for a lunch break and a pit stop at the same time I realized my car was almost on empty. After glancing at the gas gauge, I searched for a gas station and instead saw the familiar van parked in the back area of a complete dive of a bar.

I screeched to a halt, fortunately with no traffic behind me to smash in the rear end of my car.

"Sara!" Alex exclaimed, apparently mortified by my juvenile reaction. "First of all, do you even know how to drive? Then, can you just draw a little more attention to us out here? Screeching wheels might take the covert efforts out of this surveillance."

"Sorry!" I said, realizing what a stupid thing I'd done, and grateful that no movement near the van was apparent. "I'm pulling into the gas station down the way. Please fill it for me and stay there. I'm going to get a closer look and see if Tony is in the van or the bar."

"I want to go with you!" Alex insisted.

"Well," I thought through this. You can come back and pull into the bar. Tony won't recognize this car. I'll signal you somehow from wherever I find some cover, but you'll have to go into the bar. I'll call you when you've been in there for a few minutes."

Alex pouted. "Ok. Be careful please. If something goes wrong, you could be zipped off in his van. I don't want kidnapping to become a regular occurrence for you. I kinda promised Alan I'd look out for you today. I think he knows we're up to something, but was wise enough not to ask. Don't make me break that promise."

"I won't. Is your cell on? I'm switching mine to vibrate mode." We pulled into the station. I gave Alex my ATM card. I looked him in the eye.

Alex nodded and starting pumping gas while I called Eckert to give him a heads up that I'd be needing him soon. I went over the evidence I'd obtained so far, but left out the part about cashing and forging a stolen check and giving Simons his money back. I had a hard time hearing him, as acid rock music blasted in the background.

"I'm at Recycled Records with McKayla," he explained. "Can't you do this later?"

"Well, bring her along," I shrilled at him, ticked off that he'd drag his feet after I'd placed a golden opportunity in his lap. "I've laid out a huge bust for you, and I want it over with before these guys figure out who I am. Come now. Please?"

"Your evidence was obtained by means that are less than legal. I doubt I can use it. Besides, Paul and Eric found a bunch of rare records for us, and we're listening to them. There's a whole stack here. They spent a lot of time getting these for us, and McKayla even took the day off to spend this afternoon with me, you know."

Paul was the owner of the Recycled Records store, which had recently moved to a new location. It was the only real used records, movie and cd place in town, and the guys that worked there, like Eric, had been with Paul forever. They could find about any media item you wanted, even rare and out of print stuff. Even better, they helped you find new music based on what you liked. There wasn't a style of music they didn't know. It was a favorite place of mine because they never laughed at what I asked for, not even during my Spice Girls phase.

"Well, maybe I can arrange to have copies found in Tony's van when you pull it over. Then the evidence would be found, well, more ethically."

"Why am I going to pull it over? You said it's always parked. I can't get him for not having his seatbelt on if it's not moving. I'll have no grounds to even approach him unless he's illegally parked or something.

The lights went on. "His windows!" I exclaimed, practically doing a dance to match the enthusiasm I felt.

"Windows?"

"They're practically black, and have to be tinted at least beyond what is legal in the city. You can ticket him for that, and just happen to stumble on the rest."

"And just how will "the rest" get there?"

"Don't worry about that; just be ready when I call. Please promise you'll come when I call, but in no case less than twenty minutes because he's here now. I'm trying to keep my nose out of more trouble, but I'll probably stumble into it if you're not here soon."

"Now that, I believe. Hold on a sec; What?" he asked someone on his end, probably McKayla. I could hear her telling him he'd be there for me. When he got back on the line, he said, "Okay, looks like I'm coming when you call or in twenty minutes, whichever comes first."

"Thanks," I said as we disconnected, and I left Alex still pumping gas as I walked across the non-busy intersection to make my way to the bar. I hoped with everything I had that there would be somewhere for me to stay out of sight while I figured out if Tony was actually there. He'd better be since I'd just told Eckert he was.

I'd swapped out the Stephanie slutty heels for some tennis shoes, and the short skirt for jeans, but I still had the big hair and overdone make-up job.

"Good luck," Alex whispered as he watched me cross the street. I gave him a thumbs up as I walked down to the bar, finally finding a solid wall to hide behind while I checked out the whole parking lot.

I scanned the outside wall of the bar, trying to look like I was digging through my purse. When I got to the back of the building, I found a trash enclosure next to the van. I opened the gate and quickly shut it closed, grateful for the plastic green slats that were woven through the chain link fence of the enclosure.

The smell was horrendous, and I was pretty certain that a few folks had used this area for a urinal. I cringed at the odor and the thoughts of what might have caused them and wrinkled up my nose, but quickly got in a position where I could watch the van. As I waited, I pulled out my hand sanitizer and put some under my nose and on my hands with the hope of masking the putrid odors. Why were my escapades always connected somehow with trash bins?

I was motionless for four or five minutes. A bum appeared in the parking lot and started to walk back towards either the van or the trash bin. Crap! I didn't want to have to explain my presence if this was his personal toilet.

Fortunately, he knocked on the door of the van, and the side door opened up. I got a glimpse of Tony's head as the bum came into the van. After a mere second, Tony reappeared outside of the van, pushing the bum out in front of him.

"Do you ever shower or change clothes, Maitland?" Tony muttered in disgust. He was holding his nose, "You smell like a sewer. You promised you'd clean up after your last drop off."

"Sorry," said Maitland. "I spent my money too fast."

"Well, never mind, stay out of my van though. Just show me what you have."

Maitland gave Tony a dirty brown grocery bag full of mail. I assumed by the way Tony went through it that Maitland was one the guys Tony used for stealing items from mailboxes.

His review of the bag's contents took less than two minutes. He kept 20 pieces of mail out of the 100 that must have been in the bag.

Tony re-entered the van, then came back out and shoved some bills in the man's hand.

"Is that all?" the man complained, counting the bills in his hand.

"I told you a hundred times what I'm looking for. I hate going through my own junk mail, much less someone else's."

"Man, it's hard enough just to empty the boxes and not get caught; I just take everything."

"Well weed it out before you bring it to me," Tony looked at the man, his disgust turning somewhat to empathy. "Here," he said and handed the man another bill.

"Thanks, man. I'll see what I can come up with by next week. I'll call from a different pay phone just like you said."

The man started to run off, and Tony yelled after him, "Stay smart, Maitland." His cell phone rang at that moment, and I saw Alex pull into a parking space by the bar. I wanted to hear the conversation, but somehow let Alex know where I was.

Tony lit up a cigarette as he talked, and turned away from the trash bin. For such a neat freak, I wondered how he dealt with the horrid smell emanating from the place. While he was turned away, I opened the gate of the enclosure and made eye contact with Alex. He made a point not to stare at me, as Tony kept moving around.

I motioned for Alex to call Eckert. Alex and I had agreed in the car that we'd ask Eckert to pull him over for his windows being tinted too dark for city regulations. For some reason, Alex seemed to get a better response out of Eckert than I did, so he would make the call and tell him whatever details he needed to get him to come by.

Alex nodded in assent, and entered the bar. I picked up right away that Tony was talking to Carlos. His tone was defensive, and I knew something had gone wrong. Could they tell I'd cashed that check already? I kept straining to hear, impeded by a huge cement truck that chose that opportunity to drive by.

"It's a flash drive cap, Carlos," Tony explained, obviously cut off by the other speaker.

"No, I don't know. I'm looking through everything now to see if anything's missing." He turned again, pulling at his hair, probably enduring quite a grilling from Carlos.

"Yes, it means my computer got hacked but I have no idea what information was taken. I told you already, I have nothing in there that connects us," he lied,

"I'm at the 4th Street location," he said. He finally ended the call with a dejected, "Yeah, I'll be here."

"Damn it!" he yelled, then jumped into the van, slamming the side door.

A moment later, my cell vibrated. It was Alex, who was watching from the kitchen window in the back.

"What's going on?" he asked.

"I think Carlos is coming here. Did you call Eckert?"

"Yes he said he'd be here in ten minutes."

"Thank God. Just stay there. What did you do to get in the kitchen?" I asked as I spotted his beautiful face through the grimy window.

"The bus boys recognized me and I'm chatting with them. I told 'em I was spying on you, and they loved it. I think we can get five guys out there if anything goes wrong."

I shook my head, "No, don't think that way. I'm waiting here for Eckert."

"K, out."

I snapped my phone shut, and was surprised to see a huge Hummer pull into the lot and park near Tony's van. Two huge men got out of the front, and one held open the back door and a suave looking Hispanic man came out.

He had a nice crew cut, and was dressed like someone right out of an ad for Harvard University. He had a button down shirt, nice slacks, a sweater wrapped around his shoulders and loafers. He couldn't have been more than my age, and definitely less than thirty-five. He pushed up his sunglasses from his eyes and nodded to his men with the authority of someone used to having their orders followed to the letter. Crap – Carlos was here already!

41

Tony came out of the van, apparently as surprised as I was at the speed of Carlos' arrival. He actually stammered a greeting, obviously intimidated by the muscular goons flanking Carlos. I was too, even though I was safely hiding out of sight. They didn't look like nice folks at all.

"Hey, Carlos," Tony said in greeting, and nodded to the other men. They remained quiet, their arms folded and jaws squarely set, just staring at him. I could have sworn at least one of them used to fight in the WWE, and both had their hair shaved to the scalp, ears pierced and looked every inch the part they were playing in this game.

Carlos didn't greet Tony. He walked up to him, and at full height was not much taller than the frightened man. I felt even worse for Tony when Carlos cocked his arm back and sank his fist into Tony's face.

Carlos adjusted his sweater, which had fallen from his shoulders during the movement, and seemed disgusted when Tony cried out in pain.

"I shoulda made you knock off this ridiculous side business ages ago. It's peanuts compared to what you get in cuts from me. You work for me, you punk."

Tony, who had only reeled back slightly from the blow, held a hand to his face and nodded in agreement. Blood dripped from his nose and stained the front of his shirt.

"We're confiscating your van 'cause I'm having my guy take apart your computer. I want to know what exposure I have, thanks to you getting your system hacked," he said in a harsh tone that was meant to come across as such.

Carlos turned to look at his men, tapping his fingers to his mouth like he was thinking deeply.

"First we get news some of our overseas operators have been exposed. Cowards, they turned tail and ran." He turned back to face Tony. "The word is that you got fingered by one of them. You been entertaining any cops lately, or would you even be wise enough to know if you had?"

"I, I don't know what you mean. No cops have been sniffing around me," Tony stammered, his voice reaching to a low whisper.

"I'm not taking the chance. You've been a good man, but I shoulda kept you as my secretary, not a source. You're good with paperwork, but you can't read people. You're not tough enough for this game, and I'm not letting any little rat get me in hot water."

He looked to his biggest gorilla. "See what happens when I take risks boys? Gomez, take care of this for me."

Tony's face looked horror stricken as the man approached. What did "take care of" mean in Carlos' world? As Gomez started towards Tony, I stepped backwards and knocked over a beer bottle I'd somehow overlooked. It shattered, and all eyes and ears were suddenly searching for the source of the sound.

Gomez stopped in his tracks, and the other goon started walking towards the trash bin. How was I going to get out of this one?

"Someone's in there, Carlos," the man said with a sneer

"Get 'em out here then, Kagel," Carlos snapped, and motioned for Gomez to get back to Tony.

Kagel found me in a second. I didn't have time to jump into the bin, although it may not have helped me anyway. He flashed an evil grin full of white and silver teeth, then roughly grabbed, dragged and dropped me at Carlos' feet.

I got up and brushed myself off, still feeling the man's rough hands on me. I prayed that Alex was still watching from inside the bar, but hoped he had enough sense to call for help and stay inside. I felt Kagel's gun in his coat pocket when he grabbed me.

Tony somehow freed himself from Gomez when he saw me, excited enough to escape the muscle man's clutches. "I should have known it was you, you little bitch."

He charged at me in a fury of motion, but I stood my ground, not expecting his own fist to land a blow on my mouth. My knees buckled from the blow, and I tasted blood from the area of my mouth that was stinging.

Gomez caught Tony again by the collar of his shirt, and hustled him back to the van, this time throwing him in and standing in front of the door. I thought it was stupid, as Tony could have a weapon in the car, but I was probably no safer from Tony's wrath than from Carlos'.

. "Who is this?" Carlos demanded.

Kagel grabbed my purse and rummaged through it until he found my wallet. He dumped the rest of the contents on the ground and stepped on them.

Tony squeaked out, from behind Gomez's hulking figure.

"Her name is Stephanie. I sold her some I.D.s. She invited me to party last night, but never showed. She's the one that must have downloaded information from my computer. Probably followed me home or something. It has to be her!"

Carlos fingered my driver's license in his well manicured hand. "Says here your name is Sara Blake," he drawled then thrust the I.D. at Gomez, who put it in front of Tony. "Is it one of yours, T-man?"

Tony looked it over carefully and then shook his head.

"Was there a badge in there, Kagel?"

Kagel shook his head.

"Let's get out of here guys, something smells real bad here. I'm not letting this little slut get her fingers in my business." He grabbed me by the hair. "You'll tell me everything in no time," he breathed into my ear.

"Think so?" I asked with a smart tone, and got a back hand to the mouth for my efforts.

"Sure do, bitch. No one plays in my game without my express permission, and no one can ever connect me to it. No one alive, that is. I don't care what you pulled from Tony's computer, 'cause the cops haven't been able to pin me down yet. Ya know, I don't even think you're a cop. I can smell 'em, and I've taken out more than a few over the years. You'll be joining them, and your new friend here, at the bottom of Lake Tahoe. Soon, real soon."

My mouth stung, now readily pouring blood. Carlos looked around to ensure the parking lot was still visibly empty, and then landed a punch to my eye and nose area, practically incapacitating me with pain.

To Gomez he ordered, "Do him now, and put her in back with him."

I heard the van's door shut part way, a muffled scream and then a quiet shot. What blood wasn't dripping from my mouth and nose froze in my veins, and I tingled from my head to my toes as my stomach turned over. This was for real, and I was sure that Tony had been shot and presumed he was dead. Where was Eckert? Where was Alex? I was grateful he hadn't come out and offered himself as another body for Carlos to collect and toss in the lake, but we'd been here long enough for some help to arrive.

"Kagel, put her in and drive. Gomez," he said and Gomez re-opened the van's sliding door enough to hear his instructions, "keep her quiet until I get her home. Then we'll have a little chat." He finished his sentence and kicked me in the gut.

I hadn't the energy to get back up, so Kagel grabbed me and handed me to Gomez, who tried to get me in the van. I kept my arms locked on the sides of the door, trying to resist Gomez while Kagel took the wheel and started up the car.

My arms were weakening so that my grip on the van was precarious at best. Carlos gave me another hard kick on my backside. I fell to the ground, but fought even more against both of them in their efforts to get me inside. If I could just keep them from getting me into the van for another few seconds, maybe help would get here in time. As much as I wanted to, I didn't dare call out for Alex's help and get him a trip to Tahoe too. I had to keep faith that he'd escalated this to a 911 call.

Gomez pulled at my hair, and then karate chopped me in my elbows to get them to bend. I used my legs, wrapping them around the outside sections of the door as Carlos physically lifted me up to push me through the opening. I had just about given up the fight when a siren sounded behind us. *Thank God,* I thought.

Carlos dropped me, and ran for the Hummer. Kagel already had the van in gear, so Gomez made a last ditch effort to get me either in or out of the door's way. Now I was trying to prevent the door's closing, and Gomez slammed it hard onto my hand, which I felt crunch under the force.

Behind me, I could see flashing lights, and Kagel moved the van forward as Gomez made another attempt to close the side door. I was holding my broken hand out of the way, already throbbing in pain, as the door slammed. I tried to back away, but somehow my hair got caught in the door and became tightly held in it when it finally closed completely.

The van pulled away, dragging me with it. The cop cars were trying to corner the van and Carlos at the same time, preventing an easy exit from the lot. I was now a part of the van, moving forward with its slow but forceful momentum. I tried to free my hair with my good hand and had no luck. I'd be smashed in between cars in no time, as the van appeared to be making a move to get out of the lot through a back alley area.

A blur passed me, and suddenly I was pulled free from the door and thrown into an area away from the moving vehicles. I felt the ripping of hair from my scalp, and tried not to pass out from the pain. I heard an ear-splitting crash, and voices yelling words like "freeze" and "hands up".

I realized I was safely out of harm's way and relaxed. A pair of steady arms was holding me. My vision was hazy, clouded from the fear and pain that were already dimming. When I looked up, Eckert's concerned eyes met mine for the second before I passed out.

I came to moments later, as paramedics were inspecting my hand, face and head. An army of police cars in the lot now, and Carlos and his goons were being cuffed. Tony was being prepped for a trip to the hospital in an ambulance, the paramedics working on him in a frenzy that meant life or death was still pending.

Eckert was speaking to a few other cops who had apparently just arrived at the scene, and a crowd had gathered, held back by yet more uniformed cops. Cops cars and flashing lights were everywhere, and media personnel appeared on the scene concerned that another channel would scoop the story first.

"Is he?" I asked no one, since I was propped up on the side of the building by myself, as the sole paramedic still working on me went to his ambulance for something.   I spotted Alex, who was using his phone to record the event until I heard him curse. He saw me awake and ran over.

"Sara!" he exclaimed. "Sorry I left you there. Are you okay?"

I nodded. "I'm a mess again, huh?"

Alex stifled a laugh, and nodded. "I got most of the events on my video phone. I had another guy using his phone too.   That bastard will have a hard time evading charges with this evidence. I have him hitting you, the sounds of Tony getting shot, the..."

I interrupted and bluntly asked, "Is Tony dead, Alex?   I feel awful. If I hadn't meddled,"

Alex now cut me off. "He's still alive, Sara, and rather pissed off at Carlos and his goons. I think he'll be singing like a lark in no time." His eyes drifted to the scene.

"He made his bed, Sara, and chose to play a game with some dangerous folks. It's not your fault. Not at all."

Some of the media people caught sight of Alex and apparently recognized him. They hollered his name.

"I'm fine, Alex. Your frenzied, faithful fans await. The story of the soon to be TV detective fighting crime in real life should get you an Emmy nod before your show even starts. Go."

By the time my ambulance was ready to depart, Alex was in the midst of cameras and microphones. *Sure hope he leaves me out of it*, I thought as my ambulance zoomed off for yet another trip to the hospital.

42

Eckert dropped by the next morning. Alan opened the door, and the two exchanged less than warm glances of greeting. I wondered if Eckert would be able to tell that things had changed between Alan and me, but I didn't have to wonder long as Alan asserted his claim by taking my good hand to lead me to the living room and planting a kiss on me that told the room that it was more than just a friendly gesture.

June invited him into the living room and served coffee and pastries, which Eckert eagerly helped himself to, probably trying to avoid registering a reaction to Alan's display of male dominance. June settled me on the couch with a fuss, once again being the patient to her nurse. I should be paying her.

My night had been spent getting a hand cast, various cuts and abrasions cleaned, avoiding news media and having to explain to my mother what I'd been up to this time. My face was a mess. I had earned a cut and swollen lip, a blackened, puffy eye and bruises across my cheek and nose for my efforts. At least my nose hadn't been broken.

Alex, as I suspected, had made the story into national news, using his forays as an amateur detective of sorts into gossip fodder for his upcoming TV role. Unfortunately, he hadn't kept me out of it, although as he explained, it was because he had only played the role of sidekick to me and wanted me to have the credit for it. One person's logic is another man's chaos. I couldn't be mad at him. The media can pull anything out of you once they get at you. That was the very reason I was staying away. I'll let them speculate all they want.

"Well, Sara, I think you have a lot of explaining to do," Eckert started, then put down a pastry and wiped off his hand, "other than what Alex has told the world already, I mean. Maybe the less I know, the better."

He gave me the once over, and stopped at my now bald again spot. Alan glared at him, maintaining his claim on me and daring him to say anything about my damaged body. Somehow, he remained still, sitting quietly in the chair furthest from Eckert, arms folded and intently awaiting to hear what other news he'd brought.

Sam came in from the kitchen to hear the latest. He showed none of the patience that the rest of us had, and started in on Eckert.

"Well?" he demanded, grabbing a pastry. "Is she in trouble or a hero again?"

Eckert shook his head, and I feared the worst. I knew I looked a sight, having had a full night for my lip to swell up and the scratch on my cheek to heal enough to make a lovely solid line across it.

"First off, Tony died last night," he said softly, and allowed a moment of silence to pass before continuing, recognizing that it would have a big effect on me.

I couldn't bring myself to cry for him, as Alex had convinced me that I was not to blame, but I still felt bad. Plus, his testimony would be monumental in keeping me out of trouble. I had anticipated that my statement to the police would not have to go beyond what had happened yesterday, but now, who knew?

"Sam, you want to know how the police views Sara in terms of hero or villain?" Eckert rhetorically questioned. "I actually don't really know, as, um, it kind of depends on who you ask. I took the account analysis Sara prepared to my own financial crimes unit, and they loved it." Eckert gave me an impressed glance. "By the way, I'm supposed to tell you that you have a job in the department if Sam and June get tired of your antics. Apparently, your paperwork," he stressed the word for emphasis, "is top notch."

I beamed, and Alan hugged me around the shoulders, but the moment was short lived.

"We did get a full statement from Tony before he passed on, so," he continued, looking at me again, "I don't know yet how full of a disclosure we'll need from you.

I nodded my understanding.

"My team is going to get credit for the bust, and the feds will work with us on connecting the local and overseas connections to try to net in more participants. So I guess you're a hero for that, and for giving my department and the Feds enough evidence to take both Tony and Carlos from our custody. They'd never been able to get Carlos for anything."

"So once again, Sara's snooping gets you a promotion?" June asked unabashedly. "Sounds like a good deal for you; maybe the force should hire her."

Eckert reluctantly nodded and started to respond, but Sam cut him off.

"Heaven help the city, June," Sam said, giving me a sly wink on the side. They couldn't afford the damage control costs or her medical bills."

June and Alan laughed, and my face flushed with embarrassment. My good intentions always had consequences, and in this case, I hadn't been able to recover Sam's losses. I just didn't feel right dipping in to take more than I could trace back to its source. Sam had agreed with me, and told me the previous night that such an action could have come back to bite us both in the rear. At least I think that's what he said, as once again I was under the effects of pain medication. I was starting to worry about addiction to the things.

Eckert had paused for some coffee and some bites of a pastry, and we all remained silent until he dished some more. "I could only hold them for your assault and Tony's attempted and now actual murder, but the stolen mail I found," he emphasized the "I" as an indicator that this was how the factual story had to continue, "was a clincher for getting the Feds involved. We impounded the van, but are cooperating with the Feds. They're still going through the evidence, which includes the computerized information."

I nodded, knowing that the Feds and financial crimes people would find more than I ever could, and would be able to stop at least this end of an international fraud ring in its tracks.

"So, in a nutshell, all is well," he said hesitantly, "But."

"But if I have to testify, I'll have to tell them everything I've done."

He looked down as he answered, "Yes Sara, possibly. I can't control your involvement in whatever happens next."

June looked from me to Eckert. "What do you mean?"

"I haven't shared everything I've been up to," I said. I started with the story of Albert, which Sam and June knew about, but Eckert had been unaware of the complete details. I then went over my dealings with Tony, my breaking in to his van, piecing together the records, getting back money I could prove was Simons', and my setting him up to get picked up for window tinting by Eckert. I laughed as I told that section, because the ploy had been unnecessary as Eckert had personally witnessed my getting beaten up, and I'd witnessed Tony's ultimate demise. My laugh died in my throat as I went through that part.

No one in the room had known every piece of the story. Alan sat next to me and took my hand, the unbroken one. He gently kissed me.

"I'm sure glad you're on my side," he said softly, then turning to the group he chortled, "Cause heaven help those that aren't."

Eckert grunted. "You might want to keep a closer eye on her, Alan. She can't save the world; no matter what her opinion is on the subject."

"I told her that once too," he said. "I was wrong. She's made a difference in all of our lives, and for all the right reasons. However, I'm not letting you out of my sight for a while," he added for my benefit. "I'm going to keep you so busy; you won't find some other cause to champion."

"Well, as far as I'm concerned, she's skirted the law to enforce it, and the results have made things come together to right more wrongs," said Sam, who looked fired up. He gave a hard stare to Eckert. "I know enough about the law to know that the testimony of some is not always necessary when there is enough evidence in other areas."

He had spoken the words that I'd been trying to say. There should be enough evidence, found by a police officer in plain sight as he apprehended individuals that were committing a crime. I shouldn't have to testify to get these guys jailed, but I knew I would, no matter what it meant for me.

'Well, I'm assuming Tony's statement threw Carlos under the bus to save his own neck will hold, but I did witness his getting shot, err murdered. If it comes to it, I'm prepared to do what I have to. I won't lie, but I have a really good feeling that it won't be necessary."

"Girl Friday is always prepared," Sam said, nearly the exactas he'd made the last time I'd been in and somehow gotten myself out of a bind. 'Lucky too. Remember you didn't have to testify at any trials for those awful drug people. I'll bet the same fortune follows you through this."

June looked at Eckert, who was readying to leave. "Will you keep us updated, Stephen, and try, if at all possible, not to bring in Sara or Alex's names unless absolutely necessary?"

"If Alex hasn't already told the whole world every facet of this case," Eckert said sarcastically, but then nodded, and departed.

Alan had taken the full disclosure of my news rather well. Underneath though, I knew how upset he was at the risks I'd taken.

"Sara, you are lucky, as in fortunate enough, to have my undivided attention forever. I'm not letting you out of my sight again. No more unsupervised play dates with Alex."

I thought of Alex, who was still slumbering in the cottage after a late night of talking to his agent and the local and national media.

Sam sauntered from the room back into the kitchen, his words trailing, "By the way, Sara, my health insurance rates are going up due to an employee that has continual emergency room needs."

"I'll cover it, Dad," Alan replied for me then said to me directly, "I think I'm going to have to punish you with 24 hour supervision." His eyes twinkled, and I had thoughts of his chaining me to the bed, not that I'd mind for a little while, or what other ideas were running around his brain.

June, even more than I, looked to Alan to finish naming the terms of my sentencing.

"Did I mention that this cruel and unusual punishment would begin in Hawaii?" he said.

"What?" I said in a high voice of surprise and disbelief.

"You were going to take me of course, weren't you?"

The meaning of his words took a moment to register in my mind. The tickets J. Lo had given me; that's what he was talking about. I'd wanted to keep them, but then thought of giving them to Sam and June as a gift of appreciation for their patience with me during all the time I'd spent away in pursuit of wrong-doers and getting injured on the job.

"Well Alan, I was thinking of giving them to your folks as a gift for all they'd done for me."

"They've been to Hawaii 20 times already. This trip is ours. Let's get packed."

"What? But..."

June shushed me. "No ifs, ands or buts. You go. Take my son and have a good time away from here. You've had enough excitement in the past month to last a lifetime. Your thinking of us is a nice gesture, but Hawaii is a place for young love. Besides I'm going to be busy redecorating the upstairs spare bedroom now that the furniture has started to arrive from England. I won't have time for much else for at least the next month."

June appraised me, looking over every inch of my thrashed face as she spoke, and then gently added. "I love you, Sara." She kissed my head, and threw her arms around me. "I want you to be happy, and for a change, healthy too."

"I love you, too. You mean the world to me. But I can't leave things as they are here; we've only been back for a few days."

"You sure can, and you will, she said gently, then in a firm tone she commanded, "Alan, see that she relaxes and does nothing but swim, surf, dine and enjoy the islands."

"Sorry Mom, no can do. I'm planning on lots of indoor sports," he called from the corner of the room with the computer, already pecking away for flight scheduling.

Alan was always so blunt. I blushed, but June just laughed, "Work on a grandson for me." She sounded serious, and it scared me a little. I couldn't very well surf or swim with a cast on.

Alan already had the correct site up and said, "There's a flight to Los Angeles in two hours, and a connecting flight to Oahu at 5:00 p.m. We'd better get going. Better yet, forget packing; let's just buy what we need there. Shopping is more fun in Hawaii anyway."

"My Mom will kill me," I said, stopping in my tracks. "Alan, my hair, my face, they're a mess."

"It's not just your face I'm interested in," he semi-whispered with an evil grin.

"What about my cast?" I whined, pointing to my heavy cast-encased left hand. "I want to enjoy the water while I'm there."

"Easy," Alan said with a shrug, "Waterproof casts. We'll get yours redone when we land."

"I just got back. What about Rusty, the tenants?"

June wasn't taking no for an answer, as usual. "Sara, Rusty's as happy as a clam back here with her pack. I'll be sure that she gets plenty of exercise. You already took care of what needed to be done for Sam when you got back. The tenants will be fine for a little while longer. If Sam can't find something, it's not like you'll be without a phone."

"Or a computer," Alan chimed in, "I'll bring the laptop that's networked to the house. It'll be just like you're here anyway."

I ran out of excuses, so instead, I got caught up in Alan's crazy whim and was excited by the prospect of getting away with him all to myself. No bad guys, no parental worries, and just getting to know each other without other distractions.

June had me by the hand as I went to join Alan in selecting airfare and confirming reservations at the Kahala Mandarin Oriental, which we soon found had been refurbished and was now called just The Kahala Resort.

'Err, Sara dear," she said, messing with my hair, "Your face will be what it'll be, but shall we get your hair fixed before you go? You might get sunburned there." She played with the hair trying to get the longer pieces to cover the freshly ripped out section. It was still bruised and her touch hurt a bit.

"Hold on, Alan," she called out, "We could make an appointment for another weft or maybe a certain cut or style could fix the hole. Then you'd be ready for the trip."

I grabbed my Sherlock cap, which was fortunately nearby, jammed it on my head, and ran from the room with Alan by the hand before she could insist on anything.

43

Honolulu, Hawaii was as magical as I'd imagined. As soon as we landed and settled into our magnificent hotel room, Alan took me to local urgent care and had my hand cast replaced with a waterproof one so that I could enjoy the water activities without having to think about ruining it.

We spent the first several days just lying on the beach and enjoying the hotel. Our room overlooked a dolphin lagoon, and the trainers had shows at least once a day that we could enjoy right from our balcony.

I'd called my Mom while we were on the plane. I wanted to get that conversation over with before we landed. It was a good thing, because she'd given me an earful. I'd only seen her for a short visit after arriving back from England, and of course had managed to get major news coverage yet again within a week of my return. She indicated that she was tired of learning about what was up to by watching it on the news. I couldn't disagree.

This time the story had pulled all the facts together, my past job, my assistance with the drug ring bust, Alex's rise to stardom and my "incident", and now my involvement in bringing down a local financial crimes gang that was having an international ripple effect.

Alex hadn't even begun filming his new TV show yet, and was already getting movie offers. He had been responsible for escalating the issue, and of course was enjoying the consequences. I loved my friend, but made an instant decision not to involve him in any more of my extracurricular activities, if I ever have any.

If Alan had his way, I would never again get involved in anything risky or criminal other than watching Court TV. He also informed me I'd have nothing more to do with the media. I agreed with this decision whole heartedly, but explained that I had no control

Eckert had checked in while we were away too. He also reported positive feedback on the bust, although he was upset I'd left before I gave a statement of the day's events leading up to my witnessing Tony's murder. I gave him a video statement using Alan's computer, and all was well again between us. Shel, McKayla and Megan had all called too, wanting some of the details they hadn't yet gotten from Alex or Eckert.

Unlike my previous media exposure, though, no one knew I was in Hawaii, and no one in Hawaii knew or cared who I was. I could expect another week and half of peaceful bliss while I remained in Hawaii, and I was seriously thinking about extending my stay from two weeks to forever.

I'd gotten rather sunburned during my first few days at the beach. Alan incessantly applied the strongest sunscreen made at least once an hour while we were at the beach. He would have slathered it on more often than that if I'd let him. June had rubbed off on him in many ways. Unfortunately, the strongest sunscreen can't save the whitest skin from a burn, so we had to choose other activities while I peeled and healed.

Over the next week, we went para-sailing, spent a day swimming with the turtles and sea life in Haunama Bay, and swam with dolphins at our own hotel. We visited every aquarium in the area too, and took a submarine ride with glass windows in it so that we could see what was in the water we cruised through. We also went to Diamond Head, the Pearl Harbor memorial, visited botanical gardens, and even hiked to Manoa Falls. It was overwhelming, but we wanted to see and do everything we could while we were there.

Of course our nights were as equally delightful as our days. Alan and I had taken the physical part of our relationship to another level, which sometimes encompassed only cuddling and hand holding. I had a feeling that this would continue long past the so called "newlywed" phase of a sexual relationship.

The hotel was a dream in itself, and I could see why J. Lo chose it. It was secluded, a cove away from the hustle and bustle of Waikiki, and had orchid gardens, a dolphin pool, a sea turtle preserve, and its own private beach. It didn't seem right that I'd be staying in an ancient castle's historical paradise one week, and a tropical resort in tropical paradise in practically the next.

Alan wanted to go on a special excursion into the amazing fish tank at Sea Life Park, and had somehow convinced me to go as well. We actually went into the main tank with a park employee, and watched as fish, sharks and other sea creatures swam by, only an arm's length away. We also had an opportunity to swim with and touch various rays in another area.

He'd even gotten me to "snuba" during a skin diving excursion, which is a combination of snorkeling and skin diving. You didn't have to be certified, and you air tanks remained on the surface of the water while you dove.

I was terrified of being in the water with so much sea life at first, but came to love it very quickly. When you're under the water, the serenity encompasses you fully. The absences of sound and visual beauty of Hawaii's tropical ocean waters were surreal. I wasn't a strong swimmer and I had a bad hand, so Alan stayed close by to make sure I felt safe.

On our second to the last day on the island, Alan surprised me with a visit to a private beach. He made arrangements in advance to have camping gear set up for us, and a private chef to come in the evening and cook for us.

The day and evening were amazing, and I could now add making love outdoors and in the surf to my list of firsts, which seemed to grow longer everyday.

We slept, when we actually slept, in a hammock right on the beach. We cuddled together the entire night, and it was really quite comfortable. The air was warm for the day and night time, and the sounds and smells surrounding us made it yet another unique experience.

As we headed back to the hotel the next morning, we prepared to spend our last day in Hawaii. I was ready to go home. I'd had four out of five weeks of constant traveling and excursions. I just wanted to be back in a routine at home again.

We decided to spend the last day exploring the hotel grounds one more time. In the late afternoon, we went to the hotels' private beach to take in the amazing amenities and watch the sun go down in its orange blaze of glory.

Once again, Alan had a private chef prepare dinner for us, this time on an area of the hotel's beach right outside of the cabana we'd taken for the day.

"What do you want out of life?" he asked out of the blue as we finished the meal.

"Like as in right now, tomorrow, or forever?" I asked, confused as I picked the last of the lau lau from the bone.

"Forever."

I felt put on the spot. "I don't know Alan. I know it involves you."

"What do you think about kids?"

"I love kids."

"Do you ever want to have some?"

"Of course I do."

"You're going to be 32 this year. When do you plan on fitting them into your life?"

"I guess I haven't thought that far in advance, Alan," I laughed, still concerned about his foray into serious territory. "We've only been together, like this I mean, for a few weeks."

"Are you happy?"

"I couldn't be happier," I said in my most smiling voice.

"Are you afraid of things moving too fast for us?"

I was taken aback. Not only were Alan's questions serious, his tone was too. He'd usually avoided anything serious as far as I knew.

I answered truthfully though, when I said, "No, Alan, I don't think things have gone too fast between us. Sometimes you just know when something is right."

"Well, we're on the same page then," he stated as if this were not a fact taken into evidence in a court case.

"I'm just 28, but I don't want to be 35 before I have children of my own Sara. I knew you were the one for me less than a month after you came into my life."

The significance of his admission made me wonder where he was going with it. I frankly confessed, "It took me longer, Alan, but I did manage to catch up quickly. I can see us together forever. We fit well together in personality, likes and dislikes, in so many areas. Since you asked, I do question something though."

Alan looked puzzled, alarmed even. "What is it?"

"I work for your parents, if you call what I've been doing work anyway, and you haven't been working at all."

"And?"

"I think most girls wants security, and I guess when it comes to it, I'm no different. Maybe we should focus on building up your business again, or getting into some type of venture with your folks."

Alan laughed. "You know, I'd forgotten that you didn't work for my Dad when I went through school."

I couldn't fathom how that mattered, but I counted back the years to the time that I estimated he would've graduated from college.

"Maybe a year after, or so. No bells are ringing though. Why?"

"Sara, I was considered a wunderkind of sorts. I finished college at 18, and had a master's degree by 19."

I was stunned. I had no idea, and this set my mental calendar back several years. I hadn't even known Sam then.

"You think I exist on my parent's money, right?"

I nodded, my perception of truth revealed.

"My thesis was actually a project that I submitted to school after I'd sold usage rights to it."

This was a surprise. "What kind of usage rights?" I innocently asked, clueless as to what he was talking about and wondering even more where in the world this discussion was leading.

"Every search engine on the internet has to use my patented technology."

"Wow, you mean like Ask.com, Google, Yahoo and the rest?" No one on the internet didn't use a search engine at least daily.

He nodded.

"Well, that's something, Alan. I thought you were a network guy, not a programmer."

"I do networking for fun," he said, "but I've made my fortune with programming. Last month Google offered to buy it from me outright."

"Good for you, that'll build a nice nest egg.' I exclaimed, beaming with pride in recognition of his accomplishment, even though I still didn't understand exactly what it meant.

"Nest egg? Sara, I've been getting monthly royalties on this technology for ten years already."

"Handsome, smart and well off. Well, looks like my security concerns are unfounded then."

"They should be over, Sara. My monthly income is more that your annual salary. And did I mention that I'm a saver, too?"

My mouth hung open as my mind calculated the amounts. He was well off on his own!

"I've been contemplating Google's offer, and in light of recent events," he coughed, "I think I'm going to accept it. I've been working on an enhancement to it anyway, so I can probably get royalties on that or get Google to up the offer price and include it."

"Gosh, Alan. I know it's kind of personal, but is the offer a good one?"

"Before I tell you, do you like the area my folks live in?"

"Who wouldn't?" I said, thinking of the serene area that was very different from the busy area where my condo was located. "It's lovely, quiet, and peaceful. It's also one of the few green areas in the Reno-Sparks area." Reno was brown when you really thought about it, and the Westins had a nice slice of heaven as far as our area was concerned.

"Well, it's not really a 40 acre parcel, it's two 20 acre parcels. My folks' parcel is to the right, and mine is to the left. I own that parcel. Free and clear."

This was news to me, and I thought about the layout of the property and how his statement seemed factual. "You've done well, Alan. I knew you were brilliant, but not that you'd applied yourself so early on in life. I'm shocked I didn't find out about you before. June really must brag more about her successful brood. A lawyer and a mogul. Who knew?"

Lowering my voice, I added guiltily, "I'm so sorry for assuming you were a trust fund baby. I really didn't care, but I was looking out for the future to make sure we would be on the same page there too. I'm sorry if I seemed rude, but since you were being serious, I thought I'd reciprocate."

"I'm not worried you're some gold digger, Sara. You've proven with everything you've done since I've known you that you're very practical, and so am I."

I interrupted, "Except for your little mad moment at the Sherlock

Holmes Museum."

He laughed. "I did go a little nuts there. I'm usually not an impulsive person."

"Arranging last minute trips to Hawaii and tagging along to England on a moment's notice?"

"When it comes to you Sara, I do admit to some spontaneous decisions. They've paid off though, with dividends I might add."

Well, since we're together now, I see no reason to prolong the inevitable. I've never been rash on major decisions, which is one of the reasons I've done well. I could've considered Answer.com's offer of $850,000.00 over a year ago, but I decided not to sell."

My jaw dropped at such an amount.

He continued, "Instead, I'm going to accept Google's more recent offer of 20 million dollars for the rights to my technology."

My jaw dropped opened to the floor. I had nothing to say; I think I was in shock at Alan's secret of being a multi-millionaire business magnate.

Alan let go of my hand and got up from the table. He pulled something from his pocket, and I recognized a beautiful replica enamel box I'd been eyeing in England.

He got down on one knee in front of me, and my heart sped up.

"Sara Blake. I have a place to build you a home, and enough security for you to never have to worry about money again ever in your life. More importantly, I love you, and I want to start a family with you. And finally, I want to make sure that I'm close enough to you to every day to keep you out of the trouble you seem to enjoy finding, and there's just one way I can get what I want."

He opened the box, and inside he'd refitted the box to hold a ring. Knowing me, he chose well. It was not some huge ostentatious rock, but instead a simple ring that I would appreciate. He removed it from the box and held it up to me, anticipating my hand to accept it.

"Sara Blake, will you be my wife?"

Tears filled my eyes as emotions ran through me faster than I could process them. That day's heat and my dehydration came into play at the wrong time. It was only later that I learned I fainted at the perfect moment to deny or accept Alan as a permanent fixture in my life. These things happen to everyone, right?

Look for More Titles
from *LeRue Press*

Pick Me, Pick Me
by Elizabeth Horton

Fractals of Past
by Benjamin Arnold

Life in a Limerick
by Ruby Szudajski

Naming Your Baby
by Ruby Szudajski

Wicked Tides
by Sean Kinsley

Synaptic Traffic
by Benjamin Arnold

Inked In: Shadows Between
Darkness & Light
by Karlyn Simone

Strength & Courage
by Matthew Elias Goldfin

Watch for the Contender for
"The Longest Book Title in the World'";
to be released soon!
www.leruepress.com

280 Greg St. #10, Reno, NV 89502 (775) 849-3814